The *Fake* Divination *Offense*

Other Books by Sara Raasch

The Nightmare Before Kissmas

Go Luck Yourself

The Entanglement of Rival Wizards

The *Fake* Divination *Offense*

Sara Raasch

Tor Publishing Group
New York

This is a work of fiction. All of the names, characters, organizations, places, and events portrayed in this work are either products of the author's imagination or used fictitiously.

THE FAKE DIVINATION OFFENSE

A Bramble Book
Published by Tom Doherty Associates / Tor Publishing Group
120 Broadway
New York, NY 10271

www.torpublishinggroup.com

Bramble™ is a trademark of Macmillan Publishing Group, LLC.

EU Representative: Macmillan Publishers Ireland Ltd, 1st Floor, The Liffey Trust Centre, 117–126 Sheriff Street Upper, Dublin 1, D01 YC43

The Library of Congress Cataloging-in-Publication Data is available upon request.

ISBN 978-1-250-42879-0 (trade paperback)
ISBN 978-1-250-42880-6 (ebook)

First Edition: 2026

Printed in the United States of America

10 9 8 7 6 5 4 3 2 1

You're strong enough on your own. I promise.

The *Fake* Divination *Offense*

Chapter One

"Five."

"One."

I think for a minute. Or, more accurately, the buzzing under my skin thinks for a minute. The whipping epidermal hurricane of emotions I've been carrying around most of the day.

And it decides: "Five."

To which Seb responds, "One."

Thio, from his barstool on Seb's other side, snorts into his wineglass. "I don't think you two understand how negotiating works."

Seb leans back against him. "Yeah, I do. First rule of negotiating: never back down."

"Second rule of negotiating," I add, "never apologize."

And I scroll through the bar's karaoke sign-up sheet on my phone to quickly claim five slots. Maybe six. Oops, seven?

But we're celebrating tonight.

We're *free.*

Seb's slow smile is all the further argument I get. "Eh, go crazy, big guy." His eyes dip past my shoulder and his grin sharpens. "I won't be the one using my body as a human shield to stop you, anyway."

He raises his cocktail glass for a sip, the new ring on his finger flashing in the low light. We're celebrating more than one thing tonight, and I go to add an eighth slot—

When someone bats my hand away from my phone. "No."

Ah. That's who Seb was looking at.

Darian Callabrass—human, with thin black locs pulled into a topknot, and a very deliberate rock-star vibe from his leather pants, ripped white T-shirt set off against his dark skin, and the guitar strapped to his back—has been a bard on the Hellhounds for the past three years. While I've only been part of the team for two months, he's good people.

Mostly.

"I swear, Monroe, if you bastardize another Queen song like you did at practice . . ."

I give Darian my most innocent, wide-eyed sulk. "Excuse you, I was singing along to my *personal* workout playlist, so fuck off. Your patron god loves me appreciating his music."

"My patron god has made it my new mission on this plane to get you to stop inflicting emotional damage on the unknowing public by screeching his songs."

I cut a smile I know won't faze him. "Just one Queen song tonight?"

A sudden lurking presence at Darian's shoulder has both of us glancing over. I'm rather used to these antics, getting teamed up with Marlow in practices, but Darian jumps in surprise.

"Fucking hell, you're as bad as Phei," he gasps. "I'm going to put a bell on you."

Marlow, one of the Hellhounds' rogues, slowly flips Darian off and holds out her other palm, where a cluster of clip-on earrings sits. The motion wafts the smell of saltwater that always permeates the air around her, an overpowering wave of, well, waves.

Darian snatches an earring, attaches it, and repeats, "You're as bad as Phei. I'm going to put a bell on you."

Only now, thanks to the enchanted earring, his words are subtitled below his face in slightly neon-blue script.

I take an earring, as do Seb and Thio, but they've turned to watch something on one of the TVs behind the bar.

Marlow's tan skin reddens. "A *bell*? Do you have any idea how offensive that is?" she signs. It, too, is converted into subtitles, though hers are due to a ring she wears.

Darian blanches. "Oh gods. Is that some mermaid thing?"

"No." Marlow beams, all sharp white teeth. "It's a screwing-with-you thing. Put a bell on me. I dare you."

Darian shoves her.

"Where is Phei?" I ask, cutting my gaze around. Though, from what I've learned of the Hellhounds' dryad healer, they don't exactly hold to things like schedules. Or time. Or humanoid forms. But they've surprisingly never missed a practice, so.

The bar's filling, evening swelling the crowd, chatter rising with the temperature as sweat slicks my navy Henley to my back.

"No clue," Marlow says. "They said they'd try to come, though."

At which point, conversation flatlines, and it's painfully obvious that only Darian, who was assigned to *show me the ropes* when I got traded, and as such got stuck being my friend, and Marlow, my training partner and the other newest team member, came out. Despite my invite to the whole team that drinks were on me at the Silver Hound.

"I'm sure they just had other plans." Darian adjusts his guitar's strap with a shrug. "There're only a few weeks 'til the first game. Everyone's busy before the season starts."

Marlow's crystalline eyes flash with her smile. "We'll still party."

That buzzing energy I've been riding high on threatens to morph into something other than cheerfulness, but nope. It doesn't get to do that tonight.

I'm staying in this moment. Living in this victory. It was a hard-earned win, no matter what other people might think, and enjoying the release of this stress is a necessary part of the healing process.

So says my therapist at the more frequent appointments we've had the past few months in preparation for not only the lawsuit ending but me starting a new rawball season. Lots of beginnings, lots of healing, lots of *good things*.

I power back the rest of my beer and flag the bartender. "What are you guys drinking? Sky's the limit."

Seb whirls on me. "I'll get their drinks. You need to go up for your first song, right?"

The stage is at the rear of the bar, but they haven't kicked off karaoke yet and I'm not the first slot. That was already claimed in the app by someone who put their name down as Alexo the Magnificent. Sounds more like a kid's magician than a karaoke name, but whatever, I don't judge.

Lies.

I totally judge.

If you're gonna go to all the trouble of coming up with a karaoke nom de plume, then my gods, *commit.*

Seb nudges me toward the stage, but I brace myself on the barstool. There's a weird look on his face, like he's trying to cover something. Or distract me from something?

He lists to the right and sits up taller—trying to block me from seeing over his shoulder. The TV screens.

Which is hilarious. He's a little guy—significantly shorter than me, as pale as I am but all unruly blond hair, glasses, and sass against my half-giant height and bulk—and him trying to block anything from me is like a chihuahua hurling itself in front of Cerberus.

All I have to do is flick my eyes up and to the left, and the screens are in full view.

The closest one shows a news report about—I squint, then roll my eyes. Looks like another group of Galaxrien Vossen cultists tried to resurrect him. Summon him? They can't seem to decide whether their demon lord is alive or dead in the hell-pit my patron god—Urzoth Shieldsworn—locked him in centuries ago.

This time, their ceremony involved a tuft of hair—*ew*—they swear was from Galaxrien's mortal descendant. Whoever they are. Most of the people who worship Galaxrien through the official religion have demonic ancestry, by nature of Galaxrien being a demon, so they probably grabbed hair from one of their own worshippers and called it good.

Regardless, before the ceremony could be completed, members of Urzoth's church charged in and the proceeding tussle set fire to a pizza parlor, since the resurrection ceremony had been set up in an abandoned Best Buy in a strip mall.

Because, as everyone knows, demon lords trapped in hell-pits will only deign to come to earth if they're resurrected at an electronics store.

The fuck is wrong with these cultists.

I almost reach for my phone, certain it'll be lit up with texts from my mother talking about this latest drama, complaining about the Galaxrien cultists and how idiotic it is to think they can undo Urzoth's work, and so on and so forth. I could throw a little wrench into her rant by pointing out that the Urzoth worshippers used unnecessary force, but I know exactly what she'd say to that: *Force is strength, Orok! When was the last time you challenged anyone to a fight? When was the last time you displayed your strength outside the rawball field?*

My phone stays safely in my pocket.

I frown at Seb. However shit-stirring that news report will be with my mother, that can't be what he didn't want me to see.

He's got this aggressively hopeful look on his face, wide smile and forced levity.

"Go on now." He bats my chest. "Git."

My eyes cast up again as I start to move off the barstool—and I catch the other screen.

That's my face. My headshot is next to one of the ostentatiously ragey sports reporters who always tries to have the most boisterous opinions on every single move we make during games. The reporter is gesturing wildly, stabbing his finger to make a point, his face red as he shouts, but luckily the TV's muted.

Are they talking about my trade? My stats? How I was one of the Vegas Chimeras' best defensive tanks when they won the rawball championship last season? How the Philadelphia Hellhounds got a *steal* when they traded for me?

Doubtful. Not by the way the reporter looks one blood pressure spike away from a stroke, and then the symbol for Urzoth, a stone with an axe jammed into it, flashes over my headshot, followed by *Orok Monroe: Traitor?*

Call me a traitor to the magical community for bringing down Camp Merethyl, and it's annoying, sure, but anyone who says that can fuck off.

Call me a traitor to Urzoth, and my stomach sinks, all that beer I chugged shaking up at the sudden lurch.

Because they're right.

Or they will be, at least.

Yeah, I'm definitely not looking at my phone now.

I rip my eyes away from the TV. They land, instead, on Seb, whose forced levity vanishes at the look on my face.

No.

Tonight's about freedom. About celebrating the end of a four-year-long lawsuit, but it stretches beyond that, all the way back to our childhood. To our days at the magical paramilitary training camp that became the source of all my nightmares.

Literally.

I haven't slept in months.

I scramble for some of that good feeling again.

The lawsuit ended. The verdict's in: they're guilty. Camp Merethyl's directors owe us restitution for torturing us under the guise of training. The world knows what they did and how wrong it was.

Yeah, the world *knows.*

Including people like the Chimeras' managers and my other teammates. After my testimony came out, they *knew* that someone who belonged to a god made out of stone and handled conflict with his fists was patiently fielding a lawsuit, so how bad could my experience at Camp Merethyl really have been?

If I were a true Urzoth follower, I would've fought back when these supposed *atrocities* happened.

If I were a true Urzoth follower, I wouldn't have gone through with a lawsuit; I would've challenged the head of the camp to a fight and let that victory lay out the guilty party.

The pro rawball community seems almost evenly split between *knowing* I was right to stand up against the abuse and *knowing* I'm a weak coward.

All that buzzing in my skin fatalistically shifts from excitement to anxiety, creep-crawling up my spine and wrapping around my throat.

Seb grabs my forearm. "Hey. We don't have to be out tonight. We can go back to one of our—"

Saved by the squeal of a microphone.

It wails over the crowded bar and we all flinch—well, not Marlow, who watches us and laughs—before a voice reverberates in the proceeding silence:

"Let's get this party started! It's karaoke night, bitches, and you know what that means. No heckling. No booing. Everyone's welcome. If you have siren lineage, warn us *before* your song so the audience can cast disenchantment wards. Now, first up, we have . . . Alexo the Magnificent! Let's give it up for Alexo!"

The crowd applauds. But Seb keeps his grip on my arm.

"O," he says over the din. "We can—"

"I'm gonna go closer to the stage," I say. We're still wearing Marlow's clip-ons, which are a huge help in situations like this; I know Seb can understand me even with the noise.

I pause, analytical eyes sweeping over him, and my emotions take a one-eighty. "Unless *you* want to leave?"

One corner of Seb's mouth lifts. He leans back again, where Thio, in conversation with Marlow and Darian, automatically threads an arm around his waist.

That's one of the main reasons I was able to get some much-needed healthy distance from Seb over the past few years: I knew he had Thio. I knew my best friend was taken care of.

"I'm good," Seb says with a helplessly content smile. "I'm engaged. We *won*. You're back in Philly. Everything's great." His smile dims. "Right?"

Right.

Say it.

Right, Seb. Everything's great.

Except I didn't get traded due to my stats—which is the reason Seb thinks I'm on a brand-new three-year contract with the Hellhounds. I got traded because my old team turned on me for daring to bring down the camp that almost killed me.

And my new team seems to have the same opinion on the matter.

Yes. We won the lawsuit. That era of our lives can finally be put to rest.

It's this new era that terrifies the shit out of me.

I lean forward to peck Seb on the cheek. "I'll be back. Cheer for me."

Seb still looks like he wants to keep asking if I'm okay, and I love him for it. But he relents and gives me a thumbs-up as Alexo the Magnificent's song kicks on: Journey. A pretty standard karaoke pick.

I bop Darian on the shoulder to get his and Marlow's attention. "Tab's open under my name. Go crazy." *I sure as hell will.*

Marlow cackles. "Famous last words. *Drink like a fish* is a cliché for a reason."

I grin, relieved at the feel of it, the flash of camaraderie I've been starving for.

Unease wiggles its obnoxious little way into my thoughts, reminding me not to get too attached to all this. Healthy steps. Boundaries, compartmentalization. I need to keep everyone at a distance until I can figure out my place here.

Seb gives me a probing look, but I shove off the stool with a reassuring smile, a long breath escaping as I peel farther away from my group.

A large portion of the crowd has pressed around the small stage at the back of the room, but I lumber through and score a spot right up against the edge near the wall, so I'm not blocking anyone. Alexo the Magnificent croons the first lines of "Don't Stop Believin'" and a cheer goes up, but I'm pathetically scanning faces in the Silver Hound's dim light for anyone else from the team.

If they're going to believe the fuckers saying that our claims about Camp Merethyl's cruelty were lies, that I should've handled any perceived slight through stone-cold aggression, I don't want them here.

I'd hoped this team would be different. That I could be back home in every sense of the word. No one on the Hellhounds has spoken to me about the trial yet, and everyone's been welcoming and kind, if overly formal. I knew once the verdict landed that it'd all come to a head, and I'd hoped I could get in front of it, invite everyone out, play it off as something positive before they had a chance to believe the worst of me.

We're a team. Spells, explosions, obstacles—all that and more get thrown at us every time we step onto a rawball field. Trust is what keeps us alive.

The Hellhounds don't trust me, do they? It's gonna be the Chimeras all over again.

I stretch my right arm instinctively, phantom pain radiating from the hairline fracture I got in my elbow during the championship game.

Weak. Weak to worry about all this. To be disappointed. All this, just—gods, *weakness.*

I shake my head, hard, as Alexo the Magnificent takes the midnight train going anywhere. His voice is smooth, flowing over me in a crooning wash.

My eyes drift to the stage—

And my jaw drops.

Holy.

Shit.

I take back all my previous smartass thoughts about his karaoke name. *Magnificent* is completely accurate.

He's about Seb's height and size, but thinner, slighter, wearing a scarlet satin shirt unbuttoned to his stomach so it billows away from his bare chest, with tight black pants tucked into clunky gold boots. His pale skin is covered in a dusting of rosy golden glitter, and with his overall demeanor, I can't figure out if it's makeup or he's part pixie.

Alexo sways in the musical interlude between verses, eyes shut, more of that rose-gold paint shimmering across each eyelid, his messy tangle of strawberry-blond curls gleaming pink in the stage lighting.

Wow, my brain supplies. And then keeps repeating that word in a dumbstruck rollover when Alexo the Magnificent dives into the next verse.

His eyes fly open, deep onyx brown, highlighted in thick black liner and mascara, and as the music builds, rage sparks there. A small pool of it at first, then it grows and grows, spreading across his whole face until he's snarling with the swell of the words and music, *livin' just to find emotion.*

When he belts out that first long note, I don't want to look away, but my head swings back, and I catch Darian's eye. The whole damn bar is watching Alexo perform, most people slack-jawed, others bobbing to the song.

Darian meets my gaze over all the heads, and when I cock an eyebrow in an unspoken *Are you seeing this?*, he says something that gets picked up by his enchanted earring and subtitles under his face:

"This is why you leave karaoke to the professionals. You have to follow *that.*"

I roll my eyes and turn back to Alexo, because fuck Darian, that's not what I meant. I'm not sure what I meant. I just—gods, this guy is throwing his whole body into the performance, dancing across the stage, and the crowd claps along. But Alexo seems unaware of them, each word of each verse coming from the very pit of his soul. I almost wonder if I missed him telling the audience he's a siren and he'd be inadvertently casting an enchantment on us with this routine, but he doesn't have the look of someone casting spells. This is for him. Just for him.

But I take a little of it for me, too.

There's this god who fell out of favor centuries ago—Cendis, the god of small fires. Candlelight, sparks, embers, tiny touches of heat. He dropped away as people were more drawn to raging elemental fire gods, but I always found what he represented to be far more potent. He was the god of *beginnings.* Of having the ability to start a fire in the first place.

That's what I see as Alexo bares his soul with this song. Someone trying with every wisp of their existence to *begin.*

To be free.

Where the crowd is fully enjoying the song, dancing and laughing, a partying Thursday night, I go more and more slack as the music carries on. The lyrics drop in the last interlude, and Alexo's previous dance moves were a warm-up.

He pirouettes around the stage, back arching, legs kicking up to his face, arms pinwheeling in a mesmerizing braid of limbs and fluidity. All the while keeping the mic cord from tangling and playing around the karaoke machine with the lyric screen he's not once looked at—and avoiding a few reaching hands from the audience.

I jolt forward at that, shoulders bunching. I'm close enough to the edge of the stage that all I have to do is move to get the attention of the front row. When I glare, they sink back a few good inches.

Just because it's unsafe. I don't want him to trip. Obviously.

Alexo doesn't notice. He whirls back into the last swell of lyrics, clinging to the mic with both hands, and singing, *singing* his fucking heart out. Each long note becomes its own mini performance piece, his spine folding so far backward he's defying gravity, and that part of my brain still going *wow, wow, wow* now adds *he's flexible* along with pathetic little whimpers.

The song fades out as Alexo holds in the position of the final note, hands still death-gripping the microphone, eyes pinched shut.

The music barely ends when the crowd explodes, hooting and cheering and clapping.

Alexo's eyes blink open like he's coming out of a trance. He straightens up and his gaze casts over the crowd, a slow smile lifting one side of his mouth—

His eyes land on me.

Something flashes through his expression, a quick scroll of surprise—and fear.

If it isn't people fearing me for my aggressive patron god, it's people fearing me for my size. Both valid reasons, unfortunately, but I don't want this guy to be afraid of me, a want that flurries desperately in my chest.

I'm right up against the stage, arms folded over my chest, and he's got the higher ground on me from this angle. I let my arms drop to my sides and try a grin. Encouraging, awed.

Alexo lets his eyes dip down my body before they ping back up.

He smiles.

It's wide and wondrous, digging dimples into his cheeks and illuminating his dark eyes.

Oh, for gods' sakes. Give a bi guy a chance, would you? Fucking *dimples*.

Alexo eases the mic back onto the stand, faces the crowd, and sweeps into an elegant bow.

The bar manager comes out from backstage and leans into the mic. "Alexo the Magnificent, everybody!"

The crowd goes crazy again, and it kickstarts what's left of my brain so I clap along.

"Up next," the manager announces, "the Big O!"

See? I take my karaoke stage name seriously.

It catches the crowd's attention, and their cheering turns to equal groans and laughter.

The shift lets Alexo slip off the stage, on the opposite side from me. He's so damn small that I instantly lose sight of him, and I bound up onto the stage to spot him again, and—there he is. Talking with someone near the hall that leads to the bathrooms and back exit.

"Give it up for the Big O!" the manager tells the crowd. "The Hellhounds' own newest defensive tank!"

Before I have time to connect that I'm on the stage and I don't know whether the crowd might hate me, they cheer. A few chant, "O Monroe!" and "Hellhounds!"

A grin blooms across my face and some of the anxiety fighting to burst free settles.

Fans have always loved that I do shit like this, make a fool of myself in public displays of nonsensical joy. That hasn't gone away. Well, with the Silver Hound's crowd at least, but I'll take whatever support I can get.

My song starts.

And I'm suddenly aware that Alexo gave a Grammy-level performance and here I am, planning to butcher Sabrina Carpenter's "Taste."

With a self-deprecating shrug that makes the crowd laugh anew, I pull the mic stand closer, eyes flicking to the lyric screen—

But I find myself shifting back to stare at Alexo. And that guy he's talking with.

My mouth opens for the first verse when the guy leans way too close.

I can only see the back of Alexo's head, so I have no idea how he's responding to the guy's advances, if he's interested, and that's why I linger. Why the song plays on and I miss the first line.

The guy's face devolves into fury, eyes narrow, lips peeled back as he talks down at Alexo.

The crowd's gone silent, staring at me, a few errant chuckles as they assume I'm choking on stage.

But I watch Alexo shake his head at that guy—who then seizes Alexo's arm.

Alexo tries to yank away.

Nope.

Heat swells up from my stomach, soothing calm focus over me as I leap off the stage. The crowd parts in a confused shuffle when I beeline through them to reach Alexo and the guy, still in an argument. And that guy's still digging his fingers into Alexo's arm.

Nope, I think again, and I should probably think more than that, but I'm all narrow-minded goal, the meditative intensity I fall into during a rawball game. Only instead of *defend my teammates*, that narrow-minded goal is *get Alexo away from this guy*.

Again, without thinking—really cannot overstress how little I'm thinking—I do what I've done to Seb a hundred times when I want to move him somewhere:

I wrap my arm around Alexo's waist and pick him up.

He smells like fruit. Apples, maybe? Because of course he has to smell edible.

Alexo makes a disconcerted noise halfway between a chirp and a gasp.

The guy releases Alexo's arm in shock, which lets me deposit

Alexo behind me and to the side, so I can use my body as a shield between them.

By the time I'm facing the guy, one arm out to block Alexo, I realize that I made a bad move.

I know better than to just *grab* people, and shame damn near makes my knees buckle—why the *fuck* did I do that?

Before I can apologize to Alexo, the attacker guy whips his hands out in a wizard offensive stance, a green spell glowing in arcane ropes between his splayed fingers.

The crowd is watching. Dead silent.

While the instrumentals for "Taste" pulse from the stage.

I foresee an uncomfortable conversation with the team's publicists in my future about what it means to *professionally represent the team*. On top of the already uncomfortable conversation I was going to have with the team manager tomorrow. *Great.*

I lift my hands in an attempt to placate the guy. "Just back up, all right? We don't need to—"

"*You* back up," the guy snarls. He's upper-middle-aged, not dressed at all for a night out at a bar, in frumpy jeans, a wrinkled T-shirt, and an old beat-up jean jacket. His black hair's greasy, his teeth are bared, and he looks every bit ready to release this attack spell on me.

I step back and bump into Alexo—and my eyebrows pop in surprise. I figured he'd bolt after I *picked him up*.

But he's still here, and when I move into his space, he doesn't retreat. Just stays there, his warmth bleeding into my lower back and side, and I instinctively lean closer to that heat.

"Alexo," the guy snaps. "Get over here."

Alexo doesn't move.

The guy's glower goes murderous when it drops from me to Alexo. "We're leaving. *Now*."

"Maybe we should ask Alexo if he wants to leave with you," I say through my teeth.

Fuck bullies, I swear to the gods.

The guy spreads his hands, that green spell stretching, intensifying. "He's leaving with me. Now. He's *mine* to order around."

Oh, he did *not* just call Alexo *his.* Not in that tone of voice. Disrespectful asshat.

A growl rumbles in the base of my throat, my upper lip flinching in an involuntary snarl.

The crowd shifts and a few people draw closer to me, and I know without having to look that it's Seb and the rest. Does this bar have security people?

But maybe . . . maybe Alexo *is* this guy's, in some way?

I risk letting the guy out of my sight to look down at Alexo and make sure I'm not reading this situation wrong. That's the last thing I need, to keep someone from leaving with their friend, however much of a dick he is.

As I turn, all the ways I could be messing up right at this very moment come crashing through me.

Because cameras start going off. It'll be all over socials in no time, how Orok Monroe, Urzoth Shieldsworn's tank for the Hellhounds, used his strength and violence to trap a guy at a bar. I can hear the reporters now: *That's how he chooses to embody his god? He let these alleged brutalities happen at Camp Merethyl, but he channels Urzoth for a* bar fight?

But that all goes translucent with the way Alexo's gazing up at me.

This close, I can see brown freckles clustered in with the rose-gold glitter across his nose, his lashes made impossibly long by mascara.

He doesn't look afraid or annoyed that I'm stopping him from leaving. He looks intrigued. Studying me, eyes bouncing over my face.

"Do you want to go with this guy?" I ask him, a little of that growl still in my voice.

His wonder freezes. "I'd have to go with you instead?"

What? I throw my hands up, but to him, it's supplicant. "Of course not. Just—is this guy bothering you?"

Wow. Next I'll ask if he comes here often or if it hurt when he fell from the heavens.

Alexo stares at me again, studying, *studying*, before his lips part in a small huff. And with a triumphant smile—there're those dimples again, *fuuuuuck me*—he nods.

"Yeah," he says, and he drops his gaze to the guy. "Yeah, he's bothering me."

The guy makes a garbled noise of protest. "You little piece of—"

But he's cut off in an aggravated squawk, and when I look, Thio's counterspelled whatever the green glowing arcane lines were.

"Do we need to call an adventure party?" Seb asks me, but he's scowling at the guy. "They can take care of him."

Instead of showing any kind of fear at being potentially arrested, the guy laughs. A boisterous, screeching laugh, and with one last glower at Alexo, he huffs off into the crowd.

I charge after him when a small hand wraps around my forearm. It's just as debilitating for my sense of awareness as that meditative goal state.

Everything else drops away, crashes and topples to rubble, until there's just Alexo putting himself in front of me, gazing up with that awestruck wonder marred by confusion, like he's not used to people defending him. It makes my chest squeeze, that this is surprising for him.

"Thank you," he whispers.

It's so quiet in here, the crowd eating this *up*, and the music's stopped now, too, but I watch his lips and feel those words dip off his tongue.

I really intend to say *you're welcome.* Or something not quite so predatory, after all this shit.

But what comes is a runaway train of "Let me buy you a drink."

It isn't even a question.

I clear my throat and try again. "Can I buy you a drink?"

Alexo grins, and I am so, so fucked. He is some kind of siren, isn't he? Or a pixie, tossing out charms on his every exhale.

But Seb and Thio aren't affected, sharing a knowing smirk with me, then each other; and Marlow and Darian are behind them, looking concerned until Darian claps his hands loudly.

"All right, show's over!" he shouts at the crowd. "Or—has it just begun?"

He dives on stage, whips his guitar around, and starts into the first chords of "Somebody to Love." It earns a stifled applause, and the air of partying burbles back up as people peel away from gawking at me. At us.

Seb, Thio, and Marlow try to create something of a barrier between us and the crowd, a wall on our other side, but I still grimace, wondering how many of the pics people got had Alexo in them. I know what comes with my lot in life, but he sure as hell didn't ask to get embroiled in a PR moment with a pro rawball athlete who's a *traitor to his god.*

All that's for later, though.

Because right now, Alexo's brows scrunch with his smile. "You want to buy me a drink?"

"Just a drink. No expectations," I clarify. "I'm Orok." I hold out my hand.

He shakes it gently. His hand is doll-like against my thick fingers.

"Oh, I know who you are," he says.

I fight back a wince, waiting for his reaction, but he's a blank slate. So I guess, tentative, "You a rawball fan?"

"You could say that." I get the feeling that's all he'll give me, and I worry he's one of the people set against me until he grins.

He's gonna play it coy, which is fine. Enticing, actually, and prickles race down the back of my neck, fizzle straight to the base of my gut when he bites his lower lip.

But that taunting smile dims. "I have to go, though."

I keep my own smile up, hoping not to look too disheartened. Because it's dumb that I feel upset—I don't even know this guy. He's just alluring and magical, and I can still smell him, fresh, bright apples. I want to know what he was thinking about when he was singing, what happened in his life that he wants to escape from.

Whether he's had any luck with that.

Whether he can give me some tips.

I force myself to relax the muscles that'd tensed me forward.

"Can I walk you out?" Alertness sharpens my tone. "Or we really could call an adventure party, just in case."

Alexo shakes his head. "No. I'll be fine. I—I should leave."

I don't like the idea of him going out alone with that guy still gods know where. "Please let me walk you to your car. Or the bus stop."

His smile. Gods, let it be what kills me.

"You're surprising, Orok Monroe," he tells me. And before I can figure out how to respond to *that*, he lifts up onto his toes, balances with a hand in the center of my chest, and motions for me to come the rest of the way down.

I comply, and he presses a kiss to my cheek.

His lips are cloud soft, barely making a brush of contact, but their warmth plunges through me in gentle whorls and I lean into it, chasing that sensation as he lowers back down.

"Thank you," he says again, and I think he means that he's accepted my offer, but he adds, "I can take care of myself. I promise."

My mind is still fuzzy from his lips on my skin, from the pressure of his hand on my chest, so he gets a few feet toward the door before I turn after him.

Am I going to ask for his number? I don't *do* that. No numbers. No commitments. Rarely last names, even—and this is exactly why.

Because I can already feel that overpowering possessiveness scratching away at my self-control. The need to follow him, make sure he not only gets home, but that wherever he lives is in a safe location, and then check with the local adventure parties to update them on that guy who threatened him. And before I can stop it, I'll be consumed in him, pouring all my time and energy and *need* into him.

I've fixated on things ever since I was a kid; it's why I was such a good little Urzoth follower. I obsessed over the rules that the church passed down and made every aspect of them my entire personality.

I did it with Seb, too. It took me years to break my dependency on him, and our relationship wasn't even sexual; he became such a crucial part of my life that I ended up getting two full degrees I didn't want or need to stay with him.

It's usually easy to keep my walls up. I'm so obnoxiously aware of how detrimental it is for me to make attachments that I keep everything locked in tidy little compartments.

Marlow and Darian: work friends.

Seb: brother.

Thio: Seb's.

Hookups: temporary.

So what is this? *Did* Alexo cast some kind of spell?

Seb is half listening to Darian perform, half watching me.

"Enchantment spells?" I ask.

Seb shakes his head. "Only the one you're wearing." He points under his own face, where the words are subtitled in an arcane glow. Marlow's earring.

I turn, and Alexo's reached the door.

He glances back. I don't try to cover that I'm staring right at him.

He should leave. On his own. I don't need to follow him, don't need to pursue this desperation. I have way too many life shake-ups plaguing me right now. I can't risk falling into dangerous habits when I'm vulnerable.

Let him leave.

Alexo pushes out into the night.

I dive forward, using every ounce of rawball training to deftly weave through the crowded bar until I reach the door, throw it open, and burst out onto the sidewalk.

The night's warm in late summer. A few people walk by, making for one of the many bars or restaurants that pack this street. My head swivels left, right—

He's standing at the bus stop a few yards down, arms wrapped around himself, chin tucked low. Given the fact that the guy who attacked him could be anywhere, he should be doing a better job of keeping watch. But there are other people at the stop with him, safety in numbers and such.

I step to the side of the door, leaning against the bar's window, and dart my eyes up and down the street. No sign of that guy.

Alexo stays tucked into himself. He seems zoned out, unaware of anyone or anything around him. The way he was on stage, sucked into his performance.

I push at the inside of my teeth with my tongue.

That focus was sexy on stage. It's worrying here.

No, I snap at myself. Not worrying. Because he's not *mine* to worry about.

The bus rolls up to the stop.

Alexo doesn't look back as he boards. Why would he? I stayed in the bar.

I *should have* stayed in the bar.

This is as far as it goes. He's on the bus; he'll get home safe. I have to trust he meant it when he said he can take care of himself. Maybe he's a wizard, like Seb, and he was one spell vial away from fireballing that guy before I stepped in.

Back inside, Seb and Thio have claimed a standing table, while Marlow's flirting with the bartender and Darian's on his second song to an adoring crowd who have recognized him as a Hellhounds bard.

"Damn it." Thio punches my shoulder. "I bet Sebastian a—*thing* that you wouldn't come back."

Seb grins at his fiancé. "Like my prize is something you're *so* opposed to doing."

When I don't good-naturedly blanch at what's clearly foreplay, Seb's expression softens.

"You okay? Did he not want to give you his number?"

I shake my head, then amend, "No, it's not that." But my mouth hangs open.

I really, really don't want to get into it. Any of it.

Not tonight. Not when we should be celebrating.

Why hasn't this felt like a celebration?

"I'm gonna get some champagne. That's what we need." I tap a quick rhythm on the table and shove away to Seb's disgruntled "O—"

It'll take some time to settle out of the fight-or-flight reaction. That's all. I need to come down from the trauma response. My therapy appointments will be more spaced out going into the season, which will help my schedule feel normalized. I'll do my job, make sure the Hellhounds have no reason to regret accepting my trade, whether or not the team has it out for me. I'll worry about the things I can control, and fuck all the rest.

Today marks a turning point in my life, and from now on, I'm moving *forward*.

No matter what.

Chapter Two

Morning News: "Welcome to *One Shot*, your number-one source for the latest in pro rawball news. I'm your host, Diamanda Blacktalon, here with my cohost, Vaknox of the Lizard People of Tesh. Last night, Orok Monroe was spotted rescuing a singer at the Silver Hound karaoke bar. The Hellhounds' newest defensive tank is a known devotee of the stone god of strength, Urzoth Shieldsworn. A rescue mission isn't quite in keeping with a god whose followers recently burned down a pizza parlor, is it, Vaknox?"

lizard hissing noises

"Exactly. I wouldn't have believed it myself, but you can see in this clip—there, pause it there—Monroe is wearing some kind of enchanted subtitling device, and he's clearly asking if the victim is okay."

lizard hissing noises

"You're right, they seem quite cozy! Don't you worry, viewers; our best reporters are at work uncovering the identity of this mystery man, who used the karaoke name Alexo the Magnificent."

lizard hissing noises

"What a scandalous thing to say, Vaknox! One thing's for certain: Orok Monroe hasn't even played an official game with the Hellhounds yet, and he's already shaking things up in Philadelphia."

I should run.

I *need* to run.

Something's behind me. Beside me? Something's *there*, breathing down my neck; I have to go, I have to *go*.

Help me, Urzoth. Help me. Make me strong, strong enough to get through this, strong enough to stop this—

A noise jolts me awake and I fly upright in a panic, one hand in a fist, one in a defensive block. Shit, which alert was that? Do they want us in the weapons room or the potions lab today? Why can't I remember? Mistakes cause delays, and delays cause retribution, and Seb's still in a sling from the last time I fucked up.

Wait—

The bed is wrong.

This isn't the scratchy blanket and knobby cot in our barracks. The comforter's fluffy and dazzlingly white where sunlight's hitting it through the window, and out that window, the skyline shows a view my real estate agent fawned over. *On a clear day, I bet you can see all the way to the Hellhounds HQ!*

Not Camp Merethyl.

I'm in my new apartment in Philadelphia.

And the day *is* clear, an azure sky I stare blankly at, my eyes tearing as reality beats my mind into submission.

Breathe. Breathe in for—how many seconds? Let's go with four. Hold it for three? Sure. Breathe out for . . . ten. No, that feels like too many.

But I only get through one breath cycle before I realize *holy shit, I feel like crap*.

The too-bright reflection of the sun off my white comforter isn't the reason for the twinge behind my eyes; it's a headache that's already there, a thumping vein determined to bruise my skull. My mouth's dry and tastes like I licked the inside of my cleats after practice, and now that I'm upright, my stomach goes *why the fuck are you bungee jumping at this gods-forsaken hour* and lurches nauseatingly.

I bend over my lap, elbows on my knees, and—

Am I naked?

I check.

Huh. I don't usually sleep naked.

I eye my bed again, but the other side looks undisturbed, and I blow out an exhale. Okay. Probably didn't bring anyone back here, which is good, considering all I remember from last night is a third bottle of champagne and Darian agreeing to let me sing "I Want to Break Free" if he took the lead and I did *the harmonies*, whatever that means.

The noise that woke me comes again and all the muscles in my body seize, which does *wonders* for my headache and nausea.

Briefly, I hear my mother's voice, telling me true Urzoth followers don't fall prey to weaknesses like hangovers. I don't think I've ever been a true Urzoth follower, so how would I know?

But—that noise. It's a laugh? Followed by a teasing shush I'd recognize in any reality.

Feeling like I've aged several decades past twenty-eight, I haul my ass out of bed, pull on a pair of gray sweatpants, make a valiant attempt to brush my teeth, and shuffle out into the living room.

The corner apartment really does have stunning views. The main room holds an open-plan living, dining, and kitchen area, with two walls of glass windows broken up by black steel piping. I did what I did with my house in Vegas and let a designer make it livable, which apparently means the same thing here as it did there: white. Everywhere. White couches, white rugs, white marble tables, with black accents and no hint of color except gold fixtures in the kitchen, and shelves of my knickknacks on either side of the fireplace. Why designers seem allergic to color for masculine clients, I can't guess, but it's better than the TV-propped-on-cinder-blocks situation I would've done.

In the kitchen are Seb and Thio, somehow successfully cooking pancakes on a griddle at the island while wrapped up in each other.

Seb says something, and Thio laughs again—the suddenness of the noise, that was what woke me up.

It wasn't a Camp Merethyl alert.

A shiver walks down my spine, and I shake it away.

"Morning, sunshine." Seb notices me with a bright grin. "How ya feeling?"

The smell of sugary syrup and toasted butter has my stomach

unsure whether it wants to continue yelling at me, but I slump to the island and heave myself pathetically onto one of the black leather barstools. "How *should* I be feeling?"

"Like you personally cleaned out the Silver Hound's supply of champagne."

"Awesome."

"Then started on their tequila, at which point I remembered even half-giant metabolisms have limits with alcohol, and reeled you back. You're welcome."

Thio slides something across the island to me. "On that note, drink this."

I look down at what seems to be a cup of coffee, but by the empty potion vial Thio's sliding into his jeans pocket, I know it's got some kind of magic in it.

It might not be Thio's job to actively create new spells the way Seb does at his lab, but the two of them still experiment on shit together and consider it date night. They've made a lot of powerful healing potions that way.

Whatever Thio gave me, I gratefully accept it, cradling both hands around the coffee and inhaling.

I stiffen, and *gods*, my stomach clenches for an entirely new reason. "Fuck."

"You okay?" Seb asks.

I drop my head into my hands. "You spent the night of your engagement *and* lawsuit celebration taking care of my sorry drunk ass."

Something whacks me on the head.

I look up to see Seb wielding the spatula like a flyswatter. Am I the bug?

All the fixtures in my apartment were designed for my lineage, so everything's a *touch* higher or wider than average. Which means Seb has to lift himself onto the edge of the island and strain rather far to reach me over it. That's some serious commitment to rebuking me.

"*Your* celebration, too," he says and drops back down. "Thio and I got to spend the night in your cushy guestroom. Have you *seen* that bathroom? It's bonkers. Way nicer than the stall at our place and what we've come to call mandatory polar plunge showers."

I didn't know his apartment's water heater was shitty? He's never mentioned it. But I make a mental note to call his landlord and get estimates for a replacement.

Discreetly, of course.

Seb and Thio wouldn't let me buy them a place in my building, so they'll have to put up with my stealth remodeling.

"So, in a way," Seb continues, "you gave us a luxury getaway as an engagement present. Because you're thoughtful like that."

"If this is a luxury engagement getaway," I say, eyeing the pancakes, "shouldn't I be the one making you guys breakfast?"

"You forget I had a front-row seat to your cooking for many years. I'd like to survive to my wedding, thanks."

Thio hip-checks Seb out of the way and takes over pancake duty. "On that note, baby, you're burning them."

"Fuck you, I am not."

Thio flips one that does indeed look a bit charcoaled. "Burnt."

"Crispy."

They stare at each other, and I swear to the gods, how are they getting aroused from *pancakes*?

I take a gulp of the coffee, letting it scald its way down my throat. I didn't tease them last night either about the nuclear-fallout levels of sexual chemistry they're always emitting. Why?

My chest twinges and I rub at it, suddenly hit by a ghost of apples, the brush of soft lips on my cheek, the flash of pink-gold glitter over a dimpled smile.

Did Alexo get home? Is that guy staying away from him? There's no way I can check.

And I wouldn't, if I could. Because he's not *mine* to check up on.

I keep rubbing my chest until Seb and Thio finish whatever edging standoff they've got going on.

Seb nods at my hand on my sternum. "Heartburn? Geez, you are getting old." He turns like he's going to head into the guestroom. "I have a potion we've been developing at work that's supposed to help people with digestive issues. Do you have a diffuser? It does best with—"

"Not heartburn. Just—Seb, wait. I need to tell you something."

He stops. Eyes Thio, who in turn looks at me, one brow lifted in an unasked question at the heaviness in my tone. *Do you need me to leave?*

And the fact that Thio and I can have a silent conversation is testament to how thoroughly he's locked into my life now, too.

I shake my head. "You two did finish your amalgamation into one being, didn't you? Stay. I—" I roll the mug between my palms, shoulders wilting. "You didn't have to take care of me last night. But thank you."

Seb comes around the island and hefts himself onto a barstool next to me. "Of course. You never have to ask. Even though you did."

"I did what?"

"Asked me to take care of you last night."

Surprise has me blinking at him. Seb's been my better half for most of my life, and he's right; we don't have to ask each other to step in. We just *do*. So for me to *ask him* for help . . . especially after I've made a resolute effort to *not* ask him for as much these past few years . . .

"What exactly did I say?" I try.

He gives a lopsided smile and digs in his pocket to pull out—my phone? "You asked me to keep you from *calling team management and making big changes*. But then you kept saying how you'd make the change anyway because we were free now, and you wanted to be *totally free*."

He sets my phone on the island and takes my hand, threads our fingers together.

The contact is grounding, an overlap of dozens of moments like this throughout our lives when I used him as a way to calm down, to center myself.

"What change were you talking about, O?" Seb asks.

I peel my fingers out of his and push off the stool to pace behind my bright white couch. The shelves framing the fireplace are directly ahead of it, and as I walk, my eyes run over the baubles, statues, iconography, and other odds and ends I started amassing in grad school. My degree was in theological evocation, how magic gifted by gods interacts with wizardry, specifically focused on power drawn from holy items in spell work. It spurred yet another of my obsessions, but this one is more of a quirky collection. I happen to have a lot of paraphernalia from various gods and religions. People collect weirder shit.

Staring at it all now, it settles me. I have trinkets from *dozens* of gods.

Thio switches off the griddle and finishes stacking a huge mound of pancakes on a platter next to it. The potion in that coffee seems to have softened my nausea and headache, but I'm not the least bit hungry.

Seb climbs off the barstool. "You're not quitting rawball, are you?"

I stop pacing, hands beating on my thighs. "No. Not that."

"But you are quitting something?" He squints. "Or . . . changing something? You—"

"I'm going to renounce Urzoth as my patron god."

Seb's brows vault up. Thio, on the other side of the island, whistles low and mutters, "Well, shit."

Seb says nothing, his blue eyes huge behind his glasses.

"That makes it sound far more serious than it really is." I start pacing again. "*Renounce*. Like it'll be some grand ceremony. Really, I'll take his badge off my jersey. It isn't a big—"

But I can't even finish the lie.

It's a huge deal.

In particular because—

Seb closes the space between us and stops a foot away, forcing me to quit pacing. "Does your mom know?"

I bark a laugh that sends a splitting bolt of pain through my tempered headache. "Ha. Have you heard of any small towns in western Pennsylvania spontaneously combusting? No. I have not talked to my mother about it."

And I don't know how I will. I'll need to, after I tell management, but *gods*, how do I say I'm withdrawing from the thing she's built her life around? From the thing she ingrained so deeply into our family's existence that it would never occur to her that I'd want to undo it for myself?

It was hard enough to tell Seb. And I only did it because it's the eleventh hour, and I know how hurt he'd be if I did something like this without talking to him about it first.

His gaze goes more critical the longer he looks at me. Like I'm a new experiment he's trying to unlock.

Finally, he nods, but it's cockeyed and uncertain. "Okay."

"Okay?" I match his head cock. "That's it? No *why would you do that, Orok? This is a huge, crazy change you're making, Orok?*"

He gives me an unimpressed look. "In what universe would I talk to you like that? But you've been unhappy for a long time, O. Like . . . a *long* time. And I kept thinking it was all these other milestones you needed to hit to be happy. Getting out of undergrad. Getting out of grad school. Getting back to Philly. Finishing this lawsuit. But you've always been . . . held back?" He flinches. "That's not the right phrase. Like you're happy and you smile and engage people, but none of it gets to be *yours*. You make other people happy, but it doesn't ever seep back into *you*. So maybe this is it? Maybe Urzoth's been the thing holding you back from being happy."

"I am happy," I tell him. But it tastes bitter. "It's not that I'm *un*happy."

Thio comes out from behind the island and leans against one of the barstools. "Why are you separating from Urzoth now?" he asks. Not accusingly, but curious. "The lawsuit just ended. Is it too much all at once?"

He's been Mr. Caretaker since the lawsuit started. Making sure Seb was okay, making sure *I* was okay. Even though us suing the family members of his who owned Camp Merethyl caused issues for him, too, Thio's been the one to monitor our emotional states like becoming a nurse unlocked his final form.

I resisted it at first. Part of me thought he was keeping tabs on me out of obligation; I paid for his mom to stay at her previous care facility for a few months when I first got signed to the Chimeras. But Thio's a persistent bastard, and once he realized I thought he felt duty-bound to me, he actually flew out to Vegas, sans Seb, to confront me about it.

"*You're my friend, too,*" he'd said. "*And this lawsuit is a huge, suffocating life event we're all going through, and that's what friends do: help each other breathe.*"

Yeah. They do.

I never stopped helping pay for his mom's care. Her new facility has an anonymous auxiliary fund, and Thio and Seb don't know I'm one of the main donors.

I gave into Thio coddling me.

When I pointed out his mulishness, Seb sighed all dopily and said, *Isn't it sexy?*

One of the many reasons Seb and I never would've worked romantically. Who finds antagonism *sexy*?

"Yeah, it is a lot all at once." I swallow, throat dry. "That's kind of why I want to do it now. Get it all over with. Let people speculate and say whatever they want about me in one big, toxic cloud, then maybe I can move on. From everything."

"And you want to move on from your patron god?" Thio clarifies.

I nod, muscles stiff, like even saying all this out loud is going to have my mother calling me in a fury. "I need a fresh start. And Urzoth, the church—it's tied up in our past. I can't think about him without thinking about . . ." I flounder to silence.

Clear my throat, and start again.

"Being back in the city with you both, in a new team, with the lawsuit behind us . . ." I shrug, my eyes pricking. "I just need to *begin*."

Alexo bursts into my head. The fire in his eyes as he sang, the way each word felt both begging and demanding. It solidifies the torrent of emotions whipping through me—guilt over how my Urzoth-infatuated mother will react to this; resignation that it really will make me a traitor; hope that I'll get to figure out who I am beyond being forced into boxes defined by someone else.

Through it, I see Alexo belting out his song, a gilded beacon.

Seb throws his arms around me. I hug him back instinctively, even more of my chaos settling, eyes fluttering shut.

"Okay," he repeats into my chest. "I support you, whatever you want to do."

"When are you talking to team management?" Thio asks.

I squint at the clock over my stove. "A few hours."

Seb yanks back. "*Today?* You have a meeting set up with them *today?*"

"Hey, you guys marked this lawsuit ending by getting engaged; I marked it by *disengaging.*" I waggle my eyebrows, wresting some lightness into this discussion. "Get it? Because I'm *disengaging* from—"

Seb snorts. "Oh, I get it." He swats my arm. "I wish you'd told me sooner. We could've, I dunno. Talked it through."

I smile. "Nothing to talk about."

This is as much as I wanted to talk about it with him at all. I told him what I'm going to do, that I'm making this big life adjustment; it was a healthy, normal exchange.

I didn't call him in the middle of the night having a meltdown about it.

I didn't spend hours texting him all the reasons I should or shouldn't do it.

I kept this admittedly monumental decision to myself, and presented it to him in a perfectly mature, responsible way.

This is what it's like to have a *healthy* friendship. I can maintain boundaries.

I expected to feel relieved that I hit this goalpost my therapist and I have talked about. But I only feel . . . ashamed? Empty.

Unsatisfied.

Although, maybe that has more to do with being violently hungover while having this discussion, so the whole *mature* aspect is kind of nullified.

Speaking of.

I glance down at my bare chest. "Um. Why did I wake up naked?"

Thio sputters a cough that's definitely a poorly restrained laugh and whips around to face the kitchen, but not before I see his face turn *flaming* red.

Seb unleashes an evil smirk. "Oh, babe. Do you really wanna know?"

"I . . . feel like I need to?"

"Well." Seb takes a running leap at the kitchen island so he can sit on it, kicking his legs as Thio white-knuckles the edge of the counter. "I told you. You said you wanted to be *totally free* last night."

My eyes widen and my empty stomach contracts. "Oh my gods. I didn't."

"Don't worry, we got you home before you stripped down. That was just for us, apparently." Seb scrunches his nose and nudges Thio with his socked foot. "Baby?"

Thio shakes his head, shoulders heaving like he's holding back laughter.

"No," he says, voice reedy.

"He asked *you* for it."

"I don't want to."

"I asked Thio for *what*?" I choke out.

Thio goes slack with a heavy sigh and takes a second to gather himself.

He turns from the island, pulls out his wallet, thumbs free a few singles, and throws them at me.

They flutter off my stomach and I lift an eyebrow at him.

"While Sebastian was getting you some water," he starts, face still red, voice still pitchy, "you stood on your bed, told your sound system to play, and I quote, *that sexy thub-thub hubba-hubba music*, and asked me to, and again, this is a direct quote, *throw some singles all up in this bitch, please*."

My face goes slack. "*Please?*"

"It was the politest drunk striptease I've ever received."

Thio's trying hard not to laugh. He's maintaining eye contact, lips in a flat line, nodding sagely like this is a totally normal conversation to be having.

"*Orok*," I start self-mockingly, "*do you remember the exact moment you gave up alcohol?* Why, yes. Yes, I do. It was when I—oh my *fucking* gods." A memory surfaces. Pretty rude of it, honestly. "Did I helicopter my dick at you?"

"You still had your boxers on at that point, but yes. I wasn't sure what you were doing until you made propeller sound effects."

Seb cackles.

Thio finally loses it, too.

And I stare down at the three bucks Thio threw me—wow, I must've been bad at stripping; which is some bullshit, I look amazing naked—and rethink every choice that led me to this moment.

Demolishing the stack of pancakes kicks the rest of my hangover. I should be more conscious of my carb intake with the season around the corner, but that ship sailed, sunk, and turned into a coral base for marine life with all the champagne I had last night. The pancakes are just, like, an exploratory submarine at this point.

When Seb and Thio head to work, I peel out of my condo's parking garage toward the Hellhounds HQ in the southern part of the city. Right off the river, a hop, skip, and a jump from Bwararax Stadium, the whole complex is tricked out in orange-and-black Hellhounds colors, with our mascot, a brown demon dog, snarling on everything.

The parking lot is half full; our practice is in the evening today, but with our first game in two weeks, most of the team will be hitting the gym or getting in extra specialty drills while they can.

I make my way through the massive glass-and-concrete building, passing shrines to players and wins. There are several cases full of trophies, including one giant display for the three rawball championships the Hellhounds have won over their sixty-year existence. Those trophies are each half my height, shining gold, with a gilded rawball, the iconic twenty-sided icosahedron shape, right on top. It's always a bit humbling walking past these displays—this is what every player wants. More trophies, more wins.

There's a new trophy in Vegas now, the Chimeras' fourth.

Shoulders straightening, I stuff my hands in the pockets of the nice slacks I changed into. A blue button-down, a navy tie, sleek shoes; my black hair's buzzed short so there's not much to do in the way of styling it, but I trimmed my beard and facial hair, trying to be as respectful and professional as possible.

The pro rawball league's official stance on having a patron god is pretty fluid. Players aren't *required* to have one, and if they do, gods don't always intervene with the mortals who claim them. Sometimes, like with Darian, players get magic boosts from their gods the way wizards get boosts from familiars. Urzoth's never had that kind of a relationship with any of his followers; he doesn't talk to me like Darian's god talks to him, doesn't give me divine assistance. It's been a formality only.

Taking on a god or stepping away from one is seen through a lens of what's best for each player. Does their patron god contribute to better performance on the field? No? Then why are we talking about it?

The pro rawball *community*, though, has *very* strong opinions on patron gods, discussing them with zealous aplomb, mostly because a lot of the fans hold to various religions themselves.

The biggest fallout will be with my public perception, which is already in the hole thanks to the lawsuit. Why not keep digging, right?

I hope team management shares my totally flippant, completely at ease attitude. *Oh, you want to renounce Urzoth? That request could've been an email, Monroe. Get out of my office.*

The manager suites are on the third floor, a few towering doors centered around a reception desk in a vaulted space done in polished hardwood. Behind the desk is the Hellhounds logo, and when I give my name to the receptionist, he waves me toward the last door on the right.

My palms break out in a cold sweat as I knock.

It'll be fine. Even though I haven't gotten a feel yet for this team's management and have no real idea where they land on the polarizing opinions of me. But they accepted my trade even with my public testimony during the lawsuit, didn't they? They can't hate me too much.

A gruff voice calls, "Enter."

This office is as dark and imposing as the reception area, the same polished hardwood making up the floors, walls, and ceiling. Massive windows at the far end make the space not quite so cave-like, presiding over a desk and shelves displaying more Hellhounds memorabilia.

Near the door is a long leather couch and two chairs in a formal seating area, and both chairs are occupied.

The Hellhounds head manager, Roesia Sombercrown, is a werewolf who made her name as an offensive rogue twenty-ish years ago. From the few times I've met her, she's fair but cutting, no time for bullshit. I *want* to like her, but I'm still so hesitant after management turned on me in Vegas that I don't trust my own instincts.

Roesia stands from her chair, and the person sitting in the one next to her shifts to look at me.

I freeze, the door swinging closed behind me.

It's a guy, human by the looks of it, broad-shouldered and heavyset, with hair gone white from age and a pale face lined in wrinkles. He's in a simple black suit, but what has everything in my body shuddering to a halt is the symbol stitched on the pocket of his coat. And on the briefcase next to his chair. And on the folio in his lap.

An axe speared into a stone.

He's a rep for the Urzoth church.

What the fuck.

I clamp my jaw shut to avoid gaping and giving myself away. I did *not* tell the receptionist what this meeting would be about when I set it up weeks ago—I just said I needed something on the books with at least Roesia, if not the whole management team. I'm new, still getting my footing here; it wasn't unexpected that I'd want to check in. No one would've been able to guess my real purpose.

So, again, *what the fuck.*

Roesia smiles, the most she ever gives: a quick pulse of her thin lips and a flash of her orange eyes. Her brown hair's pulled back in a severe bun and she's in a sleek maroon pantsuit, her hands clasped in front of her.

"Mr. Monroe," she says. "Thank you for joining us. Please." She waves at the couch across from them.

Forget my palms sweating; I'm pretty sure I'm fauceting through my shirt.

What the fuck what the fuck what the—

But I cross the room to sink into the middle of the couch. At least it's not one of those dainty decorative ones a lot of offices have; Roesia's clearly used to hosting rawball players of massive size, because the couch doesn't so much as groan under my frame.

"Uh," I start, ever so eloquently. "I mean—"

Roesia sits, her hands poised on the armrests, those intense, predator eyes whipping from me to the man next to her.

"Oh," she says. "I assumed you knew each other; my apologies. This is Maddock Drach, the head priest of the Church of Urzoth Shieldsworn in Philadelphia. Reverend Drach, this is Orok Monroe, our newest defensive tank." She pauses, a small quirk to her lips as she looks at Drach. "Though you probably don't need that introduction."

"No, I certainly do not." Drach shifts forward to extend his hand. "Strong as stone," he says by way of greeting.

I take his hand. He's smaller than me by luck of his lineage, but his grip on my hand is unnecessarily tight. Asserting dominance. Or trying to.

I shake back, squeezing enough to let him know I recognize what he's doing. "Hard as rock," I finish, the words tasting like dust.

Drach holds my gaze for a beat. And when I think this is going to turn into a stare-down pissing match and I bite my tongue to keep from rolling my eyes, Drach drops my hand and sinks back in his chair.

His stare is assessing. "I've been following your career since the Manticores, son. You've always been one of our most beloved players."

The Manticores—my time in college. I met a few Urzoth reps while I was there, but never this guy. Either he's new to the local branch or they sent in the big guns because I'm really, really screwed.

No. I'm not screwed. Once I part from Urzoth, I won't be subject to any of the church's authority. Whatever Drach's here for won't matter.

I swallow, throat grating on itself. "Thank you, sir."

Roesia crosses her long legs. "I know you arranged this meeting with my assistant some time ago, so forgive me for hijacking it, but the timing was rather kismet. Before we get started, Mr. Monroe, what did you want to talk about?"

She watches me patiently.

So does Drach.

And my brain undergoes a full system reset in two short breaths as I piece together that they do not, in fact, know what I want to talk about. Roesia has an Urzoth rep here for some other reason, and for the life of me, I can't figure out what it could be.

But I'm not about to renounce my patron god *in front of one of his priests*. That's like breaking up with your significant other in front of their parents. Plus, with him present, he'd take my renouncing as a challenge and demand we fight so I could have the *honor* of *earning* my way out of Urzoth's graces.

It'll be way less confrontational to renounce Urzoth to only Roesia. Maybe we can take care of whatever business they have, then Drach'll leave and I can be all *actually, funny story, I'm done with that god.*

I shake my head. "Oh. That can wait. What can I do for you, ma'am?"

Roesia smiles like that was the right answer. Of course it was. She controls my team; she gets what she wants, always.

"As Reverend Drach said," she begins, "you've always been a beloved player."

I snort. I can't help it. I *should* help it, because this woman holds my career in her hands. If she and the rest of the Hellhounds hadn't taken me from the Chimeras, I don't know where I'd be. I probably could've gotten in with another team, but to be here, *home*—it's everything.

Roesia smirks. It doesn't reach her eyes. "Yes. You've had a bit of bad press recently."

It's Drach's turn to make a rude noise, only his is an aggressive throat clear. I study him, and when he shifts on his chair, his gaze meets mine with a disappointed stare I've seen enough from my mother to recognize.

Great. He's on the *lawsuit is a sign of weakness* side of this whole debate. Though, being a rep for the church, it isn't at all surprising.

Roesia flicks her shrewd eyes at him. "Would you care to touch on your church's run of bad press as well?"

My chin jerks back and it takes me a beat to realize that she's *reprimanding* him?

Maybe I do like her.

Drach's face flushes but he doesn't back down. "In due time."

Wait—Urzoth's bad press? Does she mean that nonsense with the Galaxrien cultists?

Once Roesia regains command of the room, she looks at me again. "One of the things that had the Hellhounds most interested in you is how adored you are by the public. I do not believe you will be down for long, no matter the opinions being bandied around. That being said, this is an incredibly important year for the Hellhounds. With our roster, we are poised to bring home the championship win for the first time in more than a decade—which is why we invited you on board. Your talent is one of the many pieces that will go toward reasserting the Hellhounds' place in rawball history."

The Hellhounds might not have taken home the end-of-season championship in years, but they've still ranked well in other regards. Of course, all players hope their team will make it, but with everything else going on, I hadn't let myself dream that far ahead.

The Chimeras won it last year. But it never felt like it's any part *my* win.

"Yes, ma'am," I say, sincerity prickling through me. "I'm ready to put in the work."

"I'm glad to hear it. All eyes will be on the Hellhounds—and as such, we cannot afford bad press."

My shoulders flinch. "I know, ma'am. And I apologize for the negative—"

She waves her hand. "Do not apologize, Mr. Monroe. You helped weed out unworthy members of the magical community. You have done nothing wrong."

My eyes widen.

She . . . she supports me?

Gratitude tries to make my chest take flight, and I barely restrain myself from blubbering embarrassing thanks. The backs of my eyes heat and I blink quickly, refusing to tear up here, now.

But if Roesia believes me, if she's on my side, then the rest of the team's management probably is, too. And they won't tolerate the other players being dicks about it.

My hands unclench for the first time since—gods. Maybe they've been clenched since the lawsuit began.

But Drach aggressively clears his throat again, sitting up taller, making himself look bigger. It sucks some of this supportive energy right out of the room.

For being all *brute strength above all*, no one does passive aggression like Urzoth worshippers.

Roesia looks briefly annoyed, but she smooths her expression and picks a nonexistent piece of lint off her pants. "As I was saying," she continues, "we cannot afford bad press. Which means all such instances are being taken with the utmost seriousness. Therefore, we will be working toward changing how the public views you—and you, inadvertently, gave us the perfect way of doing so."

"I did?"

Roesia picks up a tablet from the coffee table between us. She taps a button and speaks into it, "Ask Mr. Warden to begin making his way up here," and then clicks at different things on the screen. "Are you on social media?"

She's talking to me again. "No, ma'am."

"Good. Don't bother; we have a whole department whose job it is to juggle that world. But apparently, last night, you made quite an impact on several outlets."

Roesia turns the tablet to face me and my head tilts in confusion.

It's a picture of me with Alexo.

The two of us are talking close, bent into each other, so it must've been after the guy left.

At the sight of Alexo, my skin grows hot, and something dangerously close to possession frissons through my body.

I knew people took pictures of us. Between the hangover and this meeting, I hadn't gotten to the realization that I could *access* those pictures. That I could see him again.

But just as quickly, I run my tongue over my teeth. These pictures are *online*. And the way Roesia's talked, they're *everywhere* online. Strangers are goggling at us, at *Alexo*.

My arms cramp with the sudden instinct to dive in front of an attack, only the target isn't here, and the threat is in the ether.

"Urzoth works through you," Drach says, noting my tension, and it forces me to relax.

This has nothing to do with Urzoth.

"I—" I swallow again, my tongue suddenly huge. "And this was . . . good press?"

"Indeed," Drach says. "An Urzoth worshipper using his strength to save someone? The reaction has been effusive, son. Fans love you."

My brows go up in surprise that *that's* what Drach focuses on—the fact that I actually helped someone.

Roesia flips through a few more slides, images of Alexo and me. Images of me facing off with that asshole. Even a video of me talking with Alexo, and you can see everything I say thanks to Marlow's subtitle earring, so I'm clearly asking Alexo if he wants to go with this guy, if he's okay.

My eyes run over his face. The gold glitter across his nose. The streaks of it on his collarbone like neon lights.

"You're a hero," Roesia says. "Which is exactly the shift you both need."

Both?

Roesia looks at Drach with a distinctive NOW *you can talk* expression, and Drach clears his throat. Normally this time.

"I'm sure you're familiar with the uptick in Galaxrien Vossen summonings," Drach says. He doesn't stop for me to respond. "The Church of Urzoth Shieldsworn has responded to those how we *always* respond: with appropriate severity as dictated by the threat of a demonic uprising. The demon lord Galaxrien Vossen *cannot* be allowed to emerge from the Demonic Plane, and as such, his cultists *cannot* be allowed to summon him out of his hellish prison. We are protecting Earth from his—"

"Reverend Drach." Roesia gets him back on track.

"The frequency of those summonings and therefore the frequency of our responses has led the public to begin voicing displeasure over what they mistakenly view as a feud between two gods. Our approval ratings have taken a hit. We find ourselves in a similar position to yours, Mr. Monroe, and as such, we have been in contact with your team management the past few weeks to explore ways of improving both our images. After last night, we have a proposition for you."

My knee bounces.

He goes quiet, and Roesia stays quiet, and I'm left sitting here dumbly asking, "What kind of proposition?"

Whatever it is, no.

I didn't come here to ingratiate myself even more with Urzoth. They need me more than I need them—I can improve my image on my own, thanks. My bad public opinion came because I stood up to my childhood abusers; their bad public opinion came because they rationalize burning down people's livelihoods in the name of stopping absurd cult ceremonies.

In lieu of answering, Roesia hits a button on her tablet. "Is Mr. Warden here?"

A voice comes through, "Yes, Ms. Sombercrown."

"Send him in."

Fantastic. Another church rep? Is this Urzoth's way of trying to punish me for—

The door opens.

There are several patron gods for rogues, gods of stealth, thievery, and swiftness. But one is unpopular to the point of being almost forgotten, which should be reason enough for them to be the *most* popular rogue god, but they aren't taken seriously—because their name is just screaming really loud. It undercuts the point of being a god for sneaky people, but they're the god of being taken by surprise, a whole dogma built around that moment when you're going upstairs and you miss a step, or you're hammering and miss a nail. The jolt of shock, the rush of endorphins and adrenaline in tandem; fight, flight, or freeze.

My brain fills with that god's name now, a long, drawn-out scream, as Alexo walks into the room.

Chapter Three

I vault from the couch, hands splayed by my sides, living proof that the concept of *holy fucking shit* can be a religious experience.

He's *here*.

He's in baggy black joggers and an orange Hellhounds jacket over a white shirt with writing in sparkly black letters that's hard to read as he tugs the jacket over his chest. He's forgone glitter and makeup, his face clean but still dusted with brown freckles. The bar lighting made his hair more strawberry blond than what it is now, a definite soft pink color. He's alert, if a bit tired, but more important, he looks healthy—no bruises, no cuts. That guy left him alone after he got home, then.

Alexo surveys the room. "Um, I was told to—" He hooks his thumb toward the closed door before his eyes flick up to me and lock in.

With a pulse of his eyebrows, his lips form a little O, and I don't breathe at all, don't *move* until I see whatever his reaction is to me. Is he going to freak out? He was cordial to me last night, but that could've been his way of diffusing the situation.

But—how is he here?

And wearing a Hellhounds jacket?

Roesia waves him in. "Please have a seat, Mr. Warden. I believe you know Orok Monroe?"

Alexo snaps his mouth shut. Shoulders stiff, hands stuffed in the pockets of his jacket, he clocks Drach's Urzoth insignias.

His face goes the tiniest bit slack before he considers the closed door behind him.

But he makes a decision, throwing his head back, and defiance gleams in those midnight black eyes. He rounds the chairs and lowers himself to sit on the far end of the couch.

As I sit back down, there's one full cushion between us.

He's *here.*

"Hi," I can't help but say, breathy and desperate and *idiotic.*

Alexo looks at me in surprise. And confusion. Yeah, my tone was weird. Shit.

"Mr. Warden is an intern in our cheerleading department," Roesia says. That demands all my attention—he's an intern here? But when I face Roesia, she's talking to Alexo. "Are you aware of your sudden stardom?"

He stiffens, the muscle pull of preparing to run, and when his mouth opens, he doesn't respond. I stop myself from reaching out to him; he looks in desperate need of comfort suddenly, apprehension gleaming in his eyes.

Roesia carries on without his answer. "I'm sure you're aware last night's event was photographed? The internet was quick to sleuth out your identity after Mr. Monroe rescued you. It didn't take long for eager fans to go through our rosters and figure out who you are, since apparently the Silver Hound is rather popular among the team and staff."

That's how I had heard of that bar, through the grapevine of people talking about the best places to have a fun evening. Is that why Alexo was there, too?

Alexo's lips roll shut. But he stays quiet.

Roesia gives him a longer beat to say anything, but when he doesn't, she makes a soft *hm* before continuing. "I believe the correct term is that the internet is *shipping* you two."

"I—shipping?" I ask, numb.

"Yes. I've been told it's when two people make a cute couple."

"I . . . I'm familiar with what it means," I stammer. "I'm—what does this have to do with—" I point at Drach.

Who grins at Alexo, and my hackles rise.

Fuck this possession. Alexo isn't mine in any sense of the word. *Down, boy.*

"Given the reaction fans are having to your rescue of Mr. Warden," Drach says, "and the positive spin it's putting on Urzoth, our proposition is that the two of you enter into a PR relationship for the season."

My jaw plunges open.

"Excuse me?" I demand at the same time Alexo goes, "I beg your *finest* pardon?"

I dig my fingers into my knees to stop myself from looking at him. I don't need to see what his dark eyes are doing, don't need to watch for anger or hurt.

"It would only be for the season," Roesia says before Drach can jump back in. She flips through her tablet again, this time showing both Alexo and me what's clearly a contract. "You'd both sign a standard NDA, along with stipulations we've worked out for event attendance, appearances, dates, PDA—"

My brain stalls out.

PDA.

"I—ma'am, this is all—but can we—" Form a sentence, gods, *any sentence.*

It's Alexo who leans forward. "I was told this meeting was about advancing my career, but this? This isn't—no. I can't do this."

I wait to feel offended that he's so quickly shutting down the idea of pretending to date me, but all I feel is a swell of pride, and I throw him a smile. Good. Don't let them fuck you over. Don't let *anyone* fuck you over.

Alexo's eyes are aflame, his brow set in determination, and he turns on me, maybe expecting me to be insulted. But when he sees my smile, he blinks quickly, his mouth going to that little O again. Only this time, his cheeks stain the faintest shade of red.

Back up. Back allllll the way up.

"This *is* about your career, Mr. Warden," Drach says. "The Church of Urzoth Shieldsworn is prepared to sponsor you in a position with the Hellhounds cheerleading squad."

Alexo frowns at Drach. "I already have a position with the cheerleading department."

"You misunderstand me—we are sponsoring you *on the squad.*"

The room hangs quiet for a beat.

I watch the side of Alexo's face, haven't been able to look away, so I see the exact moment he transitions from flat-out refusal to—interest.

"I've been speaking with Ms. Sombercrown all morning," Drach says, gesturing at Roesia. "The Hellhounds have also had their PR team hard at work crunching preliminary numbers, and the best forecast of public image approval comes by further leaning into what the internet has already begun *shipping*. So we are playing up the *star athlete and cheerleader* optics by sponsoring you to become a starting member on the cheerleading squad."

Alexo's whole face slackens. "What?"

"The heads of the cheerleading department say you're quite talented." Roesia taps a long nail on her knee. "They said they asked you to audition, but you preferred to stay in a support role. Why is that?"

Alexo folds his arms over his chest. "What would sponsoring entail?" he asks. Very obviously avoiding Roesia's question.

Drach opens his folio and reads from a list. "Your salary, uniform, and travel would be paid for by the Urzoth Church."

"Which is similar to the situation players find themselves in when they have a patron god," says Roesia. "But the Hellhounds, at least, have never had such an arrangement for a cheerleader."

No one points out that Urzoth's church isn't paying for any of my stuff. Not for lack of offering on their part; I declined their support once I went pro.

I think I knew even then that I'd back out one day.

Alexo huffs a breath. "And in exchange I'd, what? Have to swear an oath to your church? Be required to beat people up on a regular basis?"

Drach's lips flatten, the muscles by his ears bulging and his hands fisting on his folio. I scoot to the edge of the couch, angled toward Alexo, bracing.

But Drach merely cocks his head, though he does nothing to hide his offense. "That attitude is what we are hoping to offset. While we do place value in physical prowess, the true tenets of our religion are in multifaceted strength. Our god is made of stone, but he moves and breathes and *loves*. Strength is only truly effective when it moves, breathes, and loves, too."

I sag back. Just a little.

That's what I always believed. Or tried to believe. Even as my mother pushed me to *display my strength* in as many physical ways as possible, I'd counter with how *real* strength was rarely so simply defined. No one in Urzoth's church would argue that, but most have come to uphold the easy definitions of strength—*strong as stone, hard as rock*—more than anything requiring nuance.

It's nice to hear someone high up in the church professing healthier ideals.

Drach's still a dick, though.

"But to answer your question, no," Drach carries on. "Our requirements for you would be minimal. You would wear an Urzoth symbol on your uniform, but you are not obligated to join our church unless you feel called to. Our sponsoring of you is more a . . . charity. This arrangement is to complement Mr. Monroe's standing as a current and active member."

"I'd just—" Alexo stutters, and my eyes slip shut in a beat of gathering resolve, but it's obsolete. The moment I look at him, the strongest wall of resolve wouldn't be enough to keep back the dam of my own stupidity.

He's staring at Drach, those dark eyes narrow in disbelief. "I'd be a cheerleader? Just like that? And I'd get to perform?" Almost to himself, he adds, "As a follower of Urzoth?"

Drach hands him a piece of paper out of his folio. "And you'll make real money, kid. Just like that."

Roesia's watching Alexo curiously, her chin propped in her hand, but she doesn't ask him again why he didn't audition this year. Doesn't push him as he takes the paper from Drach and sees something—a salary number, likely—that makes his eyes bulge.

He puts his fingertips to his mouth and gasps, "Oh."

Part of me dive-bombs even deeper into stupidity, pretending he's saying O, my name, and I keep digging my fingers into my knees so hard pain radiates up my thighs.

Tell them.

Tell Roesia and Drach all this is moot because I'm not claiming Urzoth as my patron god anymore.

Tell Roesia I'll happily figure out another way to improve my public image before the championship game.

TELL THEM.

Slowly, Alexo looks from the paper to me.

He swallows roughly, throat bobbing, and I'm stuck staring at that spot, remembering the sheen under the bar lights when he was on stage, the way his neck bent as he crooned about dreams and believing and *feeling*.

All those emotions he spouted last night are radiating from him now. All the hope he emitted like light beams, and there I was, photosynthesizing each and every one of them.

Before he can speak, I ask him, "Do you want this? If you don't, we can walk out that door."

"Now, wait a minute," Drach tries, but he's nothing. The only thing that matters is Alexo.

Who's looking at me the way he did last night, studying me, and I wonder what he's seeing play across my face. I'm not doing a very good job of hiding myself from him, but instead of running for the hills, he smiles.

There they are. Those dimples.

"Yeah?" he says. It's a question. "Yeah. I think I do. This is crazy, though. Right?"

It is. Certifiable. Downright demented.

I am in *all* kinds of trouble.

"If he's in," I tell Roesia, "so am I."

Alexo and I sign our lives away. It certainly feels like that; the moment we verbally agree, Roesia calls in a few people from legal, who begin going over the NDA and contracts. When someone from HR hands us each a list of PDA options and gently asks us to circle which acts we'd be comfortable doing for cameras, I swear to all the gods that a blood vessel pops in my brain.

The list is . . . *extensive*. From handholding all the way to things no one should do for cameras unless they're signing up for a whole other type of financial endeavor, and I stare at the list, stupefied.

Alexo doesn't hesitate. He circles three things and declares, "Handholding, hugging, and kissing, no tongue," with a tone that brooks *no* room for arguing.

He follows that up by looking at me, a challenge burning the side of my face before I can peel my focus away from the sheet of PDA options.

My gods, does that really say dry humping*?*

I nod at him. "Yeah. That's fine. Sure." I think I repeat that a second time. *Yeah. Fine. Sure.*

You're going to let me touch you?

Kissing, no tongue.

There go a few more blood vessels.

Alexo's brows pop up. Surprise, again. I seem to keep surprising him, but I have no extra mental space to unpick that knot. Not when I woke up this morning intending to separate from my patron god and ended up his poster boy for heroic deeds and *also* tied to a fake relationship with a guy who'd been more fantasy than reality just hours ago.

Am I still asleep? Maybe I didn't wake up this morning. Maybe this is what happens when you self-medicate with champagne.

More signatures, a few legalese speeches I only half hear. Roesia assures me my agent will get copies of everything I'm signing—*yeah, that's fine, sure*, my motto right now—and Alexo and I are both sent links to a calendar of events throughout the season.

"We'll get started today, to ride the interest from last night," a publicist says. The room's swelled to about a dozen people, and they all stand now, so I guess we're done—

Wait.

"Today?" I manage, feeling like I'm emerging from underwater. No, water would be easy to get out from. I'm emerging from under honey, sticky and tacky, and it's all over my nose and eyes, can't really breathe or see.

"Today with your first date," the publicist clarifies and nods at my phone. "It's on the calendar. We're starting you simple, a coffee in the café downstairs. We'll get a few shots of you two together, no video or sound recordings, so feel free to talk about whatever you'd like. It's all for show, remember; make it look good."

Make it look good.

All for show.

Coffee downstairs.

I do understand English, I think.

Oh gods, am I having a panic attack? It's a real possibility.

A hand closes over mine where I'm gripping the leather couch cushion. The muscles in my arm jump, recognizing his touch already, the soft flex of his hand.

I look down at him, and his expression is encouraging but cautious. The way I got when Seb used to go on an angry tear and I'd have to talk him down.

"Come on," Alexo prods. "Just coffee."

I let him pull me to stand. Which is objectively hilarious, because if I really did need him to get me to my feet, he'd probably snap in half. But as I teeter upright, it hits me that maybe he's being cautious because he doesn't know me. I could be some psycho aggressive Urzoth worshipper, and he's relegated to having to soothe me.

In a parade of PR people, we're shepherded down two floors to the Hellhounds HQ café off the main lobby. It hasn't hit the midafternoon pick-me-up time yet, so we have the place to ourselves, and as we cross the threshold, the publicity folks hang outside, leaving us to our own *make it look good* devices.

Alexo knots his hands in the sleeves of his jacket, but he's still got his defiant, chin-up stance, facing down the world and daring it to turn on him. He starts to take charge, heading for the counter to order, when I put my hand on his forearm.

"What do you want?" I ask.

His eyelashes are dark and curled, and closer now, there's a light gloss over his lips. Shimmery gold-pink. It matches his hair.

Those eyes narrow. Curious. Cautious. "Large iced oat milk latte."

"I'll get it. You pick the seat."

I head off, not waiting to see his reaction. I order his drink, get a bottle of water for me—caffeine would be a *bad* addition to my body chemistry right now—and a few pastries.

When the barista pushes the order across the counter, I scoop it up and turn to see Alexo's chosen a high table right by the glass window that looks into the lobby. The publicists will have a perfect shot of us, and something clenches in my stomach, a pang of discomfort.

This shouldn't be fake.

I'd have asked him out for real.

I could call it off and sponsor Alexo on the cheerleading team myself. Wouldn't be the weirdest anonymous donation I've told my money managers to make, but it seems like Alexo could have tried out for the cheerleading team on his own, without Urzoth's sponsorship, and he didn't. Why did this work for him?

I can find out. We'll be spending a lot of time together over the next few months. Fake relationship or not, our conversations can be real.

Determined, I head to the table and slide Alexo his drink. Along with a blueberry muffin. And a chocolate donut. And a Danish. And a yellow cake pop.

Wow. Really?

Alexo looks at the spread of pastries before cocking a bemused grin up at me. "Hungry?"

"Uh—no, actually." While Seb was right, my half-giant metabolism is impressive, I'll hate myself tonight at practice if I eat any more crap. "I just—maybe you are?"

Alexo takes the muffin and tears off part of the top, but hesitates. "I guess I need to think about an athlete's diet now. I've seen how the cheerleaders eat, and my gods, no one should be physically able to consume that amount of celery per day."

I finally take the tall chair across from him instead of lurking by the table. "There's always room for sweets. I ate my weight in pancakes this morning to counteract an equally absurd amount of alcohol last night, so I'll pass. But you should eat. Your body's perfect." Heat burns my cheeks. "I mean—" *No*, nope. I physically squish my lips together to keep from overcorrecting and making what I said worse.

Alexo, muffin piece still lifted, watches me, eyes sparkling.

He takes mercy on me and pops the bite into his mouth. I let my lips relax.

After a beat, his smile dims. "I need to thank you again for what you did last night."

"No, you don't. In fact, I—" My gaze moves to the window, where out in the lobby, the publicists are taking our picture, and I clench the water bottle as I face Alexo, putting my shoulder to the glass. "I need to apologize to you. I shouldn't have lifted you up. I'm sorry."

With another bit of muffin halfway to his mouth, Alexo gawks at me.

He drops the muffin, dusts off his hands, and bends over the table. His jacket parts as he moves, showing the text on his shirt. Black type says, THE MOST IMPORTANT THING IS THAT BOTH TEAMS HAVE FUN.

I grin.

But Alexo shakes his head at me. "Okay, I do *not* get you. You're Urzoth's golden boy. Star defensive tank. Big, bad rawball player. Brings down a corrupt arcane training camp. And you're—you're—" he stammers, waving at me, seemingly encompassing, well, everything.

"I'm what?" I ask, honestly curious. "You expected me to be violent and domineering? I'm sorry if I gave you that impression, but I promise, that's not me."

That seems to derail him. He winces and looks down at his muffin.

When his gaze swings back up to me, it's from under his dark lashes, and I don't think he necessarily means it to be coquettish, but it is. That look spears through me and I go rigid at the table, jostling it enough that his latte sloshes.

"You're right," Alexo says softly. "I don't know you. I was making assumptions." His lips curve up. "Now *I'm* sorry."

"Aw." My smile stretches. "Was that our first fight?"

His eyes bulge in a stifled chuckle and he resumes picking at the muffin. "You think *that* was a fight?"

"Well, an issue, at least. Look at us, tackling conflict resolution like champs. We're such good fake boyfriends."

He laughs. Bright and tinkling, showing his dimples, and it injects liquid fire straight into my veins.

"And as your fake boyfriend," I continue, liking too much how that word feels in my mouth, "I want to know: What about this arrangement was so appealing to you?"

Alexo sobers. Almost instantaneously. Smiling to a stationary look of shock. I hadn't expected the question to hit him like that, but he tugs his jacket over his chest and folds his arms.

I see the moment he realizes that isn't a posture that'll look good for the cameras. He straightens, lays his hands on the table, shifts to lean more casually in his chair.

"You don't have to tell me," I amend. "I just thought, if we're going to be spending all this time together, that I could get to know you." I clear my throat and amend even further with, "I *want* to get to know you."

Alexo's gaze narrows. "Do you? Why?"

His question is cutting. Accusatory.

My mouth drops open. "*Why?*" I echo.

"Yeah. *Why?* Because I was some manic pixie dream guy you helped last night? Or because your god has an *interest* in me?"

"Because after you sang that song, I wanted you to know that you aren't alone."

Alexo slams his mouth shut.

"And yeah." I shrug. "I was fascinated with you last night. You were magical—the way you danced, the way you performed like you were putting your whole heart into the words. Which is why I want to take this opportunity for what it is and get to *really* know you. Maybe it was some sort of divine intervention that brought us back together, but no god will get credit for whatever we make out of this, and what I want to make out of this is—" *Something real.*

I cut myself off.

And everything I've said comes crashing back over me.

I haven't even *tried* to temper myself. I've been so swept up in confusion and wonder from the moment I saw Alexo in Roesia's office that I didn't put up any of my usual healthy relationship barricades. This whole thing already started in the weirdest way possible; nothing *real* could come out of it. And I don't do real, for exactly this reason.

Because I gave up a massive life change for a guy *I don't actually know.*

Gods, I'm a pushover.

Weak. That word beats in my head, throbs like an angry vein. *Weak.*

I close my eyes on a soul-deep groan and scrub a hand over the back of my neck. "I think the publicists got enough pictures." I shove up from the chair. "Forget I said anything. We'll see each other at the next—"

"I want to perform."

My gaze hits his. "You want to—?"

"Dance." He splays his hands. "Sing. *Perform.* That's why this arrangement was appealing."

I don't sit back down. I should walk away, let this stay something professional, and go home so I can figure out what the *fuck* I'm going to do about Urzoth now.

"But," I start, "Ms. Sombercrown said they asked you to audition and you didn't."

Alexo picks at the muffin crumbs. It is now that, just a mountain of crumbs. "I had my reasons for not wanting to. But this sort of sponsorship—" He shrugs one thin shoulder, his Hellhounds jacket catching the café light in a sheen. "I couldn't say no. It solves a number of issues in my life that I didn't think were possible to solve. The Urzoth patronage is a . . . security blanket." Those dark eyes bounce back up to me. "Why did you agree to it?"

Because of you.

Just you.

I bite the inside of my cheek and throw an exasperated look out the glass window—

There's someone new inside the HQ lobby.

Someone I recognize.

The guy who attacked Alexo at the bar.

"What the hell is he doing here?" I growl.

Alexo stands on his chair's rung and leans over the table to see who I'm looking at. The moment he spots the guy, he grabs my arm as I try to leave, only the motion has him wobbling precariously. I whip back to steady him, but he's already overcorrecting, and he ends up toppling off the chair and into my arms.

I catch him. There's no other choice.

We're bent to the side, me cradling him like he's some kind of fainting damsel in distress, one arm braced under him, and he's got his hand locked around my neck, his breathing fast and hot on my face. His apple scent is corrosively sexy—maybe he's wearing a pheromone potion. That's gotta be it.

"Th-thanks," Alexo stutters.

He's only about two inches from me. Closer than he's been yet. And he smells *so good* and those big brown eyes are fucking me up inside, and—

The guy. In the lobby.

How did he find Alexo?

It's painful to set Alexo down, but I do, straightening his jacket and keeping his back to the window as I throw a glare through the glass.

That guy's standing there, hands in the pockets of his dirty jean coat. He clocks me through the café window and glowers, upper lip curling in a snarl, but he's smart enough not to approach.

My instinct is to stomp out there and chuck this asshole into the parking lot.

But Alexo isn't freaking out. He puts his hand in the center of my chest like he did last night. Only instead of lifting up to kiss my cheek, he shakes his head.

"It's okay that he's here," he says. "He's harmless. I promise."

I really thought my brain wouldn't have anything else to trip over after the unrepentant onslaught of *what the fuck* today. But I frown down at Alexo, flipping through his words, their implications, and—

Oh, gods.

"Is he your . . ." I don't want to say *boyfriend*. And it's entirely because I already feel possessive of the word in relation to the two of us, however play-pretend it is.

My self-hatred is rocketing to levels it hasn't been at in years.

Alexo hesitates.

That hesitation is a fist to the gut, socking right into my diaphragm.

But he says, "No. It's just complicated."

My eyes flick over his head to that guy, who's watching us with a sneer.

The NDAs we signed strictly forbid us from telling anyone that this relationship is fake. But if he has a—fuck—*boyfriend*, even an on-again, off-again piece of shit like that, we could make more problems for him with this fake dating charade.

"Is he someone who will have an issue with this arrangement?" I ask.

Alexo laughs. It's strained, nowhere close to the real, ringing laugh he gave me earlier. "*Oh* yeah."

Another sucker punch to the gut.

A winded, gasping grunt leaves my mouth, and before I know what I'm doing, *why*, I have Alexo's chin between my finger and thumb and I'm bending down over him.

"We don't have to do this," I say. "If us dating publicly will cause trouble for you, we don't have to do it. I can find another way to get you patronage on the cheerleading team."

Alexo's glare is sudden and intense and leaves me speechless. It's all the fire of his performance, all the yearning of his song, and for a moment, I want to beg him *not* to join the cheerleading team. I don't think I'll survive seeing him dance.

Through that look, he leaves his chin in my hand. Doesn't seem at all put off that I grabbed him like this, keeping his face tilted up to mine.

"I'm not letting this opportunity go," he tells me. It's a promise. A threat. "I'm tired of running. Of dimming myself. This is a real chance, and I'm taking it. Yeah, there might be some people who have problems with it. But *fuck. Them.*"

He punctuates the last two words with steps toward me, and I hadn't noticed how much space we still had between us until he's against my chest, his lips and breath and *being* held right up under my face.

There might be some people who have problems with it. But fuck. Them.

My eyes flutter shut.

This guy is the physical manifestation of all my inner turmoil the past few months.

I really never stood a chance.

"All right," I whisper.

It's *not* all right.

Alexo nods in my grip, and when my eyes open, he's backing away and glancing out the café window.

The publicists give us a thumbs-up and head back for the elevators. I completely forgot they've been immortalizing all this.

That guy is shaking his head, staring at Alexo, fury stark on his face.

"I have to go," Alexo says. He gathers up the trash on the table, the muffin remains, mostly. "I didn't realize what time it was. I—"

He startles as I take the trash from him and push the untouched pastries and his coffee toward him. "I got this. You need to leave?"

A lopsided smile. The ghost of a dimple on one cheek. He nods out the window, toward that guy. "He's my ride."

I think I crack a molar. That tension is all that keeps me from asking if *I* can give him a ride instead, because I don't want him alone with that guy. Do they live together?

Not my question to ask. Not my *anything*.

But I dig my phone out of my pocket and slip to a contact entry screen before extending it to him. "Give me your number?"

Alexo grips his coffee cup, contemplating the phone, then my face.

"Please," I add. "We'll need to . . . coordinate. Sometimes. For our events."

Another small smile. That pleasantly surprised smile that's an intoxicant.

He takes my phone, types in his number, and sends a text to himself. "There. *Boyfriend*," he adds with a wink.

I smile back, liking that way, way too much.

And when he leaves the café, crosses the lobby to talk with *that guy*, I clench down hard on the trash in my hand until the muffin crumbs are mushed into oblivion.

This is a business arrangement. For my career, for his. For our team.

I track Alexo and his escort as they cross the lobby, breath coming in faster pulls, shoulders rising to my ears.

The moment they leave, I toss the trash into a bin and storm through HQ to the gym. Our team drills don't start for several hours, but a lot of people will be doing their own workouts until then. So I will, too. That's fine.

Yeah. That's fine. Sure.

I change into the gear I keep stored in my locker, throw myself on the first open treadmill—one of the larger ones for those of us with ancestries like mine—and wrench the speed to the max. If my nearby teammates give me odd looks, I ignore them. I just run.

And run.

And it's too poetic, isn't it? Running and running only to get nowhere.

When I'm so covered in sweat that my tank is translucent, I punch off the treadmill and head for the outside track that loops the training field. It's a sweltering day, the sun high and bright, which keeps anyone else inside. Good. I'm alone, huffing and puffing and powerwalking through my cooldown until I yank my phone from my gym shorts.

I start to text Alexo. Ask if he got home okay.

Instead, I pull up Seb's number and know I'm going to break not only my NDA, but the promise I made to myself, that even though I'm back in Philly with Seb, I'll rely on him less. I'll keep him at arm's length.

I quit him cold turkey when I moved to Vegas four years ago. We still have a relationship, but it isn't the codependent, unhealthy domination we once had. Well, that *I* once had with him, where I'd wake him up if I had Camp Merethyl nightmares or seek him out if I was on the verge of an anxiety attack. My therapist once called Seb my security blanket, and—

Alexo's words ring in my head. That's what he called this opportunity. His *security blanket*.

Everything about him feels inadvertently familiar, and I'm right back where I was years ago, losing my mind and desperate for Seb to ground me.

I don't want to need Seb. I worked *hard* to *not* need him, and he's got Thio now. He moved on and healed and he's healthy, happy.

But this thing with Alexo is consuming me already, and I have *months* of interacting with him coming my way. How do I function when every single thing about him seems like it was made to call to me? It's not his fault, and I can't make it his problem, and *gods damn it*, I haven't been this unhinged in *years*.

I come to a stop in the middle of the track, planting my forearms on top of my head, phone loose in one hand, and breathe.

This is just a setback. I knew I'd struggle with the lawsuit ending; my therapist and I have spent the past few months preparing for expected stumbles and pain. I knew I'd struggle with Urzoth, too, even if that went a bit differently than I'd intended.

A setback doesn't mean all my years of striving to be better vanish. I can choose how I go forward from here.

And I choose to go forward as the person I want to be, not with the ghosts I'm running from.

I lower my phone and switch to a different contact, hit call, and hold it up to my ear.

"Hey, Mom," I say as soon as it connects.

"Orok!" she exclaims. I smile; it's involuntary. Seb used to tease me for what a momma's boy I am.

My smile wavers. I'd planned to call her tonight. To tell her I'd renounced Urzoth.

"How are you?" she asks. "Are you at practice?"

"In a bit. I wanted to, uh, tell you something."

Silence hangs. Even without being able to see her, I can *feel* her expression, that brief lip twist that signifies she's worried I'm going to talk about the lawsuit.

Seb specifically *stopped* teasing me about being a momma's boy once he realized that I'm only a momma's boy if we avoid certain topics. For a while, it was Seb himself and his *inappropriately weak influence* on me. For the past four years, it's been the lawsuit.

When the news came through yesterday that we won, I texted her about it. Didn't call.

My parents both left the message on read.

I don't let the silence hang for long. "I met someone."

Because if this thing between me and Alexo is meant to look real, I'd absolutely tell my mother about it.

I ignore the twinge in my stomach at the reminder that this is a lie.

She sucks in a breath. It sounds more relieved than excited. "Oh, that's wonderful! Do I know them?"

"Him. And no. Well, maybe? Have you or dad been on any pro rawball sites since last night? I wanted to tell you before it started getting too spread around."

There's a pause, a muffled conversation I can't hear, and my mom returns with, "No, we haven't been online in a bit, but we will now. What are we looking for?"

Great. I pinch the skin over my nose. "There was an . . . incident. I got into a bit of a situation at a bar, and—"

"A situation?" Her interest piques.

Just say it. All at once. "A guy was being rude to someone and I intervened, and the person I stepped in for ended up being—"

"*Orok!* A fight? How did you stop that man? How brutal was it? What did Urzoth call you to do?"

"It didn't escalate to that, but—"

"You didn't even *need* to fight him? Oh, I'm so proud of you! This is what Urzoth's strength is best used for—asserting dominance so all around know your might without you even needing to display it. Strong as stone."

"Hard as rock," I say automatically, then wince. "But anyway—the man I saved is who I'm seeing now. And the rawball tabloids are running with it, so I wanted to tell you before you saw anything. Keep you in the loop."

"Behind-the-scenes information?" There's a smile in her voice.

I echo it. "Yeah. Behind the scenes."

"Well, thank you. Will we get to meet him soon?"

My parents live a few hours from Philly, but if Alexo and I are meant to keep up this charade all season, they'll definitely cross paths.

"Yeah. I mean, if things work out. His name's Alexo."

"Well, I'm glad you're happy. And I'm glad you're using your position and fame to bring light to Urzoth. We'll pray for you and Alexo."

Back to squeezing the skin over my nose. "Thanks, Mom. I gotta get to practice."

"We love you."

She hangs up, and I hold there, phone to my ear, pinching the shit out of my nose to stem the headache pulsing behind my forehead.

A tap on my shoulder has me vaulting a foot in the air.

Marlow stands on the track behind me, outfitted for a run.

"Gods, Darian's right," I groan. "You do need a bell."

"I feed off your terror," she says, her ring translating. But she's grinning, looking almost conspiratorial, and she shimmies back and forth before signing, "So, you've got a new boyfriend?"

I scowl and pocket my phone. "How'd you even—"

"I can read lips. The subtitle earrings just make my life easier. You and the guy from the bar? You were shitfaced last night; there's no way you took him home. What happened?"

My mouth opens.

Uh.

What *did* happen?

"Turns out he works here." I wave at HQ behind Marlow. "It's a bit early to say we're *dating*, but the sites figured us out, and he *did* agree to see me, so we're taking it slow, but . . . um. Yeah. Not much to tell yet. Kind of boring, really, but I wanted to tell my mom before she saw something and erupted, ya know? Moms. And stuff. They can be. *Ya know*. Ya know?"

Oh my gods.

Did the publicity people brief us on a cover story? They might've while I was comatose in Roesia's office. Super helpful right now. I'm doing great.

Marlow blinks at me, her confused gaze going from my eyes to my lips and back again like she's not entirely sure she understood me right.

"Okaaaaay," she says, making sure to sign it in a long, drawn-out, disbelieving way I do not appreciate.

I shove the side of her head. "Race you?"

"Well, that's not fair to you. Choke on my dust, tank." And she bolts up the track.

I hurry after her, focusing on her taunting, on the heat of the sun, on the upcoming practice.

On anything else, literally *anything else*, other than Alexo. Or Seb. Or Urzoth.

Or Alexo.

Mostly Alexo.

Fuck my life.

Chapter Four

The weeks until our first game fly by. Because I *force* them to fly by.

To make sure all mention of my divisive lawsuit fades into the background, the team publicists are *building a narrative* with me and Alexo. Teasing it out, keeping it simple. Aside from our coffee date, we don't have any other face-to-face interactions scheduled until the game itself. Alexo supposedly watches one of my practices, but I *do not* look around to see him. I'm so focused on my plays that both the tank coach and the head coach tell me, in two separate asides, that if I keep playing like that, our defense will be an impassable brick wall.

I haven't seen Seb either. Because I am very focused on training, thank you. And not at all because he texted to see how my renouncing of Urzoth went, and when I told him I didn't do it—*it wasn't the right time*—we had a bit of a back-and-forth. And then a day later, he texted me a link to a pro rawball article about my coffee date with Alexo, and asked if my *sudden concern about timing had anything to do with this pretty little Urzoth cheerleader?*

No. Yes. But no.

I'm even more of a poster boy for Urzoth now—much to the exultation of the group chat between my mom, my dad, and me, where my mom has been heaping praise on Alexo while berating me for not telling her that he's a follower of Urzoth, too. Luckily, there haven't been more Galaxrien cult rituals and therefore no subsequent Urzoth responses, so mine and Alexo's Urzoth ties haven't needed to be too in-your-face. But all the positive press from me and Alexo has Reverend Drach and Roesia happy, as told to me by a publicist who prepped me for a media blitz.

It took everything in me to keep from asking how Alexo was doing. I know he leapt into practices with the same ferocity I did, but his reason was because he only had two weeks to get up to speed with the rest of his squad. I didn't ask about him because I didn't need to know about him, like I didn't text him because I didn't need to text him.

I've slotted him into a healthy box like everyone else.

Alexo: PR stunt.

Simple as that.

Before I can catch my breath, I'm heading into Bwararax Stadium for the first game of the season and I've got everything in my life so compartmentalized that I'm basically a walking, talking IKEA storage system.

Alexo and I are scheduled for an *interaction* after the game, win or lose. It'll be fine, a quick hug or something, then we'll separate until our next scheduled *interaction*.

In the meantime, I'm here to play.

And I'm going to trust that my teammates are here to play, too.

None of them have given me shit during practices. They haven't from the start, but I dunno; I expected *something* to get bad after the lawsuit announcement, a reminder that I'm a *traitor to the Urzoth community*. No one else on this team claims Urzoth as their god, though, so maybe that helps. Plus, the positive press about me and Alexo seems to have usurped the lawsuit news. Or Roesia's attitude toward the lawsuit is indicative of the whole team's stance.

There won't be any repeats of stuff like what the Chimeras pulled.

Everything's. Just. *Fine.*

The locker room's mostly full already, everyone launching into their various pregame rituals or prep.

Darian's in the corner restringing his guitar and cooing quietly to it; apparently it gets stage fright unless he assures it how good it sounds.

I've learned to take people at their word when it comes to enchanted rawball items.

Like how another of the tanks across the room is currently feeding strips of charred steak to her broadsword—yeah, how does *that* work—because if it doesn't get a steady diet of *flesh*, it'll *cut opponents too deep, and we want to* nick *them, not* mutilate *them.*

Then there are players like me, who go in with no weapons other than their body and fists, and get to pummel the shit out of the opposing team when they get too close to their designated offensive player.

Fucking love this game.

I dig through my locker for my gear. Shin guards, elbow guards, cup, chest shield, helmet, and more.

When I'm suited up, the last thing I pull out is my jersey. The Urzoth patch is sewn on the upper left shoulder.

This'll be the first time I'm wearing my Hellhounds uniform for a game. I'd hoped to go in with just the Hellhounds logo and my number, 64. Nothing more.

My thumb runs over the stitched symbol of the axe in a stone.

I had an iron pendant with this symbol when I was younger. I'd cling to it and pray and pray and *pray* at Camp Merethyl. *Begged* that pendant, begged Urzoth for strength, for the pain to stop.

Strong as stone. Hard as rock. Stones don't have feelings. Emotionless, tough, nothing hurts stone.

A door slams open and I startle, sniffing hard against the stinging in my eyes. Gets so damn dry down here.

I shove to my feet and tug on my jersey as the coaches file in.

The head coach is Arthur Riprak, an older dwarven man I'm pretty sure only shows emotion when the Hellhounds win. He claps twice. "Listen up! We got the field layout from the Gorgons."

Rawball routine: the visiting team's artificers choose and design the field's layout. Which means the home team doesn't know what they're working with until the day of the game.

We all gather in the center of the massive room that always kind of smells like sweat and hand chalk. I up-nod Darian and Marlow, and they return it.

Behind me, there's a groan like something shifting, stretching—

Then a willow tree shoots to the ceiling.

I look up at it. "Hey, Phei."

Its branches droop into the crowd and someone bats one aside.

"We talked about forms that get all up in other people's business when we're not on the field, didn't we?" that person groans. "Phei, can you—"

The tree vanishes, becoming a wobbling, see-through humanoid form made of . . . wind?

"Thanks," the same person says, and Phei's air form burbles assent.

"Are we all good?" Riprak calls. He doesn't wait for an answer. "Now, the field."

He turns to his assistant coach, who splays her hands, and a miniature version of the field appears in an arcane whorl over all our heads.

The moment it does, Marlow's eyes go huge and she leaps up onto a bench. "*Water!*"

I cock a smile.

The field is, indeed, almost entirely water, with a few sand islands scattered around. On either side of the long field are each team's goalposts. A ref will hover over us, and once they drop the ball into the center of the field, it's a free-for-all between both teams to get possession of it. We'll have to rely heavily on swimming or other underwater transportation to avoid magic attacks from the opposing team, grab the ball, then get it between the goalposts on the Gorgons' side, all while defending our own goalposts and fighting off the Gorgons.

And Marlow is *ecstatic*, pumping her fists and doing the Hellhounds bark. "My time has fucking *come*!" she signs. "It's over for you bitches. MVP! MVP!"

"Wow," I say. We all wear the subtitling earrings when we're in the locker room. "Do you talk to your mother with those hands?"

Marlow smiles sweetly at me. "Just yours."

There's a chorus of *ohhs*. Someone slaps me on the shoulder—good-naturedly, but I have to hold back a flinch.

It was a joke, and they all laughed, see?

"Keel, Monroe," Riprak says to me and Marlow, "thank you for volunteering to go over which plays we'll rely on for this type of field. Keel—get us started."

Marlow doesn't seem at all chastened by Coach's obvious calling-out, and she starts noting areas of weakness on the field and which plays would be best. I offer advice where I can, but Marlow's on a tear. This is her first game on the Hellhounds like it is mine, but it's also her first *game, period,* as a pro rawball athlete.

"Kid's got something to prove," a guy mutters next to me. Aaron. Human, one of the other defensive tanks—and the team captain.

He's gripping a rawball in one big hand, tapping the twenty-sided leather ball against his opposite palm in a nervous tic. I've trained alongside him the past few weeks, by nature of being a defensive tank, too, and he seems like a good guy. Encouraging, smart, charismatic. All things you'd expect of a team captain.

The Chimeras' captain was those things, too. But also an egotistical jackass. Aaron, so far, hasn't exhibited any asshole qualities, but around him I still feel like I'm walking on one of those glass floors in a skyscraper, only the glass is splintering and it's seconds away from shattering.

I eye him. "Yeah. And the field being water's gotta be some kind of sign for her."

"Shit." Aaron scratches his chin. "You're usually on her? All the luck to you. She's going to be a nightmare to defend with this kind of energy."

I give him a *what can you do* shrug.

It's all very . . . civil.

Honestly, it's freaking me out. Part of me wishes the team would turn on me; at least with the Chimeras, I knew where I stood.

Gods, that's pathetic. This team hasn't done a damn thing to earn my distrust, and I *want* them to be jerks? What is this, middle school? I came here to get into a better situation. And so far, it *is* a better situation; no passive-aggressive remarks in the locker room, no unnecessary force in practice drills, no outright cruelty or confrontations.

But they didn't come to the Silver Hound when I invited them. If they really didn't blame me for the lawsuit, they'd have come, right?

Yep.

This is middle school.

When Marlow finishes her breakdown, she topples off the bench and turns to Riprak like she's expecting a pat on the head.

Riprak blinks stoically.

"Nothing to add," he says. "Aaron, you got a word for us?"

Aaron moves past me. He leaps up onto the same bench Marlow was on and gives the kind of speech I've heard dozens of times before. About greatness, victory, the hope of a new season; we've all heard shit like this before, but it still serves to get everyone appropriately pumped up.

By the time he ends with "Let's suit up and kick some Gorgon ass!" we burst into Hellhound barks, hooting and woofing, a rising well of energy.

No one gives me sideways looks. No one jostles me unnecessarily in that dumbass macho threat way.

It's unity.

It claws at me, and I let it in, let it burrow deep into my chest and drag me with it.

This isn't the Chimeras.

This is a fresh start. Maybe not every aspect of a fresh start like I'd wanted, but it's a start all the same, and when we go out there, it's not wheels spinning. It's not a repeat.

It's a *beginning.*

Marlow *is* a nightmare to defend.

Not least because she's on such a high, but because she's *half mermaid*, and I might as well be a gods-damned boulder for all the buoyancy I exude by comparison. Our plays in water-based situations rely on wizards or bards like Darian throwing swim spells on those of us who need them, but a few well-placed counterspells from the Gorgons and I all too frequently find myself miserably doggy-paddling toward one of the sand islands.

Marlow zips and dives and pirouettes through the water, and while I do manage a few blocks for her, I'm pretty sure she doesn't need any assistance. She gets the ball and she's *gone*, and even the Gorgons' best defenses have trouble containing all the grit that is our rookie.

The bright side of how fully consumed I am in the game is that I don't have the time—or oxygen, when I'm sinking post-counterspell—to glance at the sidelines, where the cheerleaders perform.

Riprak pulls me after a particularly gnarly interaction where a Gorgon bard played a song that pinned my arms to my chest so I couldn't swim. It didn't feel like any of my team purposefully let the spell slip through, and Darian took the attack so personally that he's currently locked in a riff-off with that bard while I hack water out of my lungs on the player benches.

As entertaining as it is to watch Darian rip on his guitar, my eyes drift to the right.

The stadium's packed with Hellhound and Gorgon fans alike, and over the buzz of cheering, a song kicks on that has the cheerleaders dropping into a routine. I can only see the backs of them from here, so I grab my water bottle, take a gulp, and peek up at one of the projection screens over the stadium.

The image pans across all the performers, catching them as they expertly do the same series of thrusts, spins, and twirls.

There's Alexo.

He's in a Hellhounds cheerleading uniform.

I mean, of course he is.

But.

He's in a cheerleading uniform.

I blink up at the screen, certain my mouth is hanging open, but hopefully my teammates blame it on me catching my breath.

Cheerleading. Uniform.

It's skintight. Because why not.

For home games, it's black with orange trim, and from the looks of the other dancers, they all have a sleeveless top but can choose whether their lower half is a pleated skirt or impossibly small booty shorts.

He chose the booty shorts.

His is the only uniform top with a small symbol for Urzoth stitched on it, right above the snarling Hellhounds demon dog.

I look back down at the live show, spotting Alexo's pink hair now. His pom-poms flash in tandem with the rest of the cheerleaders', and though they're all supposed to be in sync, I can't help but note the difference in how he's dancing. Or maybe it's that I'm only looking at him, so I clock the fluidity in his arches, the extra pop in his spine when he snaps upright, the way he shimmies his ass in those painted-on fucking *shorts*.

"Monroe! Back in!"

I empty the rest of my water bottle straight onto my already drenched face and bolt off the bench.

Focus.

I'm here to play.

And my teammates are, too. We operate in tandem, and when I get hit by the Gorgons again, healers like Phei are right there to patch up any injuries, which keeps the plays fluid. It silences the blip of me that constantly wonders, *Did someone on my team let this happen to me?* We're all working our hearts out, lifted by Marlow's chaotic energy, and by the time the game wraps at 28–17 in our favor, we're downright *giddy*.

Every rawball team plays seventeen games a season, and the two teams who pull in the most wins go head-to-head after the new year to take home the rawball championship trophy. Starting this season with a W—especially on a new team, where we played so fucking *well*—sets a mood that has me soaring so high I almost don't need our team's wizards to help me out of the water.

Emphasis on *almost*.

Why'd it have to be water?

Dripping and far too graceless, I congregate on the side of the field with the rest of my waterlogged team as the crowd roars out a Hellhounds bark. It's a madhouse of backslaps and excited leaps and congratulatory cheers, and press swarm the area, pursuing individual players and recording our celebrations. Marlow's instantly set upon by half a dozen reporters.

I rip off my helmet, toss it on a bench, and turn away from a few other reporters who clearly want to talk. I'm not *searching* for someone, but I'm not *not* searching for someone—

A cluster of people separates a few paces ahead, and Alexo's there, being guided through the bedlam by a publicist who quickly ducks away once I'm in sight.

I don't move.

I should, I think. But I didn't get briefed on what we're supposed to do beyond *interact.* Or maybe I didn't let my brain absorb any of the details about our *interactions* because I don't trust myself not to spiral wildly at the slightest provocation.

Which is *great* right now, considering Alexo's crossing the grassy sideline toward me, still in that skimpy cheerleading uniform that makes saliva fill my mouth. It hugs every inch of his slender, cut body, his exposed skin glistening with sweat and more of that glitter. I swallow, aware I'm dripping saltwater like a giant drowned rat, but when I meet Alexo's eyes, he gives me a small, encouraging grin with his glossy lips.

Alexo: PR stunt.

Alexo: PR stunt.

Hug him or something. That's all this moment is. A shot for the cameras around us. So . . . hug him. That's easy.

He stops in front of me. The stadium is thunderous and my teammates aren't any better, so when he speaks, I have to angle down to hear him, close enough to smell his apple scent, a hint of his sweat.

"Congratulations," he tells me. "You were amazing."

He's wearing makeup again, smoky gray around his eyes and mascara thick on his lashes.

"No, *you* were amazing," I say. "You look like you've been dancing your whole life. I couldn't take my eyes off you."

Real smooth.

But I can't regret it. Not with the way Alexo smiles, dimples popping. "Yeah?"

"I hope it was everything you wanted it to be? That it made you happy? You *look* happy."

The way he's staring at me becomes a relentless knot I couldn't untie if I wanted to. The pause that follows is just as tangled, teeth fixed on his lip, a question building in his eyes.

"I don't, uh—" I swallow again, and where there'd been way too much saliva in my mouth, I'm now dry. "I'm not sure what more we're supposed to—"

He lifts up onto his toes and presses his lips to mine.

It doesn't progress beyond exactly what the PDA list detailed. Kissing, no tongue. But that mundane description failed to note what it *does* include.

Like Alexo's body, crushed to mine.

My arms around his hips.

His fingers scratching at my short, wet hair.

The glide of his gloss on my lips, the heat of his breath as I open to inhale, the taste of him like a shot thrown across my tongue, fruity and effervescent and eye-poppingly delicious. Except my eyes are pinched shut, desire streaking down my spine and out across my arms where I'm clinging to him, and I know, *I know*, that for all the time I spent plunging into deep, dark waters today, this is deeper, this is darker.

He's mine.

Seb was mine. He was my friend, and then Camp Merethyl's sadism made it so we had no one but each other, and he became my *everything*. That's the feeling eating at me now, the feeling I've spent a lifetime trying to keep caged, because I know how ruinous it can be, how dangerous. It made sense I'd feel that way with Seb, after what we went through, but with Alexo? I barely know him. *I barely know him.*

I break the kiss, the innocent, no-tongue kiss, and brace my forehead against his. I picked him up at some point, but he's holding on to me just as firmly, and we're both gasping, which makes sense. I played a game; he danced for hours. We're out of breath from that. Nothing else.

"C-congratulations," he says again, a stutter. I feel it on my sensitive lips.

"Thanks," I tell him. And instinctively hug him tighter, because—I don't know why.

"Orok Monroe!" A reporter shoves her way over, microphone out, a cameraman following. "And—" She checks her notes. "Alexo Warden?"

I set him down, my skin prickling with a combination of annoyance that she didn't automatically know him—who could *not* know him—and fury that he's the center of so much attention. It isn't safe, and I tuck him into my side but make sure to angle my body in front of him so I take the brunt of the focus.

The reporter gives a coy grin. "You two are *adorable*. Mr. Monroe, how are you feeling after your first time playing as a Hellhound?"

My brows go up, startled by her normal question. I expected something about me and Alexo, but I look out over the crowd, at my teammates, and I smile.

"Really good," I say. And I mean it. "We played as a unit. Well, most of today's win goes to Marlow Keel"—I wink, and the reporter laughs; Alexo, still tucked up against me, does, too—"but overall, I'm even more excited to see what we do this season."

"And do you think you did your god proud tonight?"

Does my smile get too forced? Am I able to hide my discomfort before the reporter and her cameraman see? I don't know—but I know Alexo feels me stiffen. I know my body jerks against him, muscles seizing. I know he looks up at the side of my face.

I smile for the reporter. "The whole team played their best."

She pauses, expecting me to say more. I *should* say more. I'm repping Urzoth even more boldly than before, if only to keep Alexo in their good graces.

But I can't get my jaw to open, and I keep my fake smile plastered to my face.

Eventually, the reporter pulls her mic back and clears her throat. "And you, Mr. Warden." She turns to him. "How was *your* first experience performing?"

Alexo blushes. It makes his freckles pop, and I run my thumb up and down his side.

He shivers at the motion and leans into me a little more, so I feel every vibration of that shiver, every ripple of his body in a way that has me suddenly glad I'm wearing a cup so the reporter won't be getting a whole other type of headline story.

"I, um—" He glances up at me, dazed, before he seemingly hears the reporter's question in a delayed rebound. Fuck, I get that.

Alexo steps toward her, a flash of determination, and he looks straight at the camera as he says, "It was great. I want everyone watching to—" A pause. A quick inhale of breath. "To remember to keep dancing, too."

That's . . . specific. A tagline he's hoping to start? Did the publicists work that out with him?

The reporter's head rocks in confusion before she grins. "Aw, so sweet! You really are a *beauty*."

Alexo's turn to be confused. "I—what?"

She laughs. "It's one of the names people have for you two. One is Oroxo—your names, Orok and Alexo. But most are calling you Beauty and the Beast."

Alexo frowns. "He's not a *beast*."

"Hey." I nudge him. "Maybe I'm the *beauty*." There's no way, but it gets him to give me an exasperated smile.

The reporter dives away when there's a break in the hodgepodge near Marlow, and I use the opening to close in around Alexo again, creating a little pocket of semi-privacy in the midst of this very, very not-private place.

He looks up at me in another of those silent eye-locks and touches my jersey. Several layers of padding keep his hand from making contact with my skin, but I imagine there's heat anyway, a heavy warmth.

This is doing nothing to help my uncomfortable cup situation, damn it.

"Was that okay?" he whispers, making it more lip reading than anything.

I smirk. "I'm really okay with being referred to as a *beast* if it means—"

"Not that." He scowls. "Well, kind of that, but—I meant, was the . . . kiss . . . okay?" A blush overtakes his face, scarlet red, so pretty it aches. "We both agreed to it, but agreeing and *doing* are two different things."

I cup his face in my hands. My skin is getting tacky from the dried saltwater, but I run my thumbs over his jaw and the dustings of glitter on his cheeks.

"Any way you want to touch me is okay," I tell him.

His head tips in my hands, sardonic. "*Any* way? You didn't sign that broad a margin of error, Mr. Monroe."

I laugh and lean down to put my lips against his.

He makes a startled chirp but doesn't pull away. Lingers there, and it isn't a kiss; it's a mutual breath.

"Do your worst, Mr. Warden," I say.

He shivers again.

I clench my jaw and force myself to peel away from him, take my hands off his face.

Alexo: PR stunt.

"Can you—" I scratch flakes of salt out of my beard. "Um. Can I walk you back to the cheerleader locker room?"

Dazed again, Alexo nods, but it's stilted, unsteady, and pulls a breathless smile to my face.

If he's this blissed out after two barely there kisses, what would he look like after—

Don't. Do not even *finish* that question, Orok Monroe.

I cough away the tightening in my throat and hook my arm around his waist.

"I—no! Wait." Alexo bursts back to clarity and wiggles out of my grip.

I stand in the middle of the still-celebrating crowd, arms out.

"No," he repeats. Harder. An order. "I can get there on my own. Thank you. And—I'll see you next week?"

Then he's gone, slinking away into the crowd that swallows him up.

I brace against wanting to rip everyone aside until I get eyes back on him.

He doesn't want me going to the cheerleader locker room.

I scan the crowd. I clock one of the publicists near the doors to the player tunnel and beeline to her, the noise of the stadium a dull background hum.

"Is there someone waiting for Alexo?" I demand.

She blinks up at me from where she'd been entering notes on a tablet. "Um—I'm sorry, Mr. Monroe, I don't under—"

"Is there a man waiting for Alexo near the cheerleader locker room?" I try again, saying each word through my teeth. The back of my neck prickles with the urge to race in and find out myself, but I have enough prescience of mind to not do that.

"Y-yes. Oh!" She seems to have a realization. "It *is* the guy from the bar, but Mr. Warden told us it was a misunderstanding. I believe they live together. We've been assured he isn't a boyfriend, if that's what you're concerned about? Luckily, no one's seemed to focus on who the guy at the bar was, so our narrative stands, and we don't need to worry about—"

I stop listening, my awareness narrowing.

They *live* together?

That asshole lives with Alexo? And he *dared* to treat him like an object at the bar? Dared to put his *hands on him*?

Hypocrisy tastes bitter, but I'm too furious to give it more than a passing flinch.

"You knew Alexo was living with that jackass?" I snap.

The publicist trembles.

Because she's five feet nothing and I've trapped her against the recessed door's wall to growl random, accusatory questions at her.

I'm shunted out of my fugue state and throw my hands up in surrender. My damn rawball padding makes it impossible to shrink myself at all, so I take a step back, thankful the bulk of the crowd is still in the sideline area so there's plenty of room to give the publicist space.

"I'm sorry." I glance down at her name badge. "I'm sorry, Treva. I just—"

No. There's no explanation that makes either my questions or behavior acceptable.

This is true weakness.

"I'm sorry," I repeat, shaking, and shove through the doors.

What the hell is wrong with me?

Blood thunders in my ears, rushes hot and heavy through my chest as I rush to the player locker room and rip off my gear.

My next therapy session isn't for another few weeks; I spread them out during the season so my schedule isn't unmanageable. But maybe I should add an appointment or two?

I'll send the whole publicity team lunch. For the next week. Something in penance. I do *not* get to throw my weight around like that, terrifying people into doing what I want.

My jersey drops to my feet, and as I bend to toss my shoulder pads into my locker, I spot Urzoth's symbol in the folds of the fabric.

That's exactly what my mother would expect me to do. That's what she *does* think I do. Just plow my way through life in a constant high of *I am strong, therefore everyone else is weak.*

The acidic gnawing in my stomach to rip that symbol off my uniform burns and burns.

I will *not* behave like this. I will *not* be someone who makes him proud.

Their version of strength isn't real.

I throw myself into a shower, willing the water to scald away the emotions roiling inside me, the true *beast* that's been unleashed. I take a washcloth and scrub at my skin until it's red and stinging under the spray, and I imagine the soap whirling down the drain is each pulse of *mine, mine* that was echoing in my head.

Chapter Five

Morning News: "Welcome back to *One Shot*, your number-one source for the latest in pro rawball news. I'm your host, Diamanda Blacktalon. My cohost, Vaknox of the Lizard People of Tesh, is on his biannual sojourn to molt his skin in the Teshen Temple of Chaxloakka. We miss him and wish him a speedy ecdysis. Filling in for him is Luxo the artificer and his automaton, Ratchatron. Pleasure to have you, Luxo."

robot beeping noises

"Oh, Ratchatron will be speaking with us today? Wonderful. Ratchatron, things seem to be heating up between a certain couple! Alexo and Orok, our very own Beauty and the Beast, were spotted on another date, this time at the super romantic Hilliard restaurant."

robot beeping noises

"Um. That's awful, Ratchatron. I'm sorry your—uh, Luxo's wife left him at that restaurant."

aggressive robot beeping noises

"Well . . . in returning to Orok and Alexo, let's bring up the image for our viewers of Orok helping Alexo into his seat—yep, that one—"

even more aggressive robot beeping noises

"That's awfully jaded, Ratchatron. Our viewers certainly believe in love. Just look at how cute Orok and Alexo are! Oroxo—I prefer Beauty and the Beast—have definitely secured their spot as the new It couple of rawball—"

one long shrieking robot beep

"Oh dear. I apologize for my cohost's language. I—I think we'd better go to commercial."

"Thio and I will be at your game tonight."

I tap a rhythm on the steering wheel as I wind through traffic on the way to the stadium. "You know where to go to get the family tickets?"

"Yeah," Seb says through my car's speaker. "This is the one and only instance of me going raw for you this season, so make it good for both of us, will you?"

"Uh-huh. Sure."

"Crazy weather we've been having."

I look out the windshield at the blue sky. "Is it?"

"*No.* No, fuck this, Orok Monroe. I didn't even get an annoyed groan at my rawball joke, and you're okay talking about ticket mundanity and the *weather*?"

I slow to a stop at a red light, grip clenching on the gearshift. "I appreciate you coming to the game. It's been a busy month; sorry I haven't seen you much."

At all.

I haven't seen Seb *at all*.

I'm on lockdown. Self-imposed emergency preventative maneuvers.

Which includes, always does, keeping my distance from Seb. The last thing I ever want to do is glom on to him again, make him my safety net even if he swears it's fine. It's *not* fine.

But the biggest preventative maneuver: no excess contact with Alexo either.

Matching the two other games this month, while traveling and home, we had two more *dates*. One was dinner, one was another coffee meetup at a spot downtown. I was cordial for the cameras I knew were beyond the windows both times, and I paid like a gentleman, but I kept conversation surface level. And I did not look at him too long, did not note how he wore a turtleneck crop top to the dinner date, and it showed his flat stomach and a gold belly chain.

A gods-damned *belly chain.*

It got easier to keep the boundaries up when, at the end of both dates, *that guy* was nearby, for the away game, too, waiting to whisk Alexo off.

And each time, as they were leaving, that guy was clearly berating Alexo, and Alexo slumped and just took it. And I couldn't do anything. Because he's not actually *mine*.

That's the motto of this lockdown. He's not mine and I'm not obsessed with him, or anyone, and I am perfectly capable of functioning like a normal, healthy adult because I put in the work, gods damn it.

I hate this.

All of it.

The seeing him, the not seeing him, the letting him leave with that asshole, the self-imposed restraint. I'm clinging to my hard-earned composure by the skin of my teeth, and said teeth are about ground down to nubs.

Seb huffs into the phone. "You're doing it again, aren't you?"

"Doing what?"

"Honestly? I'm not sure. Pushing me away? Putting me in a box? You did it in Vegas but it took me a while to realize you *weren't* busy. We live in the same city now, dude. *You aren't this busy*. After the game tonight, I'm going to see you. Face-to-face. For longer than an affable *hello*. I'm not letting you go all distant and formal with me, O. Not again."

A car behind me honks when I miss the light change, and I slam on the gas, knuckles white.

No, I want to tell him. *I'm not strong enough to see you yet.*

I need to get my shit together. I need to not be so gods-damned needy.

But I miss him. I moved back in large part because of him, because he's still half my soul, even when I try so hard to wedge space between us.

"All right," I concede. "Yeah. That's—that'll be good."

"Try to sound more like you're getting a root canal." On Seb's end, someone calls his name. "I gotta get back to work, but I *will* see you tonight. Asshole."

I crack a smile in spite of myself. "I do want to see you. I—" My hand stretches, the leather of the steering wheel groaning. "I'll see you tonight."

"Love you."

The slightest pause. It's minuscule, but I feel it, wide and gaping. "Love you, too."

Seb doesn't disconnect right away. "We're going to talk about this, O" is the last thing he says before he hangs up.

I pull into the player lot at the stadium and sit in my car for a beat, staring at the river in the distance.

I was arguably at my most mentally healthy in Vegas. On paper. Everything was organized just so—until the trial blew up the carefully sculpted box I kept my Chimeras teammates in. And it made me realize I'd never actually gotten to *know* any of those teammates, because when the smoke cleared as all the details of the case came out, they didn't feel fuck-all loyalty to me.

Why do I think doing the same thing here is the *healthier* option?

Because I'm terrified of being a codependent, out-of-control, self-sacrificing mess again. I already *have* been—that incident with Treva was just the most jarring. But every PR update reminds me that the Urzoth church is *thrilled* by the *positive press* I'm bringing them, when I shouldn't be bringing them any press *at all*. The Hellhounds are thrilled, too—we've won two of our first three games, on top of the Oroxo/Beauty and the Beast discussions overshadowing the remaining negativity around the lawsuit.

Like Vegas, everything looks great *on paper*.

I pull up today's schedule and recheck the *interaction* Alexo and I are scheduled for. It's a home game; we're supposed to meet at the player exit afterward and be seen walking out together.

Innocent enough.

That's it though—it's not nearly *enough*.

I toss my phone into my bag and shove out of my car, all this wanting doing its best to rip me right in two.

We barely eke out a win against the Detroit Dragons, 17–15. They chose a pretty basic field, jagged rocky peaks and hidden caverns, but even with that simplicity, they were an intense opposition. It was my fourth game playing with the Hellhounds, and I'm starting to trust the team dynamics; they've got my back and I've got theirs. No ill will. Perfectly cordial. If we can keep this up, we've got a real chance of hitting the championship; well-oiled machine and all.

That's the most I wanted out of this trade. The most I hoped for.

Not anything more than *cordial.*

Alexo was stunning tonight. The way he dances is sensational, hypnotic; I don't know how the whole stadium doesn't drop everything to ogle at the screens every time he's on. He comes alive in this vivacious flow, and I wanted nothing more than to charge off the field and repeat our kiss, no tongue, from weeks ago.

But I didn't. We're meeting at the player exit. And then I'm going out with Seb. And it's all still perfectly *contained.*

After I'm showered and dressed, I head out, palms sweating, bag over my shoulder. The hall outside the locker room is packed with security, reporters, assistants, and family members, and the first person I see is Seb.

Thio's next to him, and they're both *decked out* in Hellhounds gear—orange shirts and baggy orange pants with the demon dog logo, and Seb's wearing a gods-damned demon dog foam *hat* with the dog's mouth opening around his face, while Thio's got a temporary tattoo of the Hellhounds *H* on one cheek and the twenty-sided rawball shape on the other.

Seb throws his arms out wide and screeches over the hallway's din, "My baby!"

"You're the worst," I grumble through a smile as he yanks me down for a hug.

He pulls away before I'm done and I cling to him against my better judgment. The tension has him melting back against me and he retightens his grip on my shoulders.

"Hey," he prods, knocking his head against mine. "What's up? For real?"

I blow a breath into his shoulder and—hold here. I know I

should pull away, because this is the exact behavior I don't want to let myself need.

After one more breath, I lift back and flick the foam dog on his head. "I'm sorry I've been a jerk. I'll be around more. But—" I look at Thio, behind us, hands in his pockets, and when my eyes meet his, he shifts a little closer. "You're engaged now, and I don't want to impose."

Thio cracks a smile. "I knew you were a package deal when I proposed. Don't worry about it."

Seb flattens an offended hand to his chest. "I think you mean when *I* proposed, since mine was first, but—he's right." Seb swats that hand at me. "You're never too much, O. Tell that voice in your head to shut up. I *want* you around. You being gone these past four years was miserable for me. I kind of need you, you big oaf."

And that doesn't scare the shit out of you?

I adjust my bag. "All right. I—"

"Mr. Monroe!" Treva rushes up, already gesturing for me to head toward the door. She doesn't so much as flinch when she's near me, which has me relaxing fractionally. I've seen her at other events since I cornered her after the first game, and she doesn't seem at all bothered by it. Still feel like I should apologize again, though. Maybe the full week of catering from five of Philly's best restaurants for the PR team helped? Not that they knew it was me.

"Mr. Warden is waiting at the exit," Treva says. "We're ready for some shots of you leaving together."

My eyes widen as the logistics of *leaving together* overwhelm every sensible thought.

I thought we were *walking out* together.

"I don't—we *aren't*, though? Like how far do we—"

Is he coming home with me? No. No, that's . . . *nope.*

Is he going to get in my car? Will it smell like apples when he's gone?

Treva gestures again, and I trudge along, Seb and Thio in tow. "We want some photos of you two walking out, hand in hand. Just go past the gate into the player lot." She leans in as we duck around some reporters. "It's for show, remember."

Just walking out. It's for show.

Simple. Easy.

We make our way through the stadium and to a side door that opens into the balmy September night. The player lot is ahead, behind a gate and a brick wall, while an exclusive crowd of fans lines one side of the walkway between the stadium and that gate, held back by security and fencing. They're already screaming and calling out names as my other teammates leave. I spot Darian signing a jersey.

Movement by the open doors has all my attention swinging over.

Alexo steps forward. He's changed, too, but where I'm in sweats, he's in chunky white shoes, baggy jeans, and another crop top, this one a white tank. No belly chain, thank the gods, but as he crosses the space to me, I'm stuck staring at his navel, the little line of hair on the lower part of his stomach that disappears into his jeans.

Fuuuuuck. Fuck. Fuck fuck fuck.

I pry my eyes up to his.

And then realize that Seb and Thio are still with me and Treva has abandoned us to make the pictures more *natural*.

So, like a very mature, professional guy in complete control of his faculties, I stand there. Staring.

And Alexo stands there, too. Only his eyes keep darting away, back to me, his hands clenching and unclenching on the strap of the backpack he's got hanging off one shoulder.

Seb, bless him, breaks the silence by thrusting himself forward. "Well, hello there, cutie. You must be Alexo. O's told me *so* much about you."

I have?

I barely know anything about him, so what things I *have* found out I've hoarded like a greedy little dragon protecting its gold.

"He has?" Alexo echoes my thought, but he shakes the hand Seb extends.

"He has." Seb beams at me and props one elbow on my shoulder. Only he's nowhere near my height and has to do this tugging shimmy move to get me to bend down, so by the time he's relaxed on me, any sense of casual coolness is dead. "I'm Sebastian. And that's my fiancé, Thio. We're Orok's found family, and by extension, we're yours now, too. Welcome to the nuthouse."

Seb doesn't know this thing with Alexo is fake. He thinks the photos he's seen online and all our dates are the start of a sweet romance. I haven't had anything even resembling a romance in . . . ever. It makes sense he's immediately trying to adopt Alexo the way I did Thio, and turn us all into one big, if not dysfunctional, family.

But this isn't real. Alexo won't get to fit into my life, not this way, and the image of him sitting curled up on the couch in my apartment next to me while Seb and Thio argue over cooking dinner has the breath going out of my chest in a sudden free fall of need.

I shrug Seb away. "Give me a sec," I tell him. "I'll walk him out, then we'll go."

Seb frowns at the energy coming off me. I'm stiff, hands in fists, my tone flat. He sees right through me, he's always seen right through me, and *this* is why I've avoided him, too—because he's going to make me confront this. He's going to be the killing tap on the fissure, and I'll shatter.

I extend my hand to Alexo, eyes on the carpet they've rolled out for the players.

After a beat, his hand slides into mine. Just his fingers resting on my palm.

I curl my fingers around his and walk, pulling us farther past the doors and out into the area with the crowd.

Cameras flash. Voices call out to us. But we don't need to stop for any interviews; we just need to walk. Get to the gate for the player lot, and go our separate ways.

His hand is warm. Delicate and thin. He doesn't cling to me, just lets me hold him, and I risk a glance down at him, using my body to shield him from the worst of the cameras and crowd.

He's staring straight ahead, at the gate, his jaw set, discomfort clear in the lines around his eyes and lips. He notices me watching him and only flicks his eyes to the side, not all the way to me, before he faces forward, shoulders pulling back.

There's that free-fall sensation again. Tumbling down, down, because I lost my grip on something I was never supposed to touch in the first place.

We make it to the gate and security opens it for us. I don't let go of Alexo's hand until we're blocked from the crowd by the tall brick wall, and even then, I stop walking, facing forward, keeping his hand in mine.

He's the one who pulls away.

"Until next time," he says, formal.

I've been pushing him away. I was the one to keep things surface level on our two dates—even after I told him I wanted to get to know him.

Even after our kiss.

Wanna know how many gods have been associated with regret? Exactly two. And neither are widely worshipped, or ever have been, because the concept of regret *blows*.

Alexo doesn't look at me as he walks off into the parking lot. I stretch and curl the fingers of the hand he held.

A car's running a few rows over, and he opens the passenger door but doesn't get in. He's talking to whoever's in the driver's seat, and I know very well who it is by the way Alexo's face contorts in hurt.

That hand clenches.

"What the *fuck*, O?"

I whirl to see Seb and Thio followed us out.

Seb looks more than a little ridiculous with his arms folded and his expression crooked in annoyance while that foam dog head is wrapped around his face. "He's not coming out with us? What *was* that? You two have met before, right?"

"Baby," Thio tries, his focus pinging between us, and it's really obnoxious having two perceptive people in my life now; what Seb misses, Thio picks up, and vice versa.

Seb looks at Thio, and they have a silent discussion that ends with Seb's mouth going slack at me. "Did you—are you not together anymore?"

I look back at the car. It hasn't left yet, but Alexo's inside it now, the door shut.

My nails dig into my palms. "We're still together."

"That was not the attitude of two people in the early stages of a relationship." Seb comes closer as a few more players and their families leave, a sudden burst of noise in the night-drenched lot. "He seemed . . . uncomfortable around you. What happened?"

I can't tell him.

I signed an NDA.

And we're *in public*, in a *parking lot*.

But Alexo got in the car with that guy again. And I'll have to watch them drive away together, *again*, knowing they're fighting. Is he safe? Why is that guy so pissed off with him? Why doesn't that guy *appreciate* what he has?

Why don't *I* appreciate what *I* have?

I tip my head back and unleash a frustrated growl to the sky before swinging on Seb and Thio and word-vomiting *everything*.

How it's all fake. How I didn't want it to be. How I kept Urzoth as my patron god because the church offered to sponsor Alexo, and for whatever reason having Urzoth's support was important to him, and I need him to have what he wants. How I'm trying to keep this professional but we kissed at the first game and I can't think of anything other than that guy hurting him and the way Alexo performs like they're the only times in his life he's ever fully *himself*, fully *happy*.

By the time I'm done whispering-shouting all this down at them, Seb and Thio are wide-eyed and open-mouthed.

Their heads crank toward one another and I throw a finger up. "So help me, if you two have one of your silent conversations, I swear—"

Seb takes my hand, attention going behind me, then back.

"Okay. O—we'll talk about the whole Urzoth thing later, but right now, I think you need to go after him."

"Go—what?"

I follow his gaze to see Alexo's car starting to pull out of its spot. They're leaving.

My hand twists in Seb's. "I can't go after him. He's not really *mine*."

"But he could be." Seb releases me. "You want him to be. Your instincts are telling you something's up, something's *wrong*, right? So listen. *Talk* to him. Find out what's going on so you can *make* this real, because you owe it to yourself to go after it. Now." Seb waves toward the moving car. "Go. Chase. Talk."

"I'm not—I'm not going to *chase him*. Like a stalker."

Thio winces and cups Seb's shoulder. "Fair point. Following him probably isn't the best move. When are you supposed to see him next? You could talk to him then."

"Correction: you *will* talk to him then," Seb says. "Pull up your calendar. Let me see what you're slotted for after this. I'll hold you accountable."

The car's stuck in a line waiting to get through the parking lot's exit.

Alexo and that guy will leave. Go back to the place they share.

I scrub at my hair, fingers burning on my scalp, and snarl down at Seb. "I can't. I fucking *can't*, Seb. I'm—it isn't—it's too *much*, okay? I was too much with you and I'll be too much with him and I don't—"

Seb grabs my face, silencing me. "You have never, in the history of our relationship, been too much for me, Orok. *Never*. Getting to be loved by you is a privilege, and if Alexo doesn't see it that way, that's on him. But he should at least get the chance to decide." He smiles, shifting from intense to light in a flash. "As someone very wise once told me, you like the guy. So talk to him. That's it. Sounds simple to me."

A memory pops up—back in college, when Seb was struggling with his feelings for Thio. I told him something similar. *You like the guy. That's what it is. Simple.*

Simple.

I've been clawing my way toward simple, easy, *fine* for weeks. Been sacrificing pieces of my sanity and soul to stay in these strict little boxes so I didn't explode in a confetti cannon of *too much*. Too obsessive. Too fixated. Too consuming.

But he's leaving with that guy.

And I can't *take it anymore.*

So fucking weak.

I yank Seb in, kiss his forehead, and punch Thio on the shoulder. "Thanks. Sorry to flake on tonight, but I'll call you later, I promise."

Thio's eyes burst wide. "Wait, you really shouldn't *follow him*—"

But I'm taking off across the parking lot already. Thankfully, I got a pretty close spot before the game, and I'm yanking open the door to my car, chucking my bag in the back seat, and peeling out of the spot while Alexo's car is just leaving the exit. I clock which direction it turns and snake my way to the exit, too, and by the time I'm allowed to leave, I spot them stuck in stadium traffic at a red light.

My phone rings. I answer, and Seb's voice fills my car. "You're insane."

"Thanks."

"I've since been informed of the tactlessness of my initial suggestion and have been encouraged to dissuade you from this current path," Seb says, clearly reciting what Thio told him. "*Not,*" he adds, "that I think you're in any way being *too much*; it's just, ya know, not a good look to stalk anyone."

"I'm not *stalking* him," I say.

As the light changes and I follow them onto the highway.

Where I keep a few car lengths between us.

So *that guy* doesn't realize I'm following them.

"Okay, *mildly* stalking," I amend. "I'm going to make sure he gets home okay. And that that asshole doesn't touch him."

Seb's silent for a beat. Then he chirps "Hey!" like Thio pinched him.

Rustling. Thio's muffled voice.

Seb comes back with an exasperated, flat, "Orok. Stop. Turn back. Oh, dearest friend of mine, rethink your poor life choices, lest you—*ow*! I am not being purposefully melodramatic! Well, *excuuuuse* me for thinking he should actually go after Alexo. No, you know what? I rescind my rescinding. Because I want to know what's up with him! And it's a romantic gesture! It's not *creepy*." A pause. "It's a little creepy. But—"

Alexo's car gets off the highway in the middle of Seb's one-sided conversation with Thio, and I tail them into a neighborhood that makes me grimace, my brows pulling together.

"Seb," I cut him off. "I gotta go."

"Get your man, babe. Give it to him raw." In the background, Thio makes a long, drawn-out moan, and Seb goes, "Because they met through rawball! Oh come on, it's a *little* funny."

But no. It's suddenly not funny.

Not as I hang up and Alexo's car twists down a few side streets lined with dilapidated houses and apartments surrounded by chain-link fences, the one-lane roads packed with old cars.

This neighborhood is one of the many we were warned off during freshman orientation in college so we wouldn't get swept up in the crime and danger. As if it's some sucking whirlpool that couldn't be fixed with better funding and oversight.

Alexo's car pulls into a gravel lot beside a two-story brick townhome. The engine cuts off, and I keep going, driving around the block until I find a spot to park. Most of the streetlights aren't working, so illumination comes from light pollution, but my car is still very, very visible. It isn't a sore thumb; it's a whole hand waving for attention, and I'm pretty sure when I come back from whatever it is I'm going to do, I'll find a few less parts on it.

I won't be that long, though. I'm going to . . . fuck if I know at this point. Rationalizing went out the window the moment I left the stadium. That echoing, growling voice of *mine, mine, mine* is overtaking me, obliterating the last feeble strangleholds I had on my self-control.

This is me at the point of no return, the parts I'm always fighting so hard to keep from showing. But instead of being disgusted with myself or horrified at what I'm doing, I feel . . .

Like I can *breathe*.

I walk at a quick clip around the block, my shoes swishing on the cracked sidewalk, overgrown weeds on the pavement turned to ink-black tendrils in the night. This late, most people are locked up in their homes, but a few lights are on in rooms here and there.

Back at the townhouse, the parking lot is quiet, the street and buildings around it silent and empty.

They probably went into the townhouse, but it could be a few different apartments or one complete place, so I don't—

A light comes on in the second-floor window, the one facing the street.

I tuck myself against a broken streetlight, leaning on the splintered wood pole, breath caught in my throat. The room looks like a kitchen; I see a sink from this angle, a vinyl chair.

That guy comes into view. He's waving his arms, stabbing for emphasis, yelling. The window muffles the actual words, but I can hear his volume even all the way out here, down two floors and on the sidewalk.

I fold my arms over my chest. Watching.

Watching that guy yell, and yell, and then Alexo walks past the window, fiddling with the sink. He comes up with a glass of water and says something to it, eyes downcast. That guy pushes right up behind him, yelling, and spittle flies. Alexo curls over his water glass, small.

That's it.

I shove off the streetlight and angle for the front door when the guy stomps away from Alexo. The curtain over the window moves in a gust of air—a door opened?

Sure enough, two seconds later, that guy's racing out the main door and down the front stoop.

I sink back against the streetlight, holding myself in the shadows, but he doesn't notice me. Doesn't even scan the street for threats or do anything but mutter angrily to himself, march to his car, punch it on, and drive off.

Leaving Alexo upstairs, still bent over the sink, alone.

He puts down the glass and cups his hands over his face.

I'm in motion again, body hot and twisted and *desperate*. I can't leave him like this, alone, scared, upset, and that's where the whole of my drive is focused, on *him*.

I vault the front steps and open the main door. It isn't locked, thankfully, but it itches down my spine that anyone could waltz right into his building.

Sickly yellow lights flicker over the lower floor, showing three numbered doors off a main hallway with a staircase that loops upward. I take the stairs two at a time and find an identical layout. But I know which apartment is his, so I approach, pace slowing, heart going rapid fire against my sternum to the point I can feel it in my throat.

I stop cold.

What am I doing.

I'm standing outside Alexo's apartment. I *followed him home*.

Oh my gods. Seb was right. Well, not Seb—*Thio* was right. This was such a bad idea. I wanted to make sure he got home okay, and he did. That guy even left; maybe he won't come back.

Walk away, Orok.

Turn around, and *walk away*.

I stare at his apartment door. And I can't make myself leave. Leave *him*, here. Upset.

Any chance of escaping this situation with my dignity intact evaporates when the door groans open.

Alexo's there, a full trash bag in one hand. He startles backward when he sees me *skulking here*, and he makes a frantic noise of alarm as he thrusts the garbage bag out in defense.

"Alexo," I say. "I—"

"Orok?" He doesn't lower the bag. Doesn't relax, his whole body wound so tense I can see the muscles straining in his arms, the tendons bulging in his neck. His eyes are wide, highlighted still by his makeup, and as he holds in place, frozen, they go glassy with tears.

"Oh my gods," he gasps, chest rising and falling in too-fast breaths. "Oh my gods—"

It's what happened with Treva all over again. Only several thousand times worse, because I *knew* I was doing something wrong this time.

I stumble backward, trying like hell to make myself as unthreatening as possible. My size against his feels stark now; he barely comes up to my pecs.

"I'm so sorry. This was *exceedingly* dumb. I shouldn't have followed you, and I . . . oh fuck. I'm sorry."

He still doesn't move, doesn't drop the bag, doesn't let go of the half-open door. But his terror is a little more pinched now, more like anger, and he glares at me as I fumble my way through the shittiest of shit apologies.

"I wanted to make sure you were okay," I tell him. "That isn't an excuse. Just an explanation. That's the only reason I'm here. I wanted to see you, to make sure you were okay, because honestly? That guy, whoever he is, he better *watch himself* with the way he treats you. I don't know what's going on with you two or what situation you're in, but . . . if he's dangerous. If you're not safe. I can—I want to—"

I wilt even more, eyes rolling shut.

This moment is proof that my god's as fed up with me as I am with him, because if he gave a single remaining shit about me, he'd strike me down dead in mercy.

"That's why you're here?"

My eyes fly open.

Alexo's lowered the bag. He still looks livid.

I nod. "To check on you? Yeah."

"That's it? You didn't . . . come for me?"

Come for him? Yes, but—

My brow furrows. "Yeah? Oh—oh, *fuck*." He doesn't mean . . . "I wouldn't, I would *never* do anything like—*holy shit*. I'm leaving. Now. I'm so sorry." I turn for the stairs, stop, pivot back. "If you want to call off this PR thing because of me being exponentially stupid, say the word, and I'll take care of it so you're not at fault for anything. I'll make sure you keep your place on the team and Urzoth's patronage. Again, I'm so—"

Alexo steps into the hall. He slams the door shut—seems like he *has* to, in order to get it to close properly, and my teeth grind at the security risk—but his eyes stay on me.

His anger is gone. It's like he's decided something.

Whatever it is, he's studying me again in that searching, wondering way, and I go immobile.

"You've been kind of an ass recently," he says, point-blank.

I bellow a laugh.

Calling me on my shit is *way* better than him being scared of me.

"I think that's part of why I came here," I admit. "Because I hated how things were between us. *Hate* how they *are* between us. None of this—the whole PR bullshit, the fake dates, the pretend interactions, none of it is what I want with you, and it's—" Go for honesty. Go for broke. "It's killing me. You deserve better, and I *want* better. With you."

No matter what he decides, I won't be able to keep pretending this isn't real for me. That every time we touch or have our *interactions* isn't the highlight of my day.

He doesn't say anything.

"But if you want this to stay a PR front," I continue, "it can. It's your choice, Alexo." What the hell; at this point, just say it: "I want you to be happy."

His head tips.

One corner of his mouth lifts in the barest seed of a smile that, quite frankly, I don't deserve. The upper hallway's few grainy bulbs cast us in more of that sick interrogation-room yellow, but he's still the most stunning person I've ever seen, all fire and passion trapped in a small body.

He holds the garbage bag out. "Carry this for me?"

I take it instantly. Wait—is this a dismissal? Is he saying he wants me to take out the trash as I *take out the trash*, i.e., chuck myself out of his building?

But he jerks his head for me to follow and starts up the hall, and I hurry after him like an infatuated sap.

Chapter Six

Alexo leads me to the parking lot and points at the dumpsters behind the townhouse. He stays on the sidewalk, and I jog for them, not liking him out of my sight in this neighborhood—or at all. My footsteps crunching on the gravel is the only sound around us, broken by the occasional bout of music from a building farther down and a car engine revving at the intersection up the street.

By the time I'm back to him, he's got his hands in the pockets of his baggy jeans, his head tipped to the night sky washed clean of stars from the same city light intrusion that casts the area in a dreamlike gray.

He swings his gaze not to me, but to the empty parking lot, his head moving in a slow refusal of something unsaid.

"He left," he growls at the lot, about *that guy*, I realize, and I stuff my fisted hands in my hoodie's pocket to hide how I curl them. "He yelled at me for—" He stops, chews the remainder of the sentence. One of my fingers pops. "And then *he* left. He left me here, and *you* show up, and he's *gone*."

With a frustrated shout, Alexo whirls, hands in his hair. He paces and shouts again, and I watch him the same way he's always watching me. Studying. Learning.

A hundred questions stack up in my throat, waiting to explode, to demand answers of Alexo. But I force myself to swallow them one by one. I will *not* lose myself again, not tonight. I have reached the max on what unhinged behavior I'll allow.

Besides, asking questions would only serve me right now, and Alexo's clear irritation swerves sharply into something far too close to grief when he cups his hands behind his neck and rolls his eyes shut.

"Do you want to come somewhere with me?" is the only question I let myself ask.

He turns to me and snorts. "Well, you're a polite stalker slash kidnapper, so at least you've got that going for you."

The memory of Thio saying I was the politest striptease he'd ever had immediately has my brain picturing doing a striptease *for Alexo*, and I'm glad the dim lighting out here hides the sudden blush I feel tearing up my cheeks.

"Not kidnapping you, I promise," I say.

"But you admit to the stalking."

"Unfortunately, the evidence is a bit damning."

Alexo laughs, letting his hands drop from around his neck, and I soak up the sound of his laughter like a shriveled plant in a drought.

He sighs. "You know what? Sure. Let's go somewhere. Why not?" He throws the last question at the empty parking lot, and my stomach twists.

"If this will get you in more trouble—"

"I'm twenty-three years old." He glares at me, fury blunt in his eyes. "I don't *get in trouble.* I don't answer to him. I *won't.* Let's go."

He marches off down the sidewalk.

In the wrong direction.

I clear my throat and point. "My car is—"

Alexo swivels around and resumes his frustrated stomping the right way, scowling to the cracked sidewalk.

Around the block, my car is intact, and Alexo stares at it for a long beat.

"This is . . ." He coughs. "A fancy car."

I fiddle with the keys. "Compared to some of the outrageous vehicles my teammates drive, a Maserati might as well be a soccer van, I swear."

He gives a look that says *that's your best excuse for having such an ostentatious car?*

"Hey, I'm allowed a vice," I say with a grin and step down the curb to open the door for him.

Alexo's expression swings to amusement.

"*But he was such a gentleman,*" he says, his voice intentionally too high. "*How could I not get in the car with him? It would've been rude.*"

I cock my head.

"Just reciting what I'll say to—to the adventure party who has to rescue me from you later."

I ignore his stumble and lean on the open door. "If you want, I can call a rideshare for you and have them drop you where we're going. Which is somewhere public, I promise."

Alexo narrows his eyes. "Oh, fuck all the way off."

I recoil. "What?"

"You—*this*." He waves his hand at all of me. "Your whole *knight in shining armor* routine. This level of chivalry should be illegal." But he's talking to himself now, and he sucks in a deep breath that evolves into a moan. "Idiot. I'm such an idiot," he mumbles as he slides into my car's passenger seat.

I hold, processing what happened, before I grin and shut the door.

By the time I fold myself into the driver's seat, Alexo has his seat belt on and is fiddling with the radio. He looks almost comically small in my car—I got an adjusted model for customers with bigger ancestries, and it's the same as seeing Seb or Thio here. Only with Alexo, it highlights that size difference in a few very obvious ways, and I clamp my lips against the rush of saliva that fills my mouth.

Alexo finds a radio station he seems satisfied with and glances up at me. "So. Where are we going?"

I shake out of my stupor and focus on the road. "It's a surprise."

"Hm. *A surprise* like an abandoned warehouse where no one will hear me scream, or *a surprise* like a roll of duct tape and a creepy basement?"

A laugh bursts out of me. "Okay, fair point. We're going to a magic smash room."

"A—" Alexo twists toward me. "A magic *what*?"

"A smash room." I take a turn and begin working our way toward the city. "It kind of *is* a warehouse, but other people will be there, even this late. It's full of magically warded rooms that are stacked with various obstacles or breakables—pottery, electronics.

And you can buy stuff for spells and use whatever you want to blast the shit out of things. Do you do any magic?"

I glance at him quickly, and he shakes his head.

"That's fine. They have potions that can give you temporary attack abilities. Or you don't need to use magic at all—they have weapons, too. It's a fantastic stress release."

I found it when I was in college, researching ways to help Seb with his anger issues, but I never took him; I was honestly terrified of what he'd do if he was allowed to attack shit with abandon.

Alexo's quiet for a beat. I keep my eyes on the road, but I can feel him looking at me, the heated weight of his gaze on the side of my face.

"And you think I need to relieve stress?" he asks. I can't pin his tone—is he upset?

I risk another look at him. "I think you'd appreciate not having to restrain yourself."

He blows out an exhale. The spacious interior of my car is quickly feeling very, very small, and the steady gusts of the AC swell his apple scent, filling the whole car with the saccharine aura of fruit. When he moves on the seat, arms crossing over his stomach, it wafts more of that scent, and a hint of the mint soap the stadium provides in the showers. I bet his curls smell like that, a combination that absolutely shouldn't work, peppermint and apples, but I want nothing more than to bury my face in the spot behind his ear and breathe.

"His name's Tem," Alexo says softly.

My hands spasm on the wheel and I snap my gaze forward to keep from swerving off the road. "Who?"

"The guy I live with. Tem Raussec. And he's not my boyfriend or my partner or anything romantic at all. He's like my uncle. And he can be . . . overprotective. He hates that I insisted on working with the Hellhounds, but I got the internship, and it let me be at least performance *adjacent*, so I took it. And then this whole PR thing . . ." He sighs, head thumping back against the seat. "I can't say too much. Okay? Please don't ask. But Tem's . . . he's not all bad. He hates when I'm in the spotlight. Hates me being vulnerable."

I gnaw on my response. Carefully, painstakingly select each word.

"Well. I can at least understand that. Wanting you to be safe."

He hums. "Yeah. That's all that matters, right? People being safe."

The lot for the smash room comes up. I pull into it, park, and twist to look at Alexo.

He doesn't move. The smash room is a massive warehouse in the industrial area of town, all lit up with a few people lingering outside, and Alexo stares out the windshield at it, bracing. Like he knows I'm going to push. Like he knows—suspects, fears—that I'm like Tem, wanting to overbearingly protect him.

The thought of being at all like that asshole has nausea roiling in my stomach. Yes, I want Alexo safe. But I also want him how he was when he sang at the bar. How he is when he dances.

"Is he hurting you?" I ask.

Alexo flicks his eyes to me. "Not physically."

That's loaded. I exhale through my nose, then ask, "Do you want my help with him? With getting away from him?"

Alexo hesitates, curious, and shakes his head. "No."

"All right. If that changes, let me know. I'd still very much like to date you, and I can't promise I'll always be good at not, for lack of a better word, *smothering* you, but I can promise I'll try. I don't want to force anything on you that you don't want."

His eyes are huge by the time I'm done talking. The light from the smash room fills the car, reflecting off his brown irises, and I have a moment of panic that I finally succeeded in being too much and scaring him off.

But Alexo unbuckles his seat belt, lurches forward, and kisses me.

It is decidedly *not* the PDA list's framework of kissing, no tongue.

There is tongue.

And the taste of him.

With the unendurable *flavor* of him fed directly into my mouth, buffeted at the edges by his apple scent but an onslaught on its own, syrupy, masculine, I grab the back of his head and feast. He makes a helpless, lewd moan, pushing against me so his glossed lips slip and slide and his tongue wars with mine, each brush ricocheting straight into my gut. I quickly forget that he initiated this, that I should let him lead, too lost in devouring as much of him as I can, and I distantly note that I'm memorizing out of fear this will be the only time. Memorizing the silken feel of his curls against my fingers and the warmth of his breath in my mouth and the hemorrhagic, blissed-out whimper I get out of him when I suck on the tip of his tongue.

It wells and wells, rising waters behind a dam, and where he was a solution to a drought before, now I know it's a flood.

I reel back with a wet gasp. His dark lashes are splayed on his cheekbones, swollen lips parted in ragged breaths.

He's beautifully wrecked.

"That's just for us," I whisper.

Those lashes flutter open. Beat once, twice.

"Kissing like that," I clarify. "It's just for us. Not for the cameras."

Alexo smiles. It's small and wondrous. "Possessive, huh?"

You have no idea.

The constant, crushing echo of *mine* is silenced, though. Satisfied. I imagine a contentedly purring lion curled up in my chest.

I sweep my thumb across the diaphanous skin under his eye. "Come on." I grin. "We have some shit to destroy."

Because if we stay in this car, I'll spend the rest of the night learning every divot and dip inside his mouth. And while that isn't the worst idea, I do want to do this with him, for him.

We climb out and head for the front doors. A few groups are still clustered around; there's a food truck nearby. It's late, but the smash room doesn't close until midnight, and there's a general atmosphere of relaxed fun as I hold the door open for Alexo.

The main room is small, a glass counter and shelves holding

spell components and weapons. A siren woman with bright blue hair and translucent aqua eyes greets us with a smile, and after signing safety waivers, we look through a photo book of smash room options. One is filled with electronics, one with ceramic dishware, another with concrete blocks. Alexo flips through pictures, chuckling incredulously, until he gets to one of the last.

His smile falls. "That one." He stabs his finger on the picture.

He might as well have stabbed that finger directly into my solar plexus for the way I stagger.

Of all the options, he chose this one?

It's a room filled with religious statues. Not unlike the shelves I have at home, but whereas most of the stuff I collect are antiques, these are sculptures of various sizes depicting gods. It's meant for *friendly competition* between customers with patron gods; one time when I was here, that room was reserved for followers of two rival gods of charity, and they were duking it out in a controlled, safe way before they were due to collaborate on a project.

I nod at the owner, smiling to cover the pitch of my nerves. "Is it free?"

She looks from the room picture to me and her eyes brighten with recognition. "Oh, you're Orok, right? It's been a while since we've seen you around. Heard you went and got famous on us."

My smile is tighter than I mean it to be. I wasn't sure if she'd remember me; it's been about four years since I last came here. "Ah. Yeah. Moved away," I say with a shrug.

She takes pity on my clear discomfort and lets it drop to check her computer. "The room's free. Our records say you usually use a sledgehammer—would you like that again? We can get extra Urzoth statues set up to—"

"No," I cut her off. "It's, um, fine the way it is, I'm sure. But we'll take a"—I look at the glass case—"fireball potion? And . . ."

I turn to Alexo. And I know I come across as pleading, hoping he didn't connect several dots.

He smiles and points to the shelves of weapons. "I want a mace."

My brows hitch up.

The one he's pointing at is almost as tall as he is, a long black leather-wrapped pole with a gruesome spiked ball on the end. But I don't question it, too busy picturing him swinging that weapon and decapitating a statue of Urzoth. Or, ya know, any of the dozens of god statues in that room, whatever.

I swallow, throat thick. "Yeah. Anything he wants."

The smash room owner rings us up. She hands me a vial of fireball potion before hoisting the mace off the wall and passing it to Alexo. He takes it, his slender arms bulging with the effort, but his face is impassive as he hikes it onto his shoulder and stands there, waiting for me, other hand on his cocked hip.

The bright white light in here shows all the facets of his rose-gold hair, burnished and gorgeous, and his eyes are alight with excitement.

He sees me gawking at him and his bottom lip snags between his teeth.

I clench the fireball potion, suddenly grateful I'm wearing sweats for the extra room, but also horrified I'm wearing sweats for how little they do in the way of hiding my current problem. A problem that started in the car the moment he kissed me and is in danger of persisting the whole damn night at this rate.

"The room's ready for you," the owner tells us. "It's warded to protect you from shrapnel as soon as you enter. I'll activate an extra ward of fire protection as well. Have fun, boys."

She sends us off with a knowing smirk, but I honestly don't care. There's nothing subtle about what's happening. This is the kind of obnoxious sexual tension Seb and Thio always have, and wow, if this is what it's like for them, it's a wonder they ever get anything done.

I lead Alexo down a hall lined with shut doors, each one spray-painted with hints at which room it is. The one we head to is covered in religious symbols, and I push it open without looking at the Urzoth one right above our heads.

Inside, the space is long and narrow, the walls graffitied in an unbroken wave of more religious signs. Statues of dozens of different gods fill the room. It's a wonder no god or their group has gotten pissy about their images being used like this—although, maybe they have. Hell if I know what drama this place might be embroiled in. I wasn't here *that* often in college.

Just often enough to have the owner recognize me years later.

The door thuds shut behind us, and Alexo prowls the room, examining the statues. He bypasses one of Urzoth. A few more for gods of the ocean, the sky, one that's a god of wealth.

He stops near the back of the room at a statue of a winged being. From here, I see only concrete feathers on either side, so it might be a god of birds.

"Are we good to start?" Alexo calls without turning.

I wind my way toward him. "Yeah. Whenever you—"

He braces his legs, hefts the mace back, and fucking *clobbers* that statue.

It explodes in a shower of dust and rock chunks, the satisfying crash of his mace into the stone echoing off the walls. A piece of the statue comes rolling toward me—the head, its face in a vicious snarl.

Alexo follows after it and crushes it with the mace.

He's panting when he looks up at me, his lips peeling into a feral grin that pops his dimples.

"Oh, I *like* this," he gasps, adjusts his stance, and wails on another statue.

I forget to take the fireball potion. I don't even need to destroy anything; it's far more entertaining to watch Alexo go absolutely wild on this room.

He decimates a statue of a nature god with a manic giggle that has heat crawling across my skin before he takes the arms off a war god. Each swing comes with grunts and curses and the occasional ecstatic chirp, and after a particularly good hit that explodes an entire statue in one swing, he turns to me with an excited, childlike look of *Did you see?*

I grin, covered in concrete dust from following him around the room.

After a few minutes, Alexo holds the mace out to me. "You haven't done anything."

"I'm good," I assure him. "This is what I wanted."

One of his eyebrows flares, shit-stirring a little. "You'll be back soon on your own anyway, right?"

My smile stiffens.

Alexo clocks it, and his expression drops. "Never mind. I have secrets; you can, too."

I grab the mace handle as he turns away. He blinks up at me, a streak of gray on his cheek where he scrubbed the back of his hand across his face.

"That," I nod to the statue behind him, the one he just destroyed, "was Warnock the Fierce. A god of piracy and sailing."

Alexo glances back at the rubble. "Huh. Thought he was some kind of fashion god. All those ruffles."

I'm already turning to the next debris pile he left in his wake. "And that's Zurduq, a god of war, but surprisingly not *violent* wars—only the wars that are *friendly challenges,* like, believe it or not, thumb wars. And that"—I don't pause for his amused snort—"was Evidione, a goddess of pollen. This place goes through a ton of her statues every time allergy season kicks in; it's cathartic. And over there . . ."

I go around the room, naming the gods he's taken the mace to, and Alexo trails me, eyes bright with interest.

When we're back to the beginning, the original winged god he smashed, I point at the fragments of its head. "And this was one of the demon lords of hell. I thought it was an avian god at first, but that snarl—it was either Foul Brariock or Dimardion. Either way, a ruler of the Demonic Plane."

Alexo's lips part. His cheeks are red, and I don't think it's entirely from exertion; he's been calm for the few minutes I've explained who these statues were.

"Do you know all of them?" he asks, waving around the room.

"Yeah." I stuff my hands in the pocket of my hoodie. "I have a Mageus in Theological Evocation. My apartment's full of relics from various religions."

"Holy shit. Really? Why?" The last word comes on a winded laugh, and one side of my lips goes up at his wonder.

"Shocked a beefcake jock has an interest outside of rawball?"

Alexo taps the mace on the floor and considers the question. "Kind of. But you keep surprising me, so I *shouldn't* be surprised."

My smile holds, even as I say, "I grew up in the Church of Urzoth Shieldsworn. My parents had a lot of expectations for me because of it. Still do. And . . . eventually, it became comforting to be reminded that my family's god isn't the only one. He isn't invincible."

The breath leaves Alexo's lungs in a punch. He looks out over the room again.

"Are any of them invincible?" he asks, a tenuous whisper.

That feels like another loaded question, but I answer simply, "No."

He scrubs his hand against his face again, leaving another streak of dust, this one tinged a bit darker, his gaze watery now.

In my silence, he rolls his eyes at me, at himself, and huffs. "You're not going to ask what that's about?" he pushes. "What *this*"—he motions to his teary eyes—"is about?"

I step closer to him. Close enough to run my fingers across his hand, wiping away some of the rock dust to leave lines on his skin.

"I don't need all your secrets. I'll take whatever you want to give me." I inhale the chalky air, unable to pick up any of his apple scent through it. "And I want you to have all the secrets of mine you need. Here's another: I used to come here a lot when I was in college. No one else in my life knows about it. I always picked this room."

"And you had them set up extra Urzoth statues?" Alexo peeks at me, prodding.

I nod.

He doesn't follow that with the obvious question. With any questions, just like I didn't push him for any answers either.

We're our own sort of religious statues, hands cupped, palms up and extended, offerings only. No reaching, no grabbing. Just gifts.

"I grew up with stupid family shit, too," he tells me, words as evanescent as the dust particles dancing through the air between us. "That's why Tem's so overbearing. It's hard to escape expectations, even when you *do* escape them. It's always—" He taps the side of his head.

I take his offering. Take it and tuck it away to pick apart later.

For now, Alexo shifts his hand so it clutches mine and pulls until I'm holding the mace. Then he points, and when I look, there's the Urzoth statue. Untouched. A god with so much dominion over strength that he's made of stone in his divine form, so having a statue of him created out of poured concrete is common to the point of familiarity.

I've seen hundreds of statues like this one over my life. Grew up around them.

I adjust my grip on the mace, eyes on Alexo, who watches me with that intense connection, visceral in its heat.

The mace leaves the ground. I swing it in a wide arch, let it fall with a clattering thud onto Urzoth's head.

All the while not breaking eye contact with Alexo, whose lips flicker with a ghost of a smile.

He sobers.

"It's getting late," he whispers.

My heart drops. He wants me to take him home. Back to that unsafe apartment and *Tem*.

But I bow my head dutifully and rest the mace against the wall.

The owner has magic on hand to help clean us up, so when we leave, we're not trailing clouds of concrete dust.

The drive back to Alexo's place is silent. It isn't uncomfortable or weighted; Alexo spends most of it tapping his knee to songs on the radio.

When we're only a few minutes from his apartment, he leans on the center console where my arm's resting, hand holding the gearshift.

Without a word, he links his fingers around my wrist. Lightly, so I can still drive.

A breathy sound leaves my throat, airy and warbling, and I don't even try to swallow it. It's living between us now, this obsession I have with him, and he's aware of it, so why fight it? He's got me, pathetically, deplorably; he's got me.

I start to pull into his building's parking lot. It's empty, so Tem hasn't come back yet. Which causes a contradictory emotional tug-of-war:

How *dare* Tem leave him alone so long? Does he have any idea what could have happened to Alexo while he was gone?

And then—thank the gods Tem's gone. I don't want him here, don't want him near Alexo, no matter how *not all bad* he is.

But Alexo points up the street. "Park there," he says, and I obey, pulling the car into a free spot by the sidewalk a few buildings down from his.

He doesn't get out of the car right away. Doesn't remove his hand from my wrist. I shut off the car then go pliant under his grip, listening to his breathing grow faster. I swear I can hear his heart thundering. It's making mine flurry just as ravenously, adrenaline bursting into my veins with no target yet, nowhere to go.

"Does . . ." He licks his lips. I hear the smack of his tongue against the pink gloss he reapplied. "Does your chair move back?"

I free my hand from the gearshift, from his touch, to undo my seatbelt and throw the seat as far back as it goes.

And, like an idiot, brain moving through melted gold, I ask, "Why?"

He wheezes a nervous laugh. "Gods, your chivalry, I swear."

It's the last thing he says before he's unbuckling his own seatbelt and scaling the center console to straddle me.

I snap back against the seat, body gone to unyielding steel as he grabs the headrest behind me and his knees spread over my hips.

My first reaction, brain still sluggish through that melted gold, is to say, "You're going to hurt your legs sitting like that," because he's so small, and my thighs aren't exactly thin thanks to my half-giant ancestry with near-daily glute and hamstring drills.

Alexo whimpers, his eyes glued to my lap. "Happily. Your thighs are a wet dream." And before I can rattle my way through sensibility enough to fully appreciate that, he's kissing me again.

A triumphant, relieved mewl trills in my throat and I attack him, tongue thrusting into his mouth, chasing that flavor I'm already addicted to. He rocks with me, and I may not greedily push him for answers, but here? Here, I will be greedy, I will take and take; but he's giving just as fervently, meeting all my needy moans with little cries that fucking *ruin* me.

My hands dart up under the back of his crop top, following each knobbed ridge of his spine until I splay my hands on the wings of his shoulder blades, feeling, *feeling*, he's letting me do this. He rocks against me, that dancer's body malleable to the point of implausibility as he fluctuates his hips and grinds on me, and my sense of awareness whites out, nothing but apples and his soft skin and the aphrodisiac *taste* of him.

His legs spread this way has me thrusting up unconsciously, the barriers of my sweats and his baggy jeans thin enough that I can feel the drag of his hard length against mine. He must feel me in turn, because he slurs a curse into the seam of my mouth and a tremor goes up his thighs.

"Orok," he whines, and I chase the reverberations of it in his mouth, biting at his tongue, dragging it between my lips with an ardency that has him squirming in my lap even more. He's all motion, constant, rippling waves that churn and froth against me—his hips gyrating and his torso swaying and his fingers scraping for purchase in my beard so he can position my jaw how he wants it.

I try to be stationary for him, let him work this dance on me, but I'm insatiable, too, and when he grinds down on me with renewed desperation, I nudge his head to the side and clamp my teeth on his collarbone. Right where he had that gold shimmer the night of his song at the bar, I kiss and lick and he thrusts down against me with a liquid plea.

"*Please*, I—"

"What do you want?" My hands grip his narrow waist, not to

hold him still, but to feel the rhythm of his movements, to try to follow his wriggling flow.

"I want. I want—I don't know, I *want* you." His eyes are heavy-lidded, and the car's barely illuminated by the gray haze that permeates this neighborhood, but I can feel the heat coming off his face, know he's flushed. I want to see, want to know what his skin looks like this way, but he moans weakly and my chest crushes with leonine need.

I thrust my hands down his body, intending to get ahold of his ass and help him grind down on me, get that last little bit of perfect leverage.

My fingers dip beneath the waistband of his jeans.

Alexo sucks in a serrated breath and snatches my wrists off him. "Wait! Wait, wait—"

I rear back, hands palm up, my already panting breaths scraping hoarse. "I'm sorry, I'm so—"

His fingers pinch on my wrists. "Stop. Don't apologize. You're perfect." Each word comes through a constricted throat, his own breaths still ramped up high, and the fog is lifting. Not just lifting—it's entirely blown away, a switch-flip so jarring I catch up in jerks and pulls.

He's still on my lap. But he's holding himself up now, not seated fully on me anymore. And he's clinging to my wrists, keeping my hands back, like he's afraid I'll grab him again. Or maybe he's pinned here, delayed in his reactions like I am. Processing, beat by beat.

I have only one second to note the way his face collapses in the dark—heavy, aching sorrow—before he's scrambling off me, back into the passenger's seat.

"Alexo—"

He whips a glare at me. "*Don't,*" he snaps, and I sink back, hands still up, unthreatening, in surrender.

He winces, that flash of anger getting overridden by the emotions that stack up in his eyes: grief, regret, sorrow, sorrow, sorrow.

I've seen how majestic this man is when he's happy. That's all he should ever be, *happy*, and yet something's keeping him caged. It's costing him something to let me see this.

"Fuck," he mutters. "I'm—I'm sorry. It isn't you. I swear, Orok."

I reach for him, but hesitate. "Can I touch you?"

He grunts an empty laugh that cracks apart and he tugs his fingers through his hair. "I'm a mess. You don't want me. You don't want to be part of this. It's easier when it's fake, okay? Let's just let it be fake."

I rest my hand on one of his forearms. He doesn't flinch, so I tug until it falls, then dip my fingers under his chin and twist him to look at me.

"Is that what you want?" I ask. "For this to only be fake?"

Please, no. Gods, I don't think I can.

He laughs again, manic this time, high and creaky and distressed. "You have no idea how much I want something real."

"I told you, I'll take whatever you want to give me. We can go at your pace. I won't touch you like that again unless you tell me to. *You* lead this."

It's killing me not to ask more. Not to demand to know what's hurting him. It might not be Tem, but *something* sure as hell is hurting him—he mentioned something with his family? My hands shake with a barely repressed quiver he has to feel where I hold his chin.

"Why?" he whispers. Not for the first time tonight.

I force a smile, force a lightness against the clawing, reawakened beast in my chest, the one now pacing and irately snarling *mine, mine, he's threatened, and he's mine.*

"Because I think we could both use something in our lives that's *good.*"

Alexo stares up at me, eyes shining in the darkness, all those heavy, awful emotions now warring with a glimmer of hope. He's a cut wildflower in a vase. A lightning bug in a mason jar. He's something wild and beautiful confined.

I don't know how long I'll be able to hold myself back from figuring out what I need to do to set him free.

Alexo leans in, but doesn't kiss me again, just tips forward until I match him and our foreheads rest together.

"Thank you," he tells me. "For tonight. It was—" An airy chuckle. "One of the best nights I've had in a long time."

"Breaking shit is soul balm," I say, but he shakes his head.

"That's not what I mean, and you know it."

I go still.

He exhales, and I bask in him for this last moment, until he leans back. As he reaches for the door handle, I dig in my pocket.

"Hang on—take this."

I hand him the unused vial of fireball potion.

Alexo's teary eyes brighten. "Oh my gods. You—"

And he cackles, laughing so hard he doubles over.

I smile at his levity. "What? It's good for protection. In case, ya know. Like a taser."

He *loses it*. "A *taser*?"

"Kind of."

"You're basically—giving me—*a bomb*." He punctuates his words with gasping breaths and more delirious giggles. "A *bomb*, Orok."

Well, when he says it like that. "You don't have to take it."

I move to stick it back in my pocket.

"No, *no*." Alexo snatches it from me. "Fuck that. It's mine. You gave it to me. It's just—most people give *flowers*. Or chocolates or some shit. But this date started via stalking and attempted kidnapping and ended with you giving me an *incendiary device*."

I snort. Distantly, I know I should be mortified, because that's exactly what happened; every moment tonight was one prolonged cry for help. My therapist will have a brain bleed.

But Alexo's laughter is still warm on the air and his cheeks are shining with happy tears, and I don't regret any of it, if it brought us here.

"Can I walk you to your front door?" I ask. "Or would that be far too normal and cancel out the creepy vibes I've spent all evening painstakingly crafting?"

Alexo's smile tempers. He bites his lower lip.

I know what that lip tastes like.

"This is enough," he says softly and cracks open the car door. "Until next time?"

I bob my head. "Until next time."

He climbs out into the night.

I wait a beat, then step out onto the street, but I hold over the roof of my car as he walks up to his building. I don't know if Tem pulled in while we were . . . *occupied*, but Alexo walks quickly for the steps.

Before he ducks inside, he looks back at me. It's too far for me to see his face, too far for him to do more than make out my silhouette. But we both hold for one, two, three seconds.

Then he's through the door and gone.

I jog up the road until I can see his apartment's window, and I wait until that curtain flutters with the door opening and shutting. Even when the fabric settles and I know he's safely in his home, probably moving around in his room, getting ready for bed, I linger, watching.

Because it's all I can do right now.

All I'll *let* myself do right now.

Chapter Seven

They took Seb from me again.

I did something wrong. Something—I dropped a sword in sparring? Yeah, that's it. I dropped a sword, and they kept Seb overnight *for extra drills*, but he always comes back from those bruised to all hell.

They've been training us to depend on each other. An ouroboros partnership—we're supposed to complete each other, be so wholly in sync that we're one unit, one being. Not all their methods work, but my gods, this one has; I can't function when Seb's not around, and they know that. When I fuck up, they *take him from me*, and he's not here, *he's not here*.

Help me, Urzoth. Please, please make me strong. I need to protect Seb. I need to be strong for him, so please, give me your strength. Or—or just stop this. You could, couldn't you? You're strong enough. You can save Seb. Help him, help me, please—

Someone else is gone this time, too.

Who else did they take?

It's only Seb. But I have the distinct feeling that someone else is missing.

Seb's gone.

He's not here—

—because this is a dream. I'm asleep, in my bed in Vegas.

No, no, Philadelphia. I'm back in Philadelphia, and I'm asleep.

So *wake up*.

My phone's in my hand before I'm even all the way awake, and I'm delirious with sleep and residual panic so I'm only half conscious of the call ringing until he answers.

"If you're calling for bail money because you got arrested stalking your little cheerleader, know I'm gonna take *soooooo* many pictures of you in the holding cell."

My eyes pop open. "Seb?"

The hindbrain part of me relaxes, muscles releasing so forcefully I press the heel of my palm to my forehead and sink deeper into my bed.

He's okay. He's okay.

Fuck, breathe.

"Yeah?" His voice hangs in the silence. "O? You all right?"

"I called you." Gods, I'm catching up like molasses this morning.

"Uh, yeah. I assume you *don't* need bail money if you're this chill? What happened?"

It's—Friday. The day after the game. I pull my phone down to check the time, thinking Seb's gotta be at work—

When I see a missed text from Alexo.

ALEXO

Dark chocolate peanut butter cups

"O?" Seb's voice is thinner with the phone away from my ear. "You there? Shit, you're not actually in jail, are you?"

Dark chocolate peanut butter cups?

"No, I'm fine." I shove the phone back against my head. "I—I need to go, sorry."

"Woah, woah, there, Mr. Felony—explain yourself."

"I did not commit a felony."

"Or whatever stalking is considered. What happened? Did you see him? Did he see you? Gods, that's a creepy question."

"I saw him, and yeah, he saw me. It was . . . wonderful, actually." I shove myself up to sit, and as I do, every detail of last night flash floods through me. Alexo's body writhing against mine. The sheer delight in his eyes as he smashed the shit out of those statues.

His panicked reaction when I grabbed his ass.

The tang of nausea burns in the back of my throat. *No*. I will not jump to conclusions. I will not overreact. If he wants to tell me what that was about, he will.

Or he'll tell me . . . dark chocolate peanut butter cups?

"Listen, Seb, I'll explain everything in a bit, okay? I gotta—"

"You called me."

"I know, I—"

"No, I mean—you didn't *intend* to call me. Did you?"

It's not the first time I've woken up in the middle of seeking him out.

When we lived together, I'd sometimes sleepwalk into his room, or he'd save himself that jump scare and fall asleep in my bed. But when I moved to Vegas, I obviously couldn't physically seek him out anymore. Sleep-calling him became a thing. A thing I was very quick to work on with my therapist, and I haven't done it in several years.

"Fuck," I growl to my bedspread. "I'm sorry. You're at work. I'll—"

"Don't you dare hang up, big guy."

I obey. If only because hearing his voice is still wiping away the last of the night's restlessness.

Was Alexo in the dream, too?

It stabs through me, a gut punch of memory.

They took someone else from me. *Him.*

No. Gods damn it, *no*. Whatever I'm doing with him *cannot* be sparking my Camp Merethyl shit. *I won't let it.* The two are entirely unrelated, and I refuse, flat out *refuse* to let him become a gods-damned trigger.

But everything I do is tied up in Camp Merethyl, isn't it? It always is.

"One call is not a failure, all right?" Seb tells me. "Do not beat yourself up about this. I swear to the gods, O—I can hear you chastising yourself from here. *Don't*. And don't push me away to punish yourself."

His words have me glaring up at nothing. "What'd you say?"

"Don't—wait, which part? Don't beat yourself up? Don't push me away to punish yourself?"

"Yeah, that." Chilling sweat breaks out across my shoulders.

Do I push him away because that's how *they* trained me to punish myself?

Every time I fucked up, they'd take him. I don't think he even realized that's what they were doing; it was always under the guise of *specialized training. He* was perfectly fine without *me*—they punished him in other ways.

But now, when I act too fixated on him, I push him away. To punish myself for being *too much.*

No—I'm not punishing myself. I'm trying to break unhealthy cycles. I'm removing a vice.

Only he's not a vice. He's my gods-damned *person*, and I *have* been treating him like an incentive.

I hunch over in bed, screwing my knuckle into my temple, and tell him about last night. Everything. When I describe the magic smash room, he does take an embarrassing amount of interest in it—"Why haven't you and I gone there? I hate you." I give him the PG version of what happened in the car; so much of these details about Alexo feel porcelain delicate, things entrusted to me and me alone.

At the end, I can *hear* Seb's smile. "Orok's got a *boyfrieeeeeend.*"

"Shut up." But I'm smiling now, too. And the dream is gone, my anxiety stable. "I really do have to go, though. I gotta get to HQ to review game-day tapes."

"Ugh. They not only make you play rawball, but you have to then rewatch what you played?"

"Oh, that reminds me—since we won when you were at the game last night, I now need you to come to all my games. I've decided you're my good-luck charm this season."

Seb lets out a defeated "Please don't ask that of me, I beg of you."

I laugh. There's something weird about it, and it takes me a minute to realize I haven't laughed like this with Seb in . . . gods, I can't even remember. Since before I moved back. I've been keeping him in such a restricted box and monitoring my every interaction with him that I haven't let myself *enjoy* him, enjoy *us*.

He laughs, too. And it sounds relieved. Lighter.

"You aren't a punishment or a reward." The words gush out of me, driven by an abrupt need to reconcile this. "I'm sorry. I'll do better."

"I don't give a shit, O. I really don't. Do better; do your worst. Just let me be a part of it."

My heart thuds, throat pinching.

"I love you," I tell him.

"Fuck yeah, you do," he says back, that grin in his voice, and ends the call.

I do need to get to HQ, but I flip to Alexo's text thread and write, *Is that a code I should know?*

He texts back while I'm getting dressed.

ALEXO
No. It's something real about me. My favorite dessert. And I figure that might be an important piece of information if you're deathly allergic to nuts.

No allergies here. No food issues at all, except eating unbearable amounts of protein throughout the season. But here's something real about me: when it's offseason, I go vegetarian.

Tell me something else real.

I get to HQ, find a seat in the theater-style room with the other defensive tanks, and while our coach is setting up last night's game footage, I watch the three dots in Alexo's text thread appear and vanish and reappear.

ALEXO
I've lived almost everywhere, and my least favorite climate is right here. Fucking hate snow. And this humidity is a bitch. Give me warm, dry crop-top weather, please and thank you.

Mm. His crop tops.

"Monroe?"

The defensive coach is looking at me expectantly, so I stuff my phone away and focus.

We take a break a while later, and I text Alexo about living in Vegas, and how the weather was amazing but the scorpions terrified me.

He responds about how he fell in love with dance—his aunt could only afford one ballet class, so his cousin took it, and would teach him the moves after every session.

He grew up with his aunt and cousin? Where? What happened to them—why does he live with Tem now? Was he married to Alexo's aunt? Is it part of the *family shit* he's dealing with?

I don't ask any questions though, and neither does he. It's offerings only still, a trade of sorts.

He's busy with cheer practice, and I'm getting pulled between my own practice and media junkets for the Hellhounds, so over the rest of the week, we don't see each other, but we text nonstop.

Our next scheduled interaction is during the away game on Thursday in Manhattan—we have the game, of course, but the evening after is a gala for a charity that works closely with the national pro rawball league. Alexo and I are scheduled to attend it together.

There's going to be overlap now, our staged PR events and things I consider real, and this is one. A big one—this charity means a lot to me, and I'm excited to not only attend with Alexo, but to have him with me in what feels like our first *real* public outing.

I content myself with texting him, and we feed each other little details:

His favorite color is pink. I almost tell him mine is, too, because of his hair, but I censor myself and say mine's orange, which has worked out well with my new team's colors.

His first job was working at a makeup store for a whole day before he accidentally stabbed a woman in the eye with a mascara brush. Mine was filing at my dad's accounting firm when I was in middle school. Showing me around his workplace was the most animated my very stoic, docile father has ever been, but the next summer, my mom enrolled me at Camp Merethyl. I was destined to be something Urzoth-worthy, with strength and physicality, not a quiet office clerk.

Pretty sure the only reason my mom married my dad is because he rolls over for whatever she wants and makes her feel like a true Urzoth follower when she quote-unquote *wins* so often.

Which is something I text to Alexo before realizing, oops, that might have been too deep for a text conversation? I pivot us back to getting-to-know-each-other ground: neither of us have had any pets, we're both only children, he's a Virgo, I'm a Taurus.

He sends me a selfie in front of the cheerleader bus as they're getting ready to depart for NYC. His tongue's sticking out, freckles highlighted in a faint blush, and his pale blue crop top reads MY BIRTHSTONE IS A GLITTER BOMB in bold sparkly font.

I hate that the players are on a separate bus. Hate that I haven't seen or touched him in five days, but I can't hate it too much, because I know things about him now. The fuzzed edges of his mysteries are starting to clear, and even though there are still large unanswered questions, a foundation is building, ready for whatever weight it'll have to bear.

Tem Raussec doesn't exist online. No socials, no news reports about him. I consider and dismiss the idea of hiring a PI to get more info on him. He didn't seem to be the source of Alexo's stress, just a jerk, and I don't want to go that obsessive. Yet.

I'm also proud of myself for not contacting Alexo's landlord like I did for Seb and throwing money at his problems anonymously. Again, *yet*.

All things considered, I'm being pretty patient and levelheaded and not spiraling wildly about Alexo, and it reaffirms that, even though I had moments of relapsing, I haven't entirely lost myself. I can be calm and rational. I can have *composure*.

Until I see Alexo on the red carpet outside the charity gala at a glitzy hotel in the middle of Manhattan. Composure? *Ha.* I barely know her.

He's in high-waisted, wide-legged black pants and heavy black combat boots, a goth counterweight to his airy satin tank top with thin spaghetti straps in a rosebud color that matches the pretty blush on his cheeks. The top droops and sways over his torso, showing all the lean, honed muscles in his arms and chest, more of that body glitter dusted across his skin. Gods, I want to roll around in it.

But it isn't just glitter that has him sparkling.

He's got some kind of gold body chain that loops around his neck and shoulders and cuts down between his pecs, dipping under his collar before it goes fuck knows where below his shirt.

The body chain goes *under his clothes*.

How far down?

My jaw's open. I know it is.

Marlow cackles at me.

We're at one end of the gala's red carpet while Treva leads Alexo to me—it's a staged procession, making sure every single journalist gets plenty of time to prepare for the rawball Beauty and the Beast's next moment.

A few reporters shout out more questions about last night's game against the New York Ghouls: 21–15, us. Mostly thanks to Marlow who, even though the field our artificers built wasn't water, zipped around those desert dunes like they might as well have been an ocean. And, okay, the main reason she was able to move so freely was because of my defenses, which is why we've spent the past twenty minutes fielding questions about our technique and partnership.

As well as questions about our next game.

It's at home.

Against the Chimeras.

Luckily, the publicists prepped me for questions like that. I have to smile and say I'm excited to see my old teammates.

So that's what I do. Lie through my teeth.

Treva deposits Alexo behind Marlow and me and gives a subtle bob of her chin.

Time for a different kind of lying that's not really lying at all.

I pluck off the enchanted earring and pass it to Marlow. She takes it, then slaps my ass as I'm walking away.

"Go get your man," she signs.

A laugh barks out of me.

The rest of the team might still be heavily cordial with me, but Marlow's blissfully just . . . *Marlow.*

Alexo's glaring at Marlow when I close in around him and Treva, and I gotta say, I don't hate the flare of jealousy in his eyes.

I slide my arm around his waist and that jealousy evaporates, getting blinked away in favor of a sudden, breathless gasp and big round eyes that look even rounder lined in coal black and streaks of shimmery gold. Alexo relaxes against me, hand on my chest, and he smiles, all those days we spent apart coming to a head.

"Dark chocolate peanut butter cups," I tell him.

His brows bend in question.

"Isn't that how we start interactions between us now?" My grin is taunting and makes him roll his eyes.

"Oh, hilarious." A deeper blush stains his cheeks, his freckles vibrant. "Mock my awkwardness. That's low-hanging fruit, Orok. I expected better from you."

"Low-hanging fruit? Are you saying you're *usually* awkward? I vehemently disagree." I lean in—I can't help it, can't stop myself when he's right here, back in my arms again—and press my face behind his ear, inhaling deep. His apple brightness streaks directly to my groin and he shivers at the pull of my breath. "You're graceful," I whisper to him. "Self-assured. And absolutely stunning, especially tonight."

Alexo makes a keening noise in his throat, and his grip on my shirt clenches into a fist.

"Gods, you two are *nailing* this," Treva interrupts, partly surveying the interviews happening with my teammates across the red carpet.

A couple of yards down, Phei is giving an interview as a fire elemental. Another publicist stands behind them with a fire extinguisher, occasionally keeping the red carpet from bursting into flames.

Treva seems unbothered. Unlike the reporter interviewing Phei, who's holding a microphone as far from himself as he can and keeps yanking his hand back with a yelp.

"Keep that up exactly as you have it. Whew, damn." Treva fans herself. "Have you been practicing?"

Part of my mouth tips up in a smile, and I look down at Alexo. "Yeah. Practicing."

He blushes again. Or still. Bites that glossy lower lip and shrugs at Treva. "We committed to the cause."

Treva flicks through something on her phone. "Okay—you need to give a short interview with a reporter before you go in. Then spend the rest of the night—"

She looks up at the way Alexo's still tucked against me and I'm unable to focus on anything other than him.

"—doing that." She hesitates, head cocking. "Are you two actually—*oh my gods*. This is amazing!"

I'm quick to spin toward her. "It doesn't change anything we've agreed to do. Our private relationship doesn't have any bearing on our public relationship."

"Oh, of course," Treva says. "I meant it's adorable! What a way to meet, huh?"

Alexo snorts. "Yeah, adorable." He dips his head and quietly adds, "A bar fight, stalking, attempted kidnapping—"

I pinch his side through his silky tank top and he lets out a devastatingly cute squeak.

Treva waves us toward a reporter near the middle of the carpet, held back with the others by a velvet rope. "Let him ask a few questions, then make your way inside. And a heads-up—he's going to ask about Urzoth. Reverend Drach wanted a more direct tie between the happy couple and the church."

My grip on Alexo tightens, muscles previously relaxed by him going rock solid.

Treva bats her hand at the sudden strain on my face. "It won't be anything preachy, just fluff stuff."

Alexo pushes his weight against me. "Okay," he tells her. "We got this."

She winks before going over to Marlow, who's still being accosted with questions and photographs. Hellhounds publicists bustle all around, dipping in and out of interviews, gallantly trying to herd us like keeping kittens in a box.

Alexo and I walk away, my arm around him, but my head's stuck on what Treva said.

Urzoth is a part of this whole arrangement. Shouldn't be shocking, derailing.

And yet.

Alexo tugs on the fist he still has in my tuxedo shirt. "Hey. It'll be fine. I can take the questions. He's my patron god now, too."

My anxiety doesn't alleviate, not at all. "No. I'll—I'll do it. It's fine. Expected, even. Don't worry about it."

"Hm." Alexo surveys my expression, cheek caught in his teeth. "You're allowed to worry about me, but I can't worry about you?"

My lips part.

We've reached the reporter, and a recording device is thrust into my face.

The reporter's smiling too big, too eager, and I'm going into this off-balance.

"Orok Monroe," he starts. "What can you tell us about the new developments in tonight's charity?"

I let some of my muscles drop. See? It's a normal interview.

And the topic does make me perk up.

"Thrive Children is a national organization the pro rawball league has partnered with for decades," I say. "I've been lucky enough to be involved since I signed. They do fantastic work helping us set up rawball camps, and we've gotten to—"

"Yes, yes, we all know the pamphlet spiel," the reporter cuts in, and I flinch.

Alexo does, too.

"Tell me about the *new* programs Thrive Children is allegedly implementing," he continues. "Something about a crisis hotline and therapy access?"

My chin draws back, shock making my grip on Alexo spasm. I should let him go; he's not a stress ball. But as I peel away, and he puts his hand over mine on his hip.

"I'm not at liberty to speak about anything in development," I manage.

How does this guy know about those programs?

We haven't gone public with anything. I'm waiting for the money to come in, and it was going to be a big announcement, one of the few projects that I'd actually attach myself to, not hide behind anonymously. It's important to break down stigmas around mental health, and if I can do so by using my fame and platform? I will.

Being the face of something like that was another thing that'd give my mother a conniption, but I wasn't supposed to have to deal with that fallout for *months.*

"Where exactly is Thrive Children getting the funds for these programs?" the reporter asks with a slick *gotcha* grin. "Rumor says it'll be the money coming from your recent lawsuit against Camp Merethyl. What does the Urzoth church have to say about you promoting programs that contradict the more physical, tough-it-out methods they usually employ? *Strong as stone, hard as rock,* those ideals. How do they feel about you funding these programs with the money you got through a lawsuit many Urzoth followers have criticized for also contradicting their doctrine?"

The blood drains out of my face.

My palm's sweating; I'm ruining Alexo's nice satin shirt. I need to let go of him.

Step back, and let go of him.

Detached thoughts bob through my head while I gape at the reporter.

Answer the question. Just—say *something.*

Weak. You're so weak. You should be handling this better.

Alexo grabs the reporter's wrist and yanks the recording device down to him.

"Hi," he says, smiling sweetly. But the way he's gripping the reporter's arm counters that, his knuckles white. "I'm Alexo Warden, a follower of Urzoth's. And while I haven't been a follower for long, I can say that assuming all Urzoth followers believe in stoic, emotionless strength is antiquated. Not that any programs like the ones you've mentioned have been *properly* announced, but if they had been, you can certainly see how natural it would be to connect them to a church that promotes strength. What is stronger than getting the assistance you need? In being able to admit that you need help? Especially for children. Don't children deserve strength like that?"

The reporter winces and subtly tries to pull his hand out of Alexo's grip. "Well, I—"

"Have you had a chance to make a donation to Thrive Children tonight?" Alexo gives him a honeyed smile, butter wouldn't melt in his mouth, and releases his fingers, one by one.

The reporter snatches his hand away. "Uh—I don't—"

"I'll have someone from the organization contact you to make sure you get the chance," Alexo says. "This is for the kids, after all. Isn't it?"

The reporter straightens with a sniff. "Of course. No further questions."

"Oh, I have something else to say." Alexo waves for the recording device to come back up, and the guy obeys, albeit with a slightly *what the fuck is he going to say now* look.

But Alexo says into it, "Remember to keep dancing."

His face drops into a searing glare that has the reporter cringing in surprise.

Without another word, Alexo loops his arm around my waist in mimicry of how I'm still holding him and wheels me away.

What the—

What just happened?

A publicist, not Treva, rushes to us as we climb the steps for the gala. "I caught the end of that—I'm *so* sorry, those were *not* the questions he was approved to ask."

"Just make sure he's encouraged to make a donation. A *big* one," Alexo tells him, and the publicist hurries off.

I'm staring down at Alexo, my chest somehow both crushing in and ballooning out, weighed down in horror and free-floating from . . . from . . . *him.*

The inside of the hotel is glamoured up in the way big, flashy charities go all out to attract big, flashy donors. But everything is a blurred haze, dripping chandeliers and fancy-dressed people; a watercolor background for Alexo, who steers me through the room until we push through a set of swinging doors into a utility hall, the wood flooring swapped for practical linoleum.

A few waiters and other staff mill around, but for the most part, Alexo and I have some privacy where he tucks us up in a corner.

He twists our hands together and holds the mass against his chest. "Are you all right?"

Am I all right.

If the reporter publishes that interview, I'll have yet another thing my parents and I don't talk about. Yet another thing Urzoth supporters will yell at me for.

Alexo stood up for me. He stepped in, and not only put that reporter in his place, but demanded *money* from the man.

Gods, that was sexy.

"Thank you," I whisper. I can't make it louder. I *need* to, need to shout it from the high-rise rooftop.

He grins. "It was my absolute pleasure, trust me. I so rarely get to tell people off who deserve it." His grin slips, dimming a fraction. "What he said—"

"I, um—" My tongue feels swollen, words jamming up, but I exhale and anchor fast to—"Why did you say that, at the end? *Remember to keep dancing*? You said it before. What is that?"

Alexo goes from concerned to . . . sad.

No. *Heartbroken.*

He shrugs one shoulder, calling my attention to the diamond sharpness of his collarbone, the perfectly sculpted contours of his bicep. "It's something my cousins and I used to say to each other."

That wall of his shoots up between us, the edge of what he'll tell me about himself.

But then he's scaling the wall. Turning his heartbreak into righteous anger.

"I want them to hear it. Maybe they're rawball fans and they're watching. I want them to know I'm thinking of them."

I can't stop the questions this time, I really can't. I'm taken too far down to the quick. "What happened to them?"

Alexo smiles, his eyes glistening. "It's a long story. But I haven't seen them in a few years." Another shrug, trying and failing to play it off. "I . . . miss them. It's a silly thing."

No. It's not silly, the heaviness of the anguish in his eyes, but I don't get a chance to ask another question before he's lobbing his own at me.

We're done being delicate with each other's offerings, turns out. Now, we're taking, too.

"Are you really working on those programs?" he whispers. "A crisis hotline, therapy access?"

I was supposed to have been free from Urzoth for months, maybe a year, before they'd be announced. I didn't even officially agree to move forward on them until after the lawsuit. Seb and I, and the other Camp Merethyl survivors, we're all due to get a huge check from it, and I wanted to have something set up so I could funnel that money straight out of my account. It isn't *mine* and it sure as hell isn't Camp Merethyl's; it'll go toward healing and hope.

But I still thought I'd have a long, long time before I'd have to deal with the kind of attention Alexo's giving me. Looking up at me with awe, like I'm some kind of hero.

"It's not a big deal," I try. "Anyone would do it if they could. I won't be the one actually administering any of the resources for the kids. I sign a check and let them plaster my face on promo materials. It isn't—"

"Orok." His face gentles. "You're incredibly strong, you know that, right?"

My laugh is humorless. "You're giving me too much credit. None of this is from *strength.* I've only ever felt like I'm grabbing up every possibility for even the smallest bit of relief."

Alexo pushes closer, warm and solid against my unmoored emotions. "You *are* strong. You're strong for sponsoring these programs when you know it'll come with the kind of scrutiny that asshole reporter showed. Just like you went through with that lawsuit when you knew Urzoth's followers prefer to solve problems with their fists and they'd judge you for going a peaceful way, even though I'd argue there was nothing *peaceful* about what you did. You're *strong.* Probably the strongest person I've ever met."

He's so earnest, all innocence and wide doe eyes.

I can't help but be lethally swept up in his belief.

Fuck, that he can look at me like this. That he can say these things to me.

I stare down at his thin fingers knotted in my thick, calloused ones, all of them cradled against the cloud-soft silk of his pink shirt.

A glance up the hall tells me that while we're less public here, we're far from alone. Staff still rush in and out, a few casting curious looks our way.

I angle my body to block Alexo from their sight. "I want to kiss you again," I tell him.

His breath rips from him, eyes darkening. "You do, huh?"

"Very much."

His thumb moves against mine, a maddeningly tender motion. "Not for the cameras?"

"Not for the cameras."

A smile.

He nods. Desperately, his rose-gold hair bobbing around him, he parts his lips to utter a throaty, anxious "Please."

Chapter Eight

Our hands are still interlocked, so I leave one to pull him along as I make my way deeper into the bowels of the hotel. I have no idea where I'm going; the way to the elevators and our rooms was behind us, but all we need right now is a private room with a lock on the door.

The first door we find is a bathroom. The next—a custodial closet, filled with racks of cleaning supplies, mop buckets, and not a soul in sight. Perfect.

I hold the door open, using it to block us from the staff up the hall, and loosen my grip on Alexo's hand as I motion to the room, the single sad bulb hazing the cleaning supplies in a gray-white.

Super romantic, Monroe. Well done.

"Only if you're okay with this," I say. "I don't want to make you uncomfortable again."

"You didn't."

One of my brows lifts.

"I mean—it wasn't from *that.*" Alexo's breath goes out in a resigned slump, and when he speaks again, he's talking to the floor between us. "I need to keep . . . certain clothes *on.* I don't—it isn't—*ugh.*" He pushes his hands into his pink curls with an aggrieved moan. "Never mind. Moment's dead. Want to know how many hookups I've killed with conversations like this? Fucking *all of them.* Gods damn it."

He spins away when I seize his wrist. But he doesn't meet my eyes. His cheeks are so red they look painful.

In the pause, his words corkscrew into my brain.

Is he saying he's a—

Holy shit.

No one's ever—

And suddenly *I* feel inexperienced and unsteady, my throat turned to sandpaper and skin too hot, too tight.

There's that beast again. *Mine, mine,* it says, ever feral.

"I'm not going to fuck you in a cleaning closet," I say, my grin lopsided. "And there's plenty we can do without getting naked."

Alexo peeks up at me, surprised but guarded. "What are you saying?"

"I'm saying I want to kiss you. And if you want, if you'll let me, I want to make you feel good."

He swallows, his neck contracting. "H-how?"

"Can I touch you over your clothes?"

Another swallow. This one comes with a pinch of his brows, a pulse of want that flares heat in his eyes. "Yeah."

The hand not holding his wrist lifts, and I take one of his curls, tuck it behind his ear. His skin's rosy still, warm under my fingers.

"Can I kiss you over your clothes?"

He shudders. Hell, I do, too. My fingers rest against the pulse point in his neck and it flurries like mad.

"Y-yes," he stammers.

"Can I—" I lick my lips, willing my breathing to stay level, to not vibrate the question before I even get it out. "Can I have you in my mouth? Clothes stay on. Just your cock."

He looks like someone socked him in the stomach. Chest concaving, lips gaping.

Then *he's* the feral one.

He leaps at me, arms locking around my neck, and the force has me stumbling back into the custodial closet. My half a brain cell not currently absorbed in what's happening reminds me to lock the door, fingers fumbling the bolt until it clicks. I barely hear it over the frantic, *panicked* whimpers Alexo's making as he kisses me just as frenzied, just as rattled.

It's a heady, overwhelming barrage of his apple scent and the flavors of him dancing across my tongue, the shift and wriggle of his body in my arms. His legs clamp around my waist and he's hard, and so am I, have been since I saw him in this outfit on the red carpet.

I rotate, resting his back on the door, and kiss my way across his jaw, to his neck, to where that gold chain starts its descent across his chest and down under his tank top. It's a shooting arrow streaking over the night sky, and I make my wishes on it, every single one.

His head throws back with a staccato cry as I lick at one of the places where the chain rests on his collarbone, and I'm quick to slam my lips back over his.

"You gotta be quiet for me, all right?" I ask. "Can you do that?"

Eyes shut, he gasps into my mouth. "I can be quiet."

He's squirming as he says it, restlessly thrusting, yanking at my shoulders, and when I stop rocking against him, he whines in a high, frustrated pitch.

I grin. "You sure about that?"

Another frustrated whine. "*Yes*. Yes, I promise. I can be good. I can be so good for you."

My hips stutter forward of their own volition.

"Fuck, Alexo," I groan, head dropping to his shoulder. "You can't just say stuff like—"

"No."

I pull back. He's not squirming anymore, stationary, and it's enough of a contrast that I'm instantly alert.

But he's not pushing me away. He's looking up at me, breathless determination warring with uncertainty.

I brush my thumb against his hip bone. "What's wrong?"

"Can you—" He winces. "Can you not call me that? Not while we're—doing this."

Call him what? Alexo?

Huh.

I offer him a smile. "Would you prefer Alexo the Magnificent?"

Confusion breaks him out of his net of emotion like I hoped it would, and he rolls his eyes. "Oh gods. My karaoke name? Really? *No*, that's not what I meant. Can you . . . call me something else? When we're like this."

I bump my nose against his. "Okay. Gimme a sec."

Baby is out—Seb and Thio call each other that. *Sweetheart?* Not too bad. Or maybe something with his hair—*Pink?* Meh.

What have the press called us? Oroxo? Or, wait—Beauty and the Beast.

"What about Belle?" I ask.

He'd been immobile since asking his question. But he tenses now, winding up, and the way he gapes at me is—afraid? No. Baffled?

"The reporters," I explain quickly. Is he offended by it? "They called us Beauty and the Beast. So, Belle. That was her name in the movie, right?" Gods, it's been years since I saw it.

But Alexo nods, and I think his eyes are tearing. Or maybe it's the shit lighting in here making him look glassy and fraying.

"Yeah," he agrees. "Belle. Call me Belle."

"All right." I lean in. "My Belle."

The air disappears between us. What little there was left. I'm not sure what's changed—everything's trapped in quiescence on the surface, but something's roiling within him, and it sucks me in, has me pressing a kiss to his lips like an inevitability.

He doesn't whine this time. Doesn't claw at me. It's slow and sweet, his mouth parting and moving under me in drowsy palpitations, both of us just—just *feeling.*

Before I can resume my trail down his body, he squirms again so determinedly I peel back and allow him to sink to his knees.

Breath yanks out of my chest. "I was going to—"

"I know." He tugs at my belt. "Change of plans."

Kneeling before me, he still has to reach up a little to get at my crotch. And that view, him straining for me, those pink curls and his big, glassy eyes, rosebud lips kiss-swollen and slick—

I teeter forward, one hand going out to brace on the door behind him, the other grabbing myself through my pants.

He gives me a questioning look.

"You sure?" I huff a slightly deranged laugh. "This is going to be fast. Like, two-pump-chump fast."

He smirks. "Did you miss the part where I said I'm a virgin? Trust me, I won't be breaking any records either."

My turn to whine. It's excruciating, but it makes him smile, and anything, anything that makes him smile is worth it.

Then he's back to work, tugging my pants down, pushing my shirt out of the way, and I let it happen as I focus on how to *inhale* because I seem to have dropped that ability somewhere.

He pulls me out of my boxers, and the sight of his pale, pretty fingers around my dick has me slamming my eyes shut, digging my knuckles into the cold metal of the door, and going over rawball plays in my head.

But—this is his first time, yeah? So *step up*.

I manage to pry my eyes open, breath punching holes through my lungs, to see him—well, gawking. At my dick.

Which is a little validating, not gonna lie.

I have giant ancestry. Proportionally.

But for someone's first blow job, a giant cock is kind of like being chucked into the deep end.

Pun intended.

Fuck, now's not the time for stupid nervous jokes.

A blush creeps up the back of my neck and I reach my free hand out to touch his jaw. "You don't have to—"

His rounded eyes ping up to me.

There's that ferocity again. The Alexo who tackled me into the closet. The *hunger.*

"I might have a bit of a size kink," he says with the same straightforwardness as if he'd said, *It's cold out, wear a jacket*.

I sputter a laugh that gets immediately bitten off in a stunned moan when he sucks the head of my dick into his mouth.

"*Belle*," I shout. "Holy shit—*mmph*—"

His cheeks hollow as he pulls back and my vision goes spotty. "Now who needs to be quiet?"

That smirk.

"Don't think you can—*oh fuck*—"

He swallows me down, taking a good few inches into his mouth before he gags—only he *doesn't pull off*. Just lingers there, choking and fighting it, his eyes watering, spit pooling over the edges of his lips and dripping down his chin. Each contraction of his throat squeezes more, and more, and he holds through it like he's trying to force-train himself.

I've died, I think. This is death. This can't be happening in reality.

"B-belle," I stutter, and my hand slips behind his head, gripping his curls for something of this world to hold on to. "Fuck, you don't have to—your first go—*fuck*."

He pulls away with a wheeze and blinks up at me, eyes dewy and spilling tears that streak black makeup down his cheeks, saliva glistening all over his mouth, his chin, hell, down his neck.

"Good?" he asks, voice raspy.

I nod, can't form words, can't *think*.

He smiles, a cute little half tilt of his mouth that pushes at one of his dimples, and he's diving back in, humming in pleasure as he sucks me down again.

Another gag, holding, holding, then he suckles on my head and twists his hand around the length he can't reach.

It's sloppy but the best thing I've ever felt, and him disheveling himself for me is my undoing.

"Careful," I croak out, muscles clenching down my spine, the tingle building, building in my groin. "Back off, sweetheart. Gonna come."

Face smeared in spit and tears, mouth full of my dick, he gives me a *look*. An *are you kidding, I fucking earned this* look.

And that's it.

Blades of light score across my eyes as my orgasm hits me like a storm, roaring thunder and torrents of hail. My hips thrust forward and I'm half aware of Alexo gagging again, but he's sucking, too, taut, single-minded draws of his mouth, and it yanks one last spurt out of me, tremors setting off uncoordinated twitches through my nerve endings.

He rocks back, shoulders hitting the door behind him, chest heaving. Sweat glosses his skin and his hair's a mess, his face utterly wrecked but matched by his satisfied, exhausted smile.

Arms numb, I reach for him. The post-orgasmic haze is throbbing through me, and I need him to come, too, need to see him fall apart—

But I note a spot on the floor between my feet and the way his pants are gaped open.

He came from blowing me.

I haul him up, but he seems too blissed out to stand yet—that's fine. I've got him.

His mouth tastes like me. I'm all over him, my scent mixing with his; I'm the reason for his tear-streaked face. I scoop him into my arms and plunge my tongue into his mouth, soaking up the combination of us, the branding of me on him.

I want to leave him this way. To walk out that door and back into that gala with him looking like this, so everyone knows—the guests, the reporters, anyone who sees pictures of the event—*everyone* knows whose he is.

I make sure he's steady on his feet before I tuck myself away, then fasten his pants. I adjust his shirt so it hangs right, and I fix his body chain that got twisted a bit on his shoulder. His hair's a riot of curls, so I do what I can to tame them back down, and I find a roll of paper towels and wet a few in a utility sink before gently wiping his cheeks, his throat, his lips, under his eyes.

He lets me, his breathing stabilizing the longer I work, his gaze on me observant, peaceful.

When he's more or less set to rights, I clean the floor, toss the paper towels, and run my hands up and down his arms, watching ripples of goose bumps set off in my wake.

"Thank you," he says into our calm silence.

I smile. "I should be thanking you. That was—"

"Awkward? Messy? Gods, I slobbered everywhere."

"Perfect." I take his chin between my thumb and forefinger. "It was perfect. *You* are perfect."

He blushes. But the hazy peace dims in his eyes and he doesn't smile, his gaze drifting down to stare at my chest.

"Mm," is all he says, noncommittal.

"Are you—"

"We should get back out there," he cuts me off and forces up a grin, framing his face with his hands. "Do I look okay, or do I look like I got face-fucked by a half giant?"

A chuckle bursts out of me. "I hardly face-fucked you."

"Hm. You're right. Next time, then."

And he's out the door before I can do more than sputter a response.

The hall is empty around our closet, thankfully, and Alexo walks a few paces ahead of me as we make our way back to the doors. He's putting distance between us, and I'm not entirely sure why. I know it has to do with the secrets he's still keeping, the things he can't let me know, the things I won't ask about.

Maybe I should ask about them. Maybe, if they're going to upset him like this, I *need* to.

I quicken my pace and snatch his hand in mine. He glances up at me, but instead of pulling away or giving me that sad look again, he smiles. Relieved.

We push through the doors that lead us back into the hotel's entryway, where the gala's in full swing. People linger around the bar here, and in the ballroom, a band plays; I'm almost certain that's Darian on guitar.

"Dance with me?" I ask Alexo.

But he's frowning at someone in the entryway, and my whole body goes icy with rage. If it's Tem here to whisk Alexo away again—

I follow his gaze, but it's a group of people talking. And looking at their phones.

In fact, most of the people in the entryway are looking at their phones and speaking in the hushed way of discussing something scandalous.

Still holding Alexo's hand, I head over to the nearest group of my teammates—Aaron and a few other defensive tanks. They all have their phones out, and I barely manage a "Hey, what's going on?" before Aaron's giving me a sympathetic look.

Sympathy?

He crooks his phone at me. "You heard yet?"

Alexo and I look down at his screen.

It's a news alert.

BREAKING: Boston, MA: Disciples of Galaxrien Vossen have once again attempted to resurrect the demon lord, this time via human sacrifice.

An adventure party apprehended the cultists and rescued the victim. The victim, a forty-year-old human male, is a member of the Church of Urzoth Shieldsworn, the known rival of Galaxrien Vossen. The cult was purportedly working off intel that Galaxrien's mortal descendant is being hidden by the Church of Urzoth to "prevent his enemy from seeking righteous revenge."

The victim has no known demonic ancestry. When informed of that, one of the cultists in custody responded, "Oops."

The official spokesperson for the Temple of Galaxrien Vossen once again issued a statement condemning these ceremonies, saying the extremists are not endorsed by the Temple, as "Galaxrien's authorized prophesied return will happen a century from now, and will not involve any mortal descendant of his, least of all a live sacrifice."

The Church of Urzoth Shieldsworn was unavailable for comment.

My stomach drops straight to my toes.

A human *sacrifice* now? Not just a piece of hair? The guy got rescued, but still.

Aaron pulls his phone back. Too late, I realize he's watching me for my reaction, and I can't work through my shock quick enough to school it off my face.

I'm a defensive tank on his team. Urzoth's my patron god; I should react to this with violent anger. Offended, rampant *fury*.

But I'm horrified.

Aaron, though, doesn't seem surprised by my reaction. He doesn't get disgusted by my quiet alarm; none of the other defensive tanks standing with him do either.

They give me solemn nods of support. Someone pats me on the shoulder.

"If you need to step out for a bit, I'll cover for you," Aaron offers.

They're—helping me?

My teammates in Vegas would have been reaming me out for being such a *soft, pathetic embarrassment.*

But Aaron and the others are dismayed by the news report, and the fact that I am, too, isn't even in question.

"Thanks," I say, gratitude heavy in my tone. I take a step past him. "I—"

Alexo doesn't move with me.

He's holding my hand—no, *clinging* to me, his other hand wrapped around my arm, all his fingers clawed in deep. And when I try again to walk us away, he refuses to budge, stone-stiff and pale, his gaze unfocused on the middle space where Aaron's phone was.

"Alexo?" I tap his chin, trying to get him to look at me.

He doesn't even blink, eyes bloodshot and frozen, his breathing going jackrabbit fast. That look of terror on his face hits me with a furor, making me want to spur to some kind of action, but I'm as stuck as he is.

Aaron and the other tanks peel away to give us privacy and I barely have the wherewithal to nod my appreciation before I'm bending to eye level with Alexo.

"Hey." I cup his face. "Alexo? Ale—Belle. Belle, sweetheart, can you—"

His eyes flash to mine.

And he breaks.

Tears drip down his face, his whole body shuddering as fear releases him, and he shakes his head, shakes it and shakes it, whispering, "No, Orok, no—"

"It's all right." I tuck him into my side. "I'll get you to your room, okay?"

He clings to me. "Can we go to yours?"

I hesitate. "Yeah?"

"Roommate in mine," he mumbles, his voice choked.

I've never been more grateful that I always pay the difference to get my own room when the team travels. "My room. Yeah. Let's go."

Rather than braving the watchful eyes around the main elevators, where a few people now look from their phones to me with more of Aaron's sympathy, I swing us around and back into the utility hall, then up through the private elevators there, the ones the team took when we first checked in.

The guest floors are quiet; most people are down at the gala or out for the night as I whisk Alexo into my suite. The door lock beeps behind us and I hit a light to illuminate the front room's table, chairs, and couch. A door on the left goes into the bedroom, and beyond that is a massive bathroom.

Alexo steps numbly into the main room, his arms around himself, shivering enough that I punch up the heat on the wall unit.

"Do you want to talk about it?" I ask. That's a stupid question; I think we *need* to talk about it.

Why did that news report scare him so much? Is it because he's so connected to it now, being a follower of Urzoth?

My phone vibrates in my pocket. Honestly, I'm shocked it's taken anyone this long, and when I pull it out, I see a few missed texts from my mom, no doubt having *very strong feelings* about the Galaxrien cultists stooping to abduct an Urzoth follower—fuck, that hasn't sunk in yet—as well as a missed call from Roesia Sombercrown's office.

My phone vibrates again, another call from the team manager.

I let it go to voicemail and toss it on the couch.

"They were going to kill that man," Alexo says suddenly. It's brittle, like he's testing the validity in the words, hoping they'll be wrong.

"They didn't. An adventure party saved him."

"But they would have killed him." He finally looks up at me, caved in on himself, so damn small and lost it makes my heart crack. "They've progressed to full human sacrifice now."

"Is being associated with Urzoth worrying you?" I step toward him and touch his elbows where he's got his arms folded.

He shrugs.

I tilt his face up to me, needing him to see, to know a little bit of what I'm always trying to suppress. The steam rising inside me, the unstoppable impetus of obsession I fight tooth and nail to keep at bay every damn second.

"I won't let anything happen to you," I promise him. My skin aches with the force of everything I want to say, all the promises and oaths I want to lay at his feet. "And if being associated with Urzoth is making you afraid, we'll undo it. I'll get you out. Say the word, say anything, and it's yours."

Alexo's eyes shift through mine, his posture wilting. "You really mean that."

"I do. Anything."

"Because you want to pull away from Urzoth yourself."

My shoulders rise slightly, a twitch wobbling my hand on his face.

His lips pulse in a sad smile. "You don't exactly hide it. And if you—"

"Hey," I cut him off, trying to be gentle. "No deflecting. Not now."

A heavy sigh, and he steps away from me, scrubbing his hands on his arms, walking in an agitated circle in front of the couch.

He faces me again, fighting hard for resolve, but exhaustion sweeps over him, making his eyelashes flutter. "It's jarring. The Galaxrien threat feels closer than it did before, that's all. It's upsetting, right? Anyone would be upset."

Yeah. They would.

Like the Urzoth church, who has now been directly affronted by the extremists.

How will they respond to that?

I scratch the back of my neck and purposefully do not look at my abandoned phone, do not think of all the messages likely pouring in from my mom, from the Hellhounds, from Reverend Drach.

"Can I stay?" Alexo whispers. "Tonight. Just to sleep."

There's so much more we should talk about. I should demand answers, real answers, about whatever he's running from. I should give *him* my own answers about Urzoth, and how I want to, need to, renounce him.

But Alexo sways, chest expanding on a deep inhale, and I cross the room to wrap my arms around him. He sinks against me with a contented groan that floods my body in warmth.

It's on my tongue to tell him no—I've only ever slept in the same bed as Seb.

But why the hell did I bring Alexo up here then? I want him to stay. I want to fall asleep with him in my arms.

"Yes," I say. I trail my thumb back and forth where his body chain cups the nape of his neck. "But, um—here's something else real about me."

He pushes away to look up at me, driven by the anxiety strumming my words like guitar strings.

"I have nightmares," I tell him. "I might wake up defensive or panicked. It doesn't always happen, but you should be aware. If you still want to stay."

He pushes up onto his toes to kiss me tenderly.

"I still want to stay," he says, and I sigh down into him.

I guide him to the bedroom and dig a T-shirt out of my suitcase for him, a white one with the demon dog logo and my number on it. Any of the pants I have would be absurd on him, but the shirt should be big enough to serve as a sleep gown. He takes the hotel-provided toothbrush since I brought my own toiletries, and I leave him in the bathroom.

By the time I've changed into plaid sleep pants and propped myself up on the bed, the bathroom door opens.

Alexo comes out absolutely *swimming* in my shirt, the collar plunging off one shoulder, the hem down around his calves. My number, 64, is huge across the chest.

My hand clenches in the sheet and I know I growl, feel it bubble up my throat, but fuck if I care.

He's in my clothes, wearing my number. Probably still smells like me from earlier, too.

He shifts nervously next to the bed, scratching the back of his ankle with his toes.

Are his toes—

Yep. They're painted pink.

Fucking kill me. Now. End this torture.

"Just sleeping," he says again, half a question.

I relax my fists. "Just sleeping. Here."

I stack some of the pillows down the center of the bed, but Alexo shakes his head.

"No. I—I trust you." He scratches his ear and mutters, "It's *me* I don't trust."

He's looking at my bare chest, his eyes following the whorls of dark hair across my pecs, down my abs, to the thinner trail below my navel. It's the first time he's seen me shirtless, and I fight the urge to flex, to really nail home the fact that yeah, I've got an athlete's build, and I work hard for it.

His lust-filled gaze meanders back up—and stops on the scar that cuts down my left shoulder.

The way he's looking at me changes, goes from appreciative and hungry to analytical.

He takes me in again, clocking other places now: the edge of a scar peeking out beneath the hair on my stomach; a dimpled spot to the side of my pec.

"Rawball injuries?" he asks.

I lean forward, elbows on my knees. "Most of them."

He looks back at the scar on my shoulder. Maybe because it's the oldest, or the biggest, white and puckered and jagged.

Unease sours my stomach, taints all the delicious feelings that bubbled up at seeing him in my clothes.

"Camp Merethyl" is all I make myself say.

Alexo's brow tugs down. He lifts the hem of the shirt to climb onto the bed, knee-walks closer to me, and lays his hand on the curve of my deltoid. His thumb barely brushes the edge of the scar and he's staring at it, a dark look on his face, a weighty drop of fury.

With the trial, a lot of the details were public. Hell, *all* the details, at least what that camp did to Seb. To me. We rehashed it in the courtroom and then people spent months rehashing it online and in the media, and by the look on Alexo's face, he knows it all.

How Camp Merethyl tried to set me and Seb up as an elite type of arcane soldier, an ouroboros partnership, they called it. A pairing they could send into remote locations, and because I was with Seb, he'd always have access to most of the components he'd need for spell work. Iron, calcium, bones, hair. I would've been his living, breathing component supply.

Our final test was a room slowly filling with water, and we could either drown, die of hypothermia, or Seb could use the iron in my blood to break the ward on the door and get us out.

I ripped open my shoulder to get him what he needed.

"I think I understand," Alexo whispers. "Why people wish you'd gone all Urzoth-rage on the camp. They deserve it."

I fight back a shiver at his touch. "They might have, but I didn't. I didn't deserve to have to do that to them."

His gaze swings to mine.

And he smiles, a half-cocked offering. "See? The strongest person I've ever met."

"No," I say. "I've thought about it a lot. Gone over every day we spent there. What could I have done differently? How could I have been stronger, been braver, been more like Urzoth? But it wouldn't have made a difference. Because when it mattered, when I really needed strength, it wasn't Urzoth who saved me. It was Seb. He did what he needed to do to get us out. Every time anyone talks about Urzoth's strength, all I can think is that I *know* true strength. I've seen it. And it was never from me or a god."

Alexo runs his fingers over the scar, following the jagged line up and down. "Would Seb say you saved him, too? That you're the reason he got out?"

A beat passes. Just a flicker of hesitation.

Because yeah. He would.

Alexo smiles triumphantly. "I'm going to make you realize you're strong if it kills me, Orok."

He's so close, hovering over me on his knees, still touching my shoulder.

I pull back the comforter on his side, mouth too dry to say anything, afraid if I do speak, I'll snivel pathetically.

"Can you—" He sighs, self-deprecating. "Can you hold me?"

Holy hell, are you kidding me, YES might be too aggressive a response, so I say, "Yeah."

His timid smile. Shit.

Shit shit shit.

All of this.

Just.

Shit.

I rearrange the pillows to give him space, and as he crawls in, puts his back to me with that bare shoulder sticking up, I clear my throat.

"If you, uh, feel anything that *wakes up* because of this position, ignore it. I will."

He cradles his head on a pillow, the side of his mouth pushing up in a grin. "Noted."

I click off the light and pull the covers over us as I shimmy down behind him.

His body *fits.* His smaller frame nestles into my larger one, his legs curled up so I slot my knees under his thighs, my chin over his head, my arm around his waist. He pushes his fingers in between mine and holds our hands against his stomach, lifting his head so my other arm can slide under his pillow. My hips bump up against his ass and I choke down the gravelly moan that wants to come out, and I think he must guess, because I feel an aborted chuckle vibrate in his chest.

I bury my face in his curls and inhale so deep my lungs hurt at the pressure. Apples and brightness and a heady musk that's *him.* I'm intoxicated.

After we both settle, our even breaths softly filling the dark room, he hums. "It's been a long time since anyone's held me. Thank you."

I pull him closer, pressing around him more firmly, immovable.

"You don't have to thank me," I say, and lay a kiss on the sharpness of his bare shoulder. "This is exactly where I want to be."

He shivers.

And I could so easily keep kissing his warm skin, trail my lips up the side of his neck and nibble on his ear until he's writhing in my arms.

I drop my head to the pillow, digging my teeth into my tongue. "Goodnight, my Belle."

"Goodnight," a pause, "my big O."

I snort into his hair and he laughs, too.

"Fuck yeah, I'm your big O," I say, and his answering squeak when I bite his neck is the sweetest send-off I could ask for.

Chapter Nine

I wake up smoothly. And I'm feeling sappy enough to attribute it to the person doing their best impression of an octopus around me.

Alexo's facing me, but I must not have moved much last night because I'm still curled toward him. He's got one arm thrown over my waist and his leg wedged between my thighs to hook around my knee, his other hand wrapped across his own stomach to cling to the wrist I have poking out beneath his body.

Sunlight streams through the window's gauzy curtains, pale light illuminating his rumpled bedhead and slack mouth, breaths puffing on my chest as he twitches in sleep.

The collar of my shirt is twisted around his shoulders and the comforter got kicked down at some point last night. Probably due to me being a raging space heater; I'm shocked Alexo's crowded so close and isn't sweating. But it lets me trail my eyes down his body, his long dancer's legs, those pink polished toes, his hips twisted in the tangled position he's knotted us in.

It pops his ass.

His ass that is currently uncovered by my shirt, showing tight black boxers that highlight his perfect bubble butt.

"Creeper," he mumbles into my chest.

I flick my gaze to his face, and he's smirking at me.

"Can you blame me? You're gorgeous." I arch down to kiss his jaw. "All soft and sleepy." Another kiss on one of his dimples. "Laid out in my bed."

He wiggles up until we're face-to-face, and morning breath be damned; my focus zeroes in on that look in his eyes, and before I realize what I've done, my hand's up under his shirt, palm flat on the warm, slick skin of his lower back.

I freeze.

He does, too, his fingers arched into my short hair, a hundred questions and hesitations and desires roiling through his eyes.

"I'm sorry," I assure him and carefully peel my hand out from under his shirt, being sure not to touch anything else.

He grabs my wrist.

Those eyes catch fire, darkening with intent as he plants my hand flat on his ass.

"No. I want you to touch me," he says, and need twists beneath my belly button, pulled by the same need glowing in his eyes. He's shaking even through that determination, and I rock forward until my forehead rests on his.

"It's okay, Belle," I whisper. "We don't have to."

"I want to," he moans. "I want to tell you. Please. I—"

There's a knock at the main door.

No—a *hammering* at the door. Thunderous fists beat on the wood and I fly up, one arm automatically going over Alexo's body, pushing him back behind me.

"The fuck?" The knock goes again, and before it wakes the whole damn floor, I leap out of bed.

Alexo's sitting up, knees curled to his chest, wide eyes fixed on the open door to the suite's living room. Another booming knock and he flurries out from under the blankets, scrambling toward the bathroom.

But not before I see the fear on his face. The same fear he showed last night, when news of the Galaxrien attack hit.

I dig through my suitcase, pull on another Hellhounds shirt, chew a few breath mints—they'll have to do—and march out into the main room.

Whoever it is now punctuates their knocks with a harsh "Open up, Mr. Monroe!"

I look through the peephole.

No way.

A glance behind tells me Alexo's still in the bathroom. Good.

I square my shoulders and open the suite's main door.

To face Tem Raussec.

Who *followed Alexo to New York.*

He's followed Alexo on other away games, so I shouldn't be surprised. But tell that to my rage.

Behind him, on either side of the door, are two people I didn't see in the peephole. They're dressed in matching light leather armor with spell component belts around their hips. Members of an adventure party?

I glower at Tem. "What the hell do you think you're doing?"

He ignores me, trying to force his way into the room, but he's a human and I'm a half-giant defensive tank on a pro rawball team; he ain't getting in.

He rebounds off my chest with an affronted snarl.

"Alexo!" he calls, eyes on me. "*Alexo!*"

I flip my glare at the nearest person behind him, a half-elven woman about my mom's age with umber skin and black hair in a braid. "What's this about?"

She puts a hand on Tem's shoulder, tugging him back. "May we come in?"

"*May* we?" Tem scoffs. "He abducted him!"

"I did *not* abduct—"

Fingers press to my bicep.

I turn and Alexo's staring past me, at Tem, with an odd mix of fear and shame. He put last night's clothes back on but they're wrinkled now, his hair still a mess, and he smells like peppermint toothpaste—and me. From sleeping in my clothes and all over my body.

I instantly hook my arm around him and try to put as much of myself in front of him as I can.

"What do you want to do?" I ask Alexo. All *I* want to do is slam the door on Tem's face, but if he called an adventure party because he thought I *abducted* Alexo . . .

Alexo flicks his eyes up to me. "Let them come in. I owe you an explanation."

Tem chokes. "You sure as hell *do not.*"

But the woman behind Tem makes a thoughtful noise. "Does he deserve your explanation, Alexo? Even with who his god is?"

The fuck does that have to do with anything? I swear, if Urzoth somehow interferes with helping Alexo right now, I'll renounce his ass so hard—

But wait a second.

Does Alexo know this woman?

Without looking away from me, Alexo nods. "He's not his god," he says to her. To me. "He's stronger."

My chest concaves. I'm not entirely sure what's happening, but I stay alert and back up, keeping Alexo against me as I make room for Tem and the two other people to get inside.

I shut the door, my fingers probably digging bruises into Alexo's side.

"This wasn't an abduction," I say to the elven woman.

The other guy surveys the living room, checking behind the curtains, the couch. He pulls a vial out and does a spell that flutters over the whole room in a wash of shimmering arcane blue before it fades.

"Secure," he says.

Secure? What the hell is happening?

The elven woman nods. "We know it wasn't an abduction, Mr. Monroe. My apologies for the abruptness of—"

"It *was* an abduction. He got *taken*," Tem growls, hands fisted. He faces Alexo. "I've been out searching for you all night. I called and called, only to discover you left your phone in the room?"

Tem yanks that phone out of his pocket and chucks it at Alexo.

Alexo swings his hands up, but I grab it before it can get anywhere close to him. With that trajectory, it would have hit him in the face.

My glare could shatter rock. I hope it does. I hope Tem feels a tremor in his bones. "Throw something else at him again, and you'll find that same object shoved down your throat."

Tem looks ready to blow, waiting, *hoping* for me to make the first move.

Normally, that anticipatory look in his eyes would have me dropping into a peaceful resolution. *Don't be what people expect of me; don't use my size, my Urzoth legacy, in ways that harm or intimidate.*

But he threatened Alexo.

And that's my line, apparently. The gloves-off line, the expectations-be-damned line.

It should scare me. Unsettle me, at the very least; I'm usually so in control.

But I will fuck Tem *up* if he tries to hurt Alexo again.

Alexo calmly, too calmly, takes his phone out of my hands and pockets it. "Don't, please," he whispers.

I'm instantly reaching for his face, brushing my thumb across his cheekbone. "Belle, what's going—"

Tem screeches. "*You told him your name?*"

The room goes quiet. Fatalistically.

Tem's huffing with fury. The guy who did the secure spell has one hand on his component belt. The elven woman looks almost bored.

And Alexo stares up at me, beseeching.

His eyes tear and he rolls them shut in a wince that trembles down to his very roots.

You told him your name.

He looks at the elven woman. His hands drop to his sides, his chin thrusting forward in part defiance, part holding back tears.

"I'm going to tell him," he says to her. "I was going to tell him before you came because we're leaving anyway, aren't we? So what does it matter. Just let me have this. Just *once*."

His last word comes with a sob, and he'd buckle in half if I weren't still hanging on to his hips. I pull him into me but he shakes his head like he can't let himself collapse, not yet.

"You're not telling him shit," Tem snarls. "Let's go. Now. You've fucked this up enough."

"What is going on?" I demand, looking at Alexo, but my words are for the room, for *anyone* to start talking *now*.

The elven woman straightens, hands behind her back. "My name is Ilbryen," she says coolly. "This is my partner, Gulus."

The other guy still has his hand near his potions where he hangs back by the window.

"And you already know Tem," Ilbryen says, but I refuse to look at him.

Tem, however, spins on her. "What are you *doing*? We need to get him out of here."

Ilbryen continues, unaffected, "And you are Orok Monroe. Son of Ghorza Monroe, a former Arcane Forces soldier, and Dave Monroe, an accountant. Defensive tank for the Hellhounds, previously the Chimeras. Graduate of Lesiara University with a Mageus in Theological Evocation and an undergrad in Theology. And, for the past few weeks, one half of a PR relationship with a cheerleader to bring positive associations to your god, Urzoth Shieldsworn."

My head cocks. Most of that information is easy enough to find; hell, one quick Google would dump all that out on any rawball tabloid site.

Except the last thing. "How do you know the relationship is for PR?"

Ilbryen smiles. It doesn't reach her eyes. "It's our job to know. We are members of a larger union of adventure parties responsible for the concealment and protection of victims of prophecy, sacrifice, and curses. Victims such as—"

She looks at Alexo. And smiles, truer this time.

Despite his earlier boldness, his eyes widen. "You'll—you'll let me?"

"You said you were going to. Do you really trust him? Even with his patron god?"

He gives a frantic nod. "I told you. He isn't—" He glances at me, and I realize it's him asking permission to talk about me and Urzoth.

"What does my association with Urzoth matter?" I ask Ilbryen. "I don't understand."

"Exactly how involved in your church are you, Mr. Monroe? Enough to be their poster child."

"Enough to give Alexo a spot on the cheerleading squad," I amend, hands clenching. I don't want to get into my complicated history with Urzoth to a complete stranger. "That's what I care about."

Ilbryen studies me, her lips thinning. "Hm." She looks down at Alexo. "If you're sure?"

He nods again, just as certain.

"Well then," Ilbryen says. "Would you care to introduce yourself?"

Tem makes a gargled noise of disgust. "What are you doing? He's an *Urzoth follower*."

"And yet," Ilbryen pins him with a glare, "he allowed us into this room without violence and has made no move to attack, even with your obvious threat. A true Urzoth follower would have exhibited *some* form of challenge or aggression by now. There is more going on here I would like to explore. Do you question me?"

Tem's stance and expression clearly say *yes*. But he proves he has at least some sense when he flattens his lips.

Alexo puts a hand on my chest, in the spot I'm coming to associate with him, laying his palm over my heart and holding it there for one fortifying moment, like he's soaking me up.

He looks at Ilbryen one last time. For encouragement? For permission?

Her gaze holds steadily on him.

He sucks in a breath before his eyes flash up to mine, swollen with uncertainty.

"My name is Bel," he says. "Belzaroth. I'm the mortal descendant of Galaxrien Vossen."

I go immobile. Systems shutting down, switch by switch.

Ilbryen holds out a vial of blue liquid to him.

Alexo—Bel—gapes at her. "Really?"

"You *can't*!" Tem is red-faced. "This is insanity!"

But Ilbryen bobs the vile toward Bel. "It's a calculated risk. I think Mr. Monroe might be useful to us." She flicks her emotionless eyes to me.

Not emotionless.

Observant. Shrewd.

Bel steps away from me and takes the vial from Ilbryen.

With a fleeting look of surrender, he uncorks it and gulps down the potion.

In spite of everything, the shock and questions and blow after blow, I lurch toward him, panicked.

Ilbryen holds up her hand. "It is safe. It's to counter the illusion spray he uses."

I stiffen in place, arms extended toward him, unable to get my thoughts to catch up with what's happening.

Bel moans softly, and then he's—changing. But also *not*. He's still him, same height, same pink hair and freckles across his nose and a lean, lithe body.

But his skin transforms, goes from pale to rose gold. Pure, *gleaming* rose gold the same shade as his hair; he's a living gilded statue, reflective and shining. His eyes are now all black with rings of gold around his pupils, and he adjusts the waistband of his pants to pull out something at the back.

A tail.

He has a tail.

That rose-gold color, nearly as long as he is tall, thin with a pointed, arrow-shaped end.

It whips agitatedly around his bare feet as he stands there, letting me stare at him.

He's part demon. The mortal descendant of Galaxrien Vossen.

Of all the scenarios I'd been forcing myself not to think about in regard to his secrets, this wasn't even possibility adjacent.

And in a stupid, simplistic way, I might be . . . relieved? Fuck, I thought Tem was doing unspeakable things to him, but Alexo—Bel, *Bel*—is in protective custody because a crazy cult is after him to summon their demon lord. A crazy cult that my own slightly less crazy religion is a sworn enemy of.

Just that.

No biggie.

My muscles twitch and pulse, worry discharging from where I've been keeping it stored since the moment I saw Bel at the karaoke bar.

Gods, I *am* relieved.

Holy shit, am I having a breakdown? Has this broken me? Possibly.

At my silence, Bel shifts uncomfortably on his feet. "I have to use the spray every twenty-four hours or else—" He waves at his body, then runs a hand through his hair, tapping at a spot an inch back from his forehead. "I, um, file down my horns, and they aren't very big, so it's not hard to hide them. But it'd be too expensive to get transformation magic to make my tail vanish. The spray only alters how things look. It can't make anything disappear completely, so I use a small portal dimension stitched into my boxers for my tail, and—it's weird. I know. All of this is so weird, but I—I wanted you to know. I'm sorry I lied to you, Orok. I'm—"

His voice catches, and I'm already moving.

I sweep his face into my hands and kiss him. Fuck everyone else watching. I kiss the hell out of him, eating up his startled cry and then his relieved, stunted sob as he clings to me.

He buries his face in my neck and I hold him. Rocking him. Murmuring, "It's okay, it's okay, I'm not going anywhere," until Ilbryen clears her throat.

Bel shudders against me. Since he seems in no hurry to let me go, I keep my arms around him as I look up.

"I'd ask how you feel knowing he's a descendant of your god's sworn enemy," Ilbryen says, "but I'd say it doesn't quite bother you, does it?"

My simple "no" feels more definitive than if I had finally renounced Urzoth.

"We have been guarding Belzaroth in one way or another his entire life," she continues. "But he has been in protective custody for eight years, since a sect of Galaxrien Vossen cultists began pursuing a ritual they believe requires part or all of his mortal descendant." She motions at Tem. "Mr. Raussec has been his handler since early summer, and when Belzaroth went missing last night, he called us in."

"Because he was *abducted* by an Urzoth follower!" Tem explodes. "And you're giving him all our secrets so he can run off to his church and have *them* slaughter the target to stop the resurrection."

The target?

Fuck. This. Guy.

I pull Bel off me so I can meet his eyes. "You know I wouldn't do that."

Cheeks tear-streaked, he manages a watery smile. "I know."

"We need to transform him back and get him out of here," Tem snaps at Ilbryen. "He's been compromised. Mostly by *you*."

Ilbryen looks at Tem. It's barely more than a flick of her eyes to him, but it's so ice-cold he reels back.

Then she looks at me, her glare softening infinitesimally, and after a long beat, she says, almost as an afterthought, "Yes."

Tem huffs and throws his arms out. "*Finally*. Belzaroth, reapply your illusion magic, and let's go."

Bel inhales quickly, his hands fisting in my shirt.

I constrict my hold on him. "No—what? Go where?"

"Telling you would quite defeat the purpose of *protective custody*," Ilbryen says. "Belzaroth will be moved to a new secure location. It appears the cultists are aware that Galaxrien's heir is connected to the Urzoth church, in light of their recent attack. They do not seem to know about Belzaroth personally, but they are getting close. While his cover as an Urzoth follower and the paramour of an Urzoth star did seem smart—hiding him in plain sight, as it were—it clearly isn't enough to merely be *associated* with Galaxrien's enemy. We must take more intensive measures. To ensure his safety."

She cuts her words with a penetrating look at me, and my mind races, hands gripping Bel's upper arms.

He tugs at the hem of my shirt, running it through his fingers. "It's all right, Orok."

I frown down at him.

"It's all right," he says again, and tries to smile, but it's full of all the heartbreak he's shown over our time together, all the little flashes of it that didn't make sense until now. "I'm—I'm used to it. I knew they'd want to move me after the news dropped last night." He fights for composure. It slips the more he talks, mine splintering right alongside his. "I wanted to tell you. I'm sorry, though; you didn't need to be pulled into this. But I . . . I wanted you to know the real me. I just . . . just wanted *one thing* that's *mine*."

A strange sense of calm settles over me, the unnerving immobility that came with seeing him transform, with finding out all his truths. Like this path was always laid, I just hadn't known I was walking it until this moment.

Tem steps closer, reaching for Bel. "C'mon, kid. The waterworks are pathetic at this point."

I seize Tem's wrist midair.

My hand clamps down on him and he buckles, eyes going wide, and I could so, so easily snap his arm.

I look past him to Ilbryen.

"I think you and I both know I'm not letting you take Bel away from me," I tell her. "So how about we stop with these fucking theatrics?"

Bel's grief pauses, confusion pinching his face.

I release Tem's wrist. Unbroken. Sadly.

He staggers back, cradling it anyway. "Asshole Urzoth follower—"

"Tem," Ilbryen cuts him off. "Shut up."

Tem gapes at her.

She gives me a curious look. "Do you have something to say, Mr. Monroe?"

"Yeah." I curl my arm around Bel's shoulders. He's stiff against me. "You're not taking him. Where would you even put him? You currently have him in an apartment that should be condemned, with a door that doesn't even close properly, guarded by an asshole who verbally assaults him and *left Bel alone*. What's your next grand plan? A shack in the woods? For how long? Bel deserves better than abuse disguised as a half-assed attempt at protecting him."

Tem surges forward, his arm covered in the glowing green of a spell, but Gulus, who's been silent and unmoving up until now, twists his hands. An arcane wall shoots up between me and Tem just as Tem's releasing his spell, and the green energy dissipates across the wall in a fizzle of sparks.

"Raussec!" Ilbryen barks. "Contain yourself, or I will do it for you!"

Tem scowls, nostrils flaring. "It was idiotic ever agreeing to let the target be part of this fucked-up PR charade, and it's idiotic now to let this guy stand here and talk about shit he doesn't understand. He's a liability."

"Quite the opposite," Ilbryen tells him, her voice back to level, controlled.

She shifts her eyes to me. Then down to where I threw myself in front of Bel the moment Tem moved, how I have him held behind my back.

"We agreed to let Belzaroth be in this *PR charade*," she obviously quotes Tem's tone with a flat look his way, "as a test of expanding his circle. The protection of the Urzoth church was an opportunity we intentionally took."

"After the target signed up without our permission," Tem grumbles.

"And I do not blame him for it," Ilbryen says. "He was given an opportunity to dance when he had long been denied it as a sad reality of his protective detail, and the arrangement provided security in a way that was worth the risk. *That* is not how we have been lacking in Belzaroth's protection," she says to me. "Our adventure parties have been stretched thin in recent years. I've known for some time that Belzaroth's situation was not ideal."

"Not ideal?" Tem guffaws humorlessly. "I've been—"

"You've been a dick," Bel cuts him off, coming out from behind me. "You've been cruel and nasty and a hypocrite. How many times did I have to pay for ward spell components with my internship money because *you* refused to *waste resources*? How many times have you walked out on me for *hours*, yet you give me constant crap about *putting myself in danger*?"

"You traitorous little *shit*!" Tem roars and I lurch between them again, but Tem doesn't get close, that arcane wall still up.

Silence falls. Ilbryen's glare on Tem is conversation enough, a potent call to the proof in his own actions.

"Mr. Monroe," Ilbryen says, letting her eyes glide from Tem to me. "What do you propose?"

"Feed him to my teammate's sword."

Ilbryen grunts deep in her throat. I realize after I hear what I said that—she laughed?

Oh. That's not what she meant.

"I mean in regard to Belzaroth's safety," she clarifies, a glimmer in her eyes.

My gaze tunnel-visions onto Bel. His lips are parted and he looks like he's standing on the edge of a cliff, knowing he has to jump but unsure of anything beyond the fall.

"What would you do?" I ask Ilbryen, voice low.

"Tem will be removed as his handler—"

Tem curses.

"—and Belzaroth will be taken somewhere not far off from what you described. Given the increase in the cultists' severity, we need to step up our protection of him. We have a number of safehouses where he will be secluded."

Bel winces. "How secluded?"

"You would have a new handler who would leave only for monthly supply runs."

Another wince. I echo it.

"For how long?" he asks, surprisingly impassive. Or maybe he's just resigned.

Ilbryen's silent for a moment. "The cultists have proven they are vicious and determined. You will always be at risk, Belzaroth, and we no longer have the resources to keep shuffling you around. I'm sorry."

So . . . indefinitely?

"*No.*" My jaw's so tight a headache lances across my skull. "There's a reason the official Galaxrien Temple keeps disavowing these damn idiot cultists. They aren't *vicious*—they're morons. The Temple doesn't have Galaxrien's authorized prophesied return happening for a full *century*, and it doesn't involve a human component at all. Meanwhile, these idiots keep saying shit like they need a piece of hair, or no, a whole sacrifice; they're resurrecting Galaxrien, or no, summoning him. They can't even get their own fanaticism right."

Ilbryen's eyes narrow. "And why, exactly, do you have knowledge of Galaxrien's prophecy?"

For a beat, Tem looks smug, still glowering behind that arcane wall.

I don't back down. "You listed my credentials when you came in. My Mageus in Theological Evocation. I know about a lot of religious rituals, not just this one, so if you're implying I have some hidden ties to the cultists, I'm sure Gulus over there has a truth potion he could lob at me. Go for it. Ask me anything, I'm an open book."

"Your point, Mr. Monroe?" Ilbryen pushes. And it is that, a *push.*

Not that I need one. This is what was always going to happen, from the moment Bel told me who he really is.

"My point is that Bel shouldn't have to give up his life for zealot dumbasses. He shouldn't have to hide in the middle of nowhere *forever*. He's bright and talented and *alive*, gods damn it; let him live. You need to increase his security, I get that, and I wholeheartedly agree. So let him stay with me."

Chapter Ten

Bel's jaw drops with a strangled huff. "What?"

I take his hands. "Move in with me. I live in a building with high-end security, and I have access to top-of-the-line safety spells." Whatever I can't buy, Seb and Thio can make. "Yeah, the cultists figured out that Galaxrien's descendant is connected to Urzoth's church, but they don't know it's *you.* This is still the safest place for you. You're attached to a"—my throat catches but I quickly swallow—"a high-profile Urzoth public figure. It's hardly the same as being a random churchgoer. No one would be able to snatch you away easily. Instead of abandoning the Urzoth ties, we double down on them. Move in with me."

I don't give anyone a chance to speak; I look at Ilbryen.

"I worked for adventure parties in college," I tell her. "Not as an adventurer, but answering calls—so I'm in your system, background checked, the whole thing. Which you probably already know. But you can run another check on me if you need, or douse me in whatever truth potions you've got. I'll follow any protocols, do whatever you demand. My training as an athlete helps, too—this isn't much different from learning an opponent's plays or what defensive maneuvers I'll need to utilize. I can do this. Let him stay with me."

One detail has my chest seizing, and I spin back on Bel.

"If you want," I say. "This is only if *you* want it."

Bel looks absolutely shell-shocked. His black eyes are glistening, those gold irises gleaming.

"You can't do this," he says, barely audible. "I—you don't know what you're offering. What you're taking on. People are trying to *kill me*, and you'd be in the middle of that. I can't ask you to do this."

"So you'll lock yourself away for the rest of your life? You aren't asking me to do anything. I *want* to do this for you."

Tears spill down his face and he shakes his head, but it's like he's refuting his own thoughts, his own arguments. "No, *no*—gods, you just found out I've been lying to you! You didn't even know my real name until *ten minutes ago.* Orok—you can't want this. You *can't.*"

He pushes his fist against his mouth to stifle a sob, his shoulders heaving.

I touch that fist, pull it to me, and kiss his knuckles. "I do want it, Bel. What do *you* want?"

His eyes scream *you*, and his face fills with so much hope, so much *need.*

But he doesn't move, doesn't react until Ilbryen breaks in with, "Belzaroth? What do you think?"

Both he and I whip toward her.

"You—you'd allow this?" he asks, faltering.

She pulses one eyebrow in the barest shrug. "Mr. Monroe has been vetted by our teams—it's why we permitted your PR arrangement to continue after you'd agreed to it. His lifestyle does allow for a level of security our current handlers are unable to provide, and his knowledge of the cultists' rituals could be beneficial as well. We would reassign the new handler you would've been given to be more of a *watch from afar* situation, similar to how we watched over you before your full protective custody—but, Belzaroth, that does not mean this situation is less dire. Merely that Mr. Monroe is an active member of your security team rather than a mere caretaker."

"Yes," I say. "Whatever you need me to do."

"Plus," Ilbryen carries on, "it is easier to keep tabs on those we protect if they're somewhere they *want* to be. This option is far better than a . . . *shack in the woods*, hm? Or"—she waves dismissively, like it really doesn't matter one way or another—"Gulus fires up a memory alteration spell, and Mr. Monroe leaves here thinking you've broken up with him before you move away."

I stop myself from barking out an argument. It'd gut me, but if that's what Bel wants, I'll submit to it.

Tem fumes. "You're making a mistake. This guy's untrained. He's not an adventurer; he's going to get the target killed."

"If I were you, I'd be more concerned with your own performance, Raussec," Ilbryen snaps.

His eyes pulse, face twitching with fury. He seems to realize he's not just been beaten, but is very likely about to lose his job.

He storms past us and out of the suite, the door banging shut behind him, Gulus's arcane wall dropping in his absence.

Bel still hasn't responded. I tug gently on his hand, pulling his focus back to me.

He's guarded, wary, like maybe this is too good to be true. It gives me enough reassurance to keep trying.

"I want you to live with me. But I also want you to be comfortable with this. I have a guestroom, so you wouldn't have to—*we* wouldn't have to—it could be whatever you want it to—"

He throws himself at me.

I catch him, crushing him to me in a way that has to knock the wind out of him, but he burrows against me.

"Yes," he says. "Gods, *yes.*"

I'm grinning like a fool. Like all my obsessive compulsions got exactly what they're clawing after. *Him.*

A shudder of concern flurries through me. This isn't . . . *healthy*, is it?

He needs the security I can offer. He *needs* protection.

He needs me.

And gods, thinking that has my whole fucked-up being sighing happily, all the effort I put into keeping myself at bay losing its footholds against the torrential rush of satisfaction.

Years of fighting to better myself. *Years* of putting up boundaries and compartmentalizing and being so aggressively *good.*

It's all gone because of one impossible situation, one man in my arms who's become astonishingly important to me.

I should fight it, at least a little bit. I *know* better.

But something about the way Bel's holding me as forcefully as I'm holding him has me feeling like maybe this fixation isn't entirely one-sided. Maybe my consuming, stratospheric-level obsessive behavior won't be unmatched.

I meet Ilbryen's eyes over Bel's shoulder. She nods at me, a small smile on her face, breaking through her icy facade.

Pretty sure this is exactly what she wanted to happen. That I got manipulated.

Fuck if I care.

She pulls her phone out of a pouch on her component belt, checks it, and motions at Gulus. "I am needed elsewhere, but I will be in touch in the next few days with the final details, Mr. Monroe. For now, Gulus will remain as a temporary handler."

Ilbryen hangs back until Bel slides out of my arms.

He smiles at her, tears leaking down his cheeks. "Thank you," he whispers.

"For what it's worth, I am sorry I allowed things with Raussec to get so out of hand," she tells him, her voice softening. "We have been short-staffed, and his addition to the team was made out of desperation, not strategy. His actions toward you on top of the leak we now apparently have—" Ilbryen stops, rocks her neck to the side until it cracks. "Well. Let's just say we will be tightening things up a bit. Again, I am sorry, Belzaroth."

He wipes the back of his hand against his face. "Thanks. I appreciate it. Do you—" He falters but catches himself. "You don't think he's the leak, do you?"

Someone told the cultists that Galaxrien's descendant is connected to the Urzoth church now. Would Tem really have been that petty and stupid?

"We are looking into it," Ilbryen says. "But if he was the leak, the cultists would have moved against *you*, yes? We will keep an eye on Raussec. For now—" She looks at me, still talking to Bel. "Do not hesitate to reach out to me if you are mistreated or unhappy. Our staffing shortage is not your burden to bear. Your safety is our priority, and we will be much, much more discerning going forward."

It's a threat to me as much as it is a promise to Bel. Tem put them on alert; I won't get away with shit.

Good—they *should* be on alert. About damn time.

With a final nod, Ilbryen leaves.

Gulus widens his stance, plants his arms behind his back, and settles in like he's planning on standing here as long as we're in the room. He's bald and pale, with calculating blue eyes as shrewd as Ilbryen's, and I know he's meant to protect Bel, but I find myself pulling Bel closer to me, eyeing Gulus's sudden intensity.

But Gulus breaks with a pulse of his lips in what must amount to a smile. "I'm kidding," he says in a flat voice. "I am sure you two wish to talk privately. I will be outside."

He vanishes without another word. Literally, actually vanishes, leaving a puff of green smoke behind.

Isn't transportation magic illegal in city limits?

Not my problem.

Bel and I are alone in the quiet main room, but it suddenly doesn't feel that way, alone or quiet. Details stack up around me, questions I need to ask and things I need to figure out. It really does feel like memorizing plays before a game, analyzing all the potential challenges and figuring out solutions:

I need to call Seb. Get him to start laying protective spells on my apartment. I'm sure Ilbryen or Gulus or whoever they assign will be able to do it, but their whole adventure party left Bel with Tem for months, *knowing* how Tem was treating him, so their judgment is seriously in question. I want to build my own quasi-adventure party for Bel, and that includes Seb—but I'll ask Bel first. It's his secret, and I want him to know he has control over his protection.

I also need to check with my building, see what it would take to upgrade their security systems.

Bel fidgets in front of me.

I've been standing in place, eyes darting over the small square of carpet where Gulus vanished, for at least a few minutes. My eyes fly up to Bel and he's chewing the corner of his lip, brows pinched, thumb picking at the finger of his opposite hand.

"Overwhelming, huh?" he asks, like he's fighting to be lighthearted when all he wants is to sob again.

How do I explain that it's overwhelming in the *best* way? That

I'm voraciously grateful I get to do this for him. That I *know* he'll be safe now, and it's made me buoyant.

I still haven't said anything. I can't figure out what *to* say that wouldn't scare him off, and after he's become dependent on me to *keep him alive*.

Shit.

Bel shifts again, his painted toes digging into the carpet, and drops his chin to his chest. It's then I realize his tail—*he has a tail*—has been carefully coiled around his ankle this whole time, like he's trying to hide it.

I take his chin between my thumb and finger and lift his face to me.

"Are you okay?" I ask him.

He sputters a wet gasp. "Am *I* okay? You're the one who just got signed up to be my *handler*. Who's going to have to share his house with me now. And who'll get paid *shit* for it, by the way—Tem complained constantly about how little he was compensated for *putting up with my annoying ass*."

My lip curls in a snarl. "One day, I'll need you to tell me everything he did or said to you. But for now, I need to know how *you* are. Fuck the money; I don't need the money. And I didn't *get signed up* for any of this—I volunteered. I *want* to do this for you. You, however, didn't have much of a choice. It was this or being shoved into a hidden safehouse for the rest of your life." I lower my hand from him no matter how much I hate not touching him. "I won't have you feeling like you need to continue our relationship in order for me to protect you. My keeping you safe is separate from that." Oh gods; I see the conclusion I'm coming to like headlights on a car barreling toward me. "We should . . . we should probably take it off the table entirely."

Bel's chest contracts. "What? Why?"

"I don't want you to feel indebted to me, like your safety is contingent on us hooking up. What if one day you want to end things, but *don't* because you feel like I'll kick you out if you do? What if—"

"What if Galaxrien's cultists find me tomorrow," he cuts me off, "and I never knew what it was like for you to fuck me?"

I choke. Full-on attack of coughing and wheezing.

Bel gives me a satisfied, bratty little smirk.

"I don't know about you," he tells me while I do my best not to asphyxiate on *nothing*. "But I won't be able to treat you like a handler. I won't be able to live in the same apartment and not touch you. Kiss you. I *want* you, Orok, and—"

He stops abruptly. Like that same car I saw coming hits him, his shoulders jolting.

He glances down at his body.

"But I know . . . I don't have to look like this. I have the illusion magic."

He pulls a small spray bottle out of his pocket and uncaps the lid with shaking hands. Instantly, the smell of apples floods the space, and he hasn't even used any yet.

I close my fingers over it. "No, you—wait. That's why you always smell like apples?"

Eyes on the floor, he nods. "I got to pick a scent to cover the smell of the illusion magic. Are apples okay? I think Ilbryen could change it if you—"

"Don't you dare."

Those gold-black eyes lock on me. They aren't the big brown eyes, but they're still him, sweet and hopeful.

"Apples or not, demonic form or not, I want *you*," I tell him. "As whoever makes you the happiest. *Of course* I want you. But it isn't about me—I need you to feel safe. And I'm afraid, if we keep the physical side of our relationship, you won't feel safe. You'll feel *obligated*."

He studies me, my hand still keeping the bottle in his grip captive. Without breaking eye contact, he frees his hand, recaps and pockets the bottle, and takes a step closer, his face tipping up, reaching for mine, open, raw, pleading before he's even spoken.

"Maybe I want to feel obligated to you," he whispers.

It shocks through me, an electric current.

No. No, I'm giving him the proper out. We can make this professional. We can—we need to—

"Bel—"

"Maybe I want to feel like I belong to you."

I slam my eyes shut, rocking like the whole damn city got hit by an earthquake and I'm absorbing the impact.

"You don't know what you're saying." He doesn't. He can't know what a throughline his words have straight to the most unhinged part of me.

"I do," he says, gradually more beseeching. "I want to feel like I'm bound to you."

A shiver walks down my spine. *Stop. Stop—*

"I want to feel like I'm *yours.*"

He's mine.

Entirely. Utterly. In every conceivable way.

The beast is raging, stalking, *hungry*; I freed it, why am I still holding it back?

Because Bel needs me to. Because this is the healthy thing to do. Because—

Bel braces his hand on my chest, his spot, and I don't have to open my eyes to know he's lifting up on his toes.

I pinch my eyes shut tighter, breaths coming in rough pulls that sound like growls; how is he not afraid? My shoulders are rising and my hands are in fists and I'm one trigger away from *snapping*, can't he see that? Why isn't he running?

Because he has no choice now. Because he can't *run. He's trapped.*

He's trapped.

He can't be taken from me.

Gods, I'm sick. I'm so fucked up.

And so gods-damned turned *on*.

Bel tugs on my neck until I lean down enough for him to brush his lips across mine, the barest hint, before he leans his forehead against my jaw. He's trembling, whether from holding himself up or the stress of this morning coming to a head.

But when he speaks again, his voice is vulnerable in a way that's my final undoing.

"Can I be yours, Orok?" he asks. "Tell me you'll keep me."

I palm the back of his head, fingers snagging in his curls, and my eyes rip open to his breathless expression, but I'm too far past gone to stop.

When I kiss him now, it's unabashed and starving, brutal and beastly. I hook my thumb around his chin to lower his jaw so I can plunge my tongue inside his mouth, tasting, tasting what's *mine*. He lets me, going pliant in a deluge of little whimpers and needy shivers as he cradles his body to me, drawing closer even though he shouldn't, he shouldn't want this.

"Last chance," I tell him. It's a lie. There are no more chances. "Last chance for this to be simple."

But he's shaking his head before I even finish talking, clawing at my shoulders, those whimpers never stopping. "No, *no*, please, Orok—please, I'm yours. Let me be yours, please."

I devour his mouth again and he croons in restless relief before I'm scooping him up and carrying him through the bedroom and into the huge bathroom.

Tem didn't actually touch him earlier, but I have the sudden need to scrub off their interaction.

I set Bel down next to the double vanity. The shower has a glass door that covers half the massive marble stall, and I reach in to get the water warming up. He hasn't moved, staying right where I put him, and I tug at the hem of his silk tank top, my throat pulsating in a growl.

Pretty sure I'll always be making some kind of sound like this around him.

Pretty sure I should be more worried about that.

He lifts his arms obediently, eyes heavy-lidded, and *fuck*, there's that growl again.

"So good," I purr. "So good for me, aren't you?"

His eyes shut with a whimper that looks like it pains him.

"Open those eyes, sweetheart. I want you looking at me."

A beat passes, and then he does, blinking as the room fills with steam and humidity.

I lift the shirt over his head, drop it to the floor, and—

The growl rips out of me this time, comes barreling past my lips, raw and grating against the hum of the shower.

Bel's chest flutters in anxious breaths, making his skin shine—and making his body chain glint and glisten in the bathroom lights.

I hadn't noticed he was wearing it again.

One of my fingers drifts down the center chain. It dangles off his neck with pieces that swoop around his shoulders, his ribs; delicate, impossibly thin strands of gold links. The center one continues down, down, vanishing below the edge of his pants.

"You put it back on," I state the obvious.

He lowers his hands. "I thought . . . thought I'd be leaving."

His eyes fly to mine, like that might somehow still be true, and his brows pulse in an unspoken plea to prove that he's not going anywhere. That I'm keeping him.

"How far down does this go?" I ask, voice gravelly.

Eyes on mine, he undoes his pants, pushes the rest of his clothes to the floor, and kicks them away.

Maybe there really is an earthquake pummeling the city. Or maybe I'm the center of it, insufferable vibrations shooting out of me, more potent than the earth shifting.

The body chain trickles over his belly button, following the line of hair to his groin, his hard cock sticking straight out toward me. The chain divides around it to encircle each thigh.

What parts of me might have still been clinging to poise are demolished. He's naked for me, his rose-gold skin gleaming with the growing stickiness of the shower, but it's that damn body chain that highlights every perfect dip and contour of his muscles, makes him look like a Grecian statue come to life.

The sight is ravaging.

Bel braces his hands on the vanity behind him, cheeks flushed, knuckles whitening, his tail coiled around his calf. His muscles strain the longer I look, let myself gorge on him.

"O-orok," he stammers.

I peel off my shirt, push my sleep pants down, and it's his turn to stare. He's seen most of me already, but the flaring of his eyes and the way his knuckles turn even whiter on the vanity send a shudder like champagne bubbles from my neck to where my dick hangs hard against my thigh.

He's soaking up the reverberations of this earthquake I'm emitting as I close in on him, letting my hand follow one of the chains around his thigh, to his ass, to where his tail connects out of his lower back.

A hiss slips through his lips, answering me before I need to ask, but I do anyway.

"Can you feel me?" I whisper.

He nods. Nods as I trail my fingers down his tail, gently prying it away from his leg. Nods and shivers and pinches his eyes shut in a restrictive collapse like he's trying so, so hard to hold himself back.

"Uh-uh." I tap his chin. "Eyes open, sweetheart. You were doing so well for me, don't stop now."

He obeys instantly and I tighten my grip around his tail. Another hiss, this one coming with a squirm and an arching of his back.

"Orok," he whines.

I let my fingers lazily meander down to the arrowed tip and he's breathing hard, eyes glazed.

"That sensitive?" I ask.

Half his mouth crooks in a self-deprecating smile. "Not really. No. I—you're touching me."

I smile. "So you'd react as strongly if I touched you . . . here?"

My fingers move to his stomach. To the valley between his abs as his belly contracts.

Bel moans. "Yeah. Yes."

"Hm. And here?"

His jaw. Where his pink curls twist in too-tempting circles, and I brush one aside to touch the hollow below his ear.

The feather of his exhale across my chest points out how close we're standing now. Close enough that all it takes is shifting my hips, and the head of his cock brushes my thigh.

He gasps, body arching again. I've barely touched him.

"Please," he whispers, hands still on the vanity, still displaying himself for me, *mine*. "Please, Orok."

"What do you want?" I twist his curl around my finger and tug, earning a low mewl.

"I want—*gods*—I want what I said out there. Please, please—"

I run my nose from his shoulder to his neck, inhaling. The faint whiff of apples. The even fainter scent of me. That won't do.

"And what was that?"

"F-fuck me, I want you to fuck me." His jaw is slack, words toppling out in a rush.

My smile stretches his skin, tugs what's already taut, so when I sink my teeth into the juncture of neck and shoulder and suck, he has no choice but to cry out at the sting.

"I don't know, sweetheart," I tell him, licking the spot, more filthy promise than apology. "Think you can take me? I don't want to hurt you."

I thrust against him, my cock rubbing over his stomach, his body chain adding an extra bite. The abrading pull is so good I grip his hair for leverage and suck at his neck again.

Bel cries out, hands finally leaving the vanity to scramble for purchase on my hips, pulling me closer to him. "I can. I can, I promise."

"How do you know? No one's fucked you before, right? How do you know what you can handle?"

"I—I've fucked myself. Toys. With toys. I know how to take it. I can take you, I promise, I swear I can. I'll be so good for you, please."

"Shh, sweetheart." I brush his hair behind his ear. Gods, I'm going to need to watch him fuck himself one day. "Toys are a bit different, though. What makes you think you can handle *me*?"

He blinks up at me, looking so thoroughly put out at the idea that I might not fuck him that I can't help but grin.

"You know you can handle me," I answer for him, planting a soft kiss on his cheek, "because you know I'll take care of you. Don't you?"

He moans, his hips rocking against my leg even as I press him into the counter. "Yes. Yes."

"You trust me to do that? To make it good for you?"

"Gods, Orok, *yes*. Can you—just *fuck me*."

"So impatient. I thought you were mine? I thought you wanted to belong to me?"

He whines when I lean into him hard enough that he's trapped to the vanity, can't rock his hips, can't get relief.

"I do. I am. *Orok*—"

"Hm. I love it when you whine for me." I nip his ear and he digs his nails into my skin. "But let me take care of you. Let me take care of what's mine."

He's practically in a daze as I guide him to the shower. The whole room is a steamy sauna by now, and the water is scalding; I adjust it to the perfect temperature and pull him under the spray. He tries to go onto his toes to kiss me, but I push him down, grab a washcloth from the ledge, and get to work cleaning him with almost clinical efficiency.

I don't linger or tease him, which seems to be its own kind of tease; he's a whimpering, fidgeting mess in no time, his arms reaching for me, his legs shifting restlessly. His cock hasn't flagged and neither has mine, not with the way he can never seem to stop and *feel*, always has to be moving, always has to be expelling his emotions in a dance all his own.

I spin him around. His feet slip on the tiles, but I keep him steady until his palms slap the wall.

"Stay," I tell him, then kick his legs wider.

His head drops between his lifted hands, that body chain perfectly following the ridges of his spine and fanning out across his back. He shivers, even with the warm water spraying down on us both.

"Want to wash you," he gasps.

I kiss his shoulder blade. "Later, sweetheart. For now . . ."

There's one place I haven't washed yet, and I get to work on it, taking the cloth and dipping it between the globes of his ass. He moans low in his throat and thrusts back against me, but I'm clinical here, too. Okay, maybe I spend a little extra time on it, enough that he's twisting his hips, trying to get away, or get closer, or *move* in that enthralling way of his.

I want to make him dance. I want him to be so overcome with pleasure it has no choice but to burst out of him in his art.

This is torture for me, too. This is torture and poetry in perfect equilibrium.

The cloth splats on the shower's floor and I lower to my knees, hold him open, and slide my tongue from his taint to the bulge of his tail.

Bel shouts, the sound echoing off the tiles. "Oh my gods, oh my gods, *Orok*—"

"Gotta get you ready for me. You okay with that?"

He looks over his shoulder, hands still plastered to the wall, and nods.

"Relax for me," I tell him, and dive back in.

If he was squirming before, he's outright flailing now, shifting and wriggling so much I have to band my arm around his hips to hold him in place. His tail thrashes, hitting the wall like a hammering fist; it whips my side and he fumbles an apology, but I grab it as he recoils.

"Touch me," I say.

He whimpers but complies, too blissed out to think or argue.

His tail curls around my thigh and he groans as I do, the constriction of him on my leg matching the way his hole contracts as my tongue prods at his entrance.

"Fuck, sweetheart, you taste so good." I nip at him and he might say something, it's all devolved into mindless babbling. The water's still pouring down on us, but I can feel his hard cock where I have my arm around his hips, and it's slick with precum; he must be leaking onto the tiles.

I hold him in place, eating him out with all the desire I've been shoring up for weeks, not backing off as his babbling and squirming intensify, as he starts begging, as he swears he's ready. His rim loosens and I slip my tongue inside, using my thumb and finger to spread him wide so I can dive even deeper, licking, reaching. His heat is so intense, a napalm shot straight to my aching dick, his silken walls rippling with every stilted cry he releases; he's sobbing against the tiles now.

I promised I'd take care of him. It's my job now. My purpose, my honor, I'm lost to it. So I keep going, adding a finger alongside my tongue, stretching, massaging his tight, tight rim; gods, he's *so tight*.

"*Orok*." He thrashes, his tail damn near cutting off the circulation in my leg. "*Orok*, please, I can't—I'm gonna—*Orok*—"

"You're almost ready." I thrust two fingers in and out of him. "You gonna come on my hand, Bel? Think you can come from this?"

Another deep lick, then a third finger.

"No—yes? I don't—*Orok*."

My name on his lips like that. I want to eat it off his tongue.

He's taking three fingers easily, but I play a little longer until I add a fourth, keeping him on the edge, this side of too much. His cries are skittering, up and down and changing pitch, the muscles in his back, ass, and legs rippling and constricting under that *body chain* in a rhythm I can't catch.

Standing on damn near useless legs, I switch off the water, fingers still in him, and Bel whips a frantic look at me.

"Please, please," he mumbles, his lips bruised, eyes unfocused, and he peels one hand off the wall to grope for me.

I take his hand, press a kiss to his palm. "Going to get you to the bed."

He makes a heartbreaking, panicked sound when I slip my fingers free. Gods, he's so far gone; I might've pushed him too much.

A kiss to his forehead. "It's all right, sweetheart. Just taking you to bed. You're doing so good for me. So good. Just a bit longer, okay?"

His answering whimper is all I get, so I grab a towel and quickly dry us both, then lift him and hurry him to the bed.

I hunt lube and a condom out of my suitcase. When I settle over him, his hands immediately anchor around my neck. Some of the focus is back in his eyes, some of the fog lifted, but it rolls away with another beautiful, grinding moan as I rub lubed fingers into his stretched rim.

"Now, now," he begs. "Now, please, fuck me, *now*."

"Shh." I press kisses to his cheeks, his jaw, his lips, easing more lube in, scissoring my fingers. His head rocks back and forth on the pillow, his wet hair splayed out around his face, and his hips shift in uneven thrusts like he can't find the tempo. I keep working him and his expression slants more and more into frustrated, reaching, *wanting*.

"Not enough," he says. "Need more, need you."

I pluck the condom out of the sheets, and at the sound of it opening, Bel's delirium angles into panic.

"No, no." He claws his fingers into my neck and blinks big eyes up at me. "You said I'm yours, right? I'm yours, make me yours. I want to feel you, I want *you*. It's fine, I've never been with anyone else. I trust you. Please, just you, just you."

My consciousness knows I need a minute to disassociate, because all I can suddenly think is how furiously grateful I am that I'm the one he's doing this with. If it'd been anyone else he was saying that to, someone with fewer morals, someone who'd take advantage?

I'm overheated, skin slick and sweaty from the shower, but protective anger burns through me.

I kiss him, tongue digging into his mouth, and he hums happily, settling with every gentle lap of my lips.

Once he's calmed, I rest my forehead on his. "We should've talked about condoms before we got started. That's on me. But I'm not letting you make this decision right now. Either I fuck you with a condom, or we wait."

He whines, his bottom lip jutting out in the most adorable pout.

"Now, please," he relents, and I kiss him one more time.

"Good boy."

A tinny, fevered cry. It yanks on my chest, has me pressing another kiss to his lips.

"So good for me," I say, and he repeats the sound. "You are. Letting me take care of you, trusting me."

I roll the condom on, add a ton more lube, and position his legs so his knees are bent, a pillow under his hips, his thighs as wide as they can go. He splays back while I arrange him, his arms up, gripping another pillow under his head.

I've never fully digested the phrase *pillow princess* until I see him like this, his rose-gold body sweat-glistened, that chain off-center from all our movements. He's so gorgeous, it's regal.

"Deep breath, okay? Push out," I tell him, and he nods, eyes on my face, lips parted.

One hand holding his thigh to the side, the other lining up my dick, I prod his rim.

Bel hisses but bears down, hands gripping the pillow above his head. My gaze flicks from his face to the eye-rolling sight of my cock disappearing into his hole.

I slide past the first ring, and a breath leaves his lungs in a punch, his erection wilting, and I know I'm leaving bruises on his thigh with the way my fingers dig in beneath that chain.

"Oh my gods." His eyes slam to mine, those reddened lips popping open. "Burns, burns—"

My heart squeezes. He's so much smaller than me; it's going to hurt him, how could it not?

I force my grip on him to loosen, rub my thumb in soothing circles on the inside of his thigh. "You opened up for me really good, but this might've been too much, too soon. I shouldn't have jumped right to—"

"*Don't stop*," Bel begs, and releases the pillow to grab me when I try to pull out. "I want this. Please, Orok."

I study his face for a long second, weighing the desperation in his gaze against what he needs. I told him I'd take care of him.

But he's also had so much of his own agency ripped away, and my heart squeezes again, this time in needing to give him what he wants.

Okay. Okay, he wants this; but I'm not going to hurt him.

"Just—just t-talk to me," he stutters.

I ease back a little before pushing in. "Gods, sweetheart, you're doing so well. Sucking me in. You want me so bad, don't you? You feel amazing, opening up for me."

He whimpers; I push a little deeper, pull back, push in, setting a steady rhythm until the pained tension on his face melts under the transition into bliss.

"So good," I promise him. "You're so good for me. Fuck, Bel. I wish you could see how sexy you look right now, spread out on the bed, flushed and perfect, your hole swallowing me up. Gods, you're taking me. That's it, sweetheart, that's it. Can you do it? Can you take all of me?"

It's a stream of nonsense more than questions, but he answers, nodding and clinging to me. His tail whips against the bed, then twitches up and wraps around my forearm.

"Kiss me," he begs. "Please, please."

I comply, abs contracting to bend down to him, the angle forcing more than half of me in, and he cries out against my mouth.

"Do you want to stop?" I ask the strain around his eyes, the nails digging puncture wounds into my shoulders, the way his dick is still flaccid.

He's sweat-soaked, his dazed eyes locking on mine, and he cants his hips, whimpering as he fucks himself deeper. "No. Tell me you won't let me go. Tell me I'm yours."

"I won't let you go. You're mine, Bel. *Mine*, and I'm not letting you go. I'll keep you safe." I give an experimental thrust, pushing more in, and he moans, the good kind of moan. "You're *mine*." Another thrust, and my hips hit his ass; he's gasping, I don't think he's even realized I'm fully in. "I'm never letting you go." Another thrust. "*Mine*."

I grab his now half-hard cock, hand still slick with excess lube, and stroke in time with my gentle thrusts. He fills in my hand while sexy little mewls get mangled in his throat. I kiss that throat, laving my tongue on his salty skin, rolling my hips in a throbbing rhythm he picks up instantly, his body writhing along with it.

"Good?" I ask, propping back so I can see his face.

"S'good," he slurs, fighting to open his eyes, to look up at me. "I—I can f-feel you. Everywhere. Oh, gods, you're deep. I'm so full, so—*more.*"

He's a vice. A hot, perfect vice clamping on my dick, and that beastly part of me knows, *knows* he was made for this, for me, and I was made for him. It's over the top but everything about this morning has been that way, and I'm so *tired* of fighting what I want.

What I want is this, exactly this, him and us in this perfect held breath of a moment. Details alchemize from mundane into anchors—the satin drag of the sheets under us. The hues of pink and gold in his hair. The smell of soap and sweat on his skin. The moan that shoots out of his throat.

He consumes me in a way that silences the world. In that silence, I'm pushed out of myself, and I realize I'm not fighting so hard to be healthy, to move on, *fighting*. That's all I ever am, *fighting*, but right now, with him, I'm *here*.

It's grounding and freeing. A foundation and a release.

The backs of my eyes burn before I can consciously acknowledge the rush of emotion swarming me. Fuck, I'm not going to cry during sex—

Pain flares, ripping me out of the onslaught, Bel's nails dragging down my back. His calves hook around my hips and he tries to get leverage, sharp ankles digging into my ass, but his legs are spread too wide to pull. He squirms with the effort and my lip curls up, eyes still damp.

"You'll take what I give you," I pant, thrusts staying smooth, careful. "You'll take what I think you can handle."

I won't hurt him. But also, I want to savor him. Want to savor *this*. I want each slow plunge, each choked gasp. I want the slick, warm hardness of his cock in my palm, how I can completely surround his dick with my hand so he can't escape sensation on it.

He shudders, tremors that ripple across his gleaming skin, and between one misfired whine and the next, he's coming. It takes him by surprise as much as it does me, his eyes bursting wide in almost panicked pleasure. His neck arches, every part of him rippling and rolling as he comes in my hand, wet release spilling between my fingers.

The moment his hips flinch, oversensitive, I pull out of him, rip the condom off, and use his cum to jack myself over his stomach. His eyelids flutter, mouth agape, his belly rounding out and concaving with his winding-down breaths.

My orgasm smashes into me, pyrotechnics firing off gold and pink, shivery sparks sizzling every nerve. A roaring shout bruises my throat as my cum pools on him, fills his navel, covers some of the body chain, and in that immediate moment post-orgasm, I'm all primal, all beast—I dip my fingers in my cum and spread it across his chest, marking him.

Bel trembles, whimpering; he has been, I think: small, exhausted whimpers that have me gathering him in my arms, mess be damned, and rolling us onto our sides. He scrambles on to me, burrowing as close as he can get. Does he know he's whimpering, does he know he's shaking?

"Empty," he moans. "It hurts."

I tug the comforter over us and rub a hand down his body, between his cheeks, softly prodding his swollen rim. His whimpers splinter apart but he hooks one leg over my hip, giving me access, and I dip two fingers back inside him.

He sighs, his face tucked under my chin, parted lips letting his breath bathe the underside of my jaw.

The tremors fade.

We only have a few hours before the buses are due to take us back to Philly. I need to get him food; he has to be starving. We need another shower. I need to get started on all the other tasks I have waiting for me now to keep him safe.

But even with the intensity of being inside him passed, that overwhelming feeling of being free hasn't.

I've been a worshipper of Urzoth my entire life. Sacrificed hours in church, devoted my younger self to a barrage of commandments. And all of it, *all of it*, was in pursuit of this feeling.

Not strength.

Peace.

I hold Bel, safe and alive and *mine*, and let touching him be the catechism that overwrites all the others.

Chapter Eleven

Morning News: "Welcome to *One Shot*, your number-one source for the latest in pro rawball news. I'm your host, Diamanda Blacktalon. My cohost, Vaknox of the Lizard People of Tesh, is not yet back from his sojourn—during his molting process, he was chosen by the lizard god Chaxloakka to seek the eternal flame of the Lizard People. We wish Vaknox all the best on his divine quest. Joining me as temporary cohost is Begmi, the pixie prince from the Forest of Neetand in the Fae Plane. Begmi, you—oh. Where'd he go? He's—oh *that's* him? That speck of dust? That's his pixie form? Oh, I'm so sorry, Prince Begmi."

the softest tinkling sound ever

"Wow, that's so kind of you to say. I *did* recently have my tusks polished, thank you. Now, we've had quite the active twenty-four hours in the rawball world! But what I want to focus on is—you guessed it—Beauty and the Beast! Our favorite It couple, Orok and Alexo, strutted their stuff at the gala for Thrive Children, and *wow*, did they steam up some cameras! I—"

the softest tinkling sound ever

"Oh, yes, there was also an abduction by the Galaxrien cult. But did you *see* Alexo's outfit? We have a clip from the red carpet; can we pull it up?"

the softest tinkling sound ever

"I . . . I hadn't thought about the ramifications of Galaxrien cultists attacking an Urzoth worshipper in terms of the larger ecumenical association of those two religions, Begmi. How—oh, oh, that's what you came on here to talk about? Um. Well. I guess we can save the outfit breakdown for after the commercials."

Bel has to ride back to Philly on the cheerleaders' bus. I have to ride back on the players' bus. I haven't seen Gulus since he vanished from our room, but he's probably lurking around somewhere, right?

It's only a two-hour trip. More or less.

I can handle that.

It'd draw unnecessary attention if I suddenly insisted on changes—we've had team travel before, and I was always fine with us being separated. But now?

I'm twitchy and keep glancing out the bus window to spot the cheerleaders ahead of us.

Next time we have an away game, I'll . . . figure something out. The coaches like the team to travel together; unity and shit, and yeah, that does matter—Darian's strumming his guitar in the back, and half the team is valiantly attempting to sing along to "Bohemian Rhapsody." Aaron's actually nailing the falsetto parts; who knew? Phei's taken the form of a coconut tree, and they're rattling around on percussion.

But Bel's away from me, vulnerable unless Gulus is hiding on his bus, and it's fucking me *up*.

The separation is only for a few hours, then we'll be back in Philly and he won't need to leave my side.

Speaking of which.

I message Seb about laying wards around my apartment. I haven't done spell work since college; if I want it done right, I need Seb and Thio. Given I provide no context for my sudden urge to lock down my place, his responding texts are appropriately confused. But I didn't get a chance to tell Bel about Seb yet, to ask if I can bring him in. I will today.

I also shoot off an email to my building's owner to start ramping up their security.

And I ignore the messages from Roesia Sombercrown, and Treva, and Reverend Drach's people. They want to talk about the cultist attack and how it affects Urzoth's church now that a member was abducted.

But talking about that will force me to acknowledge what

I've done in committing to protect Bel. How it affects my ties to Urzoth.

I'm not ready to think about that yet.

I order components for every conceivable safety spell I can think of, all on overnight delivery—

Darian plops onto the seat next to me. "No time for losers," he says, strumming his guitar.

I look up.

To see the whole damn bus staring at me.

Feels like I've missed something.

"*No time for losers,*" Darian says again, harder, and I recognize the chords for "We Are the Champions." "You're the only one not singing," he stage-whispers at me.

"I didn't think your god liked me singing his songs," I stage-whisper back. "Something about inflicting emotional damage on the unknowing public."

He smirks, all straight white teeth and potent charm. "He's in a good mood; we won, and we're on track to be *rawball champions*!" He shouts the last words and the whole bus roars ecstatic agreement.

I laugh. "Should we say that? Could jinx us."

"Meh." Darian wrinkles his nose. "Confidence cancels out the jinx. *Sing*. My god's hoping the rest of these turds singing will cover up your screeching."

"Hey," Aaron mopes.

"You all sound like shit to me," Marlow signs, and someone lobs a water bottle at her.

"*No time for losers,*" Darian prods again. "Don't be a loser."

I throw another glance out the front window. The cheerleaders' bus is still ahead of us on the highway.

With a deep breath in, I bellow out the next line of the song.

Darian grins, and soon the whole bus is back to belting out the song. Even Marlow's signing the lyrics, bending her body dramatically to stretch the words.

Darian kicks his feet up on the chair in front of him, fingers dancing over his guitar.

Aaron and another tank get *into it*, singing the chorus at each other in a way that feels like a threat.

A thought hits me square in the chest.

The Chimeras would never.

Never make fools of themselves like this. Never have *fun* like this. It was serious game play, *we are intense and intimidating always*, or nothing. That attitude is why someone connected to Urzoth *should have* fit right in.

I lean over to Darian. "Your god's happy?"

What I want to ask is, *You're happy with your god?* But that answer's obvious.

He flicks a look at me along with a slightly confused smile. "Yeah." Aaron hits a note I wasn't sure humans were capable of reaching, and Darian winces. "Well. Debatable."

I watch Darian perform and I sing along with my team, and it isn't envy that I feel. I just feel glad for him, but ultimately, nothing for me.

Because I don't want a relationship with Urzoth like Darian has with his god. If I *had* that kind of relationship with Urzoth, I would never have had a problem with the Chimeras.

But this? Singing all together, laughing at each other?

It's so much better.

By the time the buses pull into the Hellhounds HQ, I've almost stopped worrying about Bel. About the Galaxrien news. I'm a little more centered, and as I disembark, I give fist bumps to my teammates. They all return them eagerly, making jokes about the ride or the game.

Off the bus, Darian pulls me in for a hug, which surprises me enough that when I step away, I cock my head at him.

"We got you," he tells me, looping his guitar case over his head. "Next week, with the Chimeras. We all got you."

My brows vault up. I haven't told them—*anyone*—how I feel about the Chimeras. Is it that obvious? There were enough reports speculating about it, and the Chimeras players haven't exactly been subtle over their feelings in interviews about losing me to the Hellhounds.

"I . . . thanks," I manage. And smile. "They won't know what hit 'em."

"Fuck yeah!" Aaron clambers off the bus. "You're *our* O Monroe now. Vegas can kiss my ass."

Marlow follows him down the steps and winks. "They'll need to get in line, hot stuff."

Aaron blushes. Full-on chin-to-hairline *blushes.*

Marlow seems oblivious and prances away. Darian shares a *you caught that, too, huh?* look with me before he also heads off.

I smile. At all of this. And I take their assurances, the team's parting Hellhounds barks, and tuck them safely away.

Maybe we're not so cordial after all.

Maybe we're almost . . . friendly?

Bel's across the lot, digging through his bus's luggage compartment for his bag. He used the illusion spray before we left, so he's in his human form now, but his pink hair is the same.

He turns, hiking his bag over his shoulder, and his eyes lock with mine.

He smiles.

And I tuck that away as well.

At the edge of the parking lot, sitting on a bench under a tree, Gulus is dressed in casual clothes, reading a newspaper.

Okay. That's going to be kind of creepy.

Treva appears in front of me as I take a step toward Bel. "Mr. Monroe, you and Mr. Warden are needed in Ms. Sombercrown's office. *Now.*"

My stomach knots. I want to get Bel to my apartment. I need him somewhere safe.

But that exact attitude is why I told Ilbryen to let him stay with me, so Bel could get out and *live.*

"Yeah," I say, beckoning Bel over. "I figured."

It's only Roesia in her office, and I breathe a little easier that I won't have to deal with an Urzoth rep through this.

Not that anything's going to change. In fact, Drach will be

thrilled by the progression of mine and Bel's relationship. It's only in my head that I expect a bit of gloating, like he'd known I was trying to weasel my way out and somehow ended up even *more* committed to Urzoth than before.

I have Bel's hand in mine where we sit on the couch. Treva is taking notes on a tablet while Roesia leans back in her chair, legs crossed, her orange eyes going from my face to our joined hands and back.

Next to me, Bel shifts.

And shifts again.

And makes a low, pained whimper.

Oh.

We only had sex, like, five hours ago, plus the long bus ride. He's sore.

Half of me wants to find him something softer to sit on.

The other half of me is ragingly turned on, wants to caveman grunt and beat my chest.

Neither half can do jack shit right now without things getting really, really weird.

"Reverend Drach apologizes for being unable to join us," Roesia says, yanking my focus to something significantly less boner-inducing. "Had you responded to any of my assistant's attempts to reach out last night, we would have been able to set up something more formal."

My grip on Bel clenches.

I told Ilbryen we need to double down on Bel's association with Urzoth.

So I will.

"I apologize, Ms. Sombercrown," I say. "We were understandably rattled by last night's news. But, luckily, something else has been in development that I think will help offset some of the strain the Urzoth church is under. It should please Reverend Drach."

Roesia's head tips ever so slightly. "Oh?"

"Alexo and I are moving in together."

Bel leans against my arm, bringing his other hand up to play with my thumb where it's locked around his. I'm not sure what's causing the tension suddenly winding through him, but I don't lose focus. Can't. Just get through this, do this performative dance, and we can leave.

Treva, typing away, glances up. "Um. What?"

I give her a small smile. "You were right in picking up that we are really together. We have been for some time. And we're taking our relationship to the next level, which should provide an excellent opportunity for Reverend Drach to capitalize on more positive Urzoth press, which will also give me and the Hellhounds positive press." My throat swells, and I clear it. "Do you—are you aware of how the church is responding to the abduction?"

Bel goes motionless.

Roesia nods. "Their followers are understandably upset, but to channel their anger, the church is planning several demonstrations of *Urzoth's strength* in cities across the country." I must not do a good job of wiping the fear off my face, because she bats her hand. "Duels among followers, nothing that will endanger bystanders. They are trying to *improve* their image, after all."

"On that note," Treva cuts in, "Reverend Drach has asked that we pass along the message for you and Mr. Warden to *not* participate in any of the demonstrations. They don't want you associated with that aspect of the church."

Oh, darn. I was planning on heading out after this and volunteering for a duel.

Roesia taps a finger on her knee. "But yes, your relationship progressing will be a bright spot against this news. Treva?"

"Yeah, we can definitely work with this. People will eat it up. And—" Treva looks down at her tablet. "This will go a long way towards distracting from last night's abduction, but the church had their own suggestion in mind for something you two can do. It'll really shine a positive light on Urzoth and, similarly, on you and the team."

My teeth clench. "What is it?"

"They'd like to have a photo op of you and Mr. Warden with

your parents, since your mother is an active member of her local church," Treva says. "It'd be a great, wholesome moment to balance the violent demonstrations. Can they come up for next week's home game?"

Numb, I repeat, "Next week's game?"

"Yes. Against the Chimeras. Since eyes will already be on you from facing your old team, we're hoping to capitalize on that extra attention."

Introduce Bel to my parents after playing against the team that ostracized me.

My smile is more than a little exhausted. "That's fine. I'll call them and arrange it."

Treva clutches her tablet to her chest. "You're okay with us and the Urzoth church continuing to push your relationship? If it's real now, we don't want to intrude."

Roesia doesn't react to that, neither to scold Treva for offering nor to agree.

I look down at Bel's hand in mine.

No. I don't want our relationship splashed across tabloids.

And *no*, I don't want our relationship used by the Urzoth church. At all.

But renouncing Urzoth would draw too much attention, especially now. The media would pick apart my choice and everything about my life, and since my relationship with Bel is the latest big change, they'd focus on that, find some way to blame him for me leaving. It'd stir up all kinds of blood in the water for the cultists, and yeah, Bel and I would still be high-profile enough to have some protection, but it'd draw unneeded focus to us. To him.

No. I don't want *any of this*.

I smile at Treva. "Yes. We're fine with it. If that's all?"

Treva looks at Roesia for confirmation.

Roesia, who's been unnervingly quiet, has her chin in her hand and her eyes narrowed pensively.

She flicks that look to Bel. "How do you feel about things, Mr. Warden? Mr. Monroe doesn't speak for you."

I jolt. Of course I don't.

But I have been.

I try to put space between us, but Bel doesn't let go of me, yanking our hands into his lap.

"I'm fine, Ms. Sombercrown," he says. "It's great. I'm really happy."

Every single person in this room hears the lie in his voice.

My brows dip, but he keeps a forced smile up for Roesia.

Her narrow eyes don't let up. "My door is always open if you need anything."

She looks at me, and her pensive gaze turns the slightest bit hostile.

I almost call her on it. What does she think is happening here? All they should see is that we started this fake relationship at their behest, and now it isn't fake anymore, and Bel's moving in with me. Why is that worthy of her ire? Does she think I'm forcing him into it?

Her protectiveness seems to be in favor of Bel, so I'll let it stand. The more people looking out for him, the better. Even if they're looking suspiciously at *me*.

"You're dismissed," Roesia says. Then adds, "Good work, both of you." But her tone is flat.

Bel and I stand and make our way out of her office. In unspoken agreement, we leave HQ in silence; there's just the swishing of our bags against my hip where I carry them both.

Gulus is still on that bench.

I ignore him—that's for the best, right?—and head to my car in the private lot. Stiff, I open the door for Bel, toss our bags in the trunk, and climb into the driver's seat.

And sit there.

Bel wiggles on the seat and winces.

I look at him, but he doesn't look at me, his cheeks red.

"How are you feeling?" I ask.

"Fine," he says too quickly. He wanes, amends with, "I'm fine. It's sore, yeah. But . . ." His blush intensifies, flooding his cheeks, his neck. "I like the reminder of you," he whispers.

Fuuuuuuck me.

I want to ask more about *that*, but if we start talking about his ass, things are going to take a sexual turn, and there's something beneath his surface I'm not seeing.

Silence falls. Again. He keeps staring out the windshield, seemingly unaware I haven't even started the car yet, his face set in a worried frown.

"Think we should set Roesia up with Ilbryen?" I ask.

Bel flings a perplexed look at me. "*What?*"

I shrug, curling and uncurling one hand around the steering wheel. "They both give off the same alpha feminine energy. What's the phrase? *Boss bitch?* I dunno. I think they could handle each other."

Bel gapes at me. I keep filling the silence.

"It'd be pretty terrifying for the rest of us, though. But I think they'd be benevolent overlords once we surrender to their invincible team-up, so we should—"

"None of this is real, is it?"

My mouth slams shut.

Bel looks horrified that he spoke. His eyes are round, and his chest flickers in a quick inhale.

He locks his arms around himself and whips to face the windshield.

"Are we going straight to your place?" he asks in a small voice. "Or can I get some stuff from my—"

"Why wouldn't it be real?"

He drops his eyes to his lap. "Please let it go. I didn't mean to say that."

I reach across the console and pull one of his arms out to take his hand.

"I don't want to go back to letting things go with you," I whisper. "Tell me what you meant. Please?"

He swallows, still not looking at me, and fights an internal war for a few quiet moments before he snaps his eyes shut. "I'm not moving in with you and meeting your parents because you *want* me to. I mean, you might want me to live with you, but it isn't—it's only—" He thunks his head back against the seat and groans. "I hate this part. I always have. The constant lying, every action blanketed in a dozen layers of half-truths. Nothing's *real.*"

"Bel. Look at me."

He does, reluctantly.

"You and me? It's real. For me, at least. What can I do to make it real for you?"

He balks. "It can't be real for you."

"Why?"

"Because—because I'm only meeting your parents as a PR stunt, and I'm only moving in with you because you agreed to be my handler. You don't want me to *move in with you.* To *meet your parents.* Not the way you said it to Roesia."

"Ah. Okay." I turn on the seat as much as I can to face him, then take both his hands in mine. "Belzaroth—crap. What's your last name? Not Warden? Vossen?"

Though having the surname linked with Galaxrien Vossen would've painted an even bigger target on him over his life.

He sighs. "See? You don't even know my last name."

I clamp down when he tries to pull his hands away. "Tell me, or I'll make something up. Something awful."

"Orok."

"Well, that's a bit serendipitous. But anyway, Belzaroth Orok—"

"Oh my gods, you know that's not what I meant."

"Fine, then. Belzaroth Hardmeat, would you—"

He gapes. "You're not taking this seriously."

"I'm trying to, but you're being stubborn. So, Belzaroth Fine-Ass—"

"Fucking hell. It's Reynolds, okay?"

I pause, head listing to the side. "Reynolds?"

That's so . . . not demonic.

Bel grumbles, exasperated. "My great-great-great-grandmother is responsible for this esteemed line of my family tree—she was a Galaxrien worshipper and gave herself up to a horrifically risky ceremony most people don't survive, all to breed little demonic Galaxrien mortals. That first descendant *was* a Vossen. But he had kids with a regular mortal, who had kids with a regular mortal, who didn't *want* their offspring being the target of a cult, and thank the gods it gave me at least one normal thing. Can you imagine if I had to go around as a *Vossen*? It's bad enough my mom named me Belzaroth."

I keep my head tipped, silently prodding for that explanation, too.

He sighs and talks quickly, like he's trying to speak past any emotional connection. "My mom was a human who fell for my dad. He carried the Galaxrien line, and he and my mom were certain it was their destiny to *reawaken our lineage* and bring about Galaxrien; don't worry, neither of them raised me, so I'm not broken up about this. Anyway, before an adventure party captured them, they had me. Thus, Belzaroth Reynolds. Thus, you know my last name. *Thus*, can we get going now?"

He tries, again, to get his hands free, but I tighten my fingers and smile. I love these moments when he cracks open some of his past for me; I want more, want it all.

"Belzaroth Reynolds," I say. "Would you meet my parents and move in with me?"

He stops fighting and gives me an annoyed look. "I already agreed."

"Not for a PR stunt or anything like that. Would you meet my parents because you're the person I want to experience all the sappy relationship firsts with?"

Surprise chases away his irritation. "I'd be the first person you've introduced to them?"

"And I want you with me after next week's game," I say. "Because playing the Chimeras is going to suck, and having you there will make it better."

A small, pained grunt. "Orok—"

"And would you move in with me," I press on, "because I haven't been able to stop thinking about you since you sang in that bar?

Would you move in with me because you're enchanting and kind, and your strength puts every other instance of strength in this world to shame?" My tone shifts; my words come harder, more desperate, and Bel's face matches it, severity sneaking up on him. "Move in with me because I don't want to spend another minute away from you. Because I look at you, and all the noise stops; that's what you do for me. You're my calm. Move in with me because I need you."

Bel's breathing stutters. Mine does, too.

He frees one hand and touches my cheek, fingertips ghosting over my skin. That's where he looks, not in my eyes; he can't seem to, not with what I've said.

I feel the weight, too. Feel it being too *much*, right up there with *hating* still being connected to Urzoth, but I'm compartmentalizing all that in one big gathered snowball of avoidance.

For now, I'm here, soul ripped bare with someone for the first time in . . . ever.

Bel's tongue darts out to wet his lips. "Yeah," he says into the stillness of the car. "Yes. I'm yours."

"For real?" My voice is so soft it's a prayer. That's what I am now. His worshipper. *His*. "Not just sex. Not as a safety arrangement. Real."

His eyes are big and happy and dazed. "Yes. It's real."

We swing by Bel's apartment. I'm not sure where Tem got to and I know Gulus is lurking somewhere nearby, but I stay on alert the whole time we're walking up the stairs. When Bel unlocks the door and shoves it open, I do a quick sweep to make sure Tem's not lying in wait for retribution.

I didn't actually go inside the apartment that first night, so now, standing in the small front room, I analyze it and let more hatred for Tem stack up like logs on a pyre. Unfortunately not *Tem's* pyre, but a guy can dream.

The main room is a combination kitchen, dining, and living

room about the size of my bathroom, with a minuscule kitchenette, a rickety plastic table, and a threadbare love seat tucked against a peeling yellow wall. There's a TV that looks fairly new balanced on plastic milk cartons, but everything else is barren and old, and the air smells of mildew and stale food.

This is where he made Bel live? And Ilbryen, Gulus, and their whole adventure party knew about it.

I expect Bel to go to the left, toward an open door that shows a lumpy double mattress on the floor. But he heads for the love seat and crouches to pull a flat storage box out from beneath it, then undoes the coffee table by easing a piece of wood off two more plastic milk cartons. They're stuffed with toiletry containers, cases, and books.

"This is it," he says, climbing to his feet. He's in an orange Hellhounds shirt all the other cheerleaders were wearing, his tied in a knot at his side to show a sliver of belly above his jeans, and he dusts his hands on those jeans, dirt streaking across the fabric. He pulls a face but quickly resets, throwing up a strained smile.

Nope.

I point at the bedroom. "Nothing in there's yours?"

"That's Tem's room."

"Where's your room?"

Bel bends over to stack one carton atop the other. "Can you help me with these? Or the storage box—that's all my clothes and shoes, and these are—"

"Bel."

He sighs and straightens again. "I miss when we'd let each other deflect shit."

"Feel free to call me out on any of my stuff. But if—"

"Why were you acting weird in Roesia's office?"

"I didn't mean *now*, sweetheart." My look is chastising, but part of me seizes internally. Damn, he picked up on that?

Bel snatches a book out of the top carton. He deactivates some locking enchantment before it opens, then idly flips through it.

"This is my room," he says with no inflection.

I look around again. There's no bed. Just that ratty love seat with a matching pillow by the armrest, a quilt folded across the back.

Tem took the only bedroom. Made Bel sleep on that small, nasty couch.

Rage climbs my spine, burns across the back of my neck, ignites several small pulses of fury in the constant smolder directed at Tem and the whole adventure party that allowed Bel to be treated like this.

But Bel stands next to the love seat, rocking on his feet, pretending to read the book with his shoulders arched.

I cross the room, leaving my rage right there, and kiss his forehead. "There's nothing else you want to take?" I make my voice light. "You won't be coming back."

He smiles up at me. "No. I've gotten used to traveling light." The storage container with his clothes is bulging a bit, and he steps on it, tries to push it shut. "Well. Light-*ish*. I've been in Philadelphia the longest of any place, almost a year. I started to get . . . comfortable." He rolls his eyes. "Then Tem took over my handler position a few months ago, and he found this place *for a steal*, and insisted that I had to keep my stuff in containers that could be easily grabbed in case we had to leave quick. My poor clothes," he murmurs the last bit to the storage box.

"Most of the master closet at my place is empty."

Bel lifts his head, eyes brightening. But he seems to force himself to dim a bit. "I really won't take up much—"

"It's got plenty of space for your clothes and shoes. And those body chains."

He smiles, wide and pretty, cheeks flushing. "You like them, huh?"

A part of him might not believe I want this, might be concerned about the validity of our relationship as long as the dynamic is unbalanced by needing to protect him, but I'll take every opportunity I can to prove I'm all in.

I grab his hips, dragging him into me, the book smashing

between us. "I like *you*. And I want you to spread your stuff all over my apartment. Clothes, shoes, jewelry, makeup, books, whatever you got. Do your worst, Reynolds."

He shivers in my arms. "Gods. It's so weird hearing someone call me that. I—" He drops his eyes to the book he's still holding.

Hand on my chest, he pushes back to free some space, then flips the book open to a page near the middle. It's a journal, or maybe a scrapbook; I spot a few ticket stubs, some scrawled notes, a ribbon.

But the page he opens to has a photo, and he turns it to me.

It's Bel in his demon form, his rose-gold skin gleaming, sun-kissed in what looks like a park, or maybe a backyard? He's younger, his face plump, his hair long enough to brush his shoulders, his mouth open in a gap-toothed, laughing smile. He's with two human girls, one a little older than him, one younger, all squished together mid-giggle, the older girl holding the camera in a dogpile selfie. Even with him in his demon form and them as pale-skinned humans, they look like him in the nebulous way relatives do; a similar nose, a similar bone structure.

"That's Mila." Bel points to the older girl. "And Jemma. My cousins."

I gently touch the edge of the photo. "You look happy."

"I lived with them when I was growing up," he says to the picture. "I was two when the adventure party captured my parents, but I was still a descendant of Galaxrien, so they wanted to keep an eye on me. Rather than ship me off to protective custody immediately, they put me with my only other living relative: my mom's sister. Pretty sure she only agreed to take me when the adventure party paid her, because *wow*, did Aunt Orla hate me."

I scowl, and Bel looks up like he can hear it.

He shakes his head helplessly. "My dad corrupted her sister. I told you—he swept my mom up in his extremist promises to resurrect a demon lord. Aunt Orla was terrified I'd do the same thing to her kids, but she was a single mom and needed the extra income." He shrugs. "Mila and Jemma didn't hate me, though. They knew what I was—the adventure party had me do illusion magic back then, too, saw off my horns and hide my tail. My genetics aren't exactly subtle. But I got to be me sometimes." He looks fondly at the picture, the kind of fondness weighted with longing.

"They're who you're talking to?" I ask. "When you say to *keep dancing*?"

He wipes at his cheek, but when he looks up again, his eyes are clear. Probably through sheer force of will, and he smiles the same way, pushing it on his face whether it wants to be there or not.

"When the adventure party had me leave," he continues quietly, like talking louder is asking too much, "I was fifteen. I barely got to say goodbye—the Galaxrien cultists had just tried to do a ritual in the middle of the town we were living in. I don't know where Mila and Jemma are, if they were able to stay once I left. They're safe, though; Ilbryen told me that much. I can't contact them. It's better for them to not be associated with me. I . . . I just want them to know I'm still thinking of them. That I miss them."

My heart cracks. I want to offer to find them for him. I could get the info out of Ilbryen.

But he's right. As long as the cultists are after him, as long as he's a descendant of Galaxrien Vossen, he's in danger, and so is anyone who knows the truth about him.

And *that's* what's more heartbreaking than anything. That he'll never be truly safe. That he'll never be as free as he makes me feel.

In that moment, I swear to myself that I won't just keep him safe—I'll find a way to get him out of this threat permanently. Whatever it takes.

Bel's eyes tear, and he sniffs hard before snapping the journal shut and staring at the middle of my chest.

"If things get dangerous," he whispers, then huffs and shuts his eyes. "I know you're supposed to keep me safe, but I can't lose you, Orok."

"Sweetheart, look at me."

He does, red stains immediately coloring his cheeks, and I hear the echo of what I said, of me telling him to keep his eyes on me this morning.

I smile, wordlessly letting him know I caught the connection.

"Do you trust me?" I ask.

He nods.

"I will do everything in my power to keep you safe," I say, and as he's sucking in a breath to argue, I add, "and to keep *myself* safe, too. You won't lose anyone else you care about, I promise."

He looks dubious. It's an impossible promise.

Luckily, Seb and I have already survived the impossible.

"On that note," I rub my hands up and down his sides, "and since we're in a sharing mood, I need to tell you about someone important to me who can help us."

Chapter Twelve

This day has been a year long. And it isn't over yet, because I refuse to let us go to sleep without my apartment being warded; and for it to be warded properly, I need Seb. I could ask Gulus to set up some spells, but until someone figures out who in their adventure party leaked the info about Galaxrien's descendant being associated with Urzoth, and on top of seeing what kind of place they let Tem keep Bel in, that whole party's on thin ice. Given that Seb's been blowing up my phone for hours, asking *why* I need him to set up extra security for me, I know I won't get our wards without an explanation.

Bel is dozing against the window by the time I park at my place. Even though all I want to do is carry him up to my bed, I wake him.

"Hey," I whisper. "We're here."

His eyes flutter open and he blinks at the parking garage, his face set in a cute rumpled scowl.

That scowl smooths in realization, and he looks at me. "Your friend's coming over?"

"Yeah. He's on his way."

Bel nods. I told him about me and Seb, from our childhood to a brief recap of how Camp Merethyl's horrors bonded us; Bel knew some of it from the public details of the lawsuit. But I told him how I went to college and grad school to follow Seb, and that I've been working on my codependency because I know I have obsessive predispositions.

I hope Bel won't be jealous of Seb, won't be uncomfortable about our relationship. But as he sits there in the dark, orienting to being awake, his brow pinches in concern.

"You're sure you're okay with bringing him in on this?" I double-check.

Bel shifts toward me. "Yes. If you're going to do this, you need people *you* trust. You didn't ask for any of this, so the least I can do is let you use who—"

"We've been over this. I *did* ask for this. I *want* this. If I do something you disagree with, or something that makes you uncomfortable, *tell me*. Does bringing Seb in make you uncomfortable?"

He hesitates, and I'm close to texting Seb not to come when he shakes his head.

"What if he doesn't like me?" he asks, then cringes. "Gods, that's pathetic. I mean, what if he doesn't like you doing this for me? It's dangerous; Ilbryen definitely manipulated you. There are a dozen reasons why someone who cares about you would be against me. Seb's important to you, so I want him to like me. But I don't know how to—"

I lean forward and kiss him. It's been way too long since I did; when was the last time? In the hotel?

My lips find his, silencing him, and I slip my tongue along the seam of his mouth until he moans.

"You've already met Seb, remember?" I tell him. "Outside the stadium."

"I barely spoke to him."

"He knows how I feel about you, so he'll love you, and he'll hear me out about why I'm doing this. It's expected he'll have reservations, but I'll talk to him."

"We both will." Bel runs his fingers through my beard. "He can ask me anything, anything at all. My life's yours now, I swear."

I grab his wrist, those words tattooing themselves at the base of my stomach, a painful bite that I know is crossing a line.

"That's not what this arrangement means," I growl. I tell him that because I know I should, but a larger, darker part of me wants to snatch him up and make him say that again.

My life's yours now.

Bel melts into my grip and rests his lips over mine.

"Maybe not," he croons into my mouth. "But it's what we both want it to be."

Gods, this is a mistake. Seb's going to see right through how unhealthy this is and call me on it.

Fuck, what will I do if he *does* tell me I should back out? I can't. I won't see Bel shipped off to what's more or less imprisonment. But beyond that, I want him here. I need him in a way that's swept over me in a suffocating whirlwind, and yes, that's harmful. Yes, that's a red flag.

But I'm past caring.

I get us out of the car. With both our bags from the trip hooked over my shoulder and the boxes from Bel's apartment stacked in my arms, I lead us to the elevator, then up to my floor. Every security feature grabs my attention now, how I have to punch in a code to access the elevator but it stops at any floor, meaning whoever has that code can easily get in. And then there's the long expanse of open hallway leading to my door; it has a security camera, sure, but is it recording? If the building owner doesn't write me back by tomorrow morning, I'll stop at her office.

Did Gulus get in here? He's probably watching from a distance like he has been, likely in a building nearby—there's a hotel diagonal across the street. Maybe he's there?

I juggle the boxes to reach for my keys when Bel takes them from me and unlocks the apartment I point to. He swings the door open and I stumble inside, bumping on the entryway light with my elbow and setting his boxes and our travel bags on the tiled floor.

As I shut the door behind us and throw the deadbolt and chain, Bel looks around with his mouth slightly agape. It's a far cry from his old apartment, and seeing it now, fresh off being there, the differences are . . . drastic. The walls are clean and white, the fixtures all high-end, and it smells like vanilla air freshener.

"Guestroom's through there," I say, pointing to the room on our immediate left. "It has a closet that's basically empty, so if the master one is too small, feel free to expand. Straight ahead is the open-plan kitchen, living, and dining room, and off to the right is—"

"I called it, baby. He's moving his little cheerleader in."

Halfway over the threshold of the main room, I spot Seb and Thio stretched out on my oversized couch. The sun set about an hour ago, and they're lurking in the glow of their phones.

I pop on the overhead light and brace my hands on my hips.

"Did you? Move him in?" Thio tosses his phone onto the coffee table with a groan. "Just let me win *one* bet involving you. Just one."

I roll my eyes. "How often do you two bet on me?"

Seb, his head in Thio's lap, grins. "Frequently enough that you've become a regular part of our foreplay. It's creating a troubling Pavlovian response, honestly."

Behind me, Bel makes a confused chirp.

I rub the skin over my nose, sigh, and step aside. "You remember *my little cheerleader*? Seb, Thio." I point them out to Bel.

Bel inches forward, arms folded protectively around himself. "Hi."

I tug him into my side and he looks at me with a forced smile.

Seb bolts to his feet, fixing his twisted T-shirt. Oh gods, they were making out on my couch, weren't they?

"Here's what I don't get," Seb says. "You're moving in together, right?"

I hesitate. "Yes."

"Which is cause for *celebration*. My gods, O, you found someone willing to put up with your shit, and he's cute as fuck and basically an anthropomorphized woodland creature."

Bel mouths *woodland creature?*

"And yet," Seb carries on, coming closer. "You text me all that vague shit about needing to update your security, and you come in with this weird, strained energy like someone died. What's going on? Am I breaking out champagne or is there a body we need to hide?"

He's joking. Sort of. Worry slips free in the way he taps his foot.

"Okay," I start. "I'm going to need you to sit down and not freak out."

In direct contrast to that, Thio pushes up from the couch.

I grunt. "Guys, seriously. It'll be easier if you—"

"I'm the mortal descendant of Galaxrien Vossen."

My head snaps down to where Bel's still tucked up against my side, but he steps away, fisted hands unwinding from his chest and shoulders pulling back. He looks exhausted, his hair mussed from sleeping in the car, bags under his eyes. And now, facing Seb and Thio, he's got that resigned look again. Like he knows whatever's going to happen won't go in his favor, but he's accepted that inevitability.

Seb and Thio are frozen. Their faces unreadable.

"My real name is Belzaroth Reynolds," Bel continues. "And Orok agreed to be my new handler to keep me safe from the Galaxrien cultists trying to use me to resurrect him. Summon him. Free him from the pit he's trapped in on the Demonic Plane. Whatever."

He looks up at me, fatigue and gratitude and a lifetime of emotions colliding all at once.

"And he's far too nice," Bel says, talking to Seb and Thio, but looking at me. "And I'm taking awful advantage of him. I expect you to hate me. I *want* you to hate me, because then it means you're looking out for him, and *someone* should be looking out for him. I just ask that you help, not for me, but for him. So he can be safe, too."

He releases a shuddering breath and sways, face pale, before he faces Seb and Thio again. I don't know where he finds the strength; he's had his entire world flipped upside down in one day, and he's still standing.

Pride swells in my chest.

"You probably have questions," Bel offers, his hands open.

Seb and Thio are still frozen by the couch, wide-eyed and silent. Seb's focus shifts from Bel to me, and I'm not sure what my face is doing exactly, but he must read some micro expression that has him nodding conclusively.

He shares a look with Thio. Who kisses Seb's cheek and dips around him.

"We need food," Thio says.

I blink out of my stupor.

Shit. When did Bel last eat? We didn't stop for anything after we left HQ.

"Gods, sweetheart." I touch his arm. "You must be starving."

He frowns, his hands clenching again. "Um. What's happening?"

"I'm making dinner," Thio says, puttering around my kitchen, pulling out ingredients. "Any food restrictions?"

"N-no," Bel stammers. "What—"

Seb flops back down on the couch. "Pasta?" he calls to his fiancé.

"Duh."

"You're the love of my life."

Thio glances up at him with a wink.

Bel leans closer to me. "They heard what I said, right?"

I could kiss Seb and Thio for their reaction. Like it isn't a big deal, like it's any other life update; none of the shouting accusations or anger Bel was clearly expecting.

"They did," I promise. "Come on. Let's have a seat."

I tug him toward the matching white armchairs by the window, but when he goes to take his own chair, I pull him into my lap.

As Thio cooks, Seb tells me about a project at his lab, and the mundanity of it has Bel relaxing into me, bit by bit.

By the time Thio serves us each a bowl of steaming fettucine alfredo, the concrete-level tension in Bel's muscles has bled out and he's nestled back against me.

Seb catches my eye when he notices, and I shoot him a grateful smile that he returns.

"So." Seb swallows a bite of food and shoves his glasses up his nose. "Galaxrien Vossen, huh? That sucks."

It's a testament to the empathy in Seb's tone that Bel doesn't stiffen.

He stares down into his bowl, stirring the noodles. "It really, really does," he whispers. His gaze locks with mine and his face softens. "Less so recently, though."

Thio smiles, his shoulder resting against Seb's where they sit side by side on the couch. "Sounds like there's a story."

Bel gnaws on his lower lip, a question in his eyes. I smile encouragingly.

He blows out a breath and tells them everything that's happened the past twenty-four hours. Well, the PG parts, from the cultist attack in the news to the visit from Ilbryen, Gulus, and Tem. Bel also gives a brief summary of what living with Tem was like, but he's quick to gloss over any actual details, maybe sensing the way it's my turn to stiffen at the mention of Tem.

When the story's done, our bowls are empty, and Bel seems to be, too.

"This was really good pasta," he murmurs, drained, as he gingerly sets his empty bowl on the coffee table. "Thank you, Thio."

Thio's smile is cockeyed but sweet. "My pleasure. Sounds like it's the least I could do after the day you've had. Hell, the past few years you've had."

Bel sags into me on a sigh that's tinged with disbelief, like he still can't reconcile the calm way they're accepting all this information.

But I can practically hear Seb's brain spinning.

"The most pressing part of that story," Seb starts, and his analytical gaze goes to me, "is that people are trying to kill him?"

"That's why I texted you," I say, rubbing a hand up and down Bel's side. "We need the apartment warded. Like, airtight. And maybe a few warded charms he can wear at all times, in case I'm not with him. And can you make some illusion counter-potion, if I get you the components Bel's adventure party uses?"

Bel twists to look at me, surprise and confusion in his tired eyes.

"So you can be in your own form around the house," I tell him. "If you want?"

He smiles, eyes shiny. "I'd like that."

My own smile stretches. "Good."

"Consider it done." Seb claps and jumps off the couch. "First, one magical Fort Knox, coming up. Baby?"

Thio's already tugging a bag onto the couch while Seb gets to work unloading stuff from his component belt.

Bel's head lists into my neck and he lets out another disbelieving sigh. "It's that simple?"

Is it that simple?

I stare at the side of Seb's face as he works, but he doesn't look at me now.

Neither he nor Thio said much of anything through Bel's story. No real questions, no prodding. Just easy acceptance.

Too easy.

"Yeah." I press a kiss to Bel's hair. "How about you get some rest? These spells could take a while."

He lifts his head on a pout. "You have to be tired, too."

"I'll be right behind you." I nod to the hall straight off the kitchen. "My room's through there."

"And you—" He swallows. Licks his lips. "You want me there. Not the guestroom."

"This is real, remember? I want you there."

Part of Bel relaxes slightly. But he seems to realize that when he leaves, a deeper conversation will be had; he's not able to hide the shimmer of panic before he drops his head and pushes out of my lap.

"I'll just—"

I grab his hand and tug him until I can claim his mouth with mine. "It's all going to be okay now. I promise."

"We promise, too," Seb offers. "Ain't no one getting past my wards. We'll take care of you."

Bel turns to Seb and Thio, who are still setting up items on my coffee table, our discarded dishes moved to the floor.

"Thank you," he says to them, hands worrying at each other. "This isn't at all what I expected, but—thank you. Really. I don't know how to tell you—"

Thio waves him off. "You don't have to."

"I told you it was a nuthouse," Seb says with a grin. "You're part of it now."

Bel lingers, shifting on his feet, but bobs his head in reluctant acceptance.

I want to assure him again, promise it's really, truly fine, but my focus goes back to Seb and I feel unsaid things hanging over us like a storm cloud.

Everything *will* be fine. I have to make sure of it.

Bel keeps his head down as he gathers our dishes, puts them in the sink, and makes for my room, and it isn't until the door clicks shut that I let myself breathe.

"All right," I say. "Let's hear it."

Seb kneels by the coffee table as he arranges a stone, a lock, and a string. "Hear what? Thio, hand me the beeswax candle."

Thio digs in the bag. "For a protection ward? You want the soy candle."

"No—beeswax. It'll be stronger."

"*Soy* will be stronger."

Seb glares at Thio, who's holding out what's probably a soy candle.

"Seriously." I bend forward, elbows on my knees. "I know you've got opinions. So, say them, especially now, while Bel's not around to hear. He already thinks you two will blame him."

Seb gawps at me. "Why would we blame him?"

"For bringing me into this? I don't know, he feels bad. I told him it's nonsense."

"Of course it's nonsense. He didn't choose to be part of a crazy family. We all know how that is."

Thio grunts. "Genetics. Fucking brutal."

"If he feels bad because he coerced you into protecting him," Seb says, "then I'd hate him. But from the way he described it, that's not what happened, and you both have an even playing field of reasons to distrust each other, so you're kind of at a weird stalemate."

My face scrunches. "What?"

"He could've been playing you this whole time to get you to become his handler—but it didn't seem like it occurred to him that you were an option until you offered and the adventure party people agreed, and *wow*, that would've been a serious long game to play. You, on the other hand, could be planning to turn over Galaxrien's descendant to the Urzoth church, because I'm sure they'd *love* being able to eliminate a tool of their god's enemy."

A stab of nausea bolts through me at the thought of people like Reverend Drach finding out who Bel really is. It isn't just cultists I have to keep him safe from.

"But," Seb continues, "even though you and I both know you're not doing that, Bel doesn't—"

"He does."

"It's still a big risk for him." Seb shrugs. "So, stalemate. You both could be screwing each other over. But you're not. Because I think, not so secretly, neither of you are maniacal psychos. You're two big ol' saps with hearts in your eyes."

"I like him," Thio adds. "I like him for you. He's exactly who I always pictured."

"Right?" Seb knocks Thio's thigh with his fist. "A sweet little pink-haired amalgamation of Timothée Chalamet and Troye Sivan."

"Timothée Chalamet!" Thio snaps his fingers. "*That's* who he reminds me of, thank you."

I blink at Thio, then Seb. "You don't have anything else to say?"

"What more should we say?" Seb asks.

"That I rushed into this!" I hiss, fighting to keep my voice down. "It's only been, like, a month, and it started as a PR stunt, and I have to commit to Urzoth indefinitely to keep him safe, and his entire life is dependent on me now, and *this isn't healthy*."

I'm panting like that storm cloud unleashed and all the things I've been ignoring are crashing down on me at once.

Maybe the unease I felt wasn't from Seb.

Maybe it was from *me*.

Seb's expression falls. He knee-walks closer to me and takes my hands. "O. I know you don't believe this, because you've kind of made it part of your personality, but there's nothing wrong with you. You aren't broken."

I grimace. "I have not made being broken my personality."

"To be fair, we *were* broken for a very long time. And I'm not saying we're both perfectly functional, wholly healed adults—gods, no. But I think you see healing as a straight line, and any symptoms mean going backward, but I've found healing is more of a . . . squiggle." He draws his finger in the air, making a convoluted, twisting shape that, even so, progresses from left to right. "Sometimes we loop back on something we thought we'd gotten over. Sometimes we spiral around something we *know* how to overcome. But we're always a little further away from where we started, even if it doesn't feel like it. *That's* healing: recognizing that what hurt us can never have us in that exact situation again because we've chosen to keep moving forward."

My brows pinch in some strangled mix of hope and horror. "How—what the fuck, Seb?"

He frowns. "What?"

"I've been going to a therapist for almost a decade now, and he's never said anything as concise as what you just said. Where the hell did that come from?"

Thio, back to setting out components for the wards, looks up with a grin. "He reads self-help books before we go to bed."

My jaw fully distends. "*What?* Since when?"

"Since he—"

Without looking back, Seb kicks his fiancé, who grumbles when it makes him knock over a jar of herbs.

"Hush, you," Seb says. "That's not important right now."

But Thio's face gets kind of dreamy and dopey, and Seb clears his throat forcefully.

I narrow my eyes at Thio. "Since when?" I repeat.

Seb looks back at Thio, having another of their silent conversations, until Seb grunts and pokes me in the chest, more flushed and nervous than I've seen him in a while.

"Since I decided I'd like to start having kids as soon as we get married and this fool"—he shoots his thumb at Thio—"agreed for some reason, and I'd like to be a little more put together before I usher life into this world, so yeah, I read self-help books now." He picks at a string on my shorts. "And those self-help books all sound like *you*, spouting your therapizing nonsense. Only a lot of it isn't quite as nonsensical as I used to think it was."

My eyes were already tearing but they heat all over again, and my throat wells with unexpected joy. "You're going to have kids?"

"Apparently. But that's far, far off in the future, and what's here in the present with us is *you*, and the fact that no, Orok. You're not broken. That's where I was, right?"

"Right," Thio says, and drops a kiss on Seb's shoulder.

Seb blushes again.

Gods, I love them.

"Anyway." Seb slaps my leg. "This relationship with Belzaroth—Bel? It makes a lot of sense. You have a massive hero complex. I used to time how long your hookups would last by how much they needed you."

I scour a hand over my face and snort. "You didn't."

"I did. There were a few I thought you'd have more than a casual repeat with, but they always proved too independent. You need someone who needs you. You need to *save* someone, like you always tried to save me; only fuck if I'd let you." He glares suddenly. "Like, don't think for a second we don't know you're the reason our landlord suddenly redid the entire building's plumbing and installed a new shower for us. *Annual renovations* my ass."

I don't even try to deny it. Just look down at my hands. "You said your shower was crap."

"But it's not your job to save me. That's my point—you need to be needed, and I've always fought you tooth and nail over every little thing. For Bel to come along, this guy who clearly needs you, and he's open to it? You didn't stand a chance, my friend. Hook, line, and sink *him*."

"Poetic."

"Thank you. But—" He bends until I meet his gaze again. "You're doing fine. Really. Caring for people is not a weakness. I think part of you believes that because of all that fuckery Urzoth's church spews about strength in aggression only. But it's *bullshit*. You feel more than anyone I've ever met, and it's your greatest strength.

And that guy in there?" Seb nods toward my room. "He definitely needs that kind of strength right now. Stop questioning yourself."

"But what if I'm wrong again?"

I don't know where the question comes from. It doesn't even sound like me. It's brittle and trembling and small, and when I ask it, I get hit by a flash of who I was at Camp Merethyl.

That's who asked that question.

Teenage Orok, curled up on his bunk at a camp where they'd beat my best friend if I failed. They tortured us and called it *training*. All the doctrine I spent my childhood adhering to—strength in physicality—got twisted against me, and everyone who taught me those original things, my mom and our church leaders, they all told me that if I was truly strong, I wouldn't be in pain. If I was truly strong, I wouldn't let the people at Camp Merethyl hurt me.

Seb cocks his head. "Again? When were you wrong before?"

I try to stand. "I'm tired. I didn't mean to—"

"*Hell* no. Sit your ass back down. What do you mean?"

Bel's right; not being able to deflect sucks.

I drop back on the chair and stare at the coffee table, spread with components for several different protection wards. Thio's on the couch, and Seb stays at my feet.

"Urzoth," I whisper. Tears come again; one leaks down my cheek. "I was wrong about Urzoth. What if I'm wrong about loving someone again?"

Because I loved him.

I did.

I was so devoted to our faith. I was obsessed with him—that's where it started. My first obsession was Urzoth and I let it consume me, let it *own* me. *Mine* and *his* in such an intermingled knot that I barely knew where I ended and Urzoth began. I gave it my everything, gave him sweat and blood and scars and *screams*.

And when I needed him, when I really, deeply needed help, I got *nothing*.

I was wrong to trust in that obsessive love. What if I'm wrong about Bel, too?

"Do you love me?" Seb asks, a gentle nudge.

I give him a flat look, seeing where he's going with this. "Of course."

"Were you wrong about that, too?"

Sometimes. Yes. I followed him to university. Made him live with me. Used him as a crutch when my night terrors got bad, and he became my security blanket.

But I got two degrees that I did, actually, enjoy. Did they help me in my career? No, but I couldn't have foreseen playing pro rawball. And I didn't *make* him live with me; he wanted to every time, and I think he needed it, too. If *he'd* been the one having night terrors? I'd have been his blanket. I'd have done anything he needed. I *tried* to do anything he needed.

I love him, and I was consumed in him, but it didn't crush me like it did with Urzoth.

"You've been right about loving someone before, too," Seb whispers. "The better question is: What if you're right again?"

Tears come ruthlessly this time and I bury my face in my hands. "Shit," I moan.

Seb rubs my back. "Get to bed, big guy. We'll throw up these protection wards and crash in your guestroom. If that's all right?"

I drop my hands so they hang between my knees. "Yeah. Please stay." It's always better if he's nearby.

Seb smiles. "Then we'll stay." He stands, groaning as he stretches, and cracks his knuckles. "You'll want to get gone, babe. I'm gonna summon Nick."

Seb's fox familiar gives him magic boosts, but Nick's invisible and used to announce his presence by biting me. The tiny hat-wearing asshole hasn't done that in years, thankfully, but it's still a running joke.

I shudder and undercut it with a smile as I haul myself off the chair.

"Evil fox aside, you'll be a great dad," I tell him. To Thio, "You both will."

Seb beams, nearly shining with the force of his smile. "Thanks, man. And you'll be a great Uncle Orok."

I don't think I've ever giggled. I mean, I'm huge. Huge people don't tend to *giggle*.

But I do.

Because that image? *Uncle Orok*. Fuck, I *want* that.

Seb bursts out laughing, and even Thio snort-chuckles.

I leave them to their warding and head down the hall to my room.

Inside, the curtains are still wide, showing the city-washed night sky; not a star in sight, but plenty of speckled building lights, their own sort of cosmos.

A lump under my blankets is motionless.

I wash up in the bathroom and change into sleep pants before plodding quietly to the bed. The huge mattress dips as I climb in, blankets shifting around the lump to peel back and reveal Bel, wrapped in another of my too-big shirts.

He peeks up at me. His gaze holds questions, eyes reflecting the city lights, but we've talked enough today. *Done* enough today.

"I told you Seb would like you," I whisper down to him. "Thio, too."

The edge of Bel's mouth flickers. "The feeling's mutual. For both of them."

I pull him against me and he immediately complies, adjusting until he's burrowed under my arm, his head on my chest.

"Thank you," he whispers. It's massive, encompassing how very much this day has held.

The kiss I leave on his curls has him shivering and moving even closer.

"Sleep," I tell him, and he obeys.

I wake up the next morning to find Bel in his demon form on a barstool at my kitchen island, helping Thio chop vegetables for omelets and laughing with Seb, Nick presumably curled in Bel's lap, if the small floating bowler hat is anything to go by.

The simple domesticity of this scene hits me with a sudden certainty: he's worth it.

All the hookups Seb talked about me having, the years of pushing people away because, yeah, I was terrified falling for anyone would hurt me again—all of that was worth it. Bel was worth the wait, but he's also worth the *weight*, the pressure of knowing this won't be easy, from the dangers stalking him to my own baggage.

Bel's smiling eyes lock on me in the hallway, and he lights up even more.

I smile back.

Chapter Thirteen

That duffel bag on my bed was not packed when I got in the shower.

I frown at it from the bathroom's doorway, towel around my waist, humid air billowing into the bedroom.

I had my game-day stuff spread across the bed like usual, but it's tucked inside the bulging Hellhounds bag now, with the suit I planned on wearing lying next to it.

Is my suit . . . ironed?

Pieces connect and I grunt a helpless laugh. "Bel?"

Something clatters in the kitchen.

A beat later, he pops up in the doorway, drying his hands on a dishcloth. His eyes widen at my bare chest, the towel low on my hips.

Spots of deeper pink burnish his pale cheeks. "Mm. I didn't think we had time for that," he says with a salacious smirk.

No, we don't have time for *that*, but I give myself a moment to eat him up anyway, because he's here, and I can't get enough.

He doesn't have to dress up for the game-day arrival, so he's in orange sweatpants, white sneakers, and a black Hellhounds tank, his tail tucked away and body transformed to human with the illusion spray. Around his neck is a band of white faux pearls Seb enchanted—if Bel crushes one between his fingers, both Seb and I will get a magic ping in our heads letting us know that he needs help. They also emit a general protection ward, keeping him safe from enchantments and most magical attacks. He can make the whole necklace vanish with his illusion spray when he has to wear his cheerleading uniform, but he hasn't done that yet; he knows I think the pearls look sexy on him.

Bel's smirk turns a little breathless when my eyes rise back to his. "We *could* have time for it," he prods.

I shake my head and rub a hand across my trimmed beard. "No, that's not—what's *that*?"

I wave at the duffel bag.

"Your game-day stuff?" Bel's head tips to the side. "Did I pack something wrong?"

"You shouldn't have packed *anything*, sweetheart."

He blushes again, meek this time, fingers toying with the dishcloth. "It was there, I had time."

"And what are you doing now?"

The toe of his shoe digs into the carpet, and his mouth opens and closes a few times before he mumbles, "Meal prepping."

The buzzer on the washing machine chooses that moment to go off.

I arch an eyebrow at him.

"And some light laundry." Bel breaks out of his humility with a frustrated groan. "I live here, too, right? I'm doing what normal people do when they live together. Housekeeping."

I cross the room and wrap my arms around him. He falls against me, sulking to my chest.

It's been a week since he moved in. A week of carpooling to HQ for practices or meetings, and me only being okay with Bel out of my sight because he's got that necklace, and Gulus is still a nebulous shadow in the distance. A week of Seb and Thio coming over for dinner, and Bel begging Thio to teach him how to cook. A week of Bel immediately dropping his human form when the door shuts behind us. Of him rehearsing his cheer routines in the living room. Of me buying tons of stepladders and lifts to make my giant-sized apartment accessible for him, and filling an entire cupboard with dark chocolate peanut butter cups just to hear him cackle with glee.

Of this place being our own little haven.

I bend down to rest my forehead on his. "We talked about this. You don't have to earn your keep."

Bel looks up at me without disengaging our foreheads. "I'm not going to freeload off you. You won't let me pay rent, so you're going to have to get used to me cooking and cleaning."

"And packing for me?"

He pulls back and runs his fingers through my chest hair. "I'll stop doing chores if you stop the research."

My dining room table has been overtaken by old college books I pulled out of storage, texts I ordered online, and research Ilbryen shipped over when I asked for their info on Galaxrien's cult.

The official religion of the Temple of Galaxrien Vossen is well documented, but the specific ritual the cultists are obsessed with is less so. It's based on an offhanded comment made by a Galaxrien priest generations ago about their demon lord *breaking free.* The comment wasn't even a full-blown prophecy and was never officially sanctioned by the Temple; it was one guy waxing hopeful about Galaxrien escaping the pit in the Demonic Plane where Urzoth Shieldsworn trapped him.

Nevertheless, a subset of the Galaxrien faith took it as gospel, and cultists have added on over the years: someone claimed it'd happen on a spring equinox; someone else countered with summer; then it went back to spring and seems to have stuck there, despite the cultists repeatedly doing rituals on days that aren't *any* equinox. Sometimes the ritual involves a full sacrifice, sometimes a piece of his descendant's body. One cultist swears the ritual involves handcuffs to *symbolize Galaxrien's suffering*. Someone else claims it won't work unless they have a bottle of ghost pepper hot sauce to *summon the flames of hell*.

This is why the cultists' ritual changes so often. None of them knows what they're doing. And they're all dumbasses.

Ghost pepper hot sauce? Seriously?

There's been an uptick among people of demonic ancestry in the news since that attack, decrying the cultists for targeting them—even though the guy they tried to sacrifice wasn't even demonic. The Urzoth church has also been making headlines for their *demonstrations of strength* in response to their member being taken, mostly public fights organized by the church; but people seem more sympathetic to Urzoth worshippers being upset this time around.

It brought me back to another issue: How did the cultists know Galaxrien's descendant is tied to the Urzoth church now?

Ilbryen also sent over a list of everyone who knows about Bel, who might have leaked his info to the cultists. It's not a long list—Ilbryen, Gulus, Tem, three other members of their immediate adventure party, as well as a clerk who helps organize sensitive missions between their larger union of adventure parties.

I'm not exactly sure how to go about investigating. Ilbryen's doing her own investigation, but do I hire someone to dig into them? They're scattered all over the country—how do I question people who aren't even in this city? I can barely get a read on Gulus. He came to inspect the apartment, nodded in approval of my security wards, and left. Barely said four words to us. Is he the mole? Hell if I know.

There might have been a bit of validity in Tem's concerns about my qualifications. I am, when it comes down to it, an athlete with a lot of money and an interest in world religions. Is this as far as my ability to analyze plays and defensive maneuvers can go?

Is it going to be enough to keep Bel safe?

I run my thumb across his necklace. "Bel—"

"You don't need to research," he says. "I can tell you anything you want to know about the ritual or the cult. I'm a walking, talking, dancing encyclopedia of demon lord knowledge. You don't need those books. For instance, I can tell you that this"—he waves at the apartment, encompassing the wards, the general security I've offered—"is as far as you can protect me. There's no secret way out. You'd have to change who I am."

I give him an unintimidated stare. "I'm not going to stop looking for a way to save you. I'm not going to accept that this is the rest of your life."

He smiles, but it's tinged by that resignation I hate on him so much. That he's given up to his fate, like he expects the cult to get him one day, and there's no other hope.

"Do we have to think so far ahead?" he asks. "I'm happier than I've been in almost a decade. I want to enjoy being safe. With *you*. You can't stop an entire cult, and I don't expect you to. What you're doing is more than enough."

But it's not enough for me.

While Bel may only be thinking in the day-to-day, chopping survival into immediate moments, I'm greedy. I don't just want moments.

I want years.

I want a lifetime.

Rather than continue this conversation, I twist down to brush my lips across his jaw.

"Have I told you lately that I'm glad you're here?" I breathe the words into his ear and he, predictably, shivers.

I love that I know exactly what buttons to push to get reactions out of him.

"Prove it." He bumps his hardening cock against my leg, and I chuckle over a groan.

We've only traded hand jobs and sloppy blow jobs the past week. Much to Bel's disappointment—but it was risky enough fucking him with my admittedly monster cock for his first time. I want to make sure he recovers, that we ease into anything like regularity.

It has been a week, though.

And today is going to be a roller coaster of shit from the start, so maybe it'll help pad the bumps to know there's something good waiting at the end.

I bite his neck above the pearls, and suck, a flash of aggression he wasn't expecting by the way he chirps and wriggles against me.

"Orok." My name comes in a moan and I suck harder, getting a mewl, another sexy wriggle.

"Tonight," I say into the spot I abused, dragging my lips back and forth over it. "You good to give me your ass tonight, sweetheart?"

Bel whines, the roll of his exhale across my chest making my nipples tighten. "Yes. Gods, yes. Please."

I smile. Even with the stress of researching the cult and fielding today's events, my face hurts—I've been smiling nonstop.

He drags his nose through my chest hair, nuzzling, and asks, "Is that our reward for surviving lunch with your parents?"

My head drops back on a disgruntled moan. "Please don't link sex to my parents."

Bel pulls away with a laugh, his gaze dragging down my body again before he swats me with the dishcloth. "Get dressed, or we're both going to be really, really late."

"Might miss the game entirely." I loosen the towel and let it drop. "Oh no. That'd be awful."

Bel adjusts himself through his sweatpants, eyes hot on my hard dick.

Would it be so bad if I . . . didn't play today?

Yes. No less because I'd lose my contract and be unable to pay for Bel's safety.

But I'd also look like a coward to my old team.

I grab my boxers next to the suit—did he iron these, too? Gods—and tug them on as Bel's hungry look fades.

"You're going to kick the Chimeras' asses today," he tells me. "Like, an embarrassing win. They're going to cry."

As long as we're speaking today into existence: "And my parents will not be at all overbearing in pushing Urzoth's doctrine on you."

"Mm. Then we'll come home, and you'll rail me so deep I'll feel you in my throat."

A cough, a laugh, and a bark try to come out of me all at once.

Bel flutters his fingers and skips out of the room.

Fuck, he is a demon, isn't he? Sent straight from hell to drag me down.

And I'm so eager for it.

The Chimeras chose a cityscape for their rawball field layout. Skyscrapers, alleyways, even subway tunnels under the street. Levitated cameras fly all around to catch every piece of the action and broadcast it to the screens over the stadium and the fans at home, feeding the energy of the crowd, a constant dull roar of cheering and applause and noise.

One screen pans across the cheerleaders, and I spot Bel thrusting his hips and flurrying black pom-poms, and it settles me.

This is any other game. I have my role to play, and I'll do it, and I'm *good* at it.

Marlow's glowering next to me where the two of us stand on a rooftop midfield, waiting for the game to start. She's not a fan of any field configuration that requires climbing, and I nudge her, giving her an encouraging smile when she looks at me.

"We got this," I sign. I've been learning.

Marlow gives me a horrified look. "*Of course* we got this. We're going to decimate them. I won't accept anything less."

Surprise has my brows popping up, and Marlow rolls her eyes.

"Seriously?" She punches my shoulder. "What'd you think I was upset about? These assholes are your rivals, so they're *our* rivals. We told you."

She nods to a building across the road, where Aaron and one of our team's wizards crouch in a rooftop garden. They see us looking and do a Hellhounds bark, which gets picked up by other teammates here, there, farther out; a chorus of hooting and growling.

They don't even know how bad things got with the Chimeras, just that I've been roiling in nerves over the game. And they're still this eager to throw down for me.

Really inconvenient time to get mushy. But damn.

Marlow jostles my arm. "See? We're out for blood."

The ref blows a whistle. The game ball drops, and it's go time.

I shake off the emotions and focus. No room for distractions; if my team's this zealous for me, the best way I can pay them back is to crush this game.

Marlow darts forward, propelling herself off the building; I follow suit. Aaron's wizard hits us with slow-fall spells so we drop to the sidewalk easily, then both of us take off, zipping through the city streets toward where the ball fell. I keep my eyes sharp for any movement in alleys or from above while Marlow ducks her head and *runs*, her singular objective to get that ball, get it across the field, and score in the Chimeras' goal. Meanwhile, *my* singular objective is to let her be able to do that.

Somewhere downfield, an explosion goes up, smoke billowing

with tinges of crackling blue—a lightning spell? I know my team holds back on anything so violent until later in the game, so it's gotta be the Chimeras, which has me gritting my teeth.

They're the ones coming into this game like they've got something to prove?

Marlow reaches an intersection and lets me gain on her so I can go out first and take whatever might be waiting for us. Above, Aaron and his wizard should be leaping rooftops, keeping pace with us—unless the Chimeras got to them. But no ref has called the play yet, so the ball's still active, and we have to trust that our unit of the team is functional.

More explosions come from a distant part of the field and the crowd cheers, the screens above reflecting other parts of the game and stadium.

Muscles loose, I barrel into the intersection, angling left, up a wider road. I have one beat of thinking the road's clear before a body smashes into me, so solid it feels like a spell, but no—hands grab me as I'm dazed and lift me in the air.

Few people can lift someone of my size. *One*, actually, that I've met:

A minotaur defensive tank on the Chimeras.

I lurch against his grip, looking down at Naell's winded, cruel smirk. His massive horns poke out of his helmet and he scuffs his feet, his tail twitching in aggravation.

"Weakling," he bellows before hurling me across the road.

Marlow might be close by, but she doesn't have magic to soften my fall; and Aaron and his wizard clearly aren't close enough, because I go down *hard*.

My pads and helmet absorb most of the impact, but I still crash to the street and skid across the pavement, only coming to a stop when I slam against the curb.

Pain streaks out from my shoulder, radiates in dizzying flares up my neck.

For the briefest of seconds, I'm at a different game. A different field layout. But the same assholes are targeting me, only they were on my team then. They saw the opposition readying an attack, and instead of defending me, they grinned and walked away.

No.

Not this time.

Trembling, my shoulder on fire, I drag myself to my feet.

By the time I'm standing, another Chimera has Marlow pinned to a wall. Aaron and his wizard are on the ground, held at bay by Naell and four more Chimera defensive tanks—too many to make sense for any play.

A camera's on us. Did it catch what Naell did? Will the refs see? Not that it matters; he didn't do anything illegal. Just wasteful since Marlow and I didn't even have the fucking ball, but I can see our standoff on one of the screens. Can see me holding my useless arm to my chest, jaw thrust forward, face red and furious behind my face mask.

The camera cuts to Bel with the cheerleaders. His focus is lifted, presumably looking at a screen, seeing me, injured. He has a hand to his mouth and his eyes are wide with fear.

I linger on that shot of him. I should be looking at Naell and the Chimeras.

Bel, on the screen, is talking with another cheerleader, who wraps her arm around him and tries to comfort him, but he's shaking his head and clearly asking, *What happened? What happened?*

A whistle trills. Somewhere on the field, the ball's gone out of play.

At the edge of my awareness, most of the Chimeras file off the street to reset for the next play, casting smug glowers back at us.

Marlow heaves after them, retribution on her face, but Aaron catches her around the waist.

"Stop, Marlow!" I shout and sign—or try to, with one good arm. "They're not worth it."

Marlow scowls, and Naell, who lingered, barks a disgusted laugh.

"Stopping your teammate from getting revenge?" he snarls. "How far you've fallen. You're a gods-damned embarrassment,

Monroe. Can't believe they're using *you* as my god's poster child. You're a *coward*."

Naell taps the emblem on his uniform. The one that matches mine, an axe in a stone.

His shoulders lift to his ears and his hands are fisted like he expects me to attack. Like all this was to get me to redeem myself somehow, or maybe to prove I'm weak.

Months ago—hell, *weeks* ago—this confrontation would've been shattering. Yes, I am weak; because no, I'm not going to attack, so everything that's said about me is true. *Weak, traitor, embarrassment, coward*—it's all true.

But now?

Naell's right to be offended that I claim to represent his god, because I *don't*. Urzoth's a tool I'm using to secure the thing in my life that makes me *truly* strong.

The pain in my shoulder is intensifying, stars speckling across my vision, but I smile at Naell almost pleasantly. Exhaustedly, more like; I was done with this attitude, this prejudice, with *Urzoth* a long time ago.

A barrage of whistles blow. Refs descend on us, forcing us off the field.

Aaron comes over and helps me away while Marlow signs violently at Naell, enough cursing that a ref calls a penalty on her. She reels it in with a frustrated groan and marches off, fuming.

Naell watches me go, his wound spring of challenge releasing in confusion when I don't react.

The pain from my shoulder sinks into nausea and dizziness, but I fight to stay coherent as Aaron helps me to the sidelines. Phei fusses over me, making me down healing potions that take the edge off, casting spells to find broken bones or torn muscle.

"Dislocated?" Coach Riprak clarifies.

Phei's flower-petal form flickers in a pantomime of a nod.

Riprak curses. I'd echo the sentiment but I'm suddenly locked in this weird amorphous numb state, all emotion dulled. Am I in shock? Maybe.

"My fault, coach," I say. Riprak's busy scratching notes on his game plan clipboard.

Phei should be able to heal me, but no way will I be recovered enough to make the rest of the game.

Riprak scowls down at me. "Huh?"

"I should've been ready for them to pull something like that," I say, eyes on the field. My teammates are getting into position for the next play. "I should've known they'd go dirty."

Riprak's anger deepens. "Don't blame yourself, Monroe. *I* should've known and put more people on you. Fucking Chimeras. They've always been vindictive bastards."

I nod stiffly and he pulls away to talk to the other coaches.

The shitty thing is—it wasn't anyone's fault. There was nothing anyone could've done to prevent the Chimeras from wanting one last bit of reprisal, especially Naell. More defenses, better plays; hell, even if I had managed to renounce Urzoth before the season, they would've piled that onto the list of reasons they hate me.

But what I care about, what has me stuck in that numb sensation, is that Bel was right.

I can't take down an entire cult, can I?

Some things are inevitable. When people's actions are based in rigid belief, no amount of us doing the right thing will alter their course. Bad things *happen*, and we're left in the aftermath even if it isn't our lesson to learn.

How do you handle preordained failure?

How do you function when the rules you're playing by don't apply to the people you're fighting against?

Phei gets to work on spells to reset my shoulder, and I distract myself by looking up at one of the screens. After a few seconds, it flashes back to Bel and the cheerleaders. He still looks concerned, but he's dancing, his smile performative.

Are his cousins watching? Have they recognized him? Do they know he's okay?

It's one thing to accept the Chimeras targeting me because of their hatred.

It's another to accept Bel getting *killed* because of cultists' beliefs.

Fuck the rules.

He's going to survive this.

Of course this is the game my parents come out to see, one where I not only spend most of it on the sidelines with an injury, but one we lose.

The score ends at 15–13, so it's close, but still a loss that bumps down our odds of making it into the championship.

A publicist informs me that even though Bel tried to get to me on the sidelines after the game, they didn't want that kind of photo op again because it would *focus too much on weakness,* aka, my injury.

The publicist isn't Treva, and it confirmed that she hasn't spread news of mine and Bel's relationship being real; either way, I make sure the publicist knows to tell the others that if Bel ever wants to get to me, *he gets to me,* photo ops be damned.

I don't feel bad when I make that publicist pale. They kept Bel from me; that shit doesn't fly. He hasn't activated the charm that alerts me to trouble, though, so I know he's fine.

In the locker room, my teammates apologize like they let me down somehow. Marlow, who was so livid with the Chimeras that she ended up getting another penalty before the game was done, is still beyond furious. I can't catch half of what she says between her angry gestures and repeated use of the word *fuck.*

I promise her that I'm fine. I promise *all* of them that I'm fine.

Because, weirdly, I am. In no small part thanks to their support, and as I leave, I thank each of them, making sure they know how much I appreciate them having my back.

We lost to the Chimeras. My arm's in a sling. I have to get through a staged lunch with my parents and Bel after I meet them by the player lot.

But I feel more centered than I have in a while, like this game was a tipping point I hadn't even known I needed.

Everyone else can change the rules to fit their own agendas. Why can't I?

When I'm prepping for a game, no matter what play I study, I know I have to operate within the bounds of general rawball rules. Which, to be fair, aren't many; it's a pretty brutal sport. But all told, the rules are so ingrained in me that I unconsciously don't question them.

And I've been approaching the Galaxrien cult the same way, keeping general rules of logic as a self-imposed restriction. I've been hoping I can figure out a way to prove their beliefs wrong, but that wouldn't stop them from acting on their beliefs, would it? It wouldn't free Bel from the danger of his demonic ancestry.

I'm going to come at it from a different angle. No fucking around this time, no keeping myself within set parameters. Fuck the rules, right? Bye-bye, logic; hello, demented.

I've got a sense of peace coming down the hall, my bag over my good shoulder—right up until I approach the turn that'll take me to the player chute, where I'm supposed to meet Bel and my parents. There's a publicist waiting for me, the one who told me they kept Bel from getting to me; he shuffles in place, still looking cowed, and thrusts a paper toward me.

"Talking points," he says and motions to the corner behind him.

People usually clog that hall, a clash of journalists and families, so outlets get the fluffy pictures of partner hugs or parent tears.

I frown at the publicist until my eyes hit the paper.

It's a list of things to say to reporters. How I'll keep fighting despite my injury; this setback won't hold me down; Urzoth makes me unstoppable.

My shoulder throbs along with the sudden sinking of my heart.

"The Urzoth church requested it," the publicist says, looking uncertain at my silence. "I assume this is all right? It seems in keeping with their doctrine."

"Yeah. It's—it's fine." I shove the paper back at him. "I got it. Thanks."

He nods, relieved, and hurries off.

I'm lucky none of the cameras picked up Naell's taunting. If they had, I'd . . .

What? Be outed as someone who's given up on Urzoth? Would that really be so bad?

Yes. Because Bel needs this cover to stay safe.

I take a deep breath as I round the corner and pull up my best smile. It's plastic and doesn't reach my eyes, but no one calls me on it; of course they wouldn't.

Every time a reporter stops to ask me about the game or my injury, I recite one of the canned responses like a good little prop, meditating on my mantra of *this will keep Bel safe*.

It doesn't matter that I credit Urzoth for my healing. That I talk about how much strength he gives me to push on. It doesn't matter how much I lie, because it's all for Bel, and I've made my peace with that.

Peace.

Undeniably peaceful.

So peaceful my good hand is digging crescent moons from my nails into my palm by the time I get through the gauntlet of reporters and notice Treva standing by the player exit with Bel at her side.

Tension bleeds out of me, a breath releasing, my fist unclenching.

Bel spots me. With a relieved cry, he shoves his bag to the floor and sprints forward. I reach for him and wince when my shoulder pulls, the sling reminding me not to move it too much.

"Fuck, Orok." Bel stops in front of me, hands hovering between us, like he's afraid to touch me. "What—"

I grab him with my good arm and haul him up to me, dropping my head to burrow down into him as much as I can. He only has a moment of resisting, a feeble protest of "I don't want to hurt you," before he throws his arms around my neck and nestles into me.

Even more of my strain vanishes, swept away by his body against mine.

My thumb trails along the small of his back, and I push my face into his shoulder until I feel that his necklace is still on. It's covered by the illusion magic.

"Gods," he whispers. "Are you okay?"

"Phei bandaged me up." I kiss behind his ear because I can, because doing it makes both of us relax. "They said the soreness will wear off in a few hours. I'm okay."

"What happened?"

I hesitate.

He catches it and shoves back with a glare.

"It was your old teammate, wasn't it?" Stark, unbridled fury fires over him; I have a disconnected thought that he and Marlow could scorch the earth together. "No one saw exactly what happened, but someone said that tank—Naell?—they said he was talking shit before the game."

Bel looks around like Naell might appear in this hall, his jaw bulging by his ears.

"I'll kill him," he growls. "He's fucking *dead*—"

"Glad to see one of you is honoring our god."

My eyes slip shut.

I allow myself one more second of Bel in my arms before I lower him to the floor and look up to see my parents next to Treva.

My mother is taller than I am, the giant ancestry undeniably from her side, with the same black hair as me, only hers is always styled in a huge arch of curls that makes her even taller. She's got a Hellhounds sweatshirt on, a massive leather purse on one shoulder, and a frown of disappointment on her face.

My dad, on the other hand, is all human, nearly half her size. His receding hairline makes his pale scalp shine in the harsh hall lights, and he looks like he just came from the office even though it's Saturday, wearing a button-down shirt and pressed khakis. He's behind my mom, deferring to her, eyes on his phone.

"Hi, Mom," I say. "Dad."

Dad nods at me. "Good game, son."

"*No*," my mom snaps. "It was *not* a good game. Weren't you watching? Orok let himself get hurt!"

Bel, one hand still in my shirt, tightens his grip. "*Excuse* me—"

But I jerk him closer to me and his eyes flip to mine in question.

I give a subtle shake of my head. He looks like he'll argue, but he nods, lips pursing.

Treva, next to my mom, cringes and mouths *I'm sorry*. "Your mother demanded to speak with you," she says. "I tried to keep her outside, but—"

Mom pushes forward, shutting Treva out of the conversation. I'm reminded of how I treated Treva after the first home game, throwing my size around the way Mom is.

I know my expression drops, but I can't stop it, and Mom zeroes in on it.

"We do not linger on weakness, Orok," she says, sizing up my sling. "Do you have to wear that to lunch? Aren't there going to be photos?"

"I have to keep it on for a few hours."

"A *sling* does not honor Urzoth. Why did you let this happen?"

Bel stiffens again. "He didn't *let* anything happen," he says through his teeth. "He got injured."

Mom's whole countenance changes. From accusatory to fawning, like she'd forgotten Bel was here.

"You must be Alexo? I've heard *so* much about you. What was it you were saying about going after whoever was responsible? That's exactly the sort of thing that will bring honor to Urzoth—a challenge of strength. Isn't that right, Dave?"

"Yes, dear," my dad says to his phone.

Mom eyes Bel again, head to toe, and grimaces. "You are . . . *capable* of fighting, aren't you? The Chimeras players are awfully large, and you are—not. We can't have you losing this challenge, not after Orok's injury. We need a *win*. I've spoken at length with Reverend Drach—now *that's* a strong man—and I have so many ideas about ways to enhance how you two are portraying Urzoth—"

"Mom." I lean a little more heavily on Bel than I normally

would. I'm just so tired suddenly. "Maybe we can have this discussion over lunch?"

"Not if Alexo is going to challenge a Chimeras player before we go. Can your publicist arrange it?" She turns to where Treva has since fled.

Bel does, in fact, pause, a flicker of consideration passing over his face.

"*No,*" I snap. "No, he's not fighting anyone." For fuck's sake. "I've already handled the press. We're good to leave. It's done."

Bel looks up at me, defiant. "Someone hurt you. *On purpose.* Maybe I want to hurt him. *On purpose.*"

I swear lovebirds circle my mom's head.

"Oh, Orok," she coos. "You've picked a good one."

I clamp my jaw shut.

Well.

I wanted my parents to like the first person I ever introduced them to, didn't I?

Chapter Fourteen

We have reservations to grab a late lunch at a place within walking distance of my apartment, so I'm able to lure my mom and Bel away from any fight challenges by reminding them that we'll be late. My mom, especially, doesn't want to miss the photo op.

Photographers pack the sidewalk in front of the restaurant. Which makes it easier to remember there are parts of this that need to *remain* staged. Bel's identity, of course; but also my true feelings about Urzoth.

We're seated at a table by the window. Bel pulls the chair out for me and I flex my good hand at him.

"Still got a few functioning appendages, sweetheart."

He sticks his chin up. "I'm allowed to baby you. You got hurt. Sit your butt down."

Mom and Dad, already seated across from us, watch this exchange in horror. Well, Mom watches it in horror; Dad's studying the menu like it's a fascinating read.

"Alexo," Mom says through her teeth, then smiles, remembering the cameras. "Orok isn't really *hurt.*" She gives me a look. "I can't believe you're clinging to this charade, Orok. What is this doing for your image? For Urzoth's image? *Take off the sling.*"

I sit, and Bel follows me into his own chair, his face wound with barely repressed anger.

I refuse to let dangerous lulls in the conversation happen. "Mom, I didn't actually introduce you. This is Alexo. Alexo, this is my mom, Ghorza, and my dad, Dave."

Mom gets a knowing smile on her face. "And Alexo is your . . . ?"

I take Bel's hand under the table.

"I moved into Orok's apartment," Bel offers.

"Oh yes, Orok told me *that.*" Mom bats her hand. "I meant what label are you using now. I don't see a ring?"

Bel makes a strangled squeak.

"*Mom,*" I say, and she shrugs.

"What? You need to lock this one down, Orok. He's so much better for you than Sebastian."

I bristle. "Seb and I were never together. And there's nothing wrong with him."

Mom hums, unconvinced, and opens her menu with a flourish.

Thankfully, the waiter comes, and we all order drinks. I'm not even sure what I ask for, my hand cramping around Bel's.

Once the waiter leaves, Mom props her elbows on the table, making herself look bigger. An intimidation tactic I'm not even sure she knows she's doing, it's so ingrained in most Urzoth worshippers.

Bel is unfazed. He moves my arm from holding hands to looped around his shoulders and settles into my side, his palm dropping to rest on my thigh.

"So, Alexo," Mom starts. "What are you doing about this awful Galaxrien business?"

I clamp my fingers on Bel's shoulder, every muscle in my body tensing.

"What?" I demand at the same time Bel gasps and mumbles, "Wh-what?"

Mom looks between us. "The cultist ritual last week. How they *dared* to abduct an Urzoth worshipper. As if we would have Galaxrien's descendant in *our* church! Which of the Urzoth demonstrations did you participate in? I couldn't find anything online about what you two did in response to that horrific attack, and Orok claims he didn't attend any of them. But *you* seem like the kind of person to not let an atrocious slight like this go unchallenged."

Bel laughs nervously. "Oh. Um—Reverend Drach didn't want us participating. He wants our relationship to help accentuate other elements of Urzoth."

"Ah, of course! See, Dave?" Mom nudges my dad, who's on his phone again. "This one has a smart head on his shoulders." She flicks a knowing look at me. "Unlike *Sebastian.*"

I suck my teeth. "Mom, enough."

"You're still friends with him, aren't you? How does *Alexo* feel about that?" She swings on him again. "Have you met Sebastian?"

"I have," Bel says, "and—"

"He's not at *all* Urzoth material. He led Orok down some very unfortunate paths."

I hold my breath. She wouldn't bring that up. Not now, not here. Would she?

"That whole messy business with"—her voice drops to a dismayed whisper—"*the lawsuit*? Sebastian's work. I want you to know it wasn't Orok's idea. He got swept up in Sebastian's schemes. He's normally *such* a great Urzoth man. Strong, relentless, passionate. It's only Sebastian's influence that swayed him to weakness."

"Mom," I manage, a choked plea for her to *stop*.

She bats her hand. "I want Alexo to know. He's a true embodiment of Urzoth. Well, a bit small, but that can be fixed. Surely he's been wondering how that lawsuit fits in with our faith? I won't have you running him off because of misperceptions. You two are doing *good* work now, bringing light to Urzoth. Representing him. Using your platforms and fame to his glory. This is too important to let the past sully it. So, Alexo, I promise, Orok's not really like that. Whatever you heard about the camp, he's better than that. If Orok had been alone there, he would have excelled—"

"*Mrs. Monroe,*" Bel barks.

Loudly.

The whole restaurant quiets. The waiter, halfway back to our table with a tray of drinks, stops, but Bel doesn't notice. His fingers are clawed into my leg and redness creeps up his neck, his dark eyes focused and *pissed*.

"Your son is *incredible,*" Bel says, his voice low and vehement. "He's the first to help whenever anyone needs it. He does *so* much for so many people and never takes credit. He constantly puts himself up against impossible odds, the kind of odds that, even if he wins, he knows will be met with attitudes like *yours*."

Mom looks taken aback, realizing Bel's upset with her. "Like mine? I don't know what you—"

"He saved me," Bel tells her, arching over the table. "He saves me every damn day, and I am so unbelievably lucky to have him in my life. And you're lucky to be able to call him your son, but you've berated him nonstop from the moment we met. Do you realize what a gift it is to have him in your life? And you're screwing it up by treating him like shit, and I won't allow you to speak to him that way. I love him, and not just because he's strong, but because he's *soft* and gentle and kind, and *that* is what makes him strong. And you should love him for that, too."

The table is silent.

The whole restaurant is silent.

Even my dad looks up from his phone.

I can't breathe, can't move, everything in my body slowly crystallizing.

Bel comes back to himself with a jagged gasp.

His gaze darts around, seeing everyone looking at him, and when his focus gets to me, it's like he hears all his words in one big ricochet.

"Oh." He smacks his hands over his mouth. "Oh my gods. *Oh my gods.* I said I love you. For the first time. *While yelling at your parents.*" He whips on my mom and dad. "I didn't mean to yell at you. Well, I did, because you're treating him terribly and he doesn't deserve this, but I—*oh my gods.* I gotta go."

He bolts out of the chair, weaving through tables until he vanishes down a hall at the back of the restaurant.

I launch after him.

"Orok!" Mom calls. "Wait—"

But I'm gone, zipping through the shocked tables and ducking down the hall.

A storage closet, an exit, and the bathroom are back here. I choose the bathroom first.

The restaurant's fairly nice and the small room reflects that, white marble on the floor and halfway up the walls. Bel's crouched in the far corner by the stalls, curled in a ball, arms around his knees, head buried in his lap.

The rest of the room is empty, so I let the door swing shut behind me and lock it.

Bel doesn't look up. Not as I approach and kneel next to him. Not as I put my hand on his wild pink curls and tug gently.

"Let me die of humiliation in peace," he moans into his legs. "Just make sure the cultists don't get my remains, okay? On principle."

"Don't even joke about that. Look at me."

He lets me pull his head back. He touched up his makeup after the game, smoky liner and black mascara and more of that pink gloss on his lips. I know now that the gold glitter across his face is from him not putting his illusion spray on as strong as he should, so parts of his real skin shine through.

I swipe my thumb under one teary eye.

If anyone ever stood up to my mom that way, I thought I'd be most worried about the fallout.

But there's only one thing pulsing in my mind.

"I love you, too," I tell him.

Bel wheezes. "What?"

"I don't know why I haven't said it yet. I accepted it as truth so easily. But." I cup his cheek. "I love you."

"Y-you love me?"

"I do."

He sputters a half-bitten-off sob. "I can't believe you're telling me in a *bathroom*."

I grin and drop my hand to his knee. "It's kind of fitting for us. Our first date happened because I stalked you."

"And kidnapped me."

"I won't admit to that."

Bel laughs, dimples popping, and he scrubs the back of his hand against his cheek.

He settles, blinking wet eyes up at me. "I'm not sorry for what I said to your mom."

"I don't expect you to be." My gaze lowers from him, unseeing on the floor. "I was going to renounce Urzoth. The day of that meeting with Roesia and Reverend Drach? I was supposed to meet with Roesia and tell her that I wasn't going to have Urzoth as my patron god anymore."

Bel moans softly. "And instead you got sucked into embodying him even more."

"No." I pin him with a look, letting all my certainty well up and out and into him. "No, I chose to be with *you*. Because I think I knew even then that you'd be important to me. All this time, when I've had to put on a front about Urzoth—I haven't been doing that. I've been choosing *us*. Only I'm realizing that lying about Urzoth, while something I can compartmentalize, is still giving the wrong message to the world."

"If you want to renounce him," Bel says, "I support you. Completely. I want you to be happy. Fuck hiding behind him—I want you to be free, Orok."

I kiss him, needing a taste. He chirps, but relents immediately, and whines when I pull back.

"It's not that easy, sweetheart," I whisper. "It's like the cultists. Both are problems that require more finesse to get out of than I'd originally hoped. But that's okay. We'll figure everything out, and as we do, we'll be together. That's all I care about. Being with you."

Bel slams his eyes shut, exhaling hard. "You can't talk like this when we have to go back out and finish lunch with your parents."

"We're not finishing lunch with my parents."

His eyes snap open. "We're not?"

"I'm taking you home." I wipe the last of the moisture from under his eyes. "We can try this again some other time, when we're—"

"No." He takes my hand and fixes me with a look of determination. "You're sweet, but no. I *want* to stay. I want to go back out there, apologize to your parents, and have lunch with my boyfriend's family."

A soft smile tugs my lips. "You're sure?"

"Yeah," he says, then gives a lopsided smirk. "Besides, how else are we going to earn that reward?"

I exhale a snort. "That's what matters most, after all."

"Have you *seen* your dick? That's *all* that matters."

My face heats as I laugh, but he squirms around me to stand and throw himself at the sink, where he quickly fixes his smudged eyeliner.

With a hard sniff at his reflection, he says, "Let's do this. Cock awaits," and marches out of the bathroom.

Gods. I really do love that man.

Bel's apology is formal but sincere—he's not sorry about standing up for me, but he is sorry about yelling and shaming my parents. In public. But his display endeared him to my mother even more, because she cuts him off by gushing about how he leapt to *defend Orok's honor*, and then goes on to list all her ideas for *further spreading Urzoth's strength.*

We both listen, and Bel asks how each of her ideas embodies Urzoth's teachings. It gets her into a probably too-deep discussion of our dogma, all that *strong as stone, hard as rock* stuff; but also the finer details, the things Reverend Drach hinted at, and the things I rarely, if ever, hear my mother admit to believing, that although Urzoth is made of stone, he is a god of strong emotions, like love.

I'm not sure I speak the whole meal. I sit there while Bel interacts with my mom, pulling these ideologies out of her and genuinely, eagerly soaking up all the information, his hand on my thigh and his body slightly leaning toward me the whole time.

As much as I love watching him win over my parents—well, my mom; my dad will like him if she does—I need this lunch to end. Now. And the longer we sit here, our plates cleared and dessert half eaten, the paparazzi outside having dispersed an hour ago, the less I listen to what Bel and my mom are saying, and the more I pay attention to the heat of his body against mine, the smell of his apple illusion magic, the way his eyelashes fan across his cheekbones when he closes his eyes in a laugh.

He loves me.

He defended me. Again.

I want you to be free, Orok.

But I already am. I am every moment I get to be with him, and finally, *finally*, Bel turns to gaze up at me, presumably to ask a question, and he notices the look I shoot him, the heat burning from my core.

I'm quick to get the check after that. I hug my mom and dad goodbye, and she fawns over Bel, promising to be in touch and get him some Urzoth books she told him about, but I'm dragging him out the door as she's still talking. Bel giggles, a delighted, sexy noise as I march him up the sidewalk, my apartment only one block away. Other pedestrians fall out of my path, and I should maybe be concerned that I'm being such a lumbering, overbearing weirdo right now, but I can't stop it.

He brings out this side of me, and it isn't even that—he's the only one I've ever felt is *worthy* of this side of me. The ferocity, the brutality, the swelling force that so many people attribute to *Urzoth's strength*. It's for Bel. It's only for him.

We surge into the lobby of my building, the doorman and security guard greeting us, and Bel says an actual hello to them, but I keep him moving. The elevator's there and I haul him into it, and before the doors are even shut, I have him caged to the wall, towering over him, burying my nose in his curls.

He smells like *him*, and the restaurant, and the soap from the stadium; I want him to smell like me. *Need* him to smell like me.

Bel sucks in a faltering breath as I lap at the skin under his jaw. "D-did we earn our reward?" he stutters. "I definitely feel like we did. We both survived, yeah? We—*gods*, that feels good—walked out of there intact."

The elevator dings, the doors peel open, and I heft Bel up.

He squeals in protest. "Orok! Your injury—"

"This arm's fine." To prove it, I sling him higher until he's draped over my good shoulder, hanging there far too temptingly. I slap his ass, and he devolves into a helpless laugh.

"Oh my gods. Tell me no one's around to see me like this."

I already have, in fact, scanned the hall. It's clear. "Uh-oh, paparazzi got ahead of us."

Bel lurches, trying to spin around. "*What?* Where? I—"

He notes the empty hall.

And drops back down to slap *my* ass. Except he barely reaches my lower back.

"Hilarious," he deadpans.

I grin and shift him to dig my keys out of my pocket, but as I unlock the door and deactivate the security wards, I lower him to press his back against the wall.

"To answer your question," I say into his open, gasping mouth, those glossy lips slick on mine, "this isn't about surviving the lunch. This is because my boyfriend"—he used that word and I'm *wild* for it; it's ours now—"won over my parents. He's earnest and brave and sexy as *fuck*, and I need to stretch him open for me so I can let him feel how much I love him."

Bel whimpers, hips rolling against my stomach as he babbles, "Yes, that. Oh my gods. Yes, please."

I get the door open and we topple inside. He tugs me down to lay kisses and bites all up my neck, interspersing his attack with progressively needier mewls, nails digging into my neck.

I spare enough composure to relock the door and reactivate the wards.

Another startled squeak when I scoop him up again, but I only take him as far as the bedroom before I'm tossing him onto the comforter. He rolls, half finding his balance, half yanking off his clothes, and he struggles around until he comes up for air, shirtless, cheeks flushed.

"Like this?" he asks on his knees, and it takes me a beat to realize what he's asking. In his human form.

"However you're comfortable," I say honestly. "Every version of you is perfect."

That flush goes to raging scarlet as he shimmies out of his remaining clothes. His tail thrashes against the bed, the only part of him rose gold, a delicate contrast of his two presentations. He's a sunset, every hue of pink in a perfectly clear sky, coral and rose and a pastel blush.

Panting, he looks up at me, coy and yearning. "You're not getting undressed."

I rock my neck side to side. The pain from my injury is all but gone. "I dunno. My shoulder's pretty sore. I think you'll have to put on a show for me."

What starts as concern quickly morphs to a popped eyebrow of interest. "Oh yeah?"

"Mhmm." I kick off my shoes, move around the bed, and sit propped against the headboard.

Phei's healing spells were potent, but I keep the sling on. This is the game, after all.

Bel immediately crawls up me, the contrast of his lithe, naked body while I'm fully clothed sending a debilitating pulse of arousal through me. I regret leaving on my jeans when he straddles my lap to grind his dick against mine. My own cock's been hard since the restaurant and the sensation's muted by the fabric, and Bel rotates his hips, his face pinching in a delicious moan.

With my good arm, I dig my fingers into his hip, helping him writhe, the flex of his muscles shuddering under my palm. "This what you want? Let you get off on me like this?"

Bel shakes his head, curls flying. "No. Want you in me again. You promised."

Gods damn, his pout. Does he know how potent it is? Does he know he could ask me for anything, in this plane or ones I can't even reach, and I'd rip apart the magic of our reality to lay it at his feet?

"All right, sweetheart. Need you to get ready for me, though."

Bel reaches for my hand, guiding it back around his ass, but I change course to drag my hand to his stomach. The muscles jump under my fingertips; I groan, thrusting up against him.

"I want to watch you," I tell him, absorbing the way those brown eyes dip further into desire, pupils blowing out, lashes fluttering. "Show me how you fucked yourself before me."

He sips in a stunted breath. "Yeah. Yeah, I can do that."

Then he's scrambling off me and racing into the bathroom, to the closet that's past the shower. He didn't have much in the boxes we brought from his old apartment, but he's somehow taken over more than half the space already, including claiming a bunch of my own clothes.

I need to take him shopping. Just pull up at a storefront, hand him my card, and let him go wild. Gods, he'd look pretty in some suits; or maybe more of those flowy satin tank tops like he wore to the charity gala. Get him something like that, but a dress version, so I could lift it and fuck him anywhere I—

Bel stumbles into the room. He fluffed his hair while he was gone and reapplied some lip gloss, his mouth now a shiny blush-pink color—and he's wearing a pair of black lace assless panties. Which he shows me by doing a quick little spin. They cup his dick but frame his tail and ass in a way that's absolutely sinful.

My jaw drops.

If possible, he's blushing even more, breathing even harder. "I bought these a while ago," he whispers. "I always hoped I'd get to—to, um, wear them. For someone."

"For me," I growl. Can't help it. My throat's gone to gravel.

His eyelashes pulse, those pretty lips parting.

He slowly rounds the bed to stand next to me.

But he doesn't climb on my lap. He fiddles with an item behind his back; I'd been so distracted by his panties that I didn't realize he brought something else out with him.

I arch an eyebrow at his hesitation, at whatever he's hiding from me.

"You said—" He licks his lips. "You said to show you how I did it before you, right?"

"Yeah. Is that okay?"

"Of course. I want to, I—"

"Bel."

His eyes fly to mine. "Just—can you—can you talk to me?"

I actually feel my eyes darken. Feel the descending of something heady and greedy, and I reach out to trickle my fingertips down his thigh. His shiver looks like it anchors him.

"You need me to tell you how good you're doing for me?" I start, gauging his reaction. He shivers again, but no, something on his face isn't quite—hm. "Or you need me to tell you to get on this bed. Get on this bed and show me what belongs to me."

There he is.

His eyes go hazy and his breathing accelerates, a clenched spasm of his lungs. Without another word, he climbs over me, past me, and kneels on the other side of the bed with his ass facing me, those panties contrasting against his pale skin.

The view alone is enough to have me adjusting my dick in my too-tight pants. I give up and take myself out, stroking slowly as he widens his legs.

"Beautiful, sweetheart," I say. "Gods, look at you. Spread your knees a bit more—that's it. You gonna get that hole opened up for me? Get it nice and loose. Take care of what's mine."

"*Mm*," Bel moans. "I—"

His head flies up and he breaks out of the fog enough to look over his shoulder, a touch accusatory.

"No condom," he tells me. "Right? We said we'd talk about it after last time but we didn't, but I still don't want to use one because you're the only person I've been with and I trust you when you said you're okay, and I—"

"Bel." I give myself a long stroke, and his gaze drops to my dick, to the sheen of moisture at the angry red tip. "No condom."

He exhales harshly. "Yeah?"

"Want me to come in you? You want to feel me dripping out of you the rest of the night?"

A shattering whimper rattles in his throat and he drops back onto his elbows, ass popping even higher. "Yes. Oh my gods. That. *Yes*."

His tail whips through the air and loops toward his head, where he messes with whatever he brought out of the closet.

I stroke myself faster—too fast, have to breathe through my nose.

Bel wiggles on the bed, and his tail arcs back around.

Clutching a thick black dildo covered in lube.

For the second time in the span of a few minutes, he makes my jaw drop.

He lines the tip of the silicone cock up with his hole and gradually, steadily begins to fuck himself open with it.

While holding it with his tail.

"Holy shit," rips out of me, and I pinch the base of my dick to thwart the rapid swell of effervescence that tries to consume me.

I told him to put on a show for me.

This is certainly one hell of a show.

The tip of the dildo pushes through that first ring and both Bel and I whimper, his back arching in a fluid ripple as his tail keeps a steady pace.

"Good?" he asks, panting.

"Holy shit," I say again. "So good. Gods, sweetheart, look at you. You're artwork. So sexy, just for me."

"Just for you," Bel echoes, and I see the blankets move as he nods. "Just yours. Say it, please, Orok—"

"Mine, Bel. All mine. You gonna take that whole thing? You'll have to, if you want to take me, too. *Fuck*, just like that—you know exactly what you're doing to me, don't you?"

His toes curl, ass flexing, and more of the not insubstantial dildo vanishes bit by bit inside him. Between his legs, his hard cock is trapped in his panties but he leaves it be, while I can't touch my own cock at all either, ecstasy pelting my senses from every angle.

He groans wantonly and shudders, keeps the thrusting pace for a few more minutes before he peers over his shoulder at me again.

That tail continues fucking him like it's got a mind of its own, and Bel's face is glossy with sweat and drool already, his eyeliner and mascara smeared across his temple as he asks, "Am I ready? Please, can you fuck me now? I need—need you in me. I'll go slow, I promise."

I nod, because I can't take anymore either.

He immediately scrambles up, holding the dildo in his ass as he moves to straddle me, and *oh my gods*. That tail. The things that tail can do. Holy shit, we are definitely exploring more of *that* later, but for now, I help him move up my lap.

My thighs are too wide for him to fit his knees on either side of me, and I have a brief moment of panic mixed with mentally doing sex physics while I try to figure out how he's going to ride me—because he's clearly determined to ride me—when he tugs at my shoulders until I slide down the bed to lay flatter. He plants his knees on my stomach, his legs folded under him along the tops of my thighs, and does a test bounce, fucking that dildo the way he'll fuck my cock.

His inhale falters, swollen lips rolling into his mouth in a moan. "Yeah?" he asks, breathy and delirious. "This okay? Your shoulder okay?"

"My shoulder's fine. This is—"

A hiss slips through his lips. He pulled the dildo out of his ass.

"Careful, sweetheart," I gently chastise. "You're supposed to take care of what's mine. I don't want you hurting. Go slow, okay? Fuck yourself open even more on me."

That delirium, that dazed look—he's only half hearing me, and honestly, I'm only half aware of what I'm saying.

The lube appears, and he coats my dick before tossing the bottle and dildo on the bedside table and grabbing my cock. With his tail.

Oh my gods.

Did not know I had such a tail kink.

Bel's head throws back as he places me against his hole and sinks down. The tendons in his neck bulge, all the sculpted muscles of his athlete's body straining to taut perfection. I can count the squares of his abs, the lean lines that fan across his pecs; I'm touching them, tracing them one by one, locked in a trance as he levers himself up, down, up again, whimpering and rocking his hips. His tail strangles the base of my cock and gods, that's needed, needed because he lifts his hands into his hair, grips those strawberry curls, and moves his torso in a sinful undulation that shouldn't be physically possible.

None of this, of him, should be possible, but he is. He's proof that gods do exist, and this, what we're doing? This is how you worship. This is how you honor the divine.

"Sweetheart," I gasp, stroking his side, up to his armpit, back down. "So perfect for me. You're dancing, do you know that? You dance while we fuck. It's the hottest thing I've ever seen, you writhing on me like my own performance. Dance for me, Bel. Make yourself feel good on me."

He seats himself fully on my cock with a crackling shout, tail unwinding from the base, those twitching waves of motion flaring out to his limbs in jerks and spasms.

"S-so much d-deeper," he manages, his eyes bursting open to lock on me like he needs that connection to orient himself. He runs his hands over his head, down his neck, his chest. His palms stop, lay flat on his stomach, and he groans, symphonic and indulgent. "I—I can feel you here. Oh my gods, Orok. You're—"

He gives an experimental bounce and keens to the ceiling, tail lassoing around my ankle so snug I can feel the bite in my skin.

"*Oh my gods,*" he wails and fucks himself on me in earnest, toppling forward to brace his hands on my pecs.

I grip one of his wrists, letting him take what he needs from me, give everything to me. His eyes stay on mine as he launches both of us interstellar, and that connection becomes tangible, becomes binding.

Blood beats in my temples, in my thumb where it presses to his pulse point, harmonizing with the rhythm of his; we're in tandem and sweeping each other away, matching intensities and driving each other higher.

It's dangerous. If we're both spiraling out, who will bring us back down?

Do we *need* to come back down?

Black makeup runs in jagged stripes down his cheeks, sweat sheening his skin mirror-bright. "Say it again. Say it, please. Tell me you love me."

"I love you," I say instantly. My fingers snag in his hair as I grip the back of his head and keep him looking at me. "I love *you*. I love you. You're mine, and I love you."

Bel lets out a sob, and he's coming, his untouched dick pulsing from beneath the lace of his panties, shooting his release up my shirt, hitting my chin. It yanks the orgasm out of me, *demands* I come, the sight of him falling apart over top of me, my body and the words *I love you* enough to get him there.

I grab his hip and thrust up into him, howling as I come inside him. Marking him. *Owning* him.

Bel's body gives out, his face burying against my sweat- and cum-slicked shirt. He's gasping, and when I curl my arm around him and try to adjust him, he whines in protest.

"No! No, don't wanna—" He grabs behind him, at where my softening cock is still in his hole.

"I got you, sweetheart. It's all right." I ease myself out, and he whines again, but I'm quick to glide two fingers inside, plugging him, relieving the emptiness, the comedown.

The added warmth and slickness in his channel—that's me. In him. A part of him.

A growl resonates in my chest, tangling with Bel's satisfied croon. I pull him higher to put a kiss on his hair. I didn't kiss him enough—I nudge his head until he looks up at me, tear-stained and disheveled and flawlessly ruined, and I kiss all over his face. His nose, his lips, his eyelids. Kissing and sealing and claiming.

He rests his cheek on my collarbone, rigidity draining out of him with each quivering breath. The feel of him breathing, his heart beating on mine, his body warm on top of me—it drains my own tension.

He's safe.

And, with him, I know I'm safe, too.

They took him.

I didn't even *do* anything this time. Did I?

Urzoth, please. I don't know what else to do. I obey all your commandments,

I do everything I'm supposed to. Why haven't you helped me? Why won't you save me? What did I do wrong? Just tell me what I did. Tell me what I need to do to get you to help me.

I had to have done *something*. They didn't take him for no reason.

But it isn't Seb they took.

It's Bel.

They have him in the same place they always take Seb, and he'll come back with his face swollen and bones broken and—

Urzoth, please, please, save him; hate me all you want, but please, give me the strength to save him.

I see Bel, his rose-gold skin covered in garish purple-and-blue bruising, blood crusted on his nose and mouth. I see him curled around himself, whimpering. They smashed his ribs because I didn't—didn't do something.

Please, Urzoth. Tell me what to do, tell me what I did wrong, why, why, HELP ME.

Why aren't you helping me?

They're punishing Bel, punishing *me*, and he *screams*.

"Orok?"

My eyes open.

I think . . . I think they might've been open already; each blink feels like sandpaper, dragging across my vision, blurring the barracks.

Not the barracks.

"You're in Philadelphia," Bel whispers. Seb told him what to do when I have a night terror; he's talking a little fast, his tone quivering, but he's calm. "You're in your apartment, in bed with me. I'm here, Orok. It's Bel. You're okay—we're in your apartment. See?"

This is the first time I've woken up like this with him.

He's next to me, clinging to my hand with both of his. My sling came off at some point, and my shoulder doesn't hurt anymore, but I'm still in my clothes, jeans gaping open, shirt covered in his dried cum. The comforter's pulled up from the other side of the bed, wrapped around Bel's mostly naked body like a cloak as he sits on his knees next to me, his lace panties twisted around his hips, his eyes big and gleaming in the dark. His illusion magic wore off; he's in his demon form.

We fell asleep. What time is it? Night, at least, and sweat turns sticky across my body, limbs twitching as the nightmare recedes. Adrenaline's always a relentless bitch of a drop, and it tugs me into the chasm of regret, of shame, of lingering waves of irrational fear.

I'm used to the nightmares about Seb. I've had them so many times over the past ten years, I compartmentalize them as easily as avoiding a sprain.

But feeling it all over again, the abandonment and helplessness, in relation to *Bel*?

A tremor runs from the base of my skull straight down my spine and I stiffen every gods-damned muscle in my body. Do not react. Not yet.

"Are you—" I clear my throat, tongue dry. "Did I hurt you?"

Bel shakes his head, lifting my hand to press it to his cheek. "No. You sat up, and you were moaning. You . . . you said my name."

My palm twitches, feeling the softness of his skin, letting it ground me.

"If you—" Gods, I have to fight to talk, my mouth scraped clean. "If you want to sleep in the guestroom—"

Bel frowns, appalled. "What? *No*, I do not want to sleep in the guestroom. This doesn't scare me. You told me that you needed me. Let yourself *need me*, because I want that, too."

A hesitation. Just one more. "Bel—"

He presses my hand to his face. "I'm yours. You said so. This is what it means, Orok. I'm yours, and I'm not going anywhere."

It's as good as permission to my nightmare-addled brain.

"At Camp Merethyl," I start, hoarse, jagged. "They paired us up. They made us—they *forced* us to—"

Bel strokes my sweaty hair, his face full of heartache. "I know, baby. I'm so sorry."

"They took Seb. When I'd mess up. They forced us to do awful things, and when I failed, they'd take Seb and beat him even worse and—and I could never save him. I could never stop it."

A sob rips out, gagging me. With a brittle cry, I yank Bel into my arms, rolling us sideways on the bed, and cling to him with everything I have.

"They took you," I whisper. "They took you this time. I couldn't save you."

Bel melts against me, scratching his fingers over my scalp, burrowing into me as strongly as I hold him. "I'm here," he says, his voice tear choked. He clears it. "I'm okay. You can feel me? I'm here with you."

I made my peace with Urzoth abandoning me and Seb. It took almost every moment of the past ten years, but I've moved on. My brain still dredges it up when I'm sleeping; in my waking moments, though, I'm *fine* with it. I'm living, I'm healing.

But Urzoth abandoned Bel.

It was a dream. I know it was a dream. *It wasn't real.*

My mind is a malleable, sleep-deprived mess of emotions and reality.

Urzoth should have *heard me*. Why didn't he hear me?

Behind my closed eyelids, I see Bel in my dream, bloodied, beaten.

A whimper claws out of my throat.

With Seb, I always tried so hard to pull myself together after a nightmare. I'd sometimes make him sleep in my bed, but I never clung to him like this, and I always talked myself carefully through all the reasons why my fears were ungrounded.

But instead, I do what Bel told me to do. I let myself need him.

Shivers rack me as relief truly sets in, untying knots through my chest, releasing the cramping in my neck and back.

"You're not leaving?" I ask. The magic wore off his necklace, too, making it visible now, and I run my fingers over it. "Gods, Bel. You can't leave me." My voice cracks. No—it *shatters*, and tears surge down my face, wet his neck and hair. "You can't leave me. Fuck, please stay."

"I'm staying," he whispers. "I'm not leaving you. I'm yours now, remember? You own me."

My whole body heats. Not just arousal, but burning righteous possession.

"I love you." His fingertips scratch my scalp again. "Shh, Orok. You're all right, and so am I."

He keeps talking, reassuring coos and promises, and I breathe him in, breathe him like a drug.

He's here. He's okay. He's not hurt, no one got him.

But they'll try.

And I know better now.

I know better than to put my trust in anyone, any *being* who hasn't proven themselves when the stakes are this high. When it matters.

My grief redirects. The adrenaline from the dream, the agony of losing Bel. It shifts, contracts, becomes an arrow targeting everyone trying to take him from me.

I keep him in my arms until his reassurances fade to the huffs and moans of sleep.

As gently as I can, I roll Bel to the side, tuck the comforter around him, and slip out of bed.

I strip off my sweat-drenched clothes and swap them for boxers. Bel stays asleep, and I brush a kiss to his forehead before I pad out to the living room.

My research is still spread across the dining room table. All the details and notes and secrets of how to protect him and stop these cultists once and for all.

I flick on the overhead light and sit down to read.

Chapter Fifteen

Morning News: "Welcome to *One Shot*, your number-one source for the latest in pro rawball news. I'm your host, Diamanda Blacktalon. While Vaknox of the Lizard People of Tesh continues his divine quest, I'm here today with yet another cohost. This one is—oh. Please don't make me do this."

oooOOOOooo

"Joining me is . . . the Red Stalker, Phantom of the Mortal Plane."

ooOOooo

"Right. Anyway, our favorite It couple has been busy! After that outburst at the restaurant—oh my, was that ever scandalous!—we've had dinners, dates to the theater—Oroxo was even spotted buying flowers at a farmer's market. Look at that picture, so domestic! I can't get enough of the way Orok watches him. Fans everywhere have been going wild for them, and I—"

oooOOOOoooOOOOO

"No, it's not invasive to have these photos! And you're a ghost, don't you haunt places? How is *that* not invasive?"

ooo

"I'm really starting to feel like I'm not taken seriously as a journalist."

Falling into a routine is luxurious.

I get to do this with him. I get to wake up every morning and have breakfast with him, Bel more often than not ending up on my lap so I can lick syrup off his tongue. We go to practices and games, home and away; and when we travel, I do my best not to be overbearing, and he texts me reassurances from the cheerleader bus or, gods, their separate plane—I can't even pretend to be okay with that arrangement.

Gulus or Ilbryen is with him for those times—their adventure party really is short on resources, if senior members are the only options for our watchdog. Or they don't trust me yet. Which is fine, considering I still don't know who among their group *I* can trust.

Regardless, when Bel's out of my sight, I'm a wreck.

My teammates, while not entirely understanding my sudden-onset travel nerves, pull me into distractions. They never once make me feel less than, never once act like having emotions is weak. Our gameplay is still fluid and cohesive, claiming us so many wins that we lock in our future before we even need to play our final season game:

The Hellhounds are going to the rawball championship.

Our managers and coaches are ecstatic. Reverend Drach is ecstatic, too, at the reception my and Bel's relationship continues to get, fans gobbling up every sighting of Oroxo/Beauty and the Beast. Any negative opinions spurred by my lawsuit are long forgotten, and more discussion is focused around us than the Urzoth church's violence or the Urzoth-Galaxrien situation. And my parents are still totally besotted with Bel, as my occasional calls to my mother are spent reassuring her I haven't *scared him off yet*.

Don't really appreciate that *yet*, but I let it go.

With things silent on the cultists' front, it'd be easy to get complacent.

But I refuse to be passive. I'm not waiting around for the cultists to attack again and I certainly won't let them get close to Bel. I spend every free moment I can poring over research, scouring texts and rereading passages until I can recite them from memory.

They think that sacrificing Galaxrien's mortal descendant, or using his body somehow, will free Galaxrien. The *whys* and *hows* don't seem to matter to them; that belief is what has taken hold, so that's the belief I have to undo to stop them.

But I can't make Bel *not* Galaxrien's descendant. Even if I could somehow *prove* that he isn't, his true form is still overwhelmingly demonic, and that alone would paint a target on him.

I want Bel completely free of this. I want him to be able to walk around as his true self, or if he wants to be in his human form, I don't care. I want it to be *his choice*. That's freedom.

I hit dead end after dead end with who might've leaked info about Galaxrien's descendant to the cultists. Mostly because it's hard to hire investigators to look into members of a highly secretive adventure party. But Ilbryen swears she's questioning things on her end.

Gods, helplessness will kill me.

Bel meets my obsessive research by deep-cleaning the apartment, and when I come out of my reading coma one day to chastise him for doing too much, he strips off his clothes and asks how I'm going to punish him.

All this research stresses him out, I know. He doesn't want me in more danger than I'm already in, and he blames himself for all of this. I can't stop, though. I *have* to keep him safe.

As the rawball season comes to a close in tandem with the winter holiday season creeping up, both Bel and I get hit with a distraction that puts all our stress in irritating perspective:

A request from Reverend Drach to attend services for one of the biggest church celebrations of the year, Urzoth Shieldsworn's birthday.

And not just attend it, but be *guests of honor*.

Gotta love the holidays.

Yeah, the Hellhounds are in the rawball championship. But who the *fuck* are we playing?

Makes me miss the college rawball schedule where we'd be all wrapped up *before* the holiday season. Fucking game stress, I swear.

I pace the bathroom, glaring at my phone where it's propped on the side of the double vanity I've come to think of as mine. The game play echoes in the marble space, crowd noise and reporter commentary overlapping in a dull roar.

"Can't believe it went into overtime," I mutter as I button my shirt.

The Hellhounds had their holiday game yesterday, on a day celebrating a werewolf god—Roesia's god, actually. We pulled in our final win of the season, which was unneeded; we had enough Ws already. Even so, it felt good. Crazy good.

The Hellhounds are undeniably a force to be reckoned with, and meanwhile, the Chimeras are scraping it out against the Dragons for the chance to go up against us.

"You're buttoning your shirt wrong," Bel offers where he's hunched over his side of the vanity on a stepstool, leaning toward the mirror. He needs the extra boost of being on his tiptoes as he swipes mascara over his lashes, and I'd swear he was doing it on purpose to pop his ass if he wasn't actually so short. Add on that he keeps his toes in a rotating color wheel of pink, Hellhound orange, and black, and it'd be a strong enough distraction; but he hasn't gotten dressed yet or put on his illusion spray, standing there totally naked, his rose-gold skin glossed with the steam of the shower we shared.

For a beat, the game fades. We blew each other in the shower but gods, that's not enough. Never will be. Just like I'll never have enough of seeing him getting ready next to me. The ordinariness makes it precious.

Then I hear what he said and look down to see—yep. My shirt's buttoned wrong.

He meets my gaze in the mirror and grins.

Eyes helplessly on him, I rebutton my white dress shirt and tuck the ends into my simple black slacks, each movement a little slower than normal. Maybe if I drag it out, we'll magically not have to go to a celebration for a god I don't want to worship anymore.

I don't know why I thought I'd be able to avoid this holiday. The church is still Bel's sponsor and I still wear their symbol on my uniform, and in all our planned PR moments, we're two big, smiling examples of how Urzoth can be loving as well as tough.

Of course Drach and the church want to capitalize on us, and beyond that, they have no reason to think we *wouldn't* want to go. That I *wouldn't* be ecstatic we're two of the select few guests of honor. That I *wouldn't* be thrilled to be asked to speak at the service.

It's tolerable. We're representing aspects of Urzoth I agree with. It's not like Drach is making me knock heads all the time; in fact, he *doesn't* want me doing that. See? It's fine.

Treva wrote a speech for me. It's . . . somewhere. I should really read it before we get there.

The game plays on behind me, still a tied score.

Gods damn it, c'mon, Dragons.

"How big will this event be, really?" Bel asks. His question would be casual if not for the way his tail taps an anxious rhythm on the bathroom floor.

We haven't had to go to any Urzoth services before, since Drach always wanted to keep our associations separate from what the services usually turn into: brutal fighting matches. But this service will be more solemn, with sermons and other guests of honor speaking. It won't devolve into any shows of brutality for a few hours.

I press a kiss to Bel's bare shoulder. "It's the main Urzoth church in Philadelphia. Hundreds of people will probably be there."

"Probably? You haven't gone?"

"When I lived here the first time, I went home and attended services with my parents. Never needed to go to this one until now."

At least my parents couldn't make the trip out here for the service, since my mom is such a high-ranking member of their own church and had to stay for their services.

Bel flicks his eyes to me but refocuses on his makeup. "Hm. *Hundreds* of people. We won't be that noticed. There are other guests of honor, right? Who'll even care that we're there?"

His tail taps, taps, taps.

I put my hand on his elbow, pulling until he stops his mascara application and faces me. "What part of this has you nervous?"

For a beat, he looks like he'll deflect. I know what his face does when he's trying to cover something up; the forced smile, his dimples nowhere in sight, his eyes turned down at the corners.

"Bel."

He clamps his lips together before, finally, looking up at me.

I hold, giving him the opening, and after a breath, he takes it.

"You have to speak to the whole congregation," he whispers. "It'll be broadcast, too. And I know you don't *want* any of this, so every time Drach says *jump* and you have to obey, I . . . I hate it."

He straightens up and points the mascara brush at me.

"That doesn't mean I'm not grateful for what you're doing for me," he says. "That doesn't mean I want you taking on my guilt on top of everything else."

My jaw thrusts to the side in thought. I can't get out of the speech. Can't step down as Urzoth's poster boy.

But . . . maybe there are ways to make this bearable.

"I can see you thinking. Stop." Bel pokes my cheek with the brush. And smirks, no doubt leaving a swipe of black behind; I don't care, let him mark me all he wants.

He rolls his eyes when I don't react and gets to work digging out a makeup remover pad from his growing collection of cosmetics. I took him shopping a few weekends ago, and I'm not sure which of us enjoyed it more: him, getting to invade half a dozen different stores, or me, getting to watch him try on outfit after outfit, and then rimming him in the dressing room of the last boutique.

As he cleans my cheek, he shoots me a chastising smirk. "I'm serious. Stop thinking."

"I'm not thinking." Because I already know what I'm going to do.

"I don't believe you. You don't need to save me from everything."

"That is literally my job, sweetheart. The sooner you accept that, the easier all this will be."

His lips part and an argument builds in his eyes, but I silence him with a kiss, tasting the mint of his toothpaste, feeling the plumpness of his lips once he surrenders. He leans into the kiss, twisting on the stepstool to press his naked body against me, and as my hand slides down the curve of his ass, he leans back, dazed and grinning.

"The Dragons won," he whispers.

My brain stalls out. "Huh?"

He points behind me, to where my phone is roaring applause now, a reporter screaming, "The Hellhounds will be playing the Dragons in the sixty-first annual rawball championship. . . ."

I gawk down at Bel, the words processing slowly, and his rising giddiness releases in a bounce against my chest.

"The Dragons won," he says again and laughs. "Fuck the Chimeras!"

Oh my gods.

The Chimeras lost.

They *lost*, and aren't going to the championship. They traded me, and won't even have the chance to defend their title.

But I have the chance to claim it again. Without them.

I scoop Bel into a kiss, ravaging his mouth with all the excitement bursting up through me. He squeals into it, arms knotting around my neck, and we really do have to go, but—fuck the Chimeras, fuck Urzoth, fuck everything but *this*.

Yeah, actually. Fuck everything but this.

I peck Bel on the cheek before grabbing my phone. "Keep making yourself even more beautiful—I have some calls to make."

"Calls—what? Tease!"

But I swat his ass and duck out of the bathroom. "Trust me!"

The Urzoth service is held in a massive cathedral downtown. The glaring stone building leaves no question as to what god it stands for, all harsh gray rock and intense statues. Inside, the main room is outfitted with pews for the first portion of the holiday service: the sermons. It'll be transformed afterward, the pews pushed aside in favor of fighting rings as Urzoth followers are pitted against each other. The *feats of strength to showcase Urzoth's power* are a lot of brawling and fistfighting and general violence as winners are declared and dethroned and declared again. It's the normal type of service cranked to a dangerous max. The floor'll be streaked with blood by the end.

Drach wants me and Bel to leave before that part.

No problem.

What *is* a problem, though, is the discomfort that seizes both Bel and me when we enter the cathedral.

Here he is, Galaxrien's mortal descendant, walking straight into an Urzoth church.

Hundreds of Urzoth worshippers pack the pews around us. More than a few hungry expressions follow us as we make our way up the aisle, and it takes me a beat to remember they have no idea who Bel really is. So they're staring at him because—

Because he looks sexy as hell.

That pearl necklace cups his throat and a slate-gray suit makes his pink hair pop. Instead of a normal solid back, the jacket has a layer of swirling lace that shows the sharp blades of his bare shoulders. He's downright edible.

I easily fall into what's expected of someone in an Urzoth church; I yank Bel under my arm and curl my upper lip at anyone who looks at us. Challenge met.

We're ushered to the second row, and I walk us to the very end, near one of the side aisles beneath the mezzanine that's held up by concrete pillars. Bel eyes me, seemingly picking up on my intent—to be able to slip out. But he says nothing and redirects his eyes to his lap when we sit. They've been down from the moment we stepped inside, focused on his balled hands or the floor, and while I should prod him to hold his chin up, keep his bearing strong and unafraid here, he doesn't need to. That's what I'm for.

The sermons start, long-winded lectures from Reverend Drach and a few other priests who go on about Urzoth's might and the importance of his birthday and how we need to stand strong against adversity.

I tune most of it out, keeping my arm around Bel, fighting to stop my knee from bouncing.

Bel puts his hand on it and squeezes.

The sermons come to a close, and Drach introduces one of the special guest speakers, a decorated arcane soldier. She gets up, talks about how grateful she is for the strength Urzoth has given her in battle, and reclaims her seat.

"And next," Drach says, looking out at the full cathedral, "we have Orok Monroe of the Philadelphia Hellhounds."

The crowd applauds. There are a few Hellhound barks, and I smile at that, the familiarity helping me stand from the pew, helping me leave Bel behind as I move to the front of the cathedral.

I step up to the podium and take the speech out of my jacket pocket. The paper crinkles as I smooth it, Treva's words short and simple but swimming before my eyes.

Hundreds of Urzoth worshippers are staring at me. Rows and rows of people who love the god I devoted my life to.

Has he ever talked to any of them the way Darian's god talks to him? It's unusual for Urzoth to talk to anyone. He's never been that kind of god, *involved.*

And yet, here we all are.

"The holiday season," I start, reading Treva's speech. Just say the words; I don't have to feel them. "Is always a special time for me. It's a time to reflect on the ways Urzoth has—"

I swallow.

Stumble a bit.

Regain myself, and carry on: "On the ways Urzoth has given me strength this year."

There's a list. A few bullet points about how Urzoth got the Hellhounds to the rawball championship, how he helped me in the bar fight months ago. Easy stuff.

Just read the list.

I clear my throat.

. . . the ways Urzoth has given me strength.

The words spin on the page. They blur.

Until I just see two: *he hasn't.*

Hand shaking, I take the speech, crumple it in my fist, and look up at the crowd.

My tongue dries and I'm going to say that, *he hasn't.* Those are the words that'll come out of my mouth, here, now. I'm going to renounce Urzoth in front of the entire church.

Oh gods. No. Not here; Bel still needs this cover. Do it for Bel. Keep your shit together for Bel—

My gaze drops to the second row and I latch on to him. He's sitting on the edge of the pew, body wound like he knows what's going through my mind, and he probably does.

He smiles, encouraging. And mouths, *It's okay.*

My chest crushes and I clamp down on the speech balled in my fist. I'm hit with such a battering ram of love for that man that I choke down those undoable words, *he hasn't,* and open my mouth and say, "The biggest sources of strength in my life have come from my relationships. Particularly now, with Alexo Warden. *He* gives me strength. And I am eternally grateful for finding him."

There's stilted applause as I duck away from the podium.

Most will attribute what I said to Urzoth; they won't get the nuance of it. And if they do? I don't care.

I wind my way back to our pew as Reverend Drach introduces the next speaker, but instead of sitting, I grab Bel's hand.

He snatches our coats off the seat and folds himself into me, and against the applause of the next speaker taking the podium, I drag him down the side aisle and out the door.

The chill December air bites into us as we step outside, and I work our coats on quickly. It isn't until we're walking to my car that Bel glances back.

"They were still doing speeches," he notes.

"Mm." I open the passenger door for him.

He eyes it, then me. "Don't we need to stay for that?"

"We fulfilled our obligation."

A slow smile stretches his face. "So . . . we're playing hooky?"

"We are grown-ass men who can make our own decisions about

how we want to spend our time." A pause. "But yes, we're playing hooky."

Bel's smile gets sheepish and tender. He pushes up onto his toes and I automatically bend down, letting him press a kiss to my cheek.

"You're my biggest source of strength, too," he whispers.

A blush heats my face, but he's already diving into the car.

I slip in on the driver's side and peel out of the parking lot.

Bel settles into the seat, but when I don't drive toward the apartment, he perks up. "Where are we going?"

"Wow." I click my tongue. "It took you this long to ask that? Do you blithely trust every strange man you get into a car with?"

He grins. There're those dimples. "Only the really sexy ones."

"Lucky me, then." I wink.

"Oh, did you think I meant you?"

I reach across the console to pinch his thigh and he chirps a laugh.

Traffic is light, so we make it across town in no time, and I parallel park in a spot right out front.

Lights are on in the bar; a few people are already there, moving beyond the glass.

That was one of the calls I made earlier: offering the Silver Hound's owner pretty much anything they asked for to reserve the whole bar on short notice.

Bel studies the exterior, his perusal transforming into a beaming grin when he recognizes the bar where we first met.

"Karaoke date night?" he asks, clearly in love with the idea.

I rest my wrist on the steering wheel, half my lips relenting in a smile. "Sort of."

He's unbuckling his seat belt, buzzing with excitement already, but stops. "Sort of?"

I rub my hand over my chin and look at the bar again.

I recognize Seb's outline through the winter-fogged window. Maybe Marlow's, too? My stomach swells with an anxious fizz I'd been doing my hardest to keep at bay through the service, but now, here, I'm hit with the same twisting worry as months ago.

It was short notice. No one might come.

Bel takes my hand. "Orok, what's going on?"

"The night we met," I say in a rush. "I'd asked the team to meet me here. The lawsuit verdict had just come out, and—" I scrub at my face again, jaw gaping in unspoken words.

Bel leans closer. Doesn't push. Just watches me until I lift my eyes and give a self-deprecating smile.

"I never felt any connection with the Chimeras," I tell him. "Never tried to. Never *wanted* to. Then I not only got traded, but got traded *home*, and I wanted it to be better. With the new team. I wasn't sure it *would* be, after that night—no one came out. It's dumb. But . . . in other ways, they've been night-and-day different from the Chimeras, so I thought we could use a team break. And with all *our* stress, you and I should blow off some steam. So. I invited them out again tonight. For a party."

"That sounds perfect," he says, his smile genuine. "For them and us."

I shrug. "They might not come again. I only let them know a few hours ago, and it *is* the holiday season, for more than just Urzoth's religion, so they probably all have plans to—"

Bel puts his free hand over my mouth. "Hey. Babbling is my thing."

"You don't babble."

"I do so. I babble so much I should sue you for copyright infringement."

I smile into his palm and press a kiss there.

He lowers his hand. "Should we go inside?"

Another wave of anxiety fizzles in my gut, but Bel clutches hard to my hand.

"Together," he whispers. "You and I will have a blast regardless of who's in there."

The one therapy appointment I had these past few weeks because of intense rawball season scheduling, my doctor said Bel sounds like he's doing me a lot of good, even though I'd braced myself to be reprimanded. I explained all the obsession and protectiveness and worry, but how I'm aware of it, and that, at least, seems to be the key—to not let those things control me.

But obsession, protectiveness, worry—turns out, that's what love is.

Seb and Thio. Marlow, Darian. Phei, in a rock formation in the corner. Aaron and the rest of the defensive tanks. Many people from the offensive line, too. Some of the friends Bel's been making on the cheerleading team. Riprak's even here, and another of the coaches, and—is that *Roesía*? Everyone's mingling, some getting drinks from the bar, a few already nibbling on plates of appetizers at the high-top tables.

Holy shit.

Bel and I hang our coats on a rack by the door, and I step past it, mouth agape. Bel's tucked under my arm, and I can see his excited smile out of the corner of my eye; but I can't stop scanning the room.

Seb is the first to race over and throw his arms around us. Thio's at the bar, his eyes on Seb as he presumably waits for drinks, and he grins when Seb shouts, "Fuck the Chimeras!"

His call gets everyone's attention and a chorus goes up. "*Fuck the Chimeras!*"

A grin cramps my face. "Hell yeah," I say and hug Seb to me.

He pulls back. "Brilliant idea with this party—I needed to get out. Work's been brutal." He waggles his eyebrows. "Pretty good turnout, huh?"

"Yeah." I clear my throat when it comes out squeaky. "Yeah, awesome turnout."

"Fuck the Chimeras!" Aaron comes over, claps my shoulder, and thrusts a chunk of rock—limestone, maybe?—at me. There's a bow on it. "And happy Urzoth's birthday."

Seb's brows shoot up over his glasses.

Bel's eyes narrow in confusion.

I take the rock.

"I wasn't sure what kind of holiday this was?" Aaron says to our odd looks. He scratches the side of his neck. "But I figured a gift's always a safe bet. And limestone, cuz, like, he's a god made of rock, yeah? That's why Phei's gone stone." He thrusts his thumb at Phei's pile in the corner.

They—wow. They did this for me?

I didn't say this was a party for the Urzoth holiday, because it isn't, but damn. This is thoughtful.

Bel takes the rock from me. "This is so sweet," he coos and nudges me, and it breaks me out of my shock.

I sniff. "I—yeah. This is—it's great. Thanks, man. I appreciate it."

A whole helluva lot, actually; Urzoth ties or not.

Seb holds his hand out to Aaron. "Sebastian Walsh. I don't think we've met; did I see you at the party Orok threw here this past summer?"

The weight in his question catches me, and I bulge my eyes at him. Seb ignores me.

"Aaron Harsaf," he says, shaking Seb's hand. "And I probably wasn't there. The team loves this place, but my schedule never seems to line up."

"It was the first Thursday in August," says Bel, his focus on making the ribbon lay flat against the rock, like he's saying something totally innocent. But there's weight in his tone, too, and my eyes fly from him to Seb, who inches closer to Bel like the two of them are suddenly partners in crime.

"Guys," I try, "it's not—"

Seb gives me a silencing look.

"Ah." Aaron snaps his finger in connection. "That's right—I don't usually go out on Thursday nights." His eyes widen and he looks at the floor in a sudden wave of dismay. "That makes me sound really boring, huh?"

"Kind of," Seb mutters, and Bel covers for him with a nose-scrunching giggle.

"Well, going out that night worked for me at least—that was when Orok and I met." He blinks up at me, still with that faux innocence. "You were celebrating your lawsuit win that night, right?"

Seb keeps his eyes on Aaron, analyzing him for a reaction.

I try again. "It's really not—"

"Oh, shit." Aaron punches my shoulder. "*That's* what that night was for? Damn, I had no idea. I thought it was another pre-season team hang. I should've been there."

Seb grins. "Let me guess: Orok's invitation was just *hey, come have a drink*? No explanation? Yeah, sounds about right."

"If I'd known it was for that, I really would've come. That was a big victory, Monroe. I was impressed you did that. Stood up for yourself. We all were." He bats his hand at the room. "You know we were hella intimidated when you got signed to us, right? Your stats, yeah, but also how you kept your composure through the lawsuit and all the press shit you got hit with. You're, like, god-tier."

Damn it, I haven't even really crossed the threshold into the bar area, and I've already been hit with far, far too much emotion.

Heat scalds my face at the sincerity in Aaron's eyes. "Thanks. I—I'm really glad to be here," is all I can muster.

Aaron grins. "Hell yeah. Let's *party.* I heard tell of karaoke?"

Darian manifests like that word summoned him. "We all need to be significantly drunker before that. Harsaf, shots." And he hooks Aaron's arm to haul him away.

Seb wings a smug eyebrow at me. Meanwhile, Bel is not so subtle, beaming as he grabs my belt and jostles me. Neither of them says anything, just living in the fallout of Aaron's words.

No. I will not cry at a bar. Without even having a drink yet.

I scrub the heel of my hand against my cheekbone. "Well. Shit."

Seb smiles at the crowd and leans toward Bel. "Who's next?"

Bel points at a rogue talking with Marlow. "Her. She's nice; there's no reason she shouldn't have been there."

Seb holds his fist out. Bel bumps it.

I grab both their wrists. "Wait—what is happening?"

They look up at me with very different, yet somehow similar, expressions. Seb's lips pucker and his head dips to the side in a clear, unspoken *isn't it obvious?* while Bel bites his lower lip to counter his grin, his eyes sparkling.

"We're going to find out why the rest of these people stood you up," Seb says.

"While the Hellhounds *do* seem like good people," Bel adds, "we should make sure, right?"

"They—I—" I shake my head. "They *are* good people. It's fine; you don't have to—"

"Oh, yes, we *do* have to," Bel interjects. "We have a mission tonight. Or, Seb and I do—I assume you don't want to come, but I am *definitely* reciting all the sweet things everyone says about you."

Seb cracks his neck. "Time to go all Protective Best Friend on these bitches."

"Hold this for me?" Bel shoves the rock into my chest. "We're keeping it, by the way. Think of a name."

My brain is having an impossible time catching up, so I fumble the rock and stutter out, "A . . . a *name*?"

I look down at the rock like it might've metamorphosed into a puppy without my noticing.

"Yeah. People keep pet rocks." Bel's face pinches in horror. "You don't think that's actually a *piece* of Phei, do you?"

"I—I doubt it."

"We can ask." Seb juts his chin across the room. "Let's question Phei, too."

"I've been with the Hellhounds for almost a whole season." Gods, it's like trying to talk down a car wreck. "There's no need to—"

"There's *every* need to." Seb pins me with an intense look, all the jokes falling away. "We're here now, and a lot of *them* are here now, and I'm not letting this opportunity pass me up."

"We'll be back!" Bel leaps up to kiss my cheek and bounces away, Seb following with a taunting wink.

Off they go, and I stand at the entrance to the bar, apparently now a rock dad, having lost control of the evening in record time.

Stunned, I wander deeper into the room, unaware of the dopey smile on my face until my eyes lock with Roesia's. She makes her way over, and I look down at the rock, but there's nothing to really do with it before she stops in front of me, sipping a glass of wine.

"Mr. Monroe," she says in greeting.

"Ms. Sombercrown." And then, because I'm mostly a reactive husk at this point, "What are you doing here?"

I messaged a bunch of the team, but it never would've occurred to me to text one of the *team managers* to come to a bar hangout.

The edges of Roesia's lips flicker up. "I was in a meeting with several members of the offensive line when they received your invitation. Is it all right that I tagged along?"

"Of course." I clear my throat. "It's great that you're here."

"Mm." She sips her drink again, those shrewd eyes on me. "And how did things go today with the Urzoth service?"

My mouth opens.

Nothing comes out.

Just say *it was fine.* That's literally all I have to say. I've lied over stuff like this so many times before; it's second nature.

But I can't get the words out. Same as when I stood up at that podium and couldn't make myself read that speech Treva'd written for me.

I don't *want* to lie anymore.

Roesia looks at me over the rim of her glass, and the silence now feels as weighty as what Seb and Bel were lobbing at me a moment ago.

"It is important to me that my players are happy, Mr. Monroe," she says as she lowers her glass. "Are you? Happy?"

My eyes flick across the room, sighting Bel where he's with Seb, talking to Phei now.

"Yes," I say easily, breathy and more than a little sentimental. "Yes, ma'am. I am."

Roesia's still studying me by the time I look back down at her. "Well, I'm glad to hear it. But if you decide you want to reevaluate your associations before next season, let me know."

"My—associations?"

"This PR arrangement has thrown your relationship with your god into an even brighter spotlight, and if doing so has made you reexamine certain things, it would not be a big matter to sever those ties. I don't want my support of this arrangement to be taken as an ultimatum."

My brows launch sky-high and I adjust my grip on the rock so it digs into my stomach.

Shit, what is with this evening? Did I turn translucent?

I laugh. It comes out as a sputter, and I scrub at my eyes, shaking my head.

"I'm sorry, ma'am," I croak. "But—gods, you're incredibly perceptive."

She smiles. Wide and true. "It's why I've had such a successful career. Now, I'll be taking my leave. I wanted to make sure you know where I stand." She glances over her shoulder, to where Bel is laughing at something Phei said. "Give my best to Mr. Warden. Everything is still good with you two?"

"Yes, ma'am." My grin is confirmation.

Roesia nods. She taps her wineglass against the rock in my hands. "Emma," she says.

"Pardon?"

"I heard Mr. Warden. Name it Emma. Emma Stone."

Oh my gods. Did she make a *joke*?

I break out in another laugh. "I'll let him know."

Roesia takes a step away. Looks back at me. "I should probably show more tact than this, but—" She sets her wineglass on a table and cups her hands around her mouth before shouting, "Fuck the Chimeras!"

The whole bar reacts with hollers and laughter, and I crack up as Roesia slips away.

This is exactly what I wanted out of tonight. This is what I wanted out of that evening months ago, when I invited everyone here the first time.

To really feel at *home*.

Darian brings me a shot—he and Aaron are clearly already several deep—and as the evening progresses, I take myself right to the precipice of contentedly buzzed while Seb and Bel pop up sporadically with reports on my teammates.

Most were like Aaron, assuming that the invite was a team hang, nothing significant; Seb swats my head at the fact that I didn't *tell* anyone *why* I was inviting them back then. Phei, it turns out, *did* come, only they were a plant. Apparently, they even tried to sing karaoke, but by that point in the evening I was too shitfaced to remember a potted fern on the stage.

Not this time—I cut myself off after the third shot, and I make sure to order a bunch of food to be spread around the tables for everyone. I want to stay coherent in case Bel needs me. And I want to remember this night.

Bel continues his rotation through the team with Seb, but the longer he does, the more my eyes drift to him. I'm in conversation with Riprak and Aaron, but looking at Bel. I'm talking with some of the offensive players, and looking at Bel. He, also, is talking to people, but looking at me, and blushing prettily, flushed with the heat of so many people in a close space, and I can't look away when he's happy.

A microphone squeals, then Darian's shouting "*KARAOKE!*" and everyone cheers.

He's on the stage at the back of the room, the neck of his guitar in one hand, mic in the other where it snakes out of the karaoke machine. "The bar manager has graciously"—he pauses to hiccup; okay, he's drunk—"allowed me control of the stage this evening. So everyone—" He points around, still gripping his guitar. "Get ready for me to heckle the *shit* out of you. Who's up first? Not you, Monroe."

I didn't even have my hand raised. "I sing like an angel, Callabrass!" I shout with a grin.

"You couldn't carry a tune if it was BabyBjörned to your chest."

I flip him off and he cackles.

An arm shoots up near the side of the room, and I already know whose it is from where he was standing. I smile as Bel scurries onto the stage, and Darian grins.

"*Here* we go! Ladies and theydies and gentlemen of all kinds, let's give it up for the Hellhound cheerleading department's own Alexo the Magnificent!"

Applause rings out, and I wind my way closer to the stage, not willing to miss a moment of this.

Bel and Darian whisper with their heads together for a second, deciding on a song; Darian laughs and nods at whatever Bel suggests. He passes Bel the microphone before strapping on his guitar and selecting the song on the karaoke machine.

Darian strums a few idle chords, and the moment the song starts, he dives into it. The crowd erupts in catcalls as Charli XCX's "Boom Clap" blares through the room. Bel's grinning and already shimmying his body in a fantastically distracting way.

And then he sings.

Bel struts across the stage, bobbing to the lyrics while Darian backs him up. The two are a harmonic convergence, and I can see Darian's smile widening with each building note between them. Bel isn't as lost in the song as he was that first night, singing because he had no other outlet; he's *happy*, dancing for the sake of it, gyrating and bouncing on his toes and playing off Darian like they've been performance partners for years.

The crowd is swept up in them, some singing along, most clapping and laughing. My throat thickens as the song rolls on, as Bel's happiness nearly leaks out of him.

Seb jostles into me, beaming; Thio's not far behind, a plate of appetizers in his hands.

"Damn, I forgot your boy can sing," Seb shouts into my ear. "We finished grilling your teammates, by the way—did he tell you? They all pass. For now. I'm keeping an eye on them, though."

I set Aaron's rock on a table behind me. "Thanks. I didn't ask you to, but thanks."

"You didn't have to." Seb loops his arm through mine. "And it's nice to know, isn't it? That most of them not coming last time was a misunderstanding?"

"Yeah, it—" I squint. "It was a misunderstanding."

I look at the room, at my teammates and coaches, all smiles, having a blast. This was what I wanted months ago, only—

Only I'd *thought* they hadn't come because they'd decided I was wrong about the lawsuit. I'd built it up as another reason, and it didn't matter that what I believed wasn't true; it still felt real to me.

It felt *real* to me.

I gasp, eyes widening, and grab Seb by the arms. "Oh my gods. That's it."

"What's what?"

I drop my voice, leaning in; the noise of the crowd and the song is enough to cover us. "The cultists. They need to *think* that Bel isn't what they need. It doesn't have to be *true*."

The cultists aren't playing by any rules, so I shouldn't either, right? Gloves are off.

We're going on the offensive.

"We make them think that Bel isn't the thing they need for their ritual," I tell Seb.

He frowns at me, not in concern, but in thought. Thio comes closer, ear cocked toward us.

"How?" Seb asks.

"We stage it," I say. "A fake ritual as convoluted as the shit they pull. We'll follow all the stupid requirements they have—the spring equinox, the hot sauce, the handcuffs—"

"Handcuffs?"

"—and we'll use magic to make someone look demonic, and we'll pretend to be cultists, and stage the whole thing. It won't work, we'll make sure it doesn't work, and report widely that it failed. They'll have *proof* that *Galaxrien's descendant* isn't what they're looking for."

Seb's face is set in that way when he's thinking through a complex problem. "There are a lot of variables we'd have to consider. What if the cultists think that *they* could do it better, and still go after him?"

My conviction wanes. "We won't change anything about his security until we're sure it worked. But—it's *something*. Isn't it?"

Thio touches my arm. "Yeah," he says with a smile. "I think we can make it work."

I grin at him. Seb, still scowling in thought, nods absently.

"Huh," he says, then pulls out his phone. "We'll need spells that—huh. What about—no. Wait. Huh."

And he dips into the crowd, typing and walking away with his head down.

Thio sighs. "I better follow him to make sure he doesn't bump into anyone. But Orok?" He squeezes my shoulder. "It's a good idea."

He ducks after his fiancé.

It might not work. Bel might still be in danger after it.

But it's something *active* instead of being so maddeningly *passive*.

The song ends. Bel and Darian twirl toward the crowd with elaborate bows and everyone goes *wild*, screaming and cheering so loud my eardrums throb.

Bel meets my eyes, beams, and takes a running leap off the stage. I catch him, consumed by his apple scent and the feel of his sweat-slicked skin through the lacy back of his suit jacket.

"You were amazing, sweetheart," I say, rubbing my nose against the shell of his ear. "I could watch you perform forever."

He pulls back, still cradled in my arms, breathless; pink curls stick to his forehead.

Gods, and to think the adventure party wanted to shut him away in a cabin somewhere, lock up all this sunshine and talent and keep the world a darker place.

I get in one kiss, one taste of his glossy lips and the sweetness of a cherry drink he had, before Marlow's begging to do a duet with him, signing while Bel sings.

After that, the evening folds into more songs and drinks and food, laughter and dancing. Bel's at the focus of it all, both with the crowd and my attention.

Seb and Thio make their way back over, and we're all cracking up about nothing, then a bit bemused when Phei does a song in their rock form. Just a pile of rocks on the stage while the instrumentals for "Sweet Caroline" play on.

Darian follows it up with a few Queen songs before Bel hops on stage and queues up Taylor Swift's "I Can Do It With a Broken

Heart," and this time he does sing his soul out, pain bleeding into the words.

The song ends, fading in applause, and I climb up next to him.

Bel's eyes are teary from his performance, and I swoop him into a hug, earning ripples of *aww* from the audience. I hold him long enough to feel his muscles relax, and when I pull back, he's smiling again, but it's soft and small and vulnerable.

I take the mic from him. "My turn."

Behind us on the stage, Darian groans. I ignore him and scroll through the karaoke machine.

I want Bel to smile again. To get back to that place of thoughtless fun, of freedom.

An older song pops up and a grin lights my face.

Bel's next to me, so he sees what I choose. A confused laugh huffs out of him. "What—"

But I hit play. Flute notes fill the bar, silencing everyone's chatter for an equally confused beat. They all look up at me with expectant smiles.

I sway to the music, pulling on an overly serious expression and holding the mic to my chest. The music swells, and I flip my eyes up, going as over-the-top cheesy as I can, and sing "My Heart Will Go On."

Bel claps his hands to his mouth to stifle his giddy shriek. Darian muffles a curse but laughs, and as I sweep my arm out wide, really hamming it up, the crowd devolves into snorts and cackles of laughter.

Sheer delight gleams in Bel's eyes, all heavy emotions gone, and it's fuel on this absurdity fire. I pivot to serenade him, pairing off-key words of maudlin love with completely inappropriate body rolls. Soon, he's holding back tears, choking on laughter, and I break with a wide smirk.

The lyrics get a little heavier suddenly, a little more real. Love *can* last for a lifetime. And it doesn't matter where he goes; near, far, I'm with him.

Bel catches my transition, the moment things go from joking

to promise. His hands lower from his mouth and his laugh slants at the edges, eyes going liquid and adoring.

The music ripples into a lull between verses, and my chest warms.

I hadn't meant to get emotional again. I wanted him to smile.

I clear my throat, the harsh grate of it echoing in the mic, and Bel breaks out of his trance with a nose-scrunching grin.

He snatches the mic from me. The final verse kicks up and he plummets to his knees.

I can't help the winded grunt that comes from the very pit of my stomach at the sight.

He arches his torso back and belts out the words, giving Celine Dion a run for her money by perfectly hitting each note, heaving his entire self into the performance like he so expertly does. The crowd *loses it,* whistling and screaming, and Bel feeds off their energy by holding the last note impossibly long until I'm sure the bar's noise can be heard all up and down the street.

The music fades out and Bel collapses forward in a bow on his knees. The applause is a torrent and I see more than a few people recording us; this is a private event, but I know the odds are good that some of this will end up online.

I take the mic from him and say, over the noise, "Remember to keep dancing."

If we stage a fake ritual and it tricks the cultists into thinking Bel isn't what they need, he'll be able to see his cousins again.

Bel's head flies up. His big eyes fix on me, chest heaving from the song.

He scrambles to his feet, grabs my hand, and hauls me offstage.

I pass the mic to Darian and go, of course I go. He's smiling again, I'm gone.

Everyone's rippling apart, alcohol and the lateness of the night peeling away inhibitions. The room is sweaty, people holding each other on their feet in intoxicated clusters or coupling up; I spot Aaron and Marlow making out in a recessed alcove. Go them.

Bel pulls me down a side hall and pins me against the wall near the restroom.

"Take me home?" he moans into my ear, his fingers hooked in the collar of my shirt.

Home. Our home. After a night out with our friends, our family.

I lick into his mouth, eating up his whimpers, cupping his ass and pulling him against me.

This is it.

This is all I ever wanted.

And I'm going to fight like hell to keep it.

Chapter Sixteen

"Amber would be better for the lightning spell than crystal," Thio says.

"Hm. Fair enough." Seb scratches out a note. "Still think lightning's overkill though. We've got smoke, thunder, fire—why lightning?"

I run down my list of things to include in our faux Galaxrien summoning. "A cultist mentioned Galaxrien would return in a *tangle of lightning*. Whatever that means. If lightning's what they want, lightning's what they get."

Seb peeks up at me over the dining room table. "Even hot sauce and handcuffs? That sounds more like a BDSM kink than a cultist ritual."

"Hell, they never said the handcuffs weren't the fuzzy kind. This ritual's going to include every single gods-damned thing any cultist has even so much as sneezed at in the years since this belief started."

I'm not leaving anything to chance. Seb and Thio are working up spells to give us all the flashy shit. We'll have a simulation of a demonic person, not Bel. And it'll take place on the spring equinox, several months from now; that seems to be the date most cultists land on.

I probably should tell Ilbryen about it. And I will—but not until it's all locked in. I'm of an *ask forgiveness, not permission* mindset. This idea carries a lot of risk, but that's part of what all this planning is going toward: making sure none of it ties back to me, and by extension, Bel. It'll be another cultist attempt, albeit one that involves *all* their professed beliefs, and it'll fail spectacularly. Which will, in turn, hopefully kill their insanity.

Gods. *This* is insanity, right?

But the cultists started this crazy game. I'm just playing it. And I'll *win*.

Thio continues perusing the book in front of him. "The biggest issue still remains with the simulacrum of a demonic person. The components alone for that spell are . . ." He whistles, eyebrows bouncing.

"Whatever you need." I bat my hand. "Just tell me what to buy."

Seb beats his pencil on the notepad. "It'll be several pounds of diamonds. *Pounds.* In addition to a few rubies, a specific type of dust shipped in from a demonic grave, and that doesn't even include the—"

I put my hand over his spastic pencil. "I got it, Seb. Don't worry about the cost."

With a sigh, he nods. "Fine. What about the—"

A tray of chicken sandwiches thuds into the center of the table. Right on all our research, books, and notepads.

"Wow," Bel says, hands on his hips. "I sure am glad I had three strapping men to help clean the table for lunch."

Ah.

Yeah.

That might've been what he sent us over here to do.

His smile is forced, but his eyes shine with a hint of amusement to cancel it out.

"Um," I start, ever so eloquently. "We were—"

"Fueling up for the championship game in a few hours?" Bel plops a stack of plates in front of me. "Good. That's what you *should* be doing. Not—*other things.*"

His voice gets a little hard with the faintest trace of discomfort.

He knows what I want to try with this ritual. And I know how he feels about what I want to try, the same reason that already clouds my head with doubt: that it might not work to get the cultists off his back. Only where I worry about unnecessarily endangering *him*, he's worried about *me* putting myself too close to this.

In the week since the Silver Hound party, we had a quiet New Year's and spent a much-needed few days off recouping.

The Hellhounds won the home stadium in the coin toss, so the Dragons get to design the field; which means I should have spent these days reviewing plays. But I don't think we left the apartment—or put on clothes—until practices started again.

The playbook was open on my bedside table most of the times we had sex, at least. A valiant effort was made.

But Bel's right. It's game day; I need to get my head around this championship match. Any ritual we do is several months off. Maybe the cult will collapse on its own before then. They've only spent eight years gaining strength.

I snap my notebook closed while Seb and Thio shut their books with the posture of scolded children.

Bel keeps his hands on his hips, and at first I think he's watching to make sure we clean up. But his eyes are on Seb's notebook, pushed off to the side.

Bel pulls the notebook to him. "What's a simulacrum?"

Seb glances up. "A physical body. A shell, really—it won't be animated or have a soul or anything. It'll *look* like a demonic person for the ritual. That way, no one's actually involved."

"And you'll . . . sacrifice this simulacrum?" Bel asks softly.

Thio moves some of the books to an empty chair but stops, his gaze narrowing on Bel. I know that look—Thio's realized something, and I frown, not seeing it yet.

"No," Thio answers. "That'll be part of the spells we set up. It isn't supposed to work, so the simulacrum won't vanish or be consumed in the ritual. There'll be a lot of smoke and noises and buildup, but the ritual will ultimately fail." His head tips, eyes locked on Bel. "It won't get hurt. And we could add extra safeguards."

"Of course it won't get hurt." Seb stretches to dump the rest of the books on a table by the window. "It won't *feel* anything. It's a shell."

But Thio's still watching Bel, and my focus pings between them. Until the same realization hits.

I shove to my feet and take Bel's arm. He's in his game-day

sweats already, illusion magic in place, apple scent rich all around him.

"No," I say.

Bel folds his arms over his chest. I don't let go of him. "No?"

"We'll use the fake body. *No*, you aren't doing this."

"I didn't suggest anything." But he pauses. "How much will this simulacrum cost you?"

"That doesn't matter—"

"A lot, right? A lot of money that you could also use for—" He stops, and I know he was going to mention my charity work.

I haven't gotten the payment from the lawsuit yet, but I'm still set to fund the Thrive Children programs; and yeah, fine, I usually throw a lot of extra money at similar stuff. But only Bel knows that.

He pivots, tongue working over his teeth. "Money that you'd use for better things. Not waste on a one-off spell. And the body just needs to *lie there*, right?" Another shrug, his eyes firming in resolve. "I can do that."

"Absolutely not."

Silence drops over the room. Thio and Seb share *uh-oh* looks. Bel's frowning up at me, his arms still crossed, my hand still on his bicep.

I hear what I said, how controlling it is, but I don't care. He's not putting himself in this.

"The point is for all the cultists to see it," I say. "To broadcast it. It'd be *your* face, *your* identity. And if it doesn't work? If cultists still go after you, only now they *know who you are*? No way in hell am I letting you participate in this."

Bel grips my tank top. I haven't put on my suit yet, just that thin layer between his warm knuckles and my skin.

"I'm *already* a participant in this," he hisses. "We can change my appearance for the ritual. Mask who I really am. I'll lie there, right? I can do that."

"No," I tell him, damn near snap at him, but he's asking to put himself in danger, and I *can't*. "We're doing the simulacrum."

Anger darkens his expression. "Just like that?"

"Just like that. You're *mine*, Bel, and I'm not letting—"

"Don't you *dare* use that against me like this."

I stop, panting, and the fury in Bel's face shifts into hurt.

This is the line. Fuck, *this* is the line, the one I'm always terrified I'll cross.

All the fight drains out of me.

"Shit. Shit, sweetheart, I'm sorry." I tug on him, and to my surprise and relief and complete unworthiness, he relents and drops against my chest. I bundle my arms around him and bury my nose in his curls, eyes stinging from the release of fear. No, of outright *terror* at the thought of him being the center of this ritual.

"I'm sorry," I say again, my throat trying to choke off the words I know I need to say. "If you—shit. If you really want to do this. We can figure it out."

His arms come around my hips, his head turning to tuck against my face.

For this beat, holding him, everything else softens.

The stiffness in my muscles from pushing so hard in training. The knots along the back of my neck from sleeping like shit and poring over research rather than going to bed. The determined tug in the base of my stomach that tells me I'm not doing enough; Bel's going to get taken from me and nothing I do will stop it.

"I want to finish this, too," he says. "I never thought it *would* be finished, that I might actually get to see my—" He cuts himself off.

I put the picture of him with his cousins in a frame. It's enchanted so we can hide it if needed, but it sits on the table next to Bel's side of the bed—right in front of Emma Stone, which Bel did insist on keeping, as well as the fireball potion I gave him after our smash room date.

My chest aches with wanting, and I can't even imagine how much *he* must ache for it, too.

"You've given me hope, Orok," he whispers. "I know it might not work. I *know* that. But I want to try."

I constrict my hold on him. "It'll kill me if you get hurt."

"Then we make sure he doesn't get hurt," Thio says.

Reminding me that we have an audience.

I meet Thio's eyes, knowing mine are desperate. "We will," I say, immutable.

Seb takes Thio's hand. "That's our top priority. Everything about this is to keep Bel safe. You know we'll have his back."

I drop a kiss to Bel's head and hold there, breathing him in, and let my fingers brush over his pearl security necklace, his illusion magic covering it.

Gods, I want him safe. I want this over.

He looks up at me. And, for a moment, I see in his eyes all the stuff he's avoiding. His own stresses that, no matter how hard I try to bear them all, still weigh on him.

A smile forces its way across his face. "Now," he exhales, "can we eat, please? Because I'd really like to go to bed with a rawball champion tonight, and you can't give me that if you pass out from hunger. Plus, if you *do* pass out from hunger, I'll have to handle your parents after the game alone. Don't do that to me."

I huff. "I'd never subject you to that, I promise. But you've *already* been going to bed with a rawball champion."

It's really never felt that way, though. Winning this game would be so much more impactful than winning for the Chimeras ever was.

Bel hums, lips pursing. "Nah, that doesn't count," he says, a close enough echo of my own thoughts that my smile gets truer. "*This* one counts, with a team that matters."

He wriggles out of my arms and sashays to the other side of the table.

"Bring me that win," Bel adds, "or I'll have to find someone on the Dragons to go to bed with."

I bark a laugh.

"Oh gods," Seb groans. "Stop making bedroom eyes at each other or I'm going to start eating without you."

Thio leans over to whisper to Seb, "I think this is what is commonly known as *payback*, dearest."

"You bet your ass it is," I say and dive forward.

Bel squeals, sprinting around the table, but I catch him in two strides and haul him into my arms, attacking his neck with bites and kisses.

Some are teasing. Some are claiming.

Each one is a promise.

The energy in Bwararax Stadium is off.

Every-fucking-one, from the rawball team to the managers, coaches, cheerleaders—hell, probably even the people selling concessions up on the main levels—we're all strung taut.

When the Chimeras made the championship last season, the energy before it had been boisterous and confident. My teammates had gone in with their heads high and spirits cranked to the max; I'd been swept along yet separated, trying to soak up their certainty.

But here?

It's like everyone's holding their breath in that clenched-up bracing of uncertainty I've been living with since finding out about Bel and these damn cultists. I hate that it feels like this negative energy is emanating out of me. Am I infecting everyone?

As we ready our uniforms after warm-up, the locker room is pin-drop silent. Usually Darian's humming or someone's murmuring spells over their enchanted items or general talk rings around. But it's quiet.

I sit on the bench near my locker, holding my Hellhounds uniform, doing what I've done before every game all season: staring at the Urzoth badge stitched on my jersey's shoulder.

Then promptly ignoring the Urzoth badge.

If we pull off this faux ritual, I'll be able to renounce Urzoth, for real this time. Bel and I both can go into next season free.

I layer on my pads and am tugging on my jersey when the main door flies open.

Roesia and the rest of the team management enter.

I stand along with everyone else. The toxic silence hangs as team management stops in the middle of the room.

Roesia sighs loudly.

"My gods," she says, fists on her hips. "Did we lose already and no one told me?"

"No, ma'am," Aaron speaks up next to me. "I apologize. This isn't the attitude we should be going into the game with."

Agreement ripples through the team.

I rub at my chest. The hell is wrong with us? We've earned our spot here. This is our stadium. What's with this dread? It's heavier than normal. It's—

An alarm rips through my head.

"*Bel.*"

Aaron hums. "I don't hear a bell."

"No, I—"

I think Roesia might be talking. Trying to convince us of our worthiness, our victory. But all I hear is the echo of that alarm in my head, the brief screaming ring that Seb said would trigger in both my head and his when Bel broke one of the pearls on his necklace. When he was in trouble.

Oh my gods.

I fly at my locker, grab my phone, but Seb's already calling me.

We're not supposed to even look at our phones this close to the game, much less when team management is talking, but I answer.

"On my way," Seb says in lieu of greeting. "He's in the cheerleader locker room?"

"Yeah. I think so. I don't—fuck, Seb—"

"Breathe, babe. Thio and I just got to the stadium, so we'll head there. You got us security passes for this reason. And Ilbryen's on him right now?"

Shit, Ilbryen. "Yeah, I'll call her next. I—"

"I'll call when we're there." He hangs up.

Numb, nearly dropping my phone, I try to call Bel first.

It goes to voicemail.

His phone's put away like mine should be. That's all.

Shaking, fighting not to spiral, I call Ilbryen. She's in the locker room with him, undercover as a media rep. Maybe he crushed a pearl by accident during his warm-up; Ilbryen will answer snappishly, assure me he's okay, and hang up.

The call rings.

And rings.

Voicemail.

My gut plummets, staggering me into the side of the locker.

No. No, no, no.

I pocket my phone and whirl—

—to find the entire Hellhounds team and management looking at me.

The championship game starts in an hour. I can't *leave.*

Only I *have* to leave.

"Bel—I mean, Alexo, something's happened to him. I don't know what, but I need to check on him. Now."

It's weak. I *hear* how weak it sounds. I don't have proof to back it up, don't have anything but this *dread* and the alarm that no one else here heard.

Roesia has every right to berate me. This is crazy unprofessional—this is—

She looks back at one of her assistants. "Contact the cheerleading squad. Locate Mr. Warden."

I blow out a noisy breath. What? Just like that?

My phone vibrates in my hand. Seb.

I'm shaking so much I'm shocked I can hold the phone to my ear. "Yeah?"

"Cheerleaders are still in the locker room," he tells me, sounding out of breath. "So says security. We're almost there. Hang on—baby, *go,* use those long legs—shit, Thio can run when he's motivated. O? You still there?"

"Yeah, I—"

Roesia's talking with her assistant, who's on the phone, too. I'm split in half; I split again when I notice the whole team's still watching me, wound with a new energy: defensiveness. Everyone leaning slightly toward me, waiting for the word, waiting to spring forward.

Seb and Roesia speak in an overlap.

"I don't see him," Seb pants. "Neither does Thio."

"Mr. Warden is unaccounted for," Roesia says, her jaw set.

The room shifts. I'm vaguely aware of hanging up on Seb, dialing Bel's phone again—it rings, rings, voicemail.

I'm barreling toward the door before I'm aware of a hand grabbing my bicep, hauling me to a stop.

I swing around, mouth open to shout when Roesia's determined face stops me.

"He's in trouble, isn't he?" she asks calmly, into the once again dead silence of the locker room.

Hollow, I nod.

He's gone. Someone took him.

My knee buckles, but I catch myself and tense everything, locking down, inertia and focus and *I will not break.* He needs me.

And then the manager of this whole team that's supposed to play the biggest game of our careers in less than sixty minutes nods decisively, and says, "All right. Let's go find him."

My chest caves. I can't think beyond the panic clawing at the edges of my brain, setting snares for every rational thought beyond *go, go, get to Bel,* GO.

"What?" I ask. "Ma'am, I—"

"What's going on?" It's Darian.

Followed by Aaron. "Your guy's missing? The fuck?"

Soon, the whole team is talking. Engaged for the first time all morning, an overlap of explanations and questions and concern.

I shake my head at Roesia. "I have to go. I'm sorry, but I can't—"

"I know," she says. "I told you, let's go find him."

She swishes past me, out the door into the hall, and I'm left in a daze.

What?

I—

What?

She should argue. She should tell me to keep my ass *here* and that Bel will show back up on his own, because maybe he's in the bathroom, or maybe he stepped out for air, or—

Marlow pats my cheek, getting my attention. "You heard her," she signs. "Let's go."

Then *she* leaves, too. And Aaron, with a shouted "We'll be back; fix the energy while we're gone."

Darian grabs my wrist. "Come on," he says, and drags me out of the room.

I go, stumbling at first, finding my footing when Darian gives me a supportive smile.

"I'm sure he's fine," he offers.

He's fine.

He has to be.

Gods, he *has* to be.

The parade of the Hellhounds' team manager, rookie rogue, a bard with a guitar on his back, and two defensive tanks in full uniform sans helmets, all barreling through the private hallways of the stadium, gets us more than a few startled looks. But we rip through the place, Roesia in the lead, and by the time we get to the cheerleader locker room, I sprint ahead to gain on her.

Seb's crouched on the ground outside the door with Thio, doing some kind of spell that involves a chalked evocation circle and several components.

He whips his head up at our approach and launches to his feet. "Can't track him," he snaps and kicks one of the components, a jar of mirror dust that clatters across the tiled floor. "Can't *fucking* track him. And I should gods-damn be able to track him—I set it into his necklace."

My throat swells, closes. I choke out the words "What does that mean?"

Seb's face goes gray, eyes flickering from furious to sorrowful. "It means whoever took him knew to ward him against tracking spells."

I wheeze.

Someone really took him.

No. *No*.

I rip my hand up, grabbing at my hair, pacing, breathing too fast. "What do we—what the fuck do we—"

Thio stands and puts a hand on my arm, asking Seb, "What about Ilbryen? Can you track her? Maybe whoever it was took them both."

"I can try. I bet anything Ilbryen's got her own wards against tracking, though. I can—" He finally notes everyone crowding the hall around me.

"Bring the cavalry?" he asks, only half joking.

Roesia nudges Seb's spell work with her toe. "No need to do another tracking spell. I can locate Mr. Warden."

I whirl on her. "What? How?"

Roesia's orange eyes rise to mine. She holds my gaze for what feels like a lifetime.

"I smelled the demonic ancestry on him the moment he stepped into my office," she says.

Every ounce of blood in my body goes to ice, my thoughts screeching to a halt.

No, Bel's illusion magic covers him. It's—that apple smell. He's protected.

Isn't he?

The apples cover the smell of the magic. Not necessarily the smell of *him*.

Spots speckle my vision. It's only through sheer force of will, of knowing Bel needs me, revelations be damned, that I don't ask Roesia a thousand questions.

"Please," I beg her, eyes burning, a jarring contrast to how cold I still am. "Please, find him."

Behind us, Darian, Marlow, and Aaron are quiet. They heard. This probably makes no sense to them. But they watch, still here.

Roesia closes her eyes. Her nostrils flare, her head tips in a move so reminiscent of a hunting dog that I flinch.

After a beat, her eyes pop open, pupils blown. "This way," she says, and she's off like a shot.

I hurry after her, trailed by Seb and Thio, and Marlow, Darian, and Aaron.

Roesia gets to an intersection. Left would take us outside; she whirls right, and a fraction of me eases.

He's still in the stadium.

Why?

Who took him? Why would they keep him here?

We get to a hall blocked by security guards. Beyond is access to the lower levels; the stadium stretches several stories belowground to accommodate for field configurations. Whatever the Dragons planned should already be locked in by their artificers, to be activated once the game starts. But right now, moments before the game? It's strictly off-limits to anyone from the opposing team.

Security tries to stop Roesia. She glares at them, every bit of her werewolf ancestry blazing out when she growls, "I am one of the owners of this stadium. Step. Aside."

They eye each other. And obey.

We fly past them, and I hear one send out a call to the head of security.

Good. Let the whole force of the security team come tumbling after us.

We descend, leaping down staircases and barreling through empty halls.

A hundred nightmares overlap. A hundred moments with Seb from the camp. Him bloodied and bruised. Him *gone*.

I reach behind me, and his hand finds mine, locks in with a reassuring grip.

Four stories belowground, Roesia stops in front of metal double doors and throws her fist up. "Here. The scent is strongest. And beyond this door, I hear—" She cocks her head again. "Six heartbeats. One unconscious. Four calm. One—" Her eyes lock on mine. "One scared."

I drop Seb's hand and march to the doors as someone hisses, "Should we plan first or—"

Fuck any plan.

They took him from me.

I punch the doors open so hard they rebound off the walls with rattling blasts, clouds of dust bursting out of the concrete.

The square room is one of many for hosting spells to adjust the field. Runes glow arcane blue on the floor and walls.

That should be it. No one should be down here; it's incredibly dangerous once the rooms start moving to accommodate whatever field the artificers planned.

But four people are centered in the room, standing in a circle, wearing black cultist robes with the hoods up.

In the corner, unconscious on the floor, is Ilbryen, her hands and legs bound.

And in the middle of the cultist circle, wearing his cheerleading tank top and shorts, his wrists chained above his head so he dangles from an I beam, is Bel in his demon form.

Tears track mascara down his cheeks. His necklace is visible, too, one of the pearls missing.

He sees me and thrashes on the chain, bare toes scraping the floor.

Orok! he mouths, but no sound comes. He says it again, *Orok, Orok—*

They put a silencing spell on him.

My shoulders arch. My hands clench into fists.

And I see. Fucking. *Red.*

One of the cultists throws his hood back. Recognizing him feels preordained.

"I won't let you ruin this again," Tem snarls. "You're too late. Galaxrien will be free!"

He's sneering, trying to be intimidating; he doesn't realize how epically he's messed up.

All that red, all that rising vehemence, has a focus.

He put the love of my life in chains.

He *took Bel from me.*

It's been years since I truly worshipped the god of strength. I renounced him, turned my back on him.

But in this moment, I don't need prayers or offerings to earn back his favor.

Because I fucking *am* the god of strength.

Chapter Seventeen

Awareness comes to me as if through water, muted, deadened.

Roesia snarls. Seb's and Thio's arms are lit up blue with readied spells. Darian's strumming on his guitar, building his own spell. Marlow's . . . gone, but that's not unusual for a rogue. And Aaron's coming around to flank me.

Teeth bared, hands in loose fists, I stomp the rest of the way into the room, envisioning my knuckles in Tem's face.

The moment I get a yard away from the cultists, a wall of translucent green shoots up, encircling them and Bel.

It doesn't stop me. I'm a tank for a reason.

I slam into the wall. A burst of electricity seizes my muscles, errant, annoying twitches that send me lurching back. Bel shouts noiselessly, thrashing again. The three cultists facing him don't react to any of this, their heads bowed under their robes.

The wall remains intact. And Tem, behind it, smirks at me.

"Give us time," Seb whispers behind me. He and Thio drop to the floor with their backs to the cultists, but they'll still know we're trying to break this wall.

I pace, mostly to keep Tem's eyes on me, not Seb and Thio; but more because if I don't move, I'll tear at the floor, slam back against the wall, anything, *anything* to get through to Bel.

Aaron rounds the barrier, stops on the side opposite me. Darian and Roesia take up other points, each of us standing near a cultist.

Tem's eyes slide around the room, and where anyone else might note that they're surrounded and trapped, he only grins. "You can't stop this. It's prophecy."

"Fuck your prophecy," I bark. "And fuck your god."

Tem's face crumbles, revulsion he quickly schools back into rage. "I shouldn't expect anything less blasphemous from a traitor to his own god. Urzoth has to be ashamed of you."

His words do nothing to me. No pinch of reaction; no fear that he's right. I don't give a shit what Urzoth thinks of me. I hope he doesn't think of me at all.

I keep pacing, moving with aggravated jerks like I'm the one in the arcane cage. "You want to talk blasphemy? Bel trusted you. *You're* the traitor."

Tem scoffs. "I have betrayed nothing; every move I've made has been in service to my lord Galaxrien. I tried to get to Belzaroth's father, but he's in a heavily fortified prison. Belzaroth, though?" He laughs, dark and cruel. "Do you have any idea how easy it was to infiltrate the adventure party once I figured out who was guarding him? They were so desperate for help that they took me on with almost no questions asked."

Just like they gave him to me.

Something clinks behind me, and Seb curses.

"Must've screwed with your plans when I took him from you," I say to keep Tem's focus.

He spreads his hands as if to say, *Did it?* "I knew his location still; I knew I could reclaim him when the time was right."

"But the time *isn't* right. Your own rhetoric says the spring equinox—"

"Yes. The spring equinox—*in the Demonic Plane*. Which is *today* in this plane. I merely needed to keep tabs on Belzaroth until the proper date."

Nowhere in any research has a cultist ever mentioned the Demonic Plane's calendar. Trust them to add a new factor because none of their other shit has worked.

Gods, I can't do this anymore.

"You're making this up as you go, aren't you?" I throw in a chuckle even though my chest is crushing in with how hard I'm fighting not to look at Bel or lose my shit.

Tem's brows pulse in a scowl. "You have no idea what I have done. Every ritual this past year has been thanks to *me*. *I* got a clipping of Belzaroth's hair to test if his lineage would indeed react to the spell. *I* had them try to do the ritual on a real person taken from

Urzoth's church as a trial run *for today*, to see how that church would react and if they would be a problem. All of this has been thanks to *me*, and in only a few moments, this room will lift into the stadium and Galaxrien's true followers the world over will see our lord *rise*!"

I don't point out that most of those rituals failed. But, wait—this room will lift into the field?

Every other ritual has been public, or at least reported on; Tem *wants* eyes on them.

The cultists begin chanting, low, murmured words I don't catch.

And the room shifts.

The walls, the floor; they groan and shudder, and I brace my legs wide as we start moving up.

I clock other items between the cultists' feet now, all things I have listed on the notepad in my apartment, the elements of the ritual. Including the gods-damned bottle of hot sauce.

My eyes fly to the chains. *Bel's* in the handcuffs.

Looking at him stabs into me, a visceral knife gouging deep. I meet his eyes, trying to wordlessly convey a dozen different things.

It's going to be okay. I'm going to get you out of here. I love you, I'm here, I'm going to save you.

I expect him to be terrified, or numb, or grieving, but he's staring straight at me, eyes aflame.

He mouths a word I don't understand. Something with an *F*.

I shake my head in confusion.

He repeats it, over and over, jutting his chin at Tem, who has his arms lifted, his head thrown back.

"Today is the day," Tem proclaims over the chanting, over the room's groans as it launches for the surface. "The blood of Galaxrien will free him. The blood of Galaxrien will free him. The blood—"

Movement yanks my focus up. Marlow's crouched along the I beam that's holding Bel.

"He's saying *fake the ritual*," Marlow signs. Thank gods I learned sign language; she's not wearing her enchanted ring.

Fake the—

I whip a wide-eyed look at Bel.

Fake the ritual.

Steal Tem's attempt at summoning Galaxrien.

The ceiling peels back so the harsh light of midafternoon plunges down on us. The I beam holding Bel stays in place, the focal point for Tem's display, and the roar of the stadium rushes in. The game shouldn't be starting yet, but the field's moving; the crowd's going crazy.

The ceiling folds back and the walls collapse as we continue to rise. In a few seconds, we'll be visible to the entire stadium. To the world.

I shake my head at Bel, panic gripping my throat. He rocks on the chain as the room twists and shudders, and he mouths, *Please, Orok.* Then, *I love you.*

That clamp on my throat releases.

We'd barely started to plan. We were supposed to be smart about it, control all the factors.

But Bel's right. We can hijack this. We can end it all, *now.*

I whirl down to Seb and Thio, who are crouched over an evocation circle, hands splayed and faces bent in focus.

"Seb," I whisper. "We're doing the fake ritual."

He stares at me for half a second.

A manic grin overtakes him, and I swear he giggles.

"Can you?" I ask. "Lightning, thunder, smoke, fire?"

He digs in his component belt. "Enough. Yeah. Keep them distracted."

The room vibrates and we all lurch to the side, the walls almost entirely gone. The crowd is a dull rumble of noise, growing louder, and distantly, I spot a speck against the sky; one of the stadium's cameras coming to see why the field's moving so early.

They'll record everything that happens. Broadcast it in the stadium and across the world. Which is what we wanted, to *show* everyone that this ritual won't work—but in our plan, we were going to alter how Bel looks. Now, he'll be at the center of this, in his true form, his identity shown to everyone. And Seb and Thio are clearly doing magic; but hopefully, those watching will think they're working to undo the barrier, which they are.

I stay in a crouch by Seb and Thio but face the cultists. They're still chanting, hands spread. Only Tem has his hood back, his face tipped up, eyes closed and a smile on his face.

Bel nods at me. *It's okay*, he mouths.

The walls collapse until only the floor and the I beam remain, and we're gliding past the field's ground, lifting higher, until we come to a warbling stop at least fifty feet in the air.

An entire stadium's attention is fixed on us, and several cameras broadcast what's left of the room. On one of the massive screens, it's clear that the runes on the floor under Bel are in the shape of a pentagram.

Aaron, Roesia, and Darian stay in a circle around the green arcane wall. Marlow's crouched on the I beam, trying to pry at the chains holding Bel. They all eye me, then the stadium, but they stay. They stay and they're ready, and I wish I could explain what's happening, but with each passing moment of strain and worry immobilizing me, I face Tem, and wait.

"The blood of Galaxrien will free him," the cultists chant. "The blood of Galaxrien will free him."

"Now," Seb whispers.

Lightning crackles around the cultists. A crack of thunder bolts through the air. Flames burst to life at the edge of the platform, billowing smoke around us. That'll help hide what Seb and Thio are doing, at least.

Tem cackles with glee. "Rise, our lord! *Rise!*"

The flames flare higher, the lightning surges blindingly white—

And then it fades.

Shimmers, pulses, and retracts. The ritual, failing.

The cultists stop their chanting, confused. Tem's smile fades and he shakes his head.

Breath saws into my lungs, fisted hands gouging my nails into my palms.

It's not going to be enough, is it?

"No, keep chanting!" Tem urges.

They'll keep trying. And trying, and Bel will never be safe, *he'll never be safe*, not until they get exactly what they want: Galaxrien Vossen.

So . . . let's give them Galaxrien Vossen.

Seb and Thio are both frantic in spell work, hands flying, components vanishing, and spells falling from their lips.

I lean over to them. "Voice projection," I murmur. "A voice projection spell."

Seb glances at me, sweat pouring down his face, his eyes slitted in confusion. "For—?"

"Galaxrien's going to make an appearance after all," I whisper.

Even over the rumbles of fading thunder, the noise of the crowd, all of it, Seb hears. Thio, too—he pats Seb's forearm and goes, "On it."

Seb shakes his head. "No, you keep breaking that arcane wall; I'll do the voice. And Orok—"

Seb's eyes flash behind me. And widen.

"*Distract him!*"

I scramble around.

And realize the full breadth of my stupidity in one heart-shattering moment.

There's a part of the ritual we haven't emulated. A part the cultists hadn't yet touched either.

The *blood*.

Tem is holding a dagger as long as his forearm.

"Thio!" I shout, banging on the arcane wall, little zaps of electricity shooting up my arms. "Get me in there!"

Bel still hangs from the beam. His eyes are round, and when he looks at me again, that resignation flashes over him.

For eight years he's run from this. For eight years he's lived dozens of lies to stay safe from this very moment, and now it's here.

A tear rolls down his face, and he tries to smile, wobbling and scared.

I love you, he mouths.

I bang on the wall again, panic clawing through me. He doesn't get to give up. *I'm not giving up.*

The cultists chant and sway. Tem faces Bel, a feverish grin stretching his lips.

"The blood of Galaxrien will free him," he says, lifting the dagger. Aiming for Bel. "The blood of Galaxrien will free him."

"*STOP!*" I scream.

"YOU FOOLS!"

The voice booms around the platform, startling a shout out of Aaron across from me.

"THIS IS NOT THE TIME OF MY PROPHESIED RETURN!" The flames around us blaze higher. "YOU HAVE SHAMED ME!"

The cultists freeze. Even Tem goes rigid, his knife still up and aimed.

Bel's fear dissolves in—amusement.

He packs it away into appropriate terror, yanking on his chains for good measure, struggling and writhing.

My shoulders arch, hands curled, *ready*.

"YOU DARE HARM MY DESCENDANT, MY ANOINTED BLOOD!" Galaxrien/Seb bellows. "FOOLS! INGRATES! RELEASE HIM! IF YOU HARM HIM, YOU WILL *FEEL MY WRATH*!"

More thunder shakes the platform; lightning flares and bursts so bright I wince. Choking smoke wraps around us, shielding Seb and Thio even more, highlighting the arcane barrier wrapped around the cultists and Bel.

The cultists cry out and drop to their knees. Only Tem remains standing, his arm with the dagger going slack.

He stares around, jaw distending, perplexity making him wilt. "My lord—"

"CEASE THIS IMPRUDENT MISSION!" Galaxrien/Seb continues. "YOU HAVE BEEN LED ASTRAY! I . . . uh . . . SMITE YOU! SMITE THEE . . . with, um . . . MY GREAT AND VENGEFUL DEMONIC POWER!"

Okay, Seb, wrap it up.

"BEGONE FROM MY SIGHT, FOOLISH MORTALS!"

The fire, the lightning, the smoke—it all vanishes at once.

"There," Thio says, then, "Orok, *now*!"

A crack, a shattering splinter as the barrier falls; the noise barely registers. I'm moving.

I dive forward, a final wave of prickling electricity sheeting over my skin as I hurl my body toward Tem.

Aaron, Roesia, and Darian move at the same time I do. I'm half aware of grunts and shouts, a snarl, a rending tear, a wail.

All I see is Tem, twisting toward me.

For one stretched-out beat, his dismay morphs into shocked fear before I tackle him.

The dagger glances off my rawball padding and clatters across the concrete with a metallic ring. Tem cries out as he thuds to the floor, my full weight crashing down on him.

Something rolls next to us—the hot sauce bottle.

I don't give him a beat to gain his breath; I grab the bottle and smash the fuck out of his face with it.

Oh, look. The hot sauce was an important part of the ritual after all.

Tem's head snaps back, skull cracking on the stone. Blood flies from his nose and hot sauce ruptures across his face in a mini explosion.

I drop the broken bottle, rear back, fist wound—

"Orok!" Darian's in front of me. "Go, I got him."

Go? Tem's unconscious but his face is still recognizable. He's still *breathing*. I'm not done yet.

"*Orok*," Darian says more firmly. "Your guy needs you."

That rips me to my feet.

Darian strums a chord on his guitar and Tem's whole body arches in a muscle spasm.

"I got him," Darian says again.

Roesia and Aaron have the other cultists restrained or unconscious. Seb and Thio lean exhaustedly on each other. Bel's hanging from the chain but Marlow's above him, legs wrapped around the I beam.

Her eyes pop upside down to mine and she quickly signs, "Get ready to catch him," before she goes back to work on the chain links.

I dive in, arms clamping around Bel's waist to hold him to me. He mouths something at me and my lungs ache as I bellow, "Someone get rid of this damn silence spell!"

I'm unhinging. The weakened seams of my composure are fraying and I have nothing, *nothing* left to hold myself together.

Darian hits a chord on his guitar and Bel sucks in a rattling breath.

"Orok," he tries, and sobs. "*Orok!*"

I kiss him, tasting my name on his lips and the salt of his tears, feeling the warmth of his exhale and the thrum of his anxiety as his body shudders in my arms. Or maybe that's me shuddering; we're both tremors and desperation.

The chain releases with a rattle of metal, and I make sure it doesn't hit Bel as it falls to the ground. Marlow drops with it and undoes the cuffs.

I take Bel's wrists and rub my thumbs over them, noting the redness, the way bruises are already forming.

I'm going to kill Tem.

Around us, everyone's stunned. Cameras are still on us; security is now levitating toward the platform.

It doesn't matter. All that matters is here, right here.

Bel's okay. He's all right. He's tear-stained and wide-eyed and shaking, but he's all right.

The tautness in my chest doesn't let up, the knot in the base of my neck doesn't untangle. I keep running my hands over Bel's arms, his back, up to his neck and in his hair, like I'm searching for wounds or checking that he's okay.

He's okay. He's all right.

Bel cups my jaw and angles me to look at him; our eyes connect.

"Hi," he whispers.

I yank him into my arms, hand to the back of his head, holding him against me, feeling him breathe.

"We're never doing that again," I tell him.

Bel burrows into me. "No arguments here." He pushes his face into my pec. "I'm sorry."

"Sweetheart—"

"I know you didn't want me to do it at all, and we rushed into it. And if it doesn't work, if they still target me, I—I don't know what it'll mean, but—"

"*Bel.*" I rock his head back, gazing down at him.

He settles, lips parted, eyes watery.

I swipe my thumbs along his cheeks, clearing the streaked mascara. "I'm so damn proud of you."

A smile pulls across his mouth. "Yeah?"

"Hell yes. I was about to lose my shit, and you kept your head on, and had us take the chance to stop all of this—you're amazing. *You* did this."

He scrunches his nose. "Well, I was no *Galaxrien Vossen,*" he says, barely a whisper.

We look over to where Seb has an arm curled around thin air. Nick, I'm guessing. Thio leans on Seb's shoulder, sweaty and winded.

They'll get the wedding of their fucking dreams after this. They would have anyway, let's be honest, but now? Whatever they want. Hell, *more* than they want. They're going to be spoiled rotten, I'll make sure of it.

I nod at Seb. *Thank you.*

He cracks a smile, and it finally pulls one out of me, too.

Until Aaron clears his throat. "So. Um. What the fuck?"

The weight of what we did hits me.

Bel's identity is out. To my team; to the world. And I dragged my teammates and manager into this.

I push Bel to the side, slightly behind me, and face Aaron, Marlow, and Darian—where's—

Roesia is crouched beside Ilbryen, who's still unconscious.

I shake my head and face my teammates. Who deserve an explanation. *So many* explanations. Security's getting closer; we probably only have a few seconds before they land on the platform, and cameras are still recording.

"Thank you," I hear myself say. "Thank you for helping me. Us. I—I can't explain everything right now, but I will, gladly. Just know that you saved him. Saved—" I look down at Bel. Who grins up at me and nods. "Bel. Not Alexo."

Darian, who's still strumming on his guitar, keeping the cultists in stasis, shrugs and smiles. "It was like an extreme training exercise."

Aaron does the Hellhounds bark, which quickly gets picked up across the stadium, until thousands of people are braying around us.

My eyes tear, because why not at this point. "Thank you. I can't say it enough."

Marlow grins. "Always."

Security clatters onto the platform. Some get to work putting magic binds on Tem and the cultists, who are, thankfully, still unconscious.

Ilbryen, however, is waking up. She blinks dazedly while Roesia seems to be . . . sniffing her? Roesia's orange eyes pulse brighter, interest like a craving flashing over her.

Ilbryen's lips flicker in the smallest, barest grin.

"Wow," Bel huffs next to me. "Did you manifest that?"

A surprised snort bursts out of me and I tighten my hold on him. I'm not sure how I'll let him go—we still have a game to play.

Bel twists into me, smiling softly, like he can see all my concern play over my face. He can, probably.

He brushes his fingertips across my lips. "I'm proud of you, too, you know. I never could have done this, would never have even *thought* to do this, without you. If this works, it's because of you." His eyes glisten, golden and black. "Do you believe me yet?"

"Believe you?" I frown, thumb rubbing against his lower back.

"That you're strong." He smiles. "The strongest person I've ever met."

I wait for the rebuttal. To argue with him or change the subject.

But nothing comes. I stare down into his smiling face while security works to fix this mess, while cameras fly all around us.

My hand moves up to my shoulder. To the corner of my jersey, to the patch I've stared at before every game. Urzoth's axe in a stone.

Eyes on Bel, fingers shaking, I grab the edge of it and pull.

With a jagged rip, the patch comes off in my hand.

We win the rawball championship game.

After our display on the platform, the Dragons were so freaked they fumbled most of their plays. Turns out taking down a crazed demon cult is a good intimidation tactic; no one on the Dragons wanted to mess with us.

Which is the opposite reaction I expected once I removed my Urzoth badge. I thought it'd open me up to claims of weakness, but actions are louder. Screamingly loud. No one questions my strength or worthiness or bravery, not now.

Well.

Almost no one.

In the player chute, my parents are standing with Reverend Drach. We're hardly alone; cameras and reporters clog the space, everyone celebrating and joyous after the win. But the three of them are solemn, Drach glowering with his arms folded.

Bel's waiting for me in the press area. Seb and Thio stayed near him through the game. Ilbryen, too, who was pissed Tem got the jump on her. But I'm anxious to get back to him.

He did the whole game, every cheer routine, in his demon form.

And *that's* why I don't think I'll ever truly believe him when he says I'm the strongest person he's ever met. Because *he's* the strongest. The bravest.

He's everything.

Head high, I cross to my parents and Drach, and don't give them a chance to speak.

"Urzoth is no longer my patron god. I'm not going to make it a bigger PR moment than it already is. I don't owe explanations or reasons, and going forward, I'll represent the team on my own, with my own strength."

My mother doesn't seem as angry as Drach; if anything, she's cautious.

But Drach puffs up his chest. "Is that right, Mr. Monroe?"

I don't rise to his challenge. Don't make myself look bigger or try to match his peacocking. "That's right, Reverend."

"One of Urzoth's chosen players defeated the cult of his enemy," Drach tries. "And Mr. Warden, this whole time, has been *demonic*? The church cannot let this pass without—"

"I appreciate everything you've done," I cut him off. "And everything you did for my boyfriend. Supporting someone of demonic ancestry will go a long way toward soothing tensions between the Urzoth church and Galaxrien followers, won't it? It'll show that the church is about more than rivalries and violence, which is what you wanted out of this arrangement all along."

Drach's mouth bobbles. His cheeks redden. "I suppose. But you cannot deny that Urzoth gave you the strength to stop the cult."

My smile is stiff. "I won't deny it. But I also won't give Urzoth credit for what I did. I hope we can all move on."

I put emphasis on the last words.

Drach bristles. Cameras flash, reminding us we're in public, and, thankfully, Treva swoops in.

"Excuse me," she says. "I'm sorry, but I need to pull Mr. Monroe away for interviews."

Drach huffs and stomps off.

My parents still haven't said anything, and my stomach sours with apprehension.

Part of the reason I put off doing this for so long is that I didn't want to lose them. But I was losing myself the longer I held on. It feels like I can *breathe* again. For the first time, maybe, in almost a decade.

"Give me a sec?" I ask Treva, who smiles politely and steps to the side.

My mom's eyes get teary and she digs in her purse to pull out—a stack of letters?

"Alexo—" She stops. "That isn't his name, is it?"

"Bel," I correct.

"Bel." She sniffs and flips through the papers. "He's been sending me letters. One a week, since our lunch."

My brows go up. He has? Why?

She holds them to her chest. "They all gush about you. He'd tell me how strong you are, all these little things you'd do for him. And I would like to—" She stops, tips her head, her smile watery. "I'd like to understand, Orok. Can we talk about your decision?"

"I'm not changing my mind."

Mom brushes the letters lovingly. "If you can inspire such a strong reaction in someone, I want to understand what you've been going through."

My eyes drop to the letters. I trust that Bel didn't tell my mom anything I wouldn't want her to know about, and I'll absolutely interrogate him about the letters' contents later. Preferably when we're both naked and I can make sure he knows how gods-damned grateful I am to have him in my life.

Throat swelling, I nod. "Yeah. Maybe I can bring Bel out for a visit soon?"

"Oh, I'd love that. *We* would. Wouldn't we?"

She elbows my dad, who's been watching us, but in his usual quiet way.

He grunts. "Yes, dear. Of course."

I hug them both, letting myself gulp in a few more of those deep, cleansing breaths that I can feel through my entire body.

The next few hours are a whirlwind of interviews, photos, and PR junkets, followed by several parties Bel and I get shuttled to along with most of the team. No one bats an eye at Bel's demon form or says anything about the cult ritual beyond *Fuckers got what they deserved.*

I spend every moment holding Bel as close as possible. There won't be one photo of me that doesn't have him in it, and vice versa. We're a package deal, and I want any lingering cultists to know that. If they still have it in their minds to come after him, they have to go through me.

By the time Bel and I stumble back to our apartment, we're nearly asleep on our feet. I reactivate the wards as soon as the door locks behind us, and the two of us stand in the dim foyer, staring at each other.

It's over.

Or it *might* be over—we won't know until we give the cultists a few months, see if there's any activity. But even if there is, Bel's out, no going back. I renounced Urzoth, also no going back.

We're free.

Like he's having the same thoughts, a smile glides across Bel's face, his lip gloss flashing in the moonlight from the living room's massive windows that barely illuminate the entryway. His outfit's been driving me wild—black crocheted sleeves connect across his collarbone, leaving most of his chest bare, showing defined planes of rose-gold skin, peaked nipples, and a thick silver belly chain looped under his navel. His tail's tucked away, and baggy black pants hang excruciatingly low on his hips.

"All night," I start, "*all night*, I kept envisioning yanking those pants down and making you sit on my lap in a way that'd steal headlines from the way we already stole headlines today."

He smirks. "Oh yeah? Why didn't you?"

I drop to my knees in front of him. His breath cuts out in a gush.

"Because," I say, crawling toward him across the marble floor. "While everyone better know who you belong to, only I get to see what you look like when I push into you."

The softest, most grasping whimper flutters in his throat.

He backs up until his spine hits the guestroom door. In this position, on my hands and knees, my head's level with his chest; I duck so I can bury my face against his belly, right over that chain.

I take it in my teeth and tug gently.

He still smells like apples. Faint, but it's there. Beneath it, he smells like *him*, like soap and the fresh, clean scent of his skin. The aroma has a snarl building in me, something feral that's been brewing since the pearl broke and alerted me that he was gone.

And suddenly, everything I've been compartmentalizing—he was taken from me; he got hurt; he almost *died*—avalanches over me, a frigid, breath-stealing assault.

Tears sting my eyes. "They took you," I say into his skin. It's barely sound, a vibration if anything.

But Bel hears. He strokes his fingers through my hair. "You saved me."

I seize his hips, yanking him up the wall so I can drop hard, open-mouthed kisses in a band across his waist. He squeals and scrambles at my head for balance, those squeals breaking into moans as I scrape my teeth over his sharp hip bones, more consumption than kiss.

His hips thrust and his torso arches, that rhythmic, sexy-as-fuck dance for me.

"Orok," he pants. "Want you. Please. N-need you."

Gods, we both need it. Both need this coming together—it's falling out of him in pleas; it's breaking out of me in hunger.

"Shh." I look up at him, supplicant and devoted. "I got you, sweetheart. Let me worship you."

He whimpers and presses back into the wall, a tremor rolling across his skin as he fights not to squirm.

I lower him long enough to hook my fingers in his pants and peel them and his boxers off, lifting first one leg, then the other to get rid of his shoes, too. His tail thwacks against the floor, and he's hard and leaking already, his body shivering despite the heat waving off us both; it's the energy of the day releasing, I know. I'm shivering, too, hands shaking as I skate my fingers up his bare legs, his muscles wound and distinct in his lean thighs.

Ravenousness burns in the pit of my stomach, my throat bobbing on a grating swallow. I'm hit with a myriad of wants so potent I get dizzy—want to wrap him in my arms, hold him for days; want to impale him on my cock so our bodies meld; want to devour him, feel every part of him connect with every part of me until I can truly accept that he's *safe* now. He's okay.

He got taken from me.

I heft him in my arms again, bracing him on the wall so his cock is level with my face, so I can be here on my knees for him. His tail twitches and wraps around my thigh; I love that outward sign of his unraveling. Want stripes of his bruises all over my legs.

I pull his hard length into my mouth and he croons, belly rippling, one hand going up to grip the guestroom door. "Orok, yes, yes, oh my gods—"

My cheeks hollow and I suck, hard, constricting the pressure around his dick and bobbing my head in a punishing rhythm. The hunger, the want, the fear and sorrow and grief are all driving me now; I'm kerosene-saturated and aflame.

Need him to come. Need him to feel good. Need him to fall apart in my mouth so I can taste him and hear those noises, see that dance.

He's okay. He's safe, he's okay.

Bel cants into me, aborted thrusts that twist into rolls. That chain, his lip gloss; he catches and sparks in the low moonlight, the barest wisp of his usual solar flare. It burns me the same, a caustic natural disaster I greedily let mark me. Cut me open in a decade, two, and there'll be a ring carved into my soul from him.

I suck harder, running my tongue around his length. Bel's hips jerk and spasm, mouth dropping open, throat elongating as he comes with a frantic wail. That sound shudders through me, stroking over my raw nerve endings like his fingertips gliding through my hair, calming, reassuring.

I ease him out of my mouth, keep hold of him as I climb his body with kisses on his stomach, his pecs, his collarbone, his jaw. He hangs in my arms, sated and limp, letting me truly worship him now, letting me drink my fill.

"So good for me," I whisper into his temple. "Giving yourself to me. Dancing for me. You're perfect."

A low whine is his response, his eyes fighting to open, his breath slowing.

"You love me," he mumbles. "Tell me."

I bite his neck, tongue the spot as he wilts. "I love you. I love you so much, Bel."

"And?"

"And," I nuzzle his jaw, "you're mine."

His jaw stretches as he smiles. "Yours. Forever."

Forever.

It isn't a flippant hope now.

It's a fact.

Morning News: "Welcome to *One Shot*, your number-one source for the latest in pro rawball news. I'm your host, Diamanda Blacktalon. With me today, after his long journey to find the eternal flame of the Lizard People, is Vaknox, now the Reigning King of the Lizard People of Tesh, Purveyor of Fire and Ash, He of the Sun, Chosen of Chaxloakka. Vaknox, I cannot begin to tell you how glad I am to have you back."

lizard hissing noises

"Aw, I missed you, too! I know you've kept abreast of everything going on in the rawball world, but there's one thing you wanted to talk about in particular, isn't there?"

lizard hissing noises

"Exactly—Orok Monroe not only helped stop a Galaxrien cult ritual during the rawball championship game, it now turns out that he's funding an entire new mental health program with Thrive Children. Swoon! There is no way for him to be any sexier, let me tell you."

lizard hissing noises

"Oh, I know, Vaknox, I know—he's locked down! Can you believe our own Beauty has been half demon this whole time? I have to ask: Do *you* think he's really the descendant of Galaxrien Vossen?"

lizard hissing noises

"Wow, Vaknox, well said. Well said indeed. We've got to go to a break, but romance is blooming on the Hellhounds for a second time: superstar offensive rogue Marlow Keel is dating team captain and defensive tank Aaron Harsaf! An in-depth look when we come back!"

Chapter Eighteen

Five Months Later

"You're sure this is the place?" Bel bounces his heel in the passenger seat's footwell.

"It's the address Ilbryen gave us."

I slow as the house comes up on our right. Plenty of spaces on the road are open to park, but as I pull into one, Bel flaps his hands with a panicked screech.

"Not yet! No—circle the block again. One more time."

"You've said that for the last three times, sweetheart." I obey though, drifting away from the curb and rounding the block, giving his thigh a firm squeeze where I've been holding it since we got in the rental car an hour ago.

He sinks into the seat, gnawing on his lip until I lift my hand to tap his chin.

"Hey. I quite like that lip. Be nice to it."

He pops it out at me in a bratty pout. But that pout dissolves quickly, leaving him with a bouncing leg and the flustered concern that's been growing larger over the past few weeks.

There's been no more Galaxrien cultist activity. No rumors, no rituals. The official church of Galaxrien Vossen reached out, wanting to meet their lord's progeny. Bel politely declined, and they've respected his wishes so far. On the other side of things, the Urzoth church quietly pulled out as his sponsor for next season, but Bel seemed relieved they were the ones to cut that tie; he doesn't need them anymore.

While none of that means all threats are gone, Ilbryen felt, after the failed ritual that got broadcast all over the world and the arrest of Tem and his closest cultists, that we could take some calculated risks with Bel's safety. I'm not about to lower my own vigilance, hell no; he's still wearing the pearl safety necklace, too.

But the one risk we can take, the one risk we *have* to take, is letting Bel see his cousins.

Bel and I both are due to start conditioning soon for the next rawball season with the Hellhounds. Before we get too busy with training and travel, we asked Ilbryen to reach out.

It was their choice. Ilbryen asked if they'd feel comfortable being a part of his life again, and *gods*, waiting on their response was the longest two days of my existence. I did what I could to distract Bel, but he was a wreck, practicing cheer routines in the living room until the late hours of the night, making Thio come over to cook with him, dish after dish we still have stuffed in our freezer.

But they said yes.

Yes, they want to see him.

Yes, they miss him as much as he misses them.

And now, we're here. Circling a suburban block in a city outside Austin, not far from the town where Bel originally lived with them. Their mother, Bel's aunt, still lives in his childhood home, but the sisters moved a few years ago. The oldest one, Mila, owns the house we've been inadvertently casing.

Bel swallows, his throat clicking against the purr of the engine. "And they're . . . they're both going to be there?" he confirms, even though he very well knows the arrangement.

I flash him a smile. "Yes. Ilbryen set it up with them."

He scrapes his palms on his baggy whitewashed jeans and snatches my hand off his thigh, clinging to it. I pulse my grip on his fingers and slow into the next turn, taking us onto the house's road again.

"They miss you," I say. The same thing I've been reminding him of, over and over, in the days since we got the green light to plan this trip. "They want to see you."

"I know, I know." He sucks in a breath. "What if this is a bad idea?"

Luckily, no other drivers are on this road, so I let the car drift to barely creeping forward. "What do you mean?"

"What if . . . what if the cultists come back? And I put Mila and Jemma in danger. Maybe it's better to stay away. It's better to not—" He frees one hand to rub at his chest, his voice small. "I don't want them to get hurt."

He's been saying some version of that since we left Philadelphia. *It's easier if I stay away. We've changed so much, why would I disrupt their lives like this?*

I've let him talk, let him get all the worry out, and I've waited for him to say what he's truly afraid of.

But we're here. No time left.

I pull his hand up to drop a kiss to his knuckles. "It's easier to keep people at a distance. No one gets hurt that way, right? Not them. Not you."

Bel peeks up at me. "I'm not . . . I'm not worried about me," he says like he's testing the words. There's no truth in them.

It'd be easier not to reunite with his cousins, in case he has to leave again.

But we're not living that way anymore. Neither of us. We love and embrace and open ourselves to all the messy parts that come with those things, because the bad doesn't get to poison the good. We *deserve* that good. It's ours.

We arrive at Mila's house again. This time, when I pull over in front of it, Bel doesn't protest. He stares at it, his rose-gold face pale.

I tug on his hand. After a beat, he reluctantly looks at me, his irises glistening with tears.

"They understand the risks," I tell him. "Just like I do. Just like Seb and Thio, and my parents, and Marlow, Darian, Aaron, and Roesia—just like the whole Hellhounds team and cheerleading squad do. Because, Bel, *you're worth the risk.*"

Listing all those people makes my eyes heat.

Gods, we're so loved.

"We won't live our lives in fear," I continue. "If you have to run again, we'll figure it out. But it won't be like last time, because the cultists don't deserve to get any part of you, least of all your happiness."

"You're my happiness," he whispers.

One side of my mouth kicks up. "You're my happiness, too."

A tear slips down his cheek. He groans and swipes at it. "Fuck. Why the hell did I even put on makeup today?"

But he settles with a heavy sigh and bites that lip again.

I tug it free. His smile is small and reticent, and he leans across the center console to brush a chaste kiss to my mouth.

He holds there, just the gentle rub of thin skin, the taste of his berry lip gloss.

"Okay," he murmurs. He pulls back, checks his makeup in the dropdown mirror, and straightens his cropped white tank. "Okay. Let's do this."

We climb out of the car.

I round the hood and stand next to where Bel stops on the sidewalk, palms scraping against his jeans again. He still sometimes chooses to use the illusion spray, but more often than not—like today—he's in his demon form. His tail's tucked away, but he's letting his horns grow back, two rose-gold knobs at the front of his pink curls.

Mila's house is a small ranch with eggshell-blue siding and a little porch where a swing rocks in the breeze. Bel's gold-black eyes shift over the door, the windows with frilly curtains.

One of those curtains moves.

A face appears, then it's gone, and before either of us can do anything, the front door opens.

Two women dash out. Both have waves of brown hair and pale skin, one's wearing jeans and a T-shirt, the other a floral dress.

I expect them to hesitate, stop and gape like Bel's doing, but they don't slow down. I catch tear-stained cheeks and a choked *oh my gods* before they're hurling themselves around Bel, a chaotic, clustered hug.

For a moment, he stands there, stiff and shocked.

But only for a moment.

He melts, looping his arms around them as they stroke his hair, exclaiming and sobbing and smiling. He's crying, too, messy and raw, and in their arms, unwinding like this, he looks so young. The fifteen-year-old version of him who was forced to run, who barely got a chance to say goodbye.

The woman in the floral dress notices me first. She pulls away from Bel and scrubs at her eyes, blows out a self-conscious laugh. "Who's this?"

Bel turns to me; his joy is the sun.

"This is Orok," he says, voice choked in tears. "My—*mine*."

My cheeks hurt with my smile. *His.*

I hold out my hand, and the woman shakes it.

"I'm Jemma," she says. "And that's—"

The other woman, Mila presumably, is already turning from Bel to throw her arms around me.

"Thank you," she whispers into my shoulder.

I return her hug. "It's my pleasure. Truly."

"Oh my gods, my manners!" Mila yanks back from me and grabs Bel's hand. "Come inside, both of you! We want to hear *everything*!"

She hauls Bel for the house, Jemma following and peppering Bel with questions about the rawball championship ritual and if he's really okay from it, though it was months ago. She promises to see him perform next season, and Mila adds how they'll come to as many games as they can.

Bel looks back at me. He's dazed, his face red from crying and laughter.

I trail them and mouth, *You good?*

He nods immediately. And says, *I love you.*

People aim too far out when they think they need to belong to a god.

All I ever needed was to belong to this one man.

Acknowledgments

The gushy part of every book! I promise not to use too many sports metaphors. But, I mean, I kinda gotsta, right? *Sports book* and all. But don't worry, I'll keep my eye on the ball.

Firstly, thanks are owed to Kristen Simmons, for being my Sports Sensitivity Reader. Look, my loves; I am not what the poets would call a "sports person." When I knew I'd be writing a sports romance, even though I found a shortcut by making up my own sport, I still wanted it to feel accurate to a fantasy version of football. Thus, I begged my darling friend to read an early draft and let me know what sporty things I messed up. Thank you, Kristen, for telling me about magical words like *downfield* and that the team captain is actually a pretty important guy. The character of Aaron got a promotion because of you; he sends his thanks, too.

Thanks also, always, to Amy Stapp. Orok doesn't interact with his fantasy sports world version of an agent, but that's only because you set the bar too high; a fictional version could not compete.

Erika Tsang, thank you for loving this book, and for encouraging my craft in ways that will make me adore you forever.

Thank you to all the marketing and publicity folks who always knock it out of the park: Jordan Hanley, Lauren Abesames, Libby Collins, Emily Mlynek, Sarah Reidy, Ariana Carpentieri, and Tyrinne Lewis.

A huge, screaming thank-you to Lilith Saur, for making this cover such a slam dunk. Each cover is better than the last; I still hold that you are magic.

Thank you, thank you to all the behind-the-scenes darlings who constantly go to the mat for me: Luisa Rozo Castaneda, Lesley Worrell, Rafal Gibek, Megan Kiddoo, Jen Edwards, Jacqueline Huber-Rodriguez, Sara Thwaite, Kira Tregoning, Katy Miller, Drew Kilman, Maria Snelling, Katy Robitzski, and Esther de Araujo.

And last but not least, a shiny gold medal to you, my ever-lovely readers. You always welcome my books and characters with open arms. This job is hard; you make it worthwhile.

Thank you, thank you, thank you.

Turn the page for a sneak peek at
Sara Raasch's next rom-com,

Lightning & Thunder

Percy Jackson but make them superheroes in an action-adventure rom-com where the offspring of gods protect humanity, and Zeus's snarky, reluctant heir is forced to team up with the globally beloved descendant of Thor.

Coming Fall 2026

He's teasing me? About things he *knows* are lies, and stuff he *knows* I've done wrong, but instead of chastising me about how I can do better, he's . . . smiling.

Who is this guy?

"Lot of weight your opinion will hold." I finish up the bacon as the elevator moves, still so unbothered, the most unbothered. "The Council may be able to justify you leaving with me, but when they find out it's so you could scamper off to a den of underground activity without the intent to bring it all crumbling down? They'll riot in the street."

Erik laughs. "Not all of our missions are overt fighting. On occasion, we do hit up seedier places for intel. This isn't too far out of my wheelhouse—as you'll learn, when you join the Hero Council."

"Oh, sweet summer child, this is nowhere close to your wheelhouse." I pole-vault over his assumption that I'll pass the final tests and make it through the Council's vote, pulling my shoulders back, all official-like. "Which is why we'll start with rule number one."

His eyes glimmer. "Two."

"What?"

"You said the first ground rule was that I don't transform into Hero Mode."

I suck my teeth. "Yes. Obviously. *As I was saying*: rule number two—"

He smirks. I want to smack him.

"—you can't ask where we're going. Do you have any tracking stuff on you?"

He pats his pocket. "My phone."

"Give it here." I hold out my hand, expecting him to bluster about how he can't do that, but he drops it into my grasp without hesitating.

My gods. He realizes what he's giving me, right?

If I slip my phone next to his, I can create a connection and dive back in later. His phone probably links to the Council's network.

This is it.

This is my way in.

I stand there as the elevator whirls us down, one hand cradling my food, the other clutching his phone.

Erik watches me, calm, trusting.

With a few taps of my thumb, I disable his location services and pass the phone back.

It's like I'm watching a B movie of myself. That's not me, harmlessly handing the phone to him. What cheap crap is this?

Erik tucks his phone away. "What else?"

What else what? What else can I fuck up by being an overemotional sap?

"Um. Number three is a version of the no-Hero-Mode promise: you let me take the lead and do *exactly* what I say. I'm accepting a huge risk bringing you. You have to listen to me."

Erik's gaze goes blistering over that smirk that seems permanent. "I can obey you, Lux. It's the other way around that's always been in question."

A strangled noise vibrates across my tongue. I smother it with the last of the pancakes.

"N-number four," I stammer. *Fuck, get your shit together, Keraunos.* "You need to wear a blindfold for the trip." I pause. "Number four point five: we need to get a blindfold. And a disguise for you. Number five: I assume the Council has a garage somewhere? Because we're going to need a car, and I'm driving. You're my passenger princess."

"Thor help me." But Erik pushes a different button on the elevator, one lower than the lobby. He's still grinning like he's enjoying himself immensely.

It makes me seventeen kinds of uncomfortable.

We're about to go somewhere that represents everything he's

always preaching against. *It's dangerous*, as he so sensibly pointed out. Bad guys, bad decisions, yadda yadda. Why does he look happy? What changed?

This elevator's too damn small. The stench of his cologne is everywhere, rich and warm; it's overpowering the free bits of air in this car.

Stupid Manhattan. Everything's so tiny.

"These rules are nonnegotiable." I lift my chin. "And I reserve the right to add more at any time, without warning. For the foreseeable future, you're my little criminal bitch-boy."

Erik's eyes heat again. "That's not the threat you think it is."

Woah. What?

He—

What?

Error 404. Page Not Found.

"Boss?" Molly's voice is a bit panicked in my ear. "Your pulse flatlined—"

"Fine." I choke, clear my throat. My hands are sweaty on the plate so I scrape one on my shorts. "Fine." I nod decisively and look anywhere, *anywhere*, but at Erik. "Fine."

About the Author

SARA RAASCH is the *New York Times* and *USA Today* bestselling author of the irreverently witty, tantalizingly sexy adult romances *The Nightmare Before Kissmas*, *Go Luck Yourself*, and *The Entanglement of Rival Wizards*. Her books have been featured in *People*, NPR, *Us Weekly*, *Elle*, *Vulture*, and more. She grew up among the cornfields of Ohio and currently lives in the historical corridor of southeastern Virginia.

sararaaschbooks.com
Instagram: @sara_raasch
TikTok: @sara_raasch